D0457914

15

The Dead House

The Dead House

By Dawn Kurtagich

Little, Brown and Company

New York Boston

Copyright © 2015 by Dawn Kurtagich

Little, Brown and Company

Hachette Book Group
1290 Avenue of the Americas, New York, NY 10104
Visit our website at lb-teens.com

Little, Brown and Company is a division of Hachette Book
Group, Inc.
The Little, Brown name and logo are trademarks of Hachette
Book Group, Inc.

First Edition: September 2015

Library of Congress Cataloging-in-Publication Data

Kurtagich, Dawn.
  The dead house / by Dawn Kurtagich. — First edition.
      pages cm
  Summary: Told through journal entries, a psychotherapist's
notes, court records, and more, relates the tale of Carly, a
teen who was institutionalized after her parents' death but
released to Elmbridge High School, where she is believed to
have a second personality or soul named Kaitlyn, and/or be
possessed by a demon.
  ISBN 978-0-316-29868-1 (hardcover) — ISBN 978-0-316-29866-7
(ebook) — ISBN 978-0-316-29865-0 (library edition ebook)
[1. Multiple personality—Fiction. 2. Dissociative disorders—
Fiction. 3. High schools—Fiction. 4. Schools—Fiction.
5. Demonology—Fiction. 6. Orphans—Fiction. 7. England—
Fiction.] I. Title.
  PZ7.1.K877De 2015
  [Fic]—dc23
                    2014044358

10 9 8 7 6 5 4 3 2

RRD-C

Printed in the United States of America

For the men and women
who saved my life

&

To my husband
and Mel (plus all the others!).

You all made miracles.

THE SOMERSET

3 DEAD, 1 MISSING IN SCHOOL FIRE

Prestigious historic high school becomes scene of horror as flames engulf building.

By DERRECK S. WESTLER

The local community was rocked when firefighters were called to the scene of a major fire at Elmbridge High School on Lord's Hill Street in Taunton at 1:08 am on Wednesday. The school, which was built in 1908, sustained substantial damage to the female dormitory wing and parts of the main building. Official reports put the number of casualties at three, though no names have been released to the press. It has also been confirmed that one student is missing. Arson has not been ruled out. Detective Chief Inspector Floyd Homes of Avon and Somerset CID, who was investigating a related missing persons case, declined to comment at this time. However, reports of an Elmbridge High student being directly involved in the fire have found their way onto a local website, where Kaitlyn Johnson has been named as a primary suspect. As of yet, no records of a student at Elmbridge High School with this name have been found. The fire burned for much of the night, but with the help of five firefighting crews, the blaze was extinguished before dawn. Elmbridge High School will be closed until further notice, and all students are being temporarily transferred to Taunton School, twenty miles away.

Report Statement

In the early hours of 2 February 2005, a fire at Elmbridge
High School in Somerset killed three and injured twenty. For
many years, little was revealed about the tragedy. However,
rumors flooded the Internet, linking "Kaitlyn" Johnson, "the
girl of nowhere," to the blaze. This was nothing more than wild
speculation.

Until now.

Along with a heavily burned "Message Book," which was used
as a method of communication, Kaitlyn Johnson's diary has been
found in the remains of the attic of the Elmbridge building. In it,
Kaitlyn reveals the thoughts of a disturbed mind...and a much
more sinister version of events than was ever made public.

What follows is a true account of what has become known as the
Johnson Incident. Included in this document is a collation of such
evidence as has been made available for examination. All Kaitlyn
diary entries have been transcribed with type-font for ease of
reading.

This witness testifies that the statements herein are accurate as
far as can be reasonably ascertained.

Yesternight, upon the stair
I met a girl who wasn't there.
She wasn't there again today.
I wish, I wish she'd...

... Carly

This altered Hughes Mearns nonsense poem was found scratched into the attic wall. It is presumed to have been cut into the wood near the end of the Johnson Incident by Kaitlyn herself.

Much of the Elmbridge building remains structurally intact, though it has recently been earmarked for demolition under the Building Act of 1984. The attic, where Kaitlyn spent much of her time and where her diary was found, remains in good condition, as does the rest of the central building. All the female dorms and wings, however, were damaged in the fire. The basement, which was initially a crime scene, then a forensic research area used by the University of Somerset, then a site of investigation into paranormal phenomena, is now condemned.

The prohibition on public access to the property remains in force after twenty years because of recurrent disappearances on the site. Despite this, it continues to attract thrill-seekers and the foolhardy.

PART I

THE
SELF
THAT
ISN'T
ME

Either the Darkness alters—
Or something in the sight
Adjusts itself to Midnight—
And Life steps almost straight.
—Emily Dickinson

She walks in beauty, like the night
Of cloudless climes and starry skies;
And all that's best of dark and bright
Meet in her aspect and her eyes...
—George Gordon, Lord Byron

1

I curse anyone who reads this book.

If you touch it, hell will be waiting.

Screw you. Happy reading.

Diary of Kaitlyn Johnson

Sunday, 29 August 2004, 12:24 am
Claydon Mental Hospital, Somerset

I am myself again.

Carly has disappeared into the umbra, and I am alone. Ink on my fingers—she's been writing in the Message Book.

Good night, sis! she writes. We'll be back at school soon. I can't wait!

I wouldn't have done this diary thing, except Carly thought it was a good idea too. See, Dr. Lansing thinks that getting my thoughts out of my head and onto paper will allow me to be free of them. She gave us both a journal with lock and key, and the instruction to "be honest and whole." Mine is black (ha ha), and Carly's is green. I'd like to think mine is black because it's Lansing's impression of my nature—solid, unchanging, hidden—but really I think she chose it because black's not a color.

You see, Diary…Dr. Lansing is convinced I'm not really here.

I'm not the diary sort, but if I'm going to record my life, I'm going to do it thoroughly. Honesty, honesty, honesty. Yes? Lansing can't tell me I don't really exist—product of trauma and all that—when my thoughts and feelings are as real as Carly's.

I am real.

I exist.

They won't ~~kill me~~ send me away.

Message Book Entry

Monday, 30 August 2004, 4pm

Kaitie, do you realize that we might never be coming back to Claydon Hospital after this year? Our LAST YEAR at school! Do you realize that? So close! We're so close! We just have to keep going. We just have to stick to it. All the lying will end as soon as we're free.

Okay, breakdown in case she tests you tonight:

Breakfast: 2 tablespoons of shredded wheat with skimmed milk

Lunch: Skipped (sorry)

Supper: Tuna sandwich, ~~half~~ a bit less than half

I love you, Kaybear. Please let us ~~sit~~ rest tonight. No breaking the rules. I really need to feel top-notch tomorrow.

xoxoxox

Carly

Diary of Kaitlyn Johnson

Tuesday, 31 August 2004, 2:14 am
Claydon Mental Hospital

A crow caws outside my window each night. I can never see him, but I know he sees me.

Elmbridge High School looms before me like some awful miasma—we return for our final school year in a few short hours! Our progress has been "admirable." What that really means is that Carly is eating again and that I haven't done anything "potentially self-harming" in weeks. Dr. Lansing thinks she did that, but it was always Carly. What it boils down to is a series of carefully planned and executed lies.

Everything is timed. Everything is coordinated. Everything is rehearsed.

Carly and I pretend to be recovering from a sickness we don't have. But when no one will believe you, you become the liar they think you are.

We work the system.

After our parents died, they sent us to Claydon. I can barely write the words without flinching. Without the deepest dread sliding over me like freezing water. Claydon is what you'd call a live-in nuthouse—excuse me, "psychiatric facility"—for troubled teens. Really it's a place for embarrassed parents to hide away their mistakes.

Carly isn't the mistake, though. I am.

We were fifteen and orphans and wards of Her Majesty. Wards of the social care system. In 2003, from January to September, they watched us, because they thought Carly might try to off herself. When it became obvious she was mostly fine, they went looking for a school. I guess Elmbridge High School won because it has a boarding facility. That was last year. We were sent back here for the summer. Until we turn eighteen (count: 274 nights), we're their problem. All the other Elmbridge High pupils go home to their families, but we don't have one of those anymore.

Elmbridge is definitely a step up from Claydon, but it's not the ultimate goal. The ultimate City of Gold is the sweet haze of urban cityscape light pollution, that rot scent of rubbish gone sour, and the endless living night that is London.

Freedom.

Where the night is vivid with noise, people, and anonymity—where the depraved live hand in hand with the righteous. London is awake all night. London is somewhere I can disappear. Or not. As I choose. I can find some kind of life.

Elmbridge is the gateway; Dr. Lansing is the gatekeeper.

Anyway—what else matters except that Elmbridge isn't Claydon? Because anywhere outside of Claydon pretty much takes the cake; a sewer in hell would be a step up. Anywhere that freedom is an option is automatically better than being locked behind a pristine white door, forgotten in a neat little cage.

I'm sorry. I really do try not to get angry. Carly says anger is a weapon, but sometimes I think it's just another cage.

So these are the goals:

Graduate—even if it kills us

Get out of Somerset and to London

Live free

The real reason we ended up in Claydon is because they think Carly's ~~crazy~~ damaged. They think the accident caused a fracture in her mind. I am, apparently, the result of trauma. They think it started that night. They think I don't exist.

It's all about "putting me away again."

See, they think I'm a personality disorder. I touched on this before. I am "a way of coping" when Carly was coping just fine. DID—dissociative identity disorder. I'm a coping mechanism...an alternative personality. I'm a symptom. They think I'm like a disease—I'm <u>infecting</u> Carly.

No one believes that I've <u>always</u> been here. Carly says it's because no one trusts the word of a teenager. And our parents, the only two people who could have told them the truth, are gone forever. I guess Jaime could tell them too, but who believes a five-year-old?

This is how it works:

I'm here courtesy of Carly. I'm anywhere because of her. Not that I'm complaining, and she'd never admit this, but I'm like the wart on her arse she'll never show, but she constantly knows is there. Where she goes, I go.

I am a prisoner of my skin. My bones are my cage. But she tells me she needs me, that I make her so happy, that she couldn't live without me, and I know it's true. It's true for both of us.

Carly and I are closer than sisters. Closer than twins. We might as well be the same person, because we share the same body. But we _are_ different. You might say she's my better half. We share one life, each getting part.

Carly gets the day.

I get the night.

We live in shifts; it's always been this way. I've always been here. Always, always, al

ways.

Wish they'd believe that.

Unfortunately, I was unlucky enough to be born to the night watch, so I'm the one nominated for ~~deletion~~ ~~integration~~

The

Big

Nothing

Dr. Lansing says it's a good thing, but I'm not much tempted by oblivion. Not today, anyway.

I don't blame Carly for being the one in the light. I love her more than anything. She's my opposite completely, and she'll say she's the weaker half of our equation, but the truth is she's my rock. She is everything I wish I were.

~~See how honest I'm being, Lansing, dear?~~

During the crossover, at dawn and dusk, just as the sun is moving behind or above the horizon, I can sometimes feel Carly coming. It's hard to describe. I get sort of dizzy…like I'm high…and just as I'm about to go, I feel her brush past me. Not quite touch…more like a familiar scent or a gentle breath. It's the closest we get to touching. I can almost talk to her in those endless minutes when we are neither one nor the other.

Almost.

But, since that's impossible, we use other methods— the Message Book and little notes scribbled on purple Post-its stuck here and there.

Gotta go—I hear the nurse coming for checks.

Remember to <u>behave</u> tonight. Only one night, OK?

　　PS: Grabbed you one of those gross marshmallow concoctions you love from the canteen. Under the bed. Also, <u>Jane Eyre</u> from the library.

Go nuts. <u>Be good.</u>

Xoxo

C

4:04 am

Where was I? Oh, yeah. Now that we're heading back to Elmbridge High School, it's safe to write in the Message Book again. For a while, back in late June, Dr. Lansing read it without our knowing, and would say things that could only have come from reading our exchanges. But we figured it out soon enough, and that was the last time we wrote in it. Lansing wanted that, of course. She saw it as Carly indulging in her alter ego—an "enabling behavior." When Carly wasn't writing to me there, Lansing probably smiled and put a neat little tick next to a task box that read "stop all messages." But she was wrong if she thought that would stop us.

We wrote to each other in the bathroom mirror, in steam. We wrote Post-it notes, which we hid in unlikely places and swallowed after reading (not the nicest thing to force down your esophagus, but they checked the bins to make sure I wasn't smoking). She forced us underground, and underground we'll stay, until the day we pack our bags and head for the city, where the night never sleeps.

For now, my nights are full of nothings, and Carly's days are full of everythings.

Session #45 Audio
Dr. Annabeth Lansing (AL) and Carly "Kaitlyn" Johnson (CJ)
Tuesday, 31 August 2004, 8:34 PM

(AL): How are you feeling tonight, Carly?

(CJ): Today was a good day.

(AL): Last day here. No anxieties about the upcoming school year?

(CJ): I like being at Elmbridge…

(AL): But?

(CJ): [Pause] They sent a notice that they're giving me a new room. Apparently, it's a little smaller. Different. It's in the "L," so I'll be able to see the boys' dorms across the courtyard, which is weird.

(AL): And it bugs you? The change?

(CJ): A bit. But it will be good being back.

(AL): Change affects us all in different ways. It'll get easier as more time passes. Tell me, how much did you manage to eat?

(CJ): I ate in the hospital canteen today. I had salad and some tuna.

(AL): I'm pleased to hear that you ate…but you know that a salad really isn't enough nourishment for the day.

[Pause]

(CJ): I know. Actually, I'm starving.

(AL): I have cookies. Would you have one?

(CJ): Okay.

[Rustling of plastic.]

(CJ): Thanks.

(AL): This is remarkable progress. Are you sure this is Carly I'm speaking to?

(CJ): You think I'm Kaitlyn?

(AL): Or maybe a new alter ego altogether. If you are, you're welcome to speak.

(CJ): I'm Carly.

(AL): Kaitlyn, I know it's you.

(CJ): [Pause] Then why ask what I ate? I know they report everything she eats to you.

(AL): It isn't as prison-like as you make it sound. Carly doesn't eat. We all know that.

[Silence]

(CJ): My answer told you who I was.

(AL): So why don't you be honest with me, huh? Tell me how you are.

(CJ): [Mumbled incoherence]

(AL): Yes, I do care, Kaitlyn. About you, about Carly. Once upon a time, you trusted me, and I did everything I could to help you. Remember?

(CJ): You keep secrets from me. You won't tell me what happened that night. You won't tell me.

(AL): We've spoken about this. Carly isn't ready to know what happened. Neither are you. You both need to work towards it. You need to integrate. [Pause] It's been a while since you mentioned the Voice. Tell me what's been happening with him.

(CJ): Why? So you can tick "crazy" on your little forms? So you can tick "Communicative"? So you can go home to Mr. Lansing and your perfect daughter and laugh about your demented patient?

(AL): Kaitlyn, you know I'd never do that.

[Silence]

Besides, Margo's not perfect. [Pause] [Sigh] She was just suspended for mooning her English professor.

(CJ): No way, don't lie. You're totally fucking shitting me!

(AL): Don't swear, please. And no, I'm not.

(CJ): [Laughing] Oh, my God!

(AL): So. The Voice—your Aka Manah. Has he been bugging you?

(CJ): You know already. I don't like to talk about him. You think he's a construct. You think he's not real.

(AL): Tell me why you chose to call the voice Aka Manah. Why that name?

(CJ): That's just his name. Arcane. Scary. Which is what he is.

(AL): And if I told you that in Zoroastrian mythology, Aka Manah was associated with evil thought? That, traditionally speaking, he was a kind of demon known to affect the mind? The thinking of people?

(CJ): So?

(AL): Don't you think it's telling? You give your auditory hallucination a name that implies he's in the mind, *influencing* the mind? You have control over that. And this is a clue.

(CJ): A clue to what?

(AL): A clue telling you—begging you to see—that Aka Manah isn't real.

[Silence]

(CJ): I'll just agree with you, shall I? Get it over with?

(AL): Kaitie, I can't help you unless you're honest with me. Unless you try. We were friends once, right?

[Pause]

(CJ): Once.

(AL): Please.

[Pause]

(CJ): [Whispering] Aka Manah used to be far away…I could tell because he shouted at me. I didn't really feel him around me. Now…sometimes…

[Silence]

(AL): Sometimes? [Gently] What, Kaitlyn?

[Rustling]

Kaitlyn, use your words. You can do it.

(CJ): I don't want to talk about him. He'll hear me.

(AL): Is he here now? [Pause] How do you know he's here?

(CJ): [Barely audible] He's closer. He'll hear you.

(AL): How do you know? Is he shouting at you?

(CJ): [Barely audible] No. He's whispering.

(AL): Whispering at you? Right now?

(CJ): [Whispering] No…at you.

[Silence]

(AL): I see.

(CJ): Sometimes…

[Silence]

Sometimes I can feel him...his breath on me. But
sometimes it's worse. I can feel him...inside me.

[Silence]

(**AL**): Kaitlyn, enough.

[Rustling]

Kaitlyn, *enough*. This isn't a game.

[Silence]

(**CJ**): Screw you, Lansy-pants. You never listen.

(**AL**): I think that will do for this evening.

(**CJ**): I want to see Jaime.

(**AL**): That's enough for this evening.

(**CJ**): I *said* that I *want* to see *Jaime*! I'm entitled to
see my little sister every month. It's been *three*.

(**AL**): Kaitlyn, that is enough.

[Scraping of chair, followed by footsteps receding]

(**CJ**): [From a distance] You never listen! You can't
stop her from visiting. Keep trying that, and you'll
see what you push me to!

[End of tape]

Tuesday, 31 August 2004

Carly continues to dissociate into
Kaitlyn. Continuing attempts at
deception indicate the need for
an adjustment in her medication.
Delusions also persist with regard to
"the Voice." Consider readmittance to
Claydon Psychiatric Hospital, inpatient
department for a few more months.

A visit from Jaime Johnson is long
overdue. I have been reluctant to grant
one in hopes that Jaime could be used
as a restraining tool, but withholding
visits has had an adverse effect, as
tonight's was the first dissociation into
Kaitlyn that Carly has experienced in at
least a month, as far as I can tell.

Dr. A. Lansing MBChB MD PhD

Several recovered fragments of Carly's journal remain intact. One has been replicated below; chronological integrity is maintained.

Diary of Carly Luanne Johnson

Wednesday, 1 September, 7am
Claydon

12 blue pills

4 white pills

16 yellow capsules

I don't know what else to write.

This morning my mouth tasted like stale cigarettes and old beer, and I dreaded opening my eyes, because sometimes Kaitie leaves me in strange places. She forgets about me. It might be on the roof or under the bed. Once it was a closet, and I understood what she meant by <u>dark</u> that day. That's why I'm so careful about where I am around sunset. I don't want to discard her in the middle of a conversation (if she has any) or cause a scene. Because Mum used to say that some of our transitions could be pretty weird-looking. Eyes rolling, all that stuff. So I'm careful.

I asked Kaitie to behave again last night, but I guess two nights of behaving were too much.

I had to mentally scan my body before I felt brave enough to open my eyes. Just like the old days when our biggest problem was Mum not understanding Kaitie's life. Her loneliness.

Dear God, save my sister.

I know she was drinking again last night. I can taste it. I really don't know how she manages it. Getting out of Claydon, especially at night, sounds impossible. And terrifying. But she did it, because here is the waxy coating on my tongue.

Leaving to go back to Elmbridge High School in a few minutes. Bags packed.

I'm sorry, Kaitie. I know you wanted us to do this whole diary thing, but I don't know what to say.

10 blue pills
3 white pills
14 yellow capsules

Left her a Post-it. "Don't flush my pills. We need them."

Carly Johnson returned to Elmbridge High School on Wednesday, 1 September 2004 at 7:54 AM. Naida Chounan-Dupré, an aspiring journalist and key witness to what was to follow, compiled a video diary of her final year at Elmbridge High School. This video diary, which was posted online to a secure blog (MalaGenie.com) at regular intervals, and was pulled from the online archive after the discovery of the Johnson journal, reveals much that was previously unknown about the Johnson Incident.

Video footage has been transcribed by [name omitted at request] and included at relevant sections throughout this testimony.

Naida Camera Footage
Wednesday, 1 September 2004, 4:00 PM
Elmbridge High Common Room

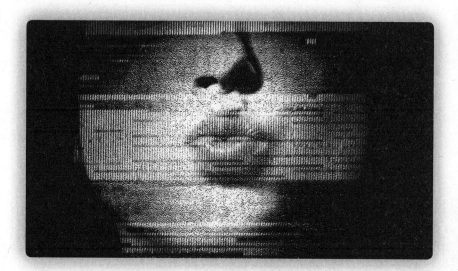

The image shakes for a moment, and then rights itself. We are staring into the face of a striking girl with pale, almost colorless eyes and black, curly hair. She puts the camera down on a shelf and steps back. She wears the Elmbridge school uniform, consisting of a white shirt sporting the Elmbridge crest and insignia, a blue tie, and a blue-and-green kilt fringed in white. Around her neck hangs a large necklace with thick black beads, and at the center, an amulet. She winks at the camera, fluffs up her corkscrew hair, and blows a kiss.

"This is it," she says. Her voice is slow and languid, a faded Scottish accent lilting every word. "Elmbridge Truthful, Episode One, Final Year, Sociology 101. Seeking documented evidence of the daily teen experience. Main players—the Best Friend, Carly Johnson—"

She picks up the camera, and it spins before focusing on Carly, a slight girl with blond hair and haunted eyes that seem shadowed. She glances up from the book she's reading. Her face waxes a deep shade of crimson, and the shadows beneath her eyes seem to lighten, chameleon-like.

"Oh, Naida—don't film me. Please."

"Come on, C!"

Carly hides behind her book. "It's invasive. Besides, you're the only one who decided to do the camera thing. You know…I think he was joking…I think he meant we should do journals. Most of us are."

"Mr. Triebourn isn't going to reward the sheep, hen," Naida says as the camera angles around the room. "He's going to reward integrity. With a shiny, beautiful A. I'm a journalist and a sociologist." The camera turns back to Carly. "Aye, I *will* capture your secrets—"

"No." Carly's face, which exudes a gentle timidity, shutters closed, and her eyes grow unexpectedly hard.

The camera drops, and through the blurry screen we hear Naida say, softly, "Please? I really need this for my Royal Holloway portfolio. If I don't have it, I won't get in, and if I don't get in, I'll have to take a job as a hack or something—for a *tabloid* newspaper. A *tabloid*, Carly! Are you going to do that to me? Really?"

The camera lifts, refocuses.

Carly frowns, visibly uncomfortable. "That is completely forbidden emotional blackmail, I hope you know." She eyes the camera with a sort of wariness, as though expecting it to be aggressive. After a moment, however, she nods, mutters, "Fine!" and then goes back to reading, subtly shrugging her hair over her shoulder to hide her face.

"*Yes!* Secrets shall be had, sugar…Nothing to be done about that."

"Yeah, yeah, paparazzi," comes a male voice from offscreen.

The camera turns to capture a lanky boy with dark skin, a little over six feet tall, with a slim frame and black hair, entering the dorm with a McDonald's paper bag dangling from his fist. He grins at Naida behind the camera.

"Turning into a scandal scavenger now?" he asks.

Naida laughs. "Subject number two: Scott Fromley, the Boyfriend, but don't ask me why. He's a clown, a slob, and a jerk most of the time."

Scott grins, looking over the top of the camera, which then jiggles as Naida leans in to kiss him. Briefly we catch a glimpse of the contact, Scott's arm wound tightly around Naida's waist, as he presses her close.

"Do you have to do that right in front of me?" Carly asks from somewhere off camera.

"You wait," Naida says, and the camera pans back onto Carly. "You'll have a beau one of these days, and your wild side will be set loose—no longer caged and celibate! Then we'll see who's making grotesque public displays of affection."

The camera turns back on Naida, close in so that we can see only her darting, penetrating eyes as she whispers, "And I think I know who that might be..."

The camera cuts away to a shot of a blond boy, around five eleven, stalking into the room. His neatly styled hair belies his casual saunter.

"Mr. Brett [surname omitted], class president, voted cutest in the year and most likely to succeed, probably owing to the fact that he is, in all honesty, pretty damn gorgeous—"

Scott, off camera, protests. "Oi!"

"—and also because his dad's [redacted]. *Yessireee*, you heard that right, lasses. We're rubbing shoulders with the elite."

"You're one to talk," Scott mutters, off camera. "Isn't your grandmother some priestess or something?"

"Aye," Naida agrees, "she's a priestess, but that's nothing next to this pretty boy."

Brett bows. "Thank you. Thank you very much. Just let my father know that I'm 'rubbing shoulders' with the likes of you, and then let's see how 'elite' I remain."

Naida, turning the camera on herself, says, "That's true. He'd disown you, for sure. Especially if he knew you joined my Mala group last year."

She sticks out her tongue, revealing a diamanté bar piercing, which she wiggles for the camera.

"Ain't that the truth," Scott says. "Hey, are we doing that again this year?"

"You know, you're more conventional than you think," Brett says to Naida, "even if you *were* born on Fair Island, the most Mala-centric and remotest place on the planet."

"Was it conventional when I taught you how to put together a *dòchas* charm?" she scoffs. "And you used it to wish for a good cricket game. God almighty."

"Oh, yeah, the hope charm. That was cool." Scott pulls Naida in for a lengthy kiss, during which the camera lowers. Brett remains in frame. He glances at Carly several times, but she fails to notice.

"Hey, man," he says, addressing Scott. "We on for Saturday?"

Scott, who plonks down onto the sofa beside Carly with little notice of her, nods. "Yeah, whatever. I don't care what we do, just so long as we're out of here for the day. I'm sick of this place already."

A shadow passes over the camera, and Naida's hand shakes; the camera almost falls.

"Whoa—"

She lifts the camera again; Carly comes into focus. "What?"

"Thought I saw...I—nothing." She laughs. "I should have got a better camera." There is a pause and then Naida adds, "Scott, Brett, can you leave us alone for a minute?"

"I'm sort of busy," Scott says, the sound muffled as though his mouth is full. A pause. "All right, fine. I've got to finish Triebourn's essay anyway. Later, though, yeah? Your room?"

"*Piss off!* Go away, now, now, now!"

"Cheers, babe. Feeling the love."

He and Brett leave.

A moment of silence followed by the squeaking of springs as Naida sits beside Carly. "What's up, C?"

"I wish you wouldn't imply things like that about Brett and me. I don't like him like that—at *all*. He's..." She shudders, shuts her eyes, and breathes deeply for a few moments. "Look, I'm never going to have a boyfriend. I don't *want* a boyfriend, Naida. I'm okay with it."

"Don't say that. You never know what might happen. One day it might be possible. Fall in love, have a family—"

"I'll never have what you have," she snaps, and then her voice softens. "And that's not your fault, Naids." Carly takes her hand. "You don't have to feel bad. The last thing I want is for you to feel bad...Just don't do that. Don't say things about Brett and me, okay? You just make everything harder."

"You don't know what is or isn't possible, though. We could put a *dòchas* charm together like last year. You could wish for love."

Carly stares at Naida; she looks like she might cry. "No. I can't."

"But why?"

Carly snatches her hand away. "Kaitlyn has a voice too, remember? We're fine like this. This is how it has to be."

"You and Kaitie...two souls in one body...it's dangerous. I told you before—"

"Your Scottish Mala stuff won't make a difference. I know...And I know what my life is going to be. I'll never have what I want. I'll never have who I love."

"You don't know—"

"I don't want to talk about that."

Naida puts the camera on the coffee table so that neither of them is in the shot. It continues to record.

"You can talk to me, you know," Naida says softly. "Maybe I can listen...if not understand or, I don't know, help."

There is a muffled exhale and a pause. "Lately...I've been feeling weird. I don't know—I can't really describe it. Just a weird feeling in my skin...like there's someone—"

The camera wobbles and then spins to face both Carly and Naida. Naida sits back down, but Carly only stares at the lens, mouth parted.

"Like there's someone...?" Naida prompts.

Carly shuts her mouth, swallows, and gets to her feet.

"Carly, wait—what is it?"

Naida picks up the camera, and we see Carly's haunted and retreating figure.

"It's nothing. Never mind."

"Hold up, this is important—"

[END OF CLIP]

Diary of Kaitlyn Johnson

Thursday, 2 September 2004, 1:42 am
Dorm

Naida's eyes are dead oceans on steroids. But when she saw I was here and that her precious Carly was safe, they warmed into something less tepid. It was kind of beautiful, kind of revolting.

It used to be Carly and me against the world—her notes guided me through the hours of darkness, and mine gave her courage in the brightness of the sun. We were each other's armor. That's a little less true these days.

And it's Naida's fault.

Naida. Carly's ~~best only~~ friend. She's probably the only person who knows about us and actually believes us. Except she thinks it's something to do with two souls in one body and an excess of power, confused spirits—blah, blah.

Last year Carly gushed about Naida the first day they met. I think that was probably the worst Message Book entry of my life. Actually, no. The worst one was the one where she told me that Naida <u>knew</u>. Knew our secret. I remember that one like it's seared on my brain. She wrote, "Naida is amazing. You will love her. She's just like you! Funny, sarcastic, reckless. Kaitie, it's so nice to have someone <u>know</u> about us! I hope you don't mind that I told her?"

I was an afterthought.

I guess Carly felt bad, because she started telling me <u>everything</u> about Naida after that, as if trying to balance the scales. Like the Mala thing.

None of us knew a damn thing about Mala before Naida. It's some weird Scottish voodoo-like—I don't know—religion? Cult? Stupid-mental-ritual practice? Witchcraft? Naida basically grew up on Fair Island,

which is this completely forgotten island in the Outer
Hebrides somewhere, and she only came to England when
she was eleven for school. I always thought Naida
was weird, even before Carly told me all this shit.
Naida's grandmother still lives on that rock in the
sea, though, so Naida goes back every summer. I think
Carly mentioned a cousin who lives a few miles away
from Elmbridge—whatever. But it's the grandmother who's
the stirrer, because Naida happened to mention to
Carly after she'd written to that old witch that our
"situation" was "unnatural." Two souls in one body—the
shock! The horror!

You read that right: "Two souls in one body."

Mostly I think I'm broken. Error on lot "Johnson-K."
Issue recall immediately.

If I'm going to do that "honest" thing, I should
tell you that I felt like I lost Carly the day she and
Naida met, and partly that's still true.

Naida stole my sister.

I've been trying to steal her back.

In any case, it all comes down to this one tragic
fact: Carly is my whole entire world. She's all I have
left, my only tie—one of the ~~three~~ two last people who
believe I'm real—and we've never even spoken. I had
a tenuous enough grip on her as it was, and now Naida
has part of that too. Except Naida has more. Naida has
her laugh, her tears, her company during the daylight
hours. Naida has her.

It's not fair.

So, you see, when I saw Naida in the corridor,
looking so relieved, I wanted to scream, "Carly's mine!"

But she just nodded once to acknowledge me, then
disappeared into her room next door, and the moment was
lost. But maybe she got the message in my eyes, the way
I get messages in hers.

I dream of her eyes, and their messages…they're
framed by the beautiful red that blood always is,
whispering I'm sorry.

Something is going on in those eyes when she looks
at me.

Later

Left Carly a note in the Message Book. I'll do what has always been done: wait for her message ~~like I have no life~~ like I'm starving.

~~I have no real use.~~

~~I'm alone.~~

My time is my own.

For all my complaining, I have a good feeling about this year. I think maybe we'll make it through without problems. So long as Dr. Lansing keeps eating the lies we tell her and never sees this book, we'll be out of here come July.

Good-bye, Elmbridge. Good-bye, Naida.

Hello, world that invites the night.

Naida and I have been talking about London. She agrees with you about it being perfect for us. That or New York. New York never sleeps either, apparently. Naida was laughing that I didn't know that. Found your sneaky Post-it on the bottom on my school shoe, by the way. You think you're so clever. Well, not only are you <u>not</u> going to find my Post-it, but even if you do, you won't be able to decode it. I can be smart too!

There's a new kid in school. He's not in any of my classes, but I've seen him around. He's got dark hair, is sort of tall, dark eyes. It's weird seeing a new student in our year. I mean, who changes school in the final year? So weird. Also, Mr. Thomas retired, and the new music teacher isn't up to his standards. I forget her name. I hate it when things change.

By the way, watch your elbow. I grazed it in PE, but the nurse cleaned it out. Sorry, Kaybear.

Love you! I've left <u>Heart of Darkness</u> under the pillow. The new Internet code is NX74SID. Don't forget to clear the history if you go into the computer room.

Xoxoxo

Carly

Diary of Kaitlyn Johnson

Friday, 3 September 2004, 12:52 am
Dorm

There's a voice in my ear. His name is Aka Manah. I have never told Carly about him because—hello, crazy.

Sometimes I feel him scratching around in there, or whispering, on and on. I think he's there to make me feel guilty for surviving when they didn't. I think he's here to make me feel as dead as they are.

I know it's because of the drugs they give Carly. The Klonopin, the Xanax, and the risperidone. They screw with my mind and not hers—how cute. I know this, and yet I don't. Because, drug-induced or not, his voice is real. As real as anything else in my life, I guess. And his words are true, even when they're just screams that sound mechanical and broken. He feels, to me, like a ticking bomb.

When he's not in my ear, he's nearby. I can't see him, but I can sense him. I can hear him. He likes to breathe. He likes to laugh under that breath, which smells moldy somehow. Like a towel left damp too long. But also hot—like burning ashes.

Tonight it's the same. I can hear him sitting in the corner, watching me; his mechanical laughs stutter and bounce along the walls around me.

I just shrug and continue writing.

Diary of Kaitlyn Johnson

Monday, 6 September 2004, 3:00 am
Elmbridge Grounds

I like to stand outside the oldest part of the school—
the real part of the school. I thought I'd show it to
you, diary. Do you mind if I call you Dee? It suits you
much better. Dee, then. I can just imagine what this
house was in the 1910s. A garish palatial home deeply
envied, full of damask silk, the finest velvet, marble
floors, and chintz.

On and on it goes, solarium, library, billiard room
(now seniors' hall), gallery, the old banquet hall, the
kitchens, old butcher's kitchen, and a few newly built
classrooms at the rear.

This—what used to be the original house before
expansion started like crazy back in 1912 and later,
when the separate wings were added for the dorms (they
look like stupid L-shaped arms sticking out on either
side, bent at the elbows)—is a mask. They bricked
over the original stonework to force it to look more
uniform. To match the stupid Oxbridge-style arm-wings
they built on either side. This part of the school is
me. A veneer. If you were to look at it from above, the
school would look like a rudimentary bird. A body with
its wings bending and turning at a ninety-degree angle.
Like I said: arms with stupid elbows. I don't get why
they didn't just make it a giant square, with a courtyard
in the middle. Wouldn't that be a better trap?

During the day, this main section is the hub and
heart of the school. You can almost sense it beating.
At night, though, it's empty. Switched off and
abandoned. God, this school is Carly and me. One thing
during the day, another at night.

It may be a redbrick, Oxbridge imitation on the outside, but within the bowels lies something far older, something far grittier, all weathered gray stone, moss stains, and watermarks. Ugly. With the suggestion of something…not quite right. This part of the school feels vaguely sinister, or <u>aware</u> somehow. There are all kinds of rumors about this part of the school.

Let's go round the side. They built two little alleys between the wings and the main house, like rabbit tunnels through the red, and near the back of the west alley are small dark windows low down on the ground. The basement windows. I nearly missed them, they're so obscure.

Elmbridge is like a church in some ways, and in others, it's like a mansion. Church<u>like</u>, in that it feels holy…no speaking over a whisper without a teacher shushing you, my dears. And that weird way you always suspect someone is watching. Even now, as I write, I feel like there is a face peering out at me from one of those windows, little hands pressed to the black glass.

I wave. Hello.

For a minute there, I thought I <u>actually</u> saw someone. A girl. A thin, grinning girl.

Mansionlike, in that you're always sure that:

a) You'll break something.

b) It's haunted.

For me, it's more like ~~my place~~ home. Couldn't explain it even if I wanted to. I hate this place, and I love it. Like the anorexic who revolts at the thing that keeps her alive. I see myself mirrored here in the fakeness of it all. Carly is my mask, of course. She's the "real" Johnson girl. I'm just the ~~imposter~~ girl of nowhere. Am I a parasite? I prefer to imagine that I'm carrying Carly, that she's asleep on a hammock inside my mind, swaying gently with every step I take.

But that's crap, because during the day, I'm nothing. I don't exist. So neither does she, at night.

I'll never tell Carly how jealous I am that she gets to walk inside every single day while I'm stuck outside at nighttime, looking at the shell.

I don't want to think about it. I don't want to be outside anymore.

I'm going in.

Ha! Try to keep me out, and I'll <u>break</u> in! Oh, I feel wonderful! ~~It's just like the old days, back in Chester with John.~~

You won't believe what I found!

I broke in through one of those smudged-up dark windows of the basement where I ~~felt~~ saw? something someone watching me earlier. I only just fit. What will they do when they notice the bro~~ken~~ wind~~ow? Whatever~~, I don't care! I'm invisible!

The ~~cellar~~ basement was

[A page has been torn from the diary.]

The top floor was where I made the real find. I was about to head back to the basement and return to the dorm when I spotted an unobtrusive black door in one of the long halls, right next to a tall grandfather clock.

It didn't look like a closet.

It didn't look like a bathroom.

It looked like a secret.

The attic, Dee, is so vast—one long, seemingly endless room. It's full of boxes that contain glass ink pots, silver-nibbed dip pens—<u>nibs!</u>—notebooks, and antiquated textbooks. Stuff that is decades older than the things stored in the basement. I found a girl's guide to etiquette, if you can believe that. Could I need anything <u>less</u>?

I could spend months up here, looking at every little thing. This might be a nice place for me. Hidden. Forgotten. Perfect.

4:34 am, Roof

Dee, I'm a bit of a spy. What else is there to do when everyone else is sleeping and you're bored? I said I'd behave, and to get out of here, it's the least I'd do.

Escapism is a window that I don't have, but I need movement. I can't sit still.

I have this horrible fear of turning to stone like I'm in an Anne Rice novel or something. Or that I'll vanish, fade like a ghost. Cease to be. Then I won't be anything, just like Lansing wants. And the thought of that, Dee, is enough to drive me up onto the roof, where I teeter on the edge and wonder why I don't just leap.

And honestly, I don't know what's holding me back anymore. But of course, I do. It's Carly.

Hurt yourself, hurt Carly.

Whatever, I digress.

Spying entertains me. The things people do when they sleep, the faces they pull and the things they say. The way they touch their bodies when they think they're alone.

Last year I sat in the dorm room of one of Naida's friends, Juliet. Right by her bed. I watched her face twitch while I tickled her nose with my hair. And, a secret? I stole from her. I took a pen from her desk drawer, wrote a note in the back of her diary—I forget what it was now, and she never found it, from what I can tell—and I did something else too. I've got to be careful what I write down…

I need to tell someone. I need to tell you.

Diary…Dee…

My confession: I cut her. I cut Juliet last year, right before summer. I took the blade out of her razor, and I sliced a little bit of her skin near her wrist. There was a tiny red line of blood, and she never even stirred.

I was horrified at myself, of course, but it was so exciting. The most exciting thing I've ever done, I think. What a thrill to tell someone! I felt a sensation deep in my stomach that I've never felt before. Can you imagine what you could do to a person while they sleep, oblivious?

I climbed out of her window, sat in the tree, and watched her. The following night, she was wearing a plaster on her wrist, but her brow was unlined as she slept—she didn't have a care in the world. It was just another inexplicable injury, forgotten in the moment it's found.

But it wasn't forgotten by me. Not after all this time, even. I made a difference, Dee. I changed something in this world. I made a plaster appear on that wrist, and it never would have happened if I didn't exist.

I've done other things since then. Taken things from students who leave their windows open. Read diaries. Did you know that joker-boy Scott Fromley keeps a diary, Dee? I read it and then I left a little message in the back, written with his own pen. I have no idea if he ever found it, and I can't remember what I wrote. I think a word. *Loser*, maybe. I couldn't see the effect it had on him, so I consider that one a failed experiment. But there were others. A strand of hair pulled from Brenda's head. A stone placed under Megan's pillow.

All of this was—is—my clever way of distracting myself from the fact that, despite Carly, I am alone.

And I always will be.

Later, Attic

I'll keep you here. I'll keep you safe.

Purple Post-it

You are a ray of sunshine at midnight.

Message Book Entry

Monday, 6 September 2004, 4pm

School was annoying today. Scott is always all over Naida. I think she noticed that it bothered me, though, because she sent him off and then we talked for ages. Mostly about you (in a good way!). She said she wishes you could hang out with us too. See? She isn't bad. She says you're feisty, and that's not a bad thing.

The downside of today was Brett. He spent all of study period passing me notes.

Anyway, how was your night? What did you get up to? I'm planning a surprise for you, but I know you hate surprises, so this is your fair warning to <u>not</u> be surprised when you find it. ☺

Also, you need to call Lansing. She'll ask about breakfast, lunch, and dinner (cereal, lasagna, and omelet) and she'll ask how choir practice was (I skipped because I felt weird, but I'm fine, don't worry).

Love you, Kaybear.

C xxx

A page has been torn from the Message Book at this point, presumably Kaitlyn's reply. The next few pages are badly scorched or destroyed entirely by the fire. It seems that the events over the following weeks prevented whatever surprise Carly had planned from coming to fruition, but mention of a need for hundreds of Post-its in what remains of Carly's journal implies an elaborate plan. It is unknown whether Kaitlyn was aware of what Carly had in mind.

7

The following Kaitlyn journal entry is the first that can be found in which Ari Hait makes an appearance. Because of his significant role in later events, all entries pertaining to Mr. Hait have been included.

Diary of Kaitlyn Johnson

Wednesday, 8 September 2004, 11:04 pm
Hill Outside Old Chapel

The chapel is organic, like it spewed up out of the ground. Not like the school, which looks more as if it fell where it sits—a meteor crashed into a crater. One a denizen of hell, the other a celestial body. Both revolt and delight me.

It's not too cold tonight, even up here at the top of the hill, but the night cuts deep, and I need… something. A filler for the space inside that's like a stygian black pit and not very pretty. I'm being melodramatic, I know. I can't help it. I guess I thought I could find something here.

Find God. Find hope. Company…I don't even know what. I'm so alone. Oh God, I wish Carly was here.

They switched the outside lights on tonight, so all the white-barked trees stand starkly orange under the new moon like lepers bent and twisted. The light is only the imitation of warmth, but I'll take what I can get.

When I was five, I asked Carly what the sun felt like, and she wrote, "Warm, Kaitie, so warm. Like a hot bath."

Even the stone walls of the chapel are illuminated, and I feel less alone somehow. But warm? No. Cold as ice, like everything else.

There's a profound stillness here, especially in the nooks where the walls cast the darkest shadows. They look like spilled ink, impenetrable. Void. Even the scratching of my pen as I write is raw and harsh in the silence, as loud to my ears as a scream. I flinch—I tear—with every stroke.

Can they hear me, the corpses beneath the little gravestones in what I call my Forgotten Garden? There are only about thirty, from a long, long time ago. Nothing but dust now, not even memories. Most of the headstones are illegible, sentiment that even stone wasn't strong enough to hold. I told you. Forgotten Garden, full of skeletons, like depressing seeds that will never flower.

I'm reading "The Fall of the House of Usher" from my Poe collection. It's so suitable.

It's been exactly 101 days since I was last here. Carly once wrote, "Naida says she understands why you go to the chapel. It's holy, she says." If ever I thought Naida was right about this being a magical place, I do tonight. It <u>feels</u> holy…synthetically warm. The closest I've ever come to God. Is this what Carly feels every single day of her life, bathing in sunlight she takes for granted? Is the sun what the hand of God is? And if so, are these uplighters the crumbs he allows me?

Dee, I don't feel warm. I feel cold and abandoned. I stand painfully alone, and, selfish as I am, I wish that some other soul stood trapped here beside me in the profound stillness.

There's nothing so terrible as the utter silence of a soul like mine. Like those souls out there. Though if I'm honest, I don't think they've lingered here. That Forgotten Garden is the <u>absence</u> of souls, which is even more pathetic. I'm alone, even among the dead. Can you begin to understand how that feels?

Except Carly is here with me…somewhere. That gives me comfort. Gives me hope. She'll never know the strength she gives me, simply by my knowing she's here.

The whole world feels like a vast, empty space, with me the only living thing in it.

Or am I dead too?

6:00 am

Dee, my hand is shaking as I write this, but I must get it all down before Carly comes. I can't risk losing any of it in the crossover. The almanac says sunrise in fifty-two minutes, but I don't trust it to be accurate. Yesternight I lost three minutes.

Onwards!

I was in the confessional, as usual. Talking to the night. Talking to silence. Talking to God knows what, to be honest. Safe in that little space. How long had I been talking?

I'm mortified by what I might have said—Oh, great. I'm having a panic attack right now.

Okay, slow and steady. Breathe.

What. Happened?

I walked into the confessional. Slid the door shut. Sighed, rested my head against the back of the booth.

"I don't think there's a God, but here's hoping." I remember I said that. "I miss Carly. I wish she were here. I wonder what she talked about with Naida today. I hate all that time they get together, especially when I'm so…Oh, God, I'm so lonely. Thank God I have you, Dee."

I kept going on and on, and then I dropped my head onto the bar separating the two sides and just let myself fill up with this horrible self-pity that made me want to tear out my eyes.

"Who's Carly?"

I gasped this breathless scream and fell out of the booth—like, literally toppled out of it and onto the floor—bashing my shoulder on the wood. The priest's side slid open, and this figure stepped out towards me. I scrambled back on my hands, gasping like a fish out of water. Like a beached octopus or something.

He followed after me. "Hey, whoa, whoa—" And then he crouched, and the vomit-orange light fell onto his face and onto the bowler hat on his head. "You're kind of skittish, aren't you?"

"Who"—gasp—"the"—gasp—"hell—"

"Are you?" he finished.

"I'm—I'm—"

"Surprised, probably. I didn't expect anyone else to be up here." He helped me to my feet. "Not the most graceful fall on an arse I've ever seen, but I'll give you points for breathlessness. Too many girls are all—" He broke off, gesturing vaguely. "Screamy."

It took a minute for the deep-boned surprise of having another living-human-person-being-thing right there to wear off.

I brushed my hands on my jeans and noticed I'd cut my hand. Carly's hand.

Damn.

"Do you always sit in confession booths and listen to private conversations?" I snapped.

"Sometimes. Do you?"

"And who the hell wears a bowler hat?"

"I do, and I have excellent taste. I'd be gay if I wasn't so straight."

I rolled my eyes. "Well, that was less than subtle. What, are you going to divulge your favorite sex position next?"

"Wheelbarrow," he challenged.

"Bank number?" I called.

"I'd tell you, but then you'd fall for me."

"Really."

"Yeah, I'm dirt poor. Very sexy. Besides, I hear that freaky people shouldn't fall for each other. Weird things happen if you break the freaky-normal, normal-normal rule."

"Okay, I have no idea what's going on here, but this is private property. My property, so get out."

"The sign outside says OUT OF BOUNDS. I'm pretty sure the school owns it." He folded his arms and cocked his head, and the stupid bowler hat stayed on his stupid head. "I don't think you really want me to leave."

I glowered at him.

"'Oh, God. I'm so lonely'?"

"Get out of here! This is *my* space, you—goddamn—" I was infuriated, lost for the word. "Watson!"

After glancing down at my book, he had the cheek to say, "You should invest in a quality hardcover of Poe's collected works. Buying cheap may be simpler and easier in the short term, but your future self is only laughing at you—or slapping you. Mentally, of course."

My future self. Ha. What a concept.

Anyway, I just stared. He talked like some kind of awkward, socially inept idiot—or genius. I honestly have no idea which.

"Or you can borrow mine," he added.

I sniggered at that. "You read Poe?"

"I read other, less trendy things too."

"Let me guess," I drawled, leaning back to consider him. "Arthur Conan Doyle?"

"Funny." He smiled. "'Cause of the hat."

It was growing early, and I could feel the change in the air as dawn began to shift and sigh, preparing for her inevitable rise.

"I have to go," I told him, and he frowned.

"Why?"

"One of the mysteries of the universe," I muttered, and left.

He said he was new. Just started. He must be the one Carly mentioned. It's got to be embarrassing to be the new kid at school on top of arriving late. Do you think I could be normal around him, Dee? Could I pretend to be a regular girl who sleeps, who dreams, who has a life ahead of her instead of an existence in which she's dragged around like an appendage by the one she loves most?

As soon as he talks to Carly, he'll know something is up. If he hasn't spoken to her already. Though, I think she mentioned that they share no classes. Maybe Naida will steal him away too. Best to let it go. Friendship is out of the question for someone like me. I know that for a fact.

Still…it would be nice to make believe for a while. And he certainly made me forget all about being lonely.

He said he just got his room in Pinewood Hall, one of the boys' dorm wings, and I told him I'm in Magpie House with the girls. I gave him my email and IM.

Isn't it funny, Dee? The world isn't empty after all.

Getting dizzy—no time. Forgot to write a new note in the Message Boo

[The entry ends here.]

8

Ari Hait and Kaitlyn Johnson communicated via Instant Message (IM) and email throughout the months that followed. Telephone records were pulled for the trial, as well as saved conversations on Kaitlyn's IM mobile service. Where relevant, those that have been made available are included in this report.

Diary of Kaitlyn Johnson
Time Index and Location Not Noted

Thursday, 9 September 2004

Proof! Proof that he was real and not some desperate wish from my warped little mind. As soon as the sun set and Carly discarded me, vanishing to wherever she vanishes when the night closes in, I found this email waiting:

From: AriHait558
To: RealxChick
Date: 9 Sept 2004
Subject: Nice Meeting You

Well, Miss Confessional. You have some pretty interesting secrets. And you're quite stunning when you're flushed. Will you have more confessions for me tonight?

Intrigued,

Ari

I'm going to print out every email we exchange and give it to you, Dee. I want to be able to figure him out, if I need to. My reply:

From: RealxChick
To: AriHait558
Date: 9 Sept 2004
Subject: Re: Nice Meeting You

Well, Mr. Watson, you're a sneaky little spy and an invader. The chapel is my base—trespassers will be shot on sight.

Armed,

Me

From: AriHait558
To: RealxChick
Date: 9 Sept 2004
Subject: Threats

Nice bait—see you then.

Ready for battle,

Ari

PS—You never gave me your name. MI5 Agent or Witness Protection?

Ari558: You never answered my email. I am mortally wounded. As my new best friend, you're off to a pretty bad start.

CONFESSIONALGRL: You are a sad, lonely little individual.

Ari558: I can go with the sad and lonely, but LITTLE?

Ari558: Okay, well, confession: you're weird.

CONFESSIONALGRL: I'm weird?

Ari558: Exceedingly.

CONFESSIONALGRL: WEIRD???

Ari558: I'm going to fix that.

CONFESSIONALGRL: Like the doctor in Star Trek? Like with a dermal regenerator, only for my personality?

Ari558: Wow.

Ari558: A Star Trek reference. I guess, kind of like that, but cooler.

CONFESSIONALGRL: If you're not a Trekkie, we cannot be friends.

Ari558: Fine, but if you're a ST: Voyager girl, I quit you here and now.

CONFESSIONALGRL: Sad, lonely LITTLE individual!

Diary of Kaitlyn Johnson

Saturday, 11 September 2004, 9:00 PM
Dorm

It's the pills. Nothing more. It's in my mind—not real, not real, <u>NOT REAL</u>.

I left Carly a Post-it on the mirror—"stop taking the pills!" If Lansing wants her to remember what happened to our parents, then I'll do it for her.

It's useless. No matter how hard I try, no matter how many synapses I burst looking for the memory, it isn't there. In the blink of an eye, Mum and Dad went from living to dead.

I don't know how they died.

Later

Some people say that night blooms. I've always said that it cuts. Like a guillotine. I guess the sun heals the wound?

Before my parents ~~died~~ ~~left~~ went away, night was full. I made it that way. I went out. I partied. I drank. I met men. I ~~stole~~ borrowed. But since we went to ~~Claydon~~ Hell and now Elmbridge, I haven't been who I was before. That destruction is still there, I think—that urge to break myself open so I can peek inside. I still climb onto the roof and wonder why I don't just ~~jump~~ fly away—even if my body cracks on the pavement below. I still break into forbidden areas.

But I don't go out to nightclubs anymore, where they sell drinks and drugs—the kind you never heard of, let alone imagined. I don't dress in masquerade, a mask behind a mask, and dance with men who touch me and then vanish without even a kiss. I don't break into bookshops, and I don't steal. I don't leave messages in weird places for people to find. Except in the back of people's diaries sometimes...

Ari reminds me of what I lost when I lost the Viking...John. You know, he used to bring me seeds and call me his bird—his pesky falcon hawk...

~~Distract yourself.~~ Distract me, Dee.

~~I miss him. John.~~ I don't want to talk about him. He's the proof that I can't have friends. He's the proof that getting close is dangerous—it just ends up hurting.

It hurts.

But I do...

~~Be honest.~~ Be honest.

<u>I miss the Viking</u>. I could really use one of his wisecracks. It's been a while since I've seen him—not since Carly and I were dragged to Claydon. I've looked for him—an email address, anything. I sent a letter to his house, but I guess they moved.

He was responsible for all these changes. He's the reason I got out of the habit of practicing my suicide note—which I left for strangers to find. At bus stops, late-night cafés, pubs, clubs. Everywhere. Anywhere. Nowhere.

I remember it line for line: "Tell the living that I was never one of you. When you find this note, my throat will be a bloody red smile."

You can say it. I have a flair for melodrama. But it really was a cry for help. ~~It still is. I'm just too scared to reach out even that much anymore. Thank you, Lansing.~~

I met the Viking at one of these masquerade clubs—Masqued, I think it was. It was all blackness with strobes, green, white, and blue. The music made the glass shiver and the floor beneath our feet hammer as if attempting to get us to quit stomping on it.

He towered over everyone and looked as if he was <u>with</u> everyone, but he was alone, like me. His mask concealed a face I instinctively knew would be a mask in itself. He was veneers upon veneers upon hidden secrets. I think I recognized myself there, and I wanted him to be my secret. Something <u>only</u> mine. Something real.

Suddenly he was beside me, his Viking helmet glinting under the strobes.

We started to dance, and he didn't touch me. Not once. We lost ourselves in the music, in the obscurity it gave us, where no words could survive, making them even more unnecessary. I took off my mask. He took off his. And we both saw, for one fleeting moment, the true self beneath before we shuttered down the iron layers we had grown over our skin.

We left without a word. He with a girl from the bar, me alone.

The following night, he was there again, same mask, just like mine. We danced, and I didn't feel or see the other masked figures gyrating around me, only him. It wasn't sexual. It wasn't anything except a small connection to another human, and even that I was skeptical of.

He left his mask down as he said, "Will we exchange names?" These words did survive.

"True or fake?" I asked.

"True."

"Dark Half."

"Barbarian."

I shook my head. No. "Viking."

And it was not an untruth. Dark Half and the Viking. That's all we were to each other. He went home with a new girl, and I went home alone.

Every night we'd dance and exchange a sentence or two. Eventually our relationship evolved out of Masqued and into the streets of Chester. We'd walk around aimlessly, among the freaks and the rejected, who all come out at night.

"Don't you have somewhere to be?" I'd ask.

"Yes," he always replied. "Here."

"Which girl tonight?"

He'd shrug. "No idea."

"You like your damsels."

"No Viking is ever without one. Pillage and plunder.

How about you? A Dark Half…implies another half. A
Light one."

I hesitated. "True."

"Want to eat?"

He always knew when I didn't want to talk about
something. He never asked too many questions. At least,
he never asked important ones. He'd state a truth and
move on to the trivial, and I liked him for it.

We ate greasy chips from a chippy off Guildford
Road.

"Got to go," I said, flipping down my mask once we
were done.

He nodded and put on his helmet-with-mask, and was
once again ~~Barbarian~~ the Viking. He turned and left.
No long, drawn-out good-byes. No hugs or air kisses. I
think I loved him because of that.

It became a regular thing.

I kept him out of the Message Book. For a full half
year, he was just mine. I accidentally mentioned him
once, and after that—after the tiny slip—he wasn't
my secret anymore. It was after the slip that I asked
Carly if I could tell him about us. She agreed, and I
did, and for a time, everything seemed sort of…perfect.

I should have memorized his number, maybe, instead
of just saving it in my phone. They took it away. Took
him away. I never even knew his surname.

I hate that I miss him. My brother. My friend. I
hate that I've been looking for signs of him on the
Internet. I hate that I'm so easy to let go.

I guess it's easy to ~~abandon~~ forget someone once
she's out of sight. Still. I can't believe the Viking
would do that. Or I couldn't, for a long, stupid time.
Some days I still can't.

And here I sit, writing about him as though he's
just a ghost from my past that still haunts me. And I
guess that *is* all he is now. Just some guy I used to
know.

Midnight, Courtyard

I'm too proud to email Ari first.

Sunday, 12 September 2004, 12:30 am

I spy on Naida sometimes too. She's going to be a serial
killer for sure. Right now I'm outside her window, up in
the giant beech tree. Juliet also has a beech outside
her window, and Brenda too, and I'm pretty well hidden.
In late autumn, when the leaves fall, I won't be able to
use it to spy, but I have other methods—besides, I have
this weird notion that I'm one with the darkness and
that I'm really nothing more than a shadow myself.

Well, it's true, Dee, isn't it?

Right now, Naida's kneeling beside her bed, facing
the window—facing me—but there's a candle burning
(probably some acacia-turnip-catnip ritual concoction),
so she's blind to my presence, I think. As far as I
know, she sneaks these candles and paraphernalia into
the dorms without permission. Where she hides them I
have no idea. In her arsecrack for all I care.

To the casual observer, it would appear (apart
from the scarves—tapestries?—on the walls and the
strangely symbolic carpets on her floor) that her room
follows school regulations. I know, however, that
the bottles that look like perfumes are actually oils
she uses for conjurations and ritual baths and that
the little pouches that look like purses are actually
full of herbs and weird stuff like that. What do they
call them? Douche charms? Hope charms? Whatever. The
cards on her dresser are kind of like tarot cards, and
she has all kinds of weird spell kits that I've seen
her riffling through under her bed (covered with long
bedclothes, of course)—**cough** Witch **cough**.

When I watch her murmur under her breath, hold a
lighter under the incense (banned incense, I might
add), and beat on a little drum she stashes under
her bed—when I watch her draw symbols on her walls
in fragrant water that no one can see and then dance
around her room—I almost feel like a part of it.

It's so…dark.

When she bounces on the balls of her feet, eyes
closed and face so serene, I'm almost pulled in with
her. I can almost hear the drum, rhythmic, hypnotic,
and I can sense the Voice in my head somewhere nearby,
slowing. Like a purr, he enjoys this. He's calmed.
Lulled, almost. He sleeps.

How strange that Aka Manah should sleep so close
to the one I hate most. It never fails to amaze me how
opposites attract. Carly, the purest, most innocent and
trusting girl alive and, well, Naida. I mean, look at
her. You see that, right? Black magic? Enough said. ~~She
should be burned at the stake.~~

Naida is rocking back and forth now, praying to
whatever goddess she serves. I wish I could hear what
she's saying. Whatever it is, she's put the Voice in my
ear into a coma.

Holy freak show, Dee. Just when I thought I was safe.

Naida saw me. Looked right up into my face like
she knew I was there the whole time. I literally froze
solid, but not just because she was looking at me.
Because, for a second, I thought my own reflection in
the windowpane was smiling at me.

Creeped.

Me.

The. Hell.

Out.

But then my eyes refocused and Naida was right at
the window, face almost pressed against the glass,
staring at me. My heart is <u>still</u> racing. Jeeeeeeebus.

It was the weirdest thing. She stared at me for a
full three seconds, then leaned forward and blew out
the candle, and the room was plunged into darkness.
Could she have known I was there all along? Maybe she's
always known that I spy on her. Maybe these creepy
rituals are for my benefit. Maybe she's just laughing.
Except she didn't seem amused, Dee.

She looked scared.

Purple Post-It

Kait, did you move my biology textbook?

The one with the anatomy diagram on the front?

I <u>really</u> need it!

NO. But if you put your books in the <u>bookcase</u> once in a while instead of dumping them in piles all over, then you wouldn't lose things! (And quit blaming me, you cheeky arsewipe— I despise structured education.) :)

10

The following video footage does not contain a time index and has been placed here because of its relation to the previous Kaitlyn diary entry.

Naida Camera Footage
Date and Time Index Missing
Magpie House Corridor

"Hey!"

The camera shakes violently as Naida moves briskly towards Kaitlyn, who is walking away from her down the hall. Kaitlyn doesn't turn.

"Why were you spying on me last night?"

Still Kaitlyn doesn't stop.

"I saw you!"

"I don't know what you're talking about."

"Outside, in that tree. I've seen you there before."

Finally, Kaitlyn turns, notices the camera, and blanches. "So?"

"So I want to help. Maybe you could, like, have a hobby? It's sort of creepy having an audience."

"Screw you."

Kaitlyn storms away and slams the door behind her, glaring through the glass for a moment before running down the stairs.

"Shit."

"Language, Naida," comes a stern voice from off camera.

Naida films the empty corridor, but we catch her reply to someone at the other end. "Sorry, Miss Chisholm."

"And you're late for lights-out. The bell went off five minutes ago."

"Sorry, miss."

[END OF CLIP]

Naida Camera Footage
Date and Time Index Missing
Naida's Dorm Room

Naida kneels before a short candle, and the shadow of the flame flickers along the floor and wall. Outside, the light is growing brighter, and the rain patters the windows in rhythmic droves. Beside her, Carly sits biting her lip. Naida first covers the candle with a small pot with holes all over it, so that the candlelight is scattered over the walls like raindrops. Then she removes a little drum from beneath her bed and begins to beat it while chanting phrases that the mic cannot pick up.

After a brief silence, during which Naida's head remains bowed, Carly glances up at Naida's mirror on the wall. It is covered with a cloth.

"So the dead can't enter," Naida says, looking up at her. "And so that our souls can't get lost or be harmed."

"Are we in danger?"

"We should be careful."

Carly blinks, swallows, nods.

Naida takes a breath. "Great Father, Gorro, aid us in our prayer for our friend. Open the doorway for this communication. But protect us from wandering ears and eyes, and keep us safe. Keep her safe. Forgive our bold request. Bring us cleanly into the spirit world and help us bring our friend—sister—peace. Accept my small offering tonight, great Gorro, majestic Karrah, and bring harmony to the school." She pours what appears to be wine or grape juice into a chalice from a silver jug, her hands shaking visibly. "Quiet any evil that may exist here and let it sleep."

She raises the chalice to her lips and drinks deeply, then hands it to Carly, who sniffs the liquid, then takes a sip.

"Finish it."

Carly does so with some difficulty, and when the chalice is empty, she coughs.

"Is it done? Will Kaitie be—"

"Blessed Father, great Gorro, honored Mother, kindly Karrah," Naida interrupts, squeezing her eyes shut. "Thank you for your communion. We close the door."

"Is it—"

"Done. Yes."

"Kaitlyn will be happier? Calmer?"

Naida hesitates. "I hope so."

[END OF CLIP]

Criminal Investigation Department, Portishead Headquarters
Avon and Somerset Constabulary, Portishead, Bristol
Tuesday, 7 June 2005, 09h20
AUDIO INTERVIEW #1, PART 1: Detective Chief Inspector Floyd
Homes (FH) and Dr. Annabeth Lansing (AL)

(FH): Detective Chief Inspector Floyd Homes, Avon and
Somerset CID, interviewing Dr. Annabeth Lansing on
the seventh of June 2005. You were Carly Johnson's
therapist?

(AL): That is correct.

(FH): In what respect were you treating Miss Johnson?

(AL): Emotionally and psychologically. Carly suffered
numerous complications after the death of her parents.

(FH): Were you the admitting doctor in Carly's case?
For Claydon, I mean.

(AL): No. Dr. Phillips admitted Carly, and I was
brought in when she was diagnosed with DID.

(FH): DID?

(AL): It's a personality disorder, normally brought on
by severe trauma. Dissociative identity disorder.

(FH): Can you elaborate?

(AL): Dissociative identity disorder is a disruption
of identity. There are usually two or more distinct
personality states.

(FH): And Carly had this disorder?

(AL): That's why I was brought in. It's my field of
expertise.

(FH): I see. [Shuffling paper] In plain English, Doctor, what are the symptoms?

(AL): Altered personality states, amnesia surrounding the trauma. Sometimes accompanied by a paranoid alter ego, a scared alter, a sexually deviant alter, a dominant or aggressive alter—

(FH): How many of these alters did Carly have?

(AL): That's what made her case so interesting. She had only one other alter, and that one was fairly normal, as far as alters go. She was fully developed, but not exaggerated, like alters can be. Another unique feature is that the alter, who called herself Kaitlyn, came out regularly, at timed intervals.

(FH): Is that unusual?

(AL): It's unheard of. Another unusual thing about the Kaitlyn alter is that she heard a voice—a voice speaking to her when there was nothing there. She called it Aka Manah.

(FH): A voice. She was delusional?

(AL): She heard a voice. We all hear voices, but we know that they are our thoughts. Kaitlyn wasn't sensitive to that. She heard the voice in her head *and* outside of herself. Most often outside of herself. She thought it was real.

(FH): I see. [Pause] When did the Kaitlyn persona come out?

(AL): At night. Kaitlyn called herself a child of darkness.

(FH): And that *wasn't* extreme?

(AL): In the scheme of things, no. It simply amounts to a normal teenager's angst about her existence. I believe it was Kaitlyn's "job," as it were, to protect Carly from the dark hours, owing to what happened to her parents. In trauma, darkness is often given personification—like an evil force.

[Pause]

(FH): Tell me about what happened at the end of
September 2004.

(AL): I only found out about all of this later, but it
was around the end of November when Carly seemed to
integrate, but she did so in a peculiar manner.

[End of tape]

Diary of Kaitlyn Johnson

Sunday, 19 September 2004, 6:30 pm
Dorm

I should throw tantrums more often.

Jaime knocked on the door before she came in, which I should have known meant something was wrong. She's grown so much that when I saw her, I thought I might actually cry. Her arms are leaner, her stomach flatter; the pudginess of her toddler years is gone. She's five years old already.

When she saw me, she paused, eyes searching mine, ~~she was afraid of me~~ but when I opened my arms, she laughed and ran into them. I picked her up—she's so heavy now!—and spun her around like I used to.

My heart was breaking.

"It's been too long, Spud," I told her. "Were those fake parents of yours trying to keep you away?"

Jaime bit her lip as I put her down, and I felt bad, but only for a minute.

"Hey," I said, bending low so that I could look her in the face. "Don't listen when they talk crap about me, okay? The Baileys are a different kind of people from our family. They don't understand."

Jaime's eyes began to well, and she nibbled on her lip. Some things don't change after all.

"What is it, Spuddy?" I took her waist and wiggled her until she laughed. "You can tell me anything, you know."

"Even a bad thing?"

"Of course, even a bad thing. And you know, when you tell someone else a bad thing, it breaks in half, so that you're only carrying a small bit of it. So come on."

"Mr. and Mrs. Bailey don't like you."

What else is new? I'm well aware that they look down their straight, pointed little noses at me, judging with their self-righteous little eyes. That Johnson girl…she has problems. <u>Mental</u> problems…Gasp! Shudder!

"I know. It's okay. They don't have to like me. But <u>you</u> have to like me because I'm your sister and I love you. That's all that counts."

"They want to keep you away. I heard them talking."

It took all my self-control not to press her for information right away. Instead, I said, "Oh?"

She nodded. "They say that you're a bad affluence—"

"Influence."

"—a bad iff-iffluence, and you should go back to prison."

Prison. What a nice euphemism for the loony bin.

"Jaime, we weren't in jail. You know that, right? We were in a kind of hospital getting better after the accident."

"Mrs. Bailey says that you have to be locked up because your personality is wrong."

Word for word, Dee. My. Personality.

                                         Is.

                                               Wrong.

I took Jaime's hands. "My personality isn't wrong. And I don't think Carly's personality is wrong. Do you?"

"No."

"Mrs. Bailey thinks our personality is wrong because she thinks one of us shouldn't be here."

"Oh."

"I want you to do something for me, okay?"

She nodded, her eyes fixed on my face. I was her big sister. I would make everything right again. I would take a world that had become bent and confusing overnight and smooth out all of the wrinkles. Her hope is a noose around my neck.

"Whenever the" — insert: Dickball — "Baileys talk about me, I want you to close your ears. Close them like you close your eyes, and don't listen.

They don't understand. They think they do, but they
don't."

"But I can't close my ears. I don't have earlids."

"Oh, you do," I said earnestly. "They're inside your
head. If you imagine them closing, they will."

Jaime considered this for a moment. "Okay."

"Now, come on, enough about the Baileys," I said,
rolling my eyes. She giggled. "Tell me about you, about
friends—everything!"

She wrapped her little arms around my neck, and I
helped her onto my lap.

"I started school, and I like it a lot. I have a
friend called Mandy, and she likes me and lets me play
with her dolls."

I frowned. School? Already?

"Oh, yeah?" I prompted.

"She has a Bratz doll that has hair that can grow,
and a Barbie doll with a tail like a mermaid, and…"

She told me the minutiae of her life, and I felt as
though I had never heard anything more interesting or
vital in my whole existence. I soaked up every little
detail—about her new crayons (green was her favorite),
the dresses she got to wear (disgusting, frilly
concoctions to make her look like a doll), the shopping
trips she and Dickball Mrs. Bailey took into London,
and the dollies that Mandy let her play with.

"Do you have a picture of Mummy and Daddy in your
room?" I asked her abruptly, because it suddenly
occurred to me what the Baileys were doing. They weren't
merely giving an orphan a place to live; they were
adopting her, absorbing her as their own, sucking out
her Johnson and injecting their Bailey! It explained
the dresses, the "keep away from Carly" mission, the
"Carly's personality is wrong" mantra—it explained why
she had started schooling so young. Indoctrination.

"I don't have any pictures from before." The words
slipped out like a bubble, too fragile to resist the
destruction of dry air.

It was like a glass smashing against a wall.

"Who do they think they are? They won't allow you to have a photo of your dead parents? That's sick!"

"I don't want one," Jaime said in a little voice, her eyes already swollen with tears.

I. Don't. Want. One.

A sledgehammer couldn't have hit me as hard.

I whispered my reply. "What?"

"I don't like to remember."

"Remember them?"

"Remember what happened."

It was like an electric shock to my head. "You remember the accident?"

She looked away, and although she didn't nod, I saw the answer in her haunted eyes.

"Jaime…tell me. I can't remember. Tell me—"

"Dr. Lasny said not to talk about it."

"Dr.—Dr. Lansing?"

Jaime nodded.

Betrayal. Betrayed. I was betrayed. Dr. Lansing is in this whole thing with the Baileys—working to make Jaime forget me and to never come see me! She only caved when I threw a tantrum and made things hard for her! They want Jaime to forget me!

I grabbed Jaime by the shoulders. "I'm your sister! I'm the oldest now they're dead, and you have to listen to what I say! You will not forget me!"

She cried out—a small, piercing shriek—and began to weep. I dropped her arms, instantly sorry, and gave her a big hug. She sobbed until she fell asleep, her head padded on my chest. I lay on my bed with her, taking in her little-girl smell (it had changed since living with the fake parents, but not so much that I couldn't smell the real her underneath).

"Don't forget me," I whispered in her ear, holding her hand—a tiny version of my own.

We lay together for an hour or so, and I thought about how things used to be. Carly discarding me in our room, always the same. Cuddling up with Jaime in her bed for a while, reading her a bedtime story—always "The Frog Prince"—and then going out into the night after (maybe) a brief chat with Mum. Looking down at Jaime sleeping beside me now, I felt the loss of that normal all over my body like an ache. I could have stayed like that forever, but she jolted awake, dizzy and confused.

"Where am I?" she asked. She was shivering.

"With me in my room, silly," I told her.

She gave a couple of sleepy grunts. "It's too cold in here. I don't like it."

I glanced at the window—it was shut firmly. And Jaime was still in her fluffy coat.

"It's not cold," I said, touching her cheeks, which were warm.

"And it smells funny."

I sniffed the air. Nothing.

"I don't like it," she said, eyes shadowed.

It was weird. Jaime loves everything, and when she doesn't, she doesn't moan about it. Those Bailey shits have got into her head.

"Come on, Jaime. It's just a room!"

"There's something bad in here."

What could I say? The Baileys have been turning her against me for months. Not in an obvious way, of course, but in subtle ways. And there's nothing I can do about it. It makes me crazy.

"I have to go," she said, climbing off my bed. There were duvet lines across her cheek, and sleep was still heavy in her eyes. "Mrs. Bailey said she would wait for me at the end of the corridor."

"Jaime?" I said, as she turned to go. "Don't let those dickballs tell you things about me."

"Okay."

"You know me better than they do," I added.

She nodded. "Okay."

As the door was closing behind her, I thought of something.

"Wait—Jaime?"

Her little head popped back. "Yeah?"

"Have you heard from Carly lately?"

"Yes."

"She sound...normal? I mean, did she sound okay?"

She just shrugged. "I have to go now."

"Okay, Beanette."

The door closed. I didn't get a chance to say "I love you," so I said it to the closed door. The words, spoken but unheard, fell to the floor, where they shattered like glass. Everything so fragile, and I love her so much. That, I think, is fragile too.

I sniffed the air, and still I didn't smell a thing.

I should have asked what it smelled like.

Later, Dorm

Kaitlyn is:

1. **A prophet**

2. **Demonstrably insane**

3. **An incredible force**

4. **Bipolar**

5. **A ghost**

6. **A big dog in a little cage**

Which of these seems likely, Dr. Lansing?

So sick of her. Sick of her ideas. Sick of it all. I am not a symptom! She's the symptom. She's sick.

Sick!

  Sick!

    Sick!

      Sick!

        Sick!

          SICK!

From: RealxChick
To: AriHait558
Date: 19 Sept 2004
Subject: A Disgrace to My Gender

So I finally caved and emailed you. What a crappy night so far.

Grumpy.

From: AriHait558
To: RealxChick
Date: 19 Sept 2004
Subject: Re: A Disgrace to My Gender

It never ceases to amaze me the rules girls put on their lives.

I saw you near the art block the other day, and you looked right through me. Hence my silence. I suppose I'm a little too weird to acknowledge during school? Maybe your friends will disown you if they find out you're secretly befriending the weird guy in the bowler hat.

A.

[There is no reply from Kaitlyn on the server.]

Sunday, 19 September 2004, 10:00 pm
Basement

You have dark hair. (I've always wanted dark hair.)
Your eyes will be brown, a color that holds secrets
well. Isn't that fitting? You're tall, because I'm
not. You have three tattoos—an asp on your left wrist,
a sparrow on your right ankle, and a dagger on your
thigh. You have plump lips that are for kissing, not
talking, and your eyes sparkle with inner light. You
like to listen.

What do you think, Dee? Have I described you
accurately? Do you need a more distinctive feature to
tell you apart from the rabble of the world? How about
this: You have one brown eye and one green eye. You
take in through the green and cage with the brown. You
have a nose stud too, and you always wear black.

Welcome to my head, Dee. Please, look around.

I'm in the bowels of the main building, exploring
the basement. It's so cold.

I swear, Dee, this place is as big as the entire
main building. Chairs, tables, boxes, uniforms,
equipment, netting, the old (and new) hall curtains,
mannequins, old mattresses from the boardinghouse,
skeletal teaching props—you name it. Not only did I
reach a point where I thought I'd never find an exit,
but I also lost track of the window that gave me entry.
Just my luck, being trapped down there with useless
things. Maybe, I thought, I'll die down here. It got me
thinking about whether I'm a prop in Carly's life, or
she's one in mine.

There's another room down there, Dee. Totally cut
off from everything else. A tiny little box of a room
with its own staircase—grimy and moist—up to a secret
servants' corridor that leads between walls and out
into the kitchen. This room is the only part of this
building not cluttered with stuff. The only thing in

there is a big Victorian cupboard—an armoire. It gave
me the chills. Even though it's just an empty room,
it felt as if someone was in there with me. Maybe more
than one person. At any rate, I felt watched.

Lame, I know.

Because, Dee, I'm the thing in the dark, just like
the Viking used to tell me. I'm the creature coming
up from the basement, the thing under the bed. I have
nothing to fear in the dark. I am the dark.

I am afraid.

Ari came to the main building looking for me. He said that when I didn't answer his email and didn't come to the chapel, he got worried (contrived much?). He saw me from the top of the hill, heading there. By the time he got there, I was already climbing out through the broken window.

"So this is where you sneak off to," he said, grinning from ear to ear.

I glanced back at the building, feeling oddly protective. "Sometimes."

"Fancy a swim?"

Dee, I had forgotten! I'd forgotten how badly I wanted to visit the swimming pool, having been so preoccupied with the attic. He grinned and nodded towards the building, and honestly, I just gave in! I showed him the window I've broken, and we climbed inside. We didn't linger long—instead, we ran up the stairs, and along the main corridor, past the billiard room, gallery, and main foyer, into the pool room, where we stripped down to our underwear and slipped in.

It was beautiful—and warm! So warm. We had to be quiet, since Coach O'Grady and Mrs. Mayle both have their apartments in this main building round the back, but it was the most fun I've had in years.

I thought, for a moment, Ari might try to kiss me, and I wasn't sure how I felt about that, but then he didn't, and we just giggled and raced quietly in the pool. I'm going to keep this to myself, Dee. I'm going to keep Ari to myself.

I'm glad he didn't kiss me.

I'm glad I'm still untouched.

Session #46 Audio
Dr. Annabeth Lansing (AL) and Carly "Kaitlyn" Johnson (CJ)
Friday, 24 September 2004, 7:57 PM

(**AL**): Am I speaking with Carly? Or Kaitlyn?

(**CJ**): Aren't you supposed to be able to tell?

(**AL**): Hello, Kaitlyn.

(**CJ**): It's Carly.

(**AL**): It's better if you're completely honest. You know that.

[Pause]

(**CJ**): Dr. Lansing, it's Carly.

(**AL**): This is excellent. I didn't see you last session.

(**CJ**): No. Kaitlyn?

(**AL**): She was concerned about not being able to see Jaime.

(**CJ**): I was wondering about that. About the delay.

(**AL**): A visit was arranged. I'm assuming Kaitlyn was around, not you.

(**CJ**): No…I was there. I meant I was wondering before the visit.

(**AL**): Tell me about the visit. How did it go?

(**CJ**): Jaime's…different. I don't want to talk about it.

(**AL**): I heard from Meredith Bailey. She tells me that Jaime was disturbed by a smell in your room.

(**CJ**): I don't want to talk about it.

(AL): Carly, you need to tell me if Kaitlyn is smoking marijuana again.

(CJ): I would have told you.

(AL): It might not be very obvious.

(CJ): I lived with Kaitlyn for a long time. I know what weed smells like. There's none.

(AL): Jaime also complained, apparently, of a strange feeling. Do you know anything about that?

(CJ): She doesn't recognize me anymore. You keep her away from me and then wonder why she doesn't feel comfortable? You want this—you want her to forget me.

(AL): Carly, I want no such thing. You know why she doesn't come to see you.

(CJ): No, I don't! Why, because they call me crazy? Because you think I have multiple personalities?

(AL): You know that's not the only reason.

(CJ): You keep saying I know what happened the day my parents died! I don't! So why don't you just stop with the theatrics and *tell* me!

(AL): [Sigh] Carly, you have that information inside you. You will remember exactly what happened when your mind can cope with it.

(CJ): So I was there. *Actually* there, not just informed afterwards?

[Pause]

I was there. I was, wasn't I?

(AL): Give the details time. You aren't ready for the information yet. If you were, you'd have it.

(CJ): And in the meantime, Jaime grows up and forgets me.

(AL): She'll never forget you.

[Pause]

(CJ): I'm not so sure.

[Rustling paper]

(AL): How about school this year? Do you feel more positive about it?

(CJ): There are new students.

(AL): And that makes you uncomfortable?

(CJ): [Pause] I…I don't know.

(AL): New faces, new names, new smells. Does it make you happy? Glad for the change?

(CJ): No. I…I want things to be the same as last year.

(AL): Of course you do. No one likes change that's unexpected. Not unless you're a destructive alter, like Kaitlyn. Do you get messages from Kaitlyn anymore?

(CJ): Sometimes.

(AL): Thank you for being honest with me, Carly. I can see that you certainly *look* well and that the summer hasn't brought back old behaviors. Apart from an appearance from Kaitlyn last week, which is to be expected, you've been doing well.

[Silence]

I wonder, though, if you're being completely honest. I know that you're intimidated by Kaitlyn, and that she's controlling. But this is a safe space. You can tell me if there is anything wrong.

[Pause]

(CJ): Nothing's wrong.

(AL): You've been wearing your school uniform to our sessions. Why?

(CJ): I don't have time to change.

(AL): And it has nothing to do with the uniform having long sleeves?

(CJ): No.

(AL): You're feeling good, then? Nothing bad from Kaitlyn? No cuts, bruises? Nothing hurting? Have you checked your body, Carly? Your…[Pause] I know it's difficult, but Kaitlyn may be taking control without you knowing it and doing things—

[Loud slamming noise]

(CJ): No!

[Silence]

(AL): Well, Kaitlyn. Out again. You sound defensive.

[Heavy breathing]

(CJ): Screw you, Lansing. I'd never hurt Carly.

(AL): Luckily for Carly, it seems you can't hurt her anymore. She was just here, after sundown. Does that surprise you? That she can exist in the darkness, just as you can?

(CJ): You're a piece of work, Doctor. Carly is everything that the day is supposed to be. And I don't appreciate you hinting at me hurting her.

(AL): You hurt yourself.

(CJ): That's different.

(AL): How? You said yourself—you share a body. What you suffer is what you inflict on her, correct?

[Silence]

Despite your sudden appearance, Carly's doing well. You're slowly integrating, Kaitlyn. You shouldn't be afraid of that. One day you'll function as a harmonious whole—you'll be a part of Carly, both of you together.

(CJ): You mean I'll be gone. Buried by her mind.

(AL): I'm afraid it's the way it's supposed to be. You won't vanish, as such. But you'll be reabsorbed. You came out at a time of profound stress. You're a coping mechanism. But Carly is the true self, and your job is done. You've protected her so well, dear, you have. You've kept that awful darkness of the nighttime away—and the memories. You've carried the burden for her, but now she's strong enough to take it back. She needs to take it back.

(CJ): You've got no clue what you're talking about.

(AL): Carly, come out.

(CJ): You think you know everything.

(AL): [Loudly] Carly, come out!

[Sigh]

[Pause]

(CJ): I…I'm—what was I saying?

(AL): We were talking about Kaitlyn being put away for good. I think you're doing remarkably well.

(CJ): Oh. Can I stop the medicine? Just a little bit? I haven't done anything reckless in so long—I haven't lost much time at all.

[Scratching of pen on paper]

(AL): In time, Carly. Soon. I'd like to see you again in, let's say…Thursday. Yes, the thirtieth, at five PM. Come straight after school.

(CJ): I have choir then. Could I come after?

(AL): Okay. [Pause] I have a meeting at…let's make it six thirty.

(CJ): All right. Thank you Dr. Lansing. For everything.

(AL): You've worked hard. A little more work, Carly, and you'll feel better.

[End of tape]

Friday, 24 September 2004, 9:35 pm
Dorm

I AM NOT A SICKNESS!

I have to get out of this room—these four walls. All I see is shadow on white paint, bleeding into vomit gray when you look hard enough. All I see is by halves, and I feel the Voice in my ear, whispering, laughing, telling me the time is coming.

Soon, he tells me. Soon.

I have to get out of here.

11:00 pm

I have this horrible feeling tonight. Like—I don't know. Like, maybe I'm starting to remember something. Just the hint of something—a hunch I can't shake. My mind was wandering, and I saw my mother, in my memory, sitting on the bed. She was wearing a blue polo-necked dress and that thick black belt. She leaned forward and said, "Isn't it funny how memories are just colors, shades, and impressions?"

She leaned back, and then she wasn't Mum anymore, she was Dr. Lansing, and she was shaking her head. "Not funny at all, really. Is it?"

I don't think our parents died in an accident like Lansing says.

Did they die...on purpose?

14

A police incident report was filed on 25 September 2004. Part of the report detailed the damage to a dorm in the Juniper House.

Berkley, Somerset
Incident Report.
25 September 2004

OFFICER REPORTING: Community Officer Seamus Rompton

DETAIL OF INCIDENT: Door to one of the dorms in Juniper wing of Elmbridge High removed and hidden (as yet missing). Mirror in the bathroom of Juniper House smashed on the floor. No sign of a weapon, and no item in the bathroom heavy or sturdy enough to inflict damage of this nature. A sixth-form student, Mike Bowers, suffered several superficial lacerations to his face, torso, and thighs. He has been removed to a local hospital for treatment and recalls nothing of how he was wounded. A brief search of the boys' wing revealed nothing untoward; however, it is noted that none of the windowpanes or doors have a locking mechanism in the student wings, and anyone might have had access. Incident resembles a student prank and will be treated as such.

Naida Camera Footage
Sunday, 26 September 2004
Time Index Not Noted
Common Room

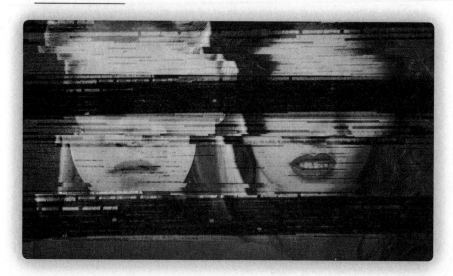

"You heard?" Naida says, putting the camera down on the common room coffee table. She sits beside Carly, who stares out the window, the back of her thumb pressed to her lips. She looks pale.

"Carly," Naida presses. "Did you hear? About Mike?"

"Hm?"

"Did you hear about Mike's room?"

Carly ignores Naida's question and turns to gaze out the window again. "Do you hear that?"

"Hear what?"

"You don't hear it? It's—shh! Listen...like someone whispering."

Naida frowns, her eyes darting as her ears search for the sound. The girls sit still for a moment, until Carly gasps and grabs Naida's arm.

"There! You heard that, right?"

"Carly, there's nothing."

Carly swallows, glancing down at her legs. "It sounds so sad."

"Sugar, you're scaring me."

Carly exhales and, with a wistful glance out the window, turns back to Naida.

"What were you saying about Mike?"

"Someone took his door clean off its hinges and hid it somewhere. *And* someone smashed the mirror in the Juniper House bathroom." Naida laughs. "They can't find the door anywhere. Not to mention that he woke up covered in tiny little cuts. Couldn't have picked a more perfect target, if you ask me. Mike's an A-hole."

"Oh. Hm."

"What's wrong? You've been acting so weird lately. Always zoning out, always tired, or else fidgeting and worried. I feel like you aren't even here sometimes. Where are you?"

"I think I'm getting sick. Or maybe it's these new meds. Dr. Lansing says they'll help me feel better once I get used to them." There is tightness in her lips and jaws as she speaks.

The light in the room changes, dimming subtly, which registers noticeably on the camera. The time index is not given, but it can be assumed it is late afternoon, or early evening. Both girls are still wearing their Elmbridge uniforms.

Naida folds her arms. "And you trust this doctor woman? Kaitie seems skeptical."

Carly frowns and scratches at her arm. "You speak to Kait?"

"When she lets me. Which isn't often."

"Yeah," Carly says slowly. "I do trust Dr. Lansing. She's trying to help me."

"Help with what?"

"Help me to remember the accident. What happened. I don't know. And I need to believe that...I just need her."

"And Kaitlyn? She wants to put Kaitlyn away, right?"

"You can't just put her away."

Naida hesitates. "Would you...if you could?"

For the first time, Carly's face grows hard, alert, and resolute. "No. Never. I would destroy myself first, okay?" Her voice turns desperate. "Do you believe me? I would never intentionally—" She breaks off with a gasp, hands flying to her throat.

"What? What—Carly, what?"

Carly's face crumples. "Don't you hear it? Don't you hear the noise?"

She stands, and her face disappears out of the shot, but we can see her hands shaking. "I hear you! I hear you! What? *What?*"

"Carly, what the hell—"

Carly's legs buckle, and she collapses onto the sofa, eyes rolling and lips trembling. She looks panicked, though unaware. Naida pushes back her hair and feels her forehead.

"Kaitie," Carly murmurs in a high, small voice, before she falls silent.

Naida sits watching, face drawn and eyes shadowed. "What the hell's going on with you?"

After a few moments, Carly's eyes snap open. She glances at Naida before sitting up and leaning away. Her posture is noticeably different, her expression visibly hardening.

"What do *you* want?"

Naida shakes her head, seemingly unable to tear her eyes away. "Nothing, Kaitlyn."

With a withering look, Kaitlyn gets to her feet and walks out of the shot. As though stung, Naida reaches out a hand.

"Kaitlyn!" she calls. "Is...is everything okay...with you?"

Offscreen, Kaitlyn's reply is curt. "Why should you care?"

"I do. I...is Carly okay?"

There's a pause. It stretches out. Has Kaitlyn left?

"How would I know?" comes the somewhat subdued reply at last.

Naida nods. "Okay...um...see you around."

Footsteps, a door closing, and then Naida bends forward, covering her face with her hands. It is unclear whether she is crying.

[END OF CLIP]

Sunday, 26 September 2004, 8:00 PM
Attic

So Mike's door was apparently taken right off its hinges while he slept, and no one can find the door. It's vanished into thin air. That's not all. The mirror in the Juniper House boys' bathroom was completely smashed—and no one heard a thing. And then there's Mike's face…cut to little pieces. Creeeeeeeeepy. The police are being all hush-hush about it too, and Mike hasn't been back to school since. I think there's something more that they're not telling us.

Principal Roth called the police. And, naturally, the police wanted to talk to me—I guess because of my parents or maybe just because of Claydon and Carly's meds. Technically, we're the only ~~people~~ person who ~~are~~ is a social-deviancy risk. This was after dinner, thank God. If they had treated Carly the way they treated me and I found out about it later, I'd have done something stupid.

As it was, I simply listened to them ask the same questions over and over.

"Do you know what happened to the door to Mike's room?"

No.

"Did you remove the door to Mike's room?"

No.

"Do you and Mike associate in school?"

No.

"Did you and Mike have a falling-out?"

No. (Get on with it already.)

"Are you currently taking your medication?"

(Screw you.) Yes. Is that all?

"We'll be in touch again."

(Goodie for me.) Uh-huh.

Automatically it's me, right? Oh, yes, Officer, I unscrewed Mike's forty-five-pound door and carried it out of the dorm on my back and then buried it in the ~~graveyard~~ Forgotten Garden, then proceeded to smash the bathroom mirror—all without anyone hearing a thing. Oh, right. I must have drugged everyone with the enormous amounts of nitrazepam they give me, which I secretly hide on the roof of my mouth, so they all slept right through it. Prick.

I'll admit that it's odd. Me, awake all night, and I didn't hear anything either. I can see into his room from across the courtyard, so, really, I should have seen something. Then again, I try to avoid being in the dorm too much. It feels like Carly's, not mine.

If I'm the accused, I want to see this for myself.

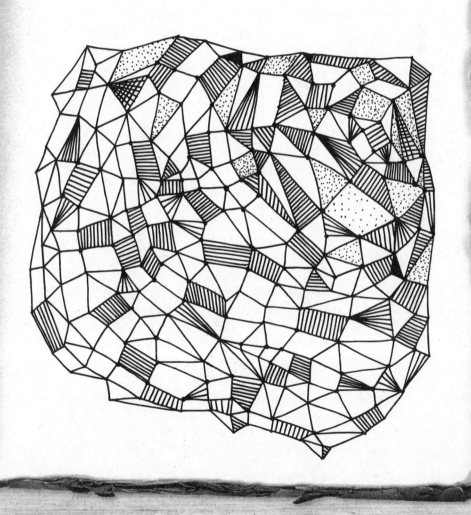

Monday, 27 September 2004, 2:35 am
Attic

I went to check out the missing-door situation. I climbed in through Mike's window, because he's gone home now, and wandered around. It smelled like guy, and I don't even know why. It just did. Instinctively, I knew that the musk in there was male, nothing more.

Much like Magpie House, the dorms in Juniper House are plain and boring, though interior decoration varies from most of the useless crap I see in the girls' rooms. More posters, less jewelry (although still some), and more clothes in unlikely places (windowsill, sink, and trash can). I wondered if Ari's room was like this. I could have found out…I thought about going to Pinewood Hall and looking into every window until I found his.

But I had to focus.

Apart from the missing door, which was kind of like a giant hole in a person's face, the room looked normal. I inspected the hinges and found them intact, if missing the door. What would I feel like if I arrived to find *my* door missing, Dee?

The bathroom was another story.

At first, everything looked completely normal. The mirror looked perfect—new, even. I couldn't believe how fast they'd replaced it, but I guess I wasn't *that* surprised. Maybe it posed a health and safety risk. Maybe Elmbridge just didn't want ugliness anywhere near it. I glanced at myself, for some reason put in mind of my reflection when I spied on Naida from out in the beech tree—how I thought I saw my reflection smile at me.

I frowned, pulling faces at myself, making sure that my reflection followed suit and in perfect time. For a minute, I was stupid enough to think that…maybe…if I looked really hard, I would see Carly in there, looking

out at me. But it was just me, of course, and I felt
like an idiot.

"Nothing," I muttered, glancing around once. "How
disappointing."

I rolled my eyes and headed for the exit. As I got
to the door, I turned back one last time—

The mirror was gone.

Utterly,

Completely,

Gone.

Not a mirror. Not my reflection looking back.

A yawning black hole.

I tried to scream, but I was frozen, locked in
place by the sight of such…nothingness. My voice was
gone, sucked into that dark expanse, which seemed
to be inhaling. One giant, terrible breath. Pulling
me closer. My heart skipped a beat, then thumped
painfully, then raced like it was trying to escape.

I just kept thinking,

This isn't real.

This can't be real.

This isn't real.

And then she was standing in the gulf, the girl
I thought I'd seen at the basement window, grinning,
her thin arm waving back and forth at me.

Hi there, she seemed to be saying, her long white
teeth shocking in the black. So real. So fucking real.

I wanted so badly to scream, to run, to escape. But
I was trapped there, my legs stuck.

Who is she?

The sink lay full of shards of glass…and they
were bloody. The girl reached slowly through the
black space, crisp and empty, and took a long shard
of mirror. She grinned wider—how was it possible?—
and slashed at her arms, flesh parting to reveal thick
spaces of black nothing inside.

I stumbled back a step, my body weak and useless
with shock, and I blinked—

And then she was gone. The black hole was now a
chipboard, and not a shard of glass was in sight. My

heart thumped once in my chest, paused, and then raced frenetically; my eyes couldn't look away. Somewhere… very close yet also very far, something was laughing at me. Raucous roars of pulsing derision.

"This isn't happening," I whispered, but the chipboard seemed to be laughing as well, and I had the sense that it was becoming more and more real. More and more…present—mocking me.

I covered my mouth to hold back my scream, and then I ran from that bathroom, from that wing, and threw myself out the window, the whole time feeling as if something was right behind me, inches away from grabbing me, right on my heels. The laughter faded the farther I went, but I didn't stop running until I got up here, safely to the attic, and to you, Dee.

I can't stop shaking. What's happening to me?

Diary of Kaitlyn Johnson

Tuesday, 28 September 2004, 1:51 am
Attic

I think that Aka Manah is trying to make me believe I'm
crazy.

5:00 am,
Dorm

Went to the chapel tonight. Ari came a little after
2 am, and the moment I saw him, everything else faded
away. I was fine. Isn't it strange? How another human
being can make the quiet seem less quiet, the unreal
more real? Even when we sat there, doing nothing. Isn't
it astonishing? Isn't it miraculous? I haven't felt
this way ~~since the Viking~~ in a while.

If I sat there with Ari for long enough, could the
thing I saw—the not-mirror, the blood—be a nothing?
Could I forget about it, brush it off?

Ari didn't mention Carly tonight, so maybe they
haven't run into each other yet? I hope so. How could I
explain it to him…Worse, how could I explain to Carly
why I kept him to myself?

"Because you've been busy, and I needed ~~someone~~."

Too cruel?

Too cruel.

So I'll keep him for myself, like the Viking. Except
this time, I won't waver. Maybe he can make me more
real. Maybe he can make what I saw in the bathroom last
night be forgotten.

~~I know what I saw~~.

Almost time to disappear. I wonder where I go.

Wednesday, 29 September 2004, 3:00 am
Attic

I like to leave myself memento mori. I draw them in everything—hidden in textbook diagrams, in the grains of the wood on the wall, under my bed.

They make shit real. But not as real as the girl staring at me from the corner.

Is that you, Dee?

Recovered Message Book Entry

Wednesday, 29 September 2004, 4:40 am

Carly, where are you? Why haven't you written?
Are you angry with me?

I think maybe I'm starting to remember
something about how it happened. Please answer.
I need to talk to you.

Session #47 Audio
Dr. Annabeth Lansing (AL) and Carly "Kaitlyn" Johnson (CJ)
Thursday, 30 September 2004, 8:34 PM

(CJ): Thank you...for seeing me. I know you canceled, but...

(AL): What's happened?

[Rustling as of material]

(CJ): Nothing, really. I just...You told me to trust you, and...

(AL): You can trust me. [Pause] Trust me.

(CL): Carly hasn't written to me. She hasn't left me any messages. It's unsettling. She *always* writes to me. Always.

[Pause]

(AL): Kaitlyn. How long since she failed to write?

(CJ): A couple of days. I mean, she still leaves me Post-its, but something's wrong. She's distant.

(AL): [Sigh] This is good. This is excellent.

(CJ): Wait...you think this is *good*? Where is she?

(AL): Kaitlyn, this is hard for you. I understand. You're holding on. It can't be easy to learn that you're not real. To learn that you're a symptom of trauma. I understand that you want to resist. To hold on. But by doing that, you're keeping Carly from healing—

(CJ): No! You're trying to confuse me. Carly
wouldn't abandon me. She wouldn't leave me all
alone! Something's wrong, I know her!

(AL): Carly is letting you go. It has to happen.
It will feel like abandonment, it will be so hard.
But, eventually, you'll find peace. You'll integrate.
Absorb.

(CJ): [Sniff] Disappear.

(AL): The way it's meant to be.

[Pause]

(CJ): I'm not nothing. I'm not meant to be nothing.

(AL): You need to free her, Kaitlyn. You need to let
her go. You need to stop being a crutch. She has to
heal.

(CJ): You want me to just...die?

(AL): [Pause] Yes.

[Lengthy silence]

[End of tape]

PART II

WE
ARE
ME

I celebrate myself, and sing myself,
And what I assume you shall assume,
For every atom belonging to me as good
belongs to you.

—Walt Whitman

You are the music
While the music lasts.

—T. S. Eliot

18

Naida Camera Footage (Raw)
Date and Time Index Missing
Naida's Dorm Room

Camera, blurry, spins and jostles, but in a few of the frames, we can see that we are in a dorm room. Shots of scarves pinned to the wall reveal that it is Naida's room.

"How do you get this stupid thing to work?" she says, peering down into the lens so that we see her eyes large and distorted.

"Give it here."

Scott takes the camera, which angles in on his face, and messes with the lens. The picture refocuses, definition sharp. He turns the camera on Naida, who reaches for it.

"Give it back, Scott! It's new. Hand it over, or I'll give you a nutshot and upload it onto the school website."

Scott laughs. "I thought that making a little 'Scott's bollocks' voodoo doll and sticking it full of pins was more your style?"

"Push me, Scotty-boy, just push me."

Scott hands back the camera, and Naida wipes the screen with her sleeve. For a moment a shadow passes over the shot—behind Naida.

"You adore me too much for that," Scott says.

"Your balls, maybe. Ugh, forget it. I need to fiddle with it some more."

"Fiddle with this," Scott says, but the camera turns off before we can see Naida's reaction.

[END OF CLIP]

Close analysis of the frames in this clip reveals two things. First, there is a sound, perhaps only static or something brushing against the microphone as Naida wipes the lens, or perhaps what it sounds like, whispering. Second, a person is standing in the closet behind Naida, the dark form of someone looking out, two pinpricks of light glinting off their eyes.

Diary of Kaitlyn Johnson

Friday, 1 October 2004, 12:24 am
Elmbridge

Tricks, trickery, manipulations.
  Lies.
  They are all lying to me.
  Lansing is a master manipulator.
  Liar.
  Trying to put space between Carly and me.
  Part of the "integration process."
  She's a murderer! She wants to kill me.
  If Carly doesn't write to me, then she won't need me.
  Tricky tricky tricksters.
  <u>Carly</u>.

3:00 am

~~I saw something by the~~
~~I'm not really sure what I saw~~
I'm not going to let Lansing and her psycho-drugs get to me. I wish Carly would stop taking them!

Searched for the Viking again online. Nothing. Always nothing.

Wrote in the Message Book:

Carly, Lansing scared me.

Where are you?

Why are you so quiet?

Lansing said—God, Lansing will do anything. Please answer.

What happened to our plan? Elmbridge, then out, remember?

Lansing...she said—she said—just write something nice. Tell me you love me. Tell me you need me. You believe I'm here. Please. Please, Carly.

Where are you??

Message Book Entry

Saturday, 2 October 2004, 7:18 am

Everything's going to be okay, Kaitie. I promise.

The "Forgotten Garden" area of which Kaitlyn speaks in the entry below is the graveyard outside St. Martha's Chapel on the hill above Elmbridge High, where Kaitlyn and Ari first met. Petitions to have a children's play area built near the site were denied thirteen times in the twelve years following the incident. No petitions have been filed in the last eight years.

Diary of Kaitlyn Johnson

Monday, 4 October 2004, 4:42 am
Forgotten Garden

There are places. Abandoned places. Forgotten places. These are the places I like to be.

Elmbridge has one of these places. Once, it was beautiful. You can tell that right away. The rain-stained gravestones among the dying grasses; the fence, rusted and half-hinged, with coils of wrought iron—once painted black or a very dark green—now flaking away; the overgrown footpath, which now leads into the impenetrable grasses that stand dry and still. A dead yellow sea.

I figure it's either a holy place, or cursed. Either way, I guess I belong here.

Redemption or Punishment.

I don't know which one I'm looking for. Each seems likely. When I first found the chapel, where no one goes, I walked around blind. The next night, I came with my flashlight and spent my hours swimming my way around the sad place, memorizing the blank graves.

Last year, I guarded this place with such jealousy that I never told Carly about it. When she asked me about my night in the Message Book, I lied, and it became a habit. Now all I do is lie.

"How are you tonight, Kait?" Oh, fine. Feeling good.

"What are you going to do tonight, Kaitie?" Probably read. Watch a movie in the common room. Have a blast.

"Are you okay, Kat?" Of course I am, Carly-bean.

"I love you." Yeah.

How quickly the tables turn. Now I'm desperate for her to tell me something real, instead of the short little lies she feeds me. Her last message to me: "Everything's going to be okay, Kaitie. I promise."

What does that even mean?

Criminal Investigation Department, Portishead Headquarters
Avon and Somerset Constabulary, Portishead, Bristol
Monday, 13 June 2005, 14h56
AUDIO INTERVIEW #2: Detective Chief Inspector Floyd Homes
(FH) and Dr. Annabeth Lansing (AL)

(FH): Detective Chief Inspector Floyd Homes, Avon
and Somerset CID, interviewing Dr. Annabeth Lansing
on the thirteenth of June 2005. Thank you for coming
in again. For the record, I will once more ask you
a few standard questions. You were Carly Johnson's
therapist?

(AL): Yes.

(FH): In what capacity were you treating Miss Johnson?

(AL): Psychologically. I was also responsible for
administering psychotropic drugs to control various
symptoms.

(FH): The DID. [Rustling of paper] The...dissociative
identity disorder.

(AL): Yes, and later for early psychosis. She was
hearing things. Sometimes seeing things. Her thought
pattern was erratic.

(FH): How was this psychosis diagnosed?

(AL): Initially, Carly was an inpatient at Claydon.
When she became stable enough that continued residence
at Claydon became detrimental to her recovery, she was
sent to Elmbridge High.

(FH): That is a rather well-known and well-thought-of
school, am I correct?

(AL): Yes.

(FH): And how did a girl with a diagnosis of early psychosis end up there?

(AL): Claydon and Elmbridge have had a partnership agreement since the thirties. Elmbridge High is a top school in the academic leagues, but it is also a feeder for some of the Claydon children who have had psychiatric treatment but are not a danger to themselves or others. Depression. Anorexia nervosa. Persistent insomnia. A number of the Elmbridge staff consult for Claydon as well. Essentially, it allows them to classify their institution as a charity for tax purposes. And Miss Johnson wasn't psychotic at that time.

(FH): Did Miss Johnson acclimatize well?

(AL): When Carly started at Elmbridge in September 2003, she seemed to be doing remarkably well, yes. She even made a friend or two. However, the Kaitlyn alter persisted, and she began to talk of seeing things. Shadows. A girl. And having feelings about other people being around at night.

(FH): Can you be more specific?

(AL): She described something touching her. No more.

(FH): So you were treating Carly for...emotional troubles?

(AL): Among other things.

(FH): Please elaborate.

(AL): I assume you have my therapy session notes. I received the court order. I surrendered everything I have.

(FH): Why don't you just humor me, Doctor?

(AL): [Pause] Carly was overcompensatory in her affairs. She was...clingy. Needy. Chatty. Her emotional state was fragile at the best of times. Too heated, too scared, too timid. She would fluctuate between

paralyzing shyness and overly tactile displays of
affection. It was dangerous, given the chaotic nature
of her Kaitlyn alter, who would climb onto roofs,
drink, smoke, and cause a lot of trouble for herself.
Carly was easily broken when someone said or did
something she felt was either a betrayal or purposely
cruel. She was anorexic—something she could control
fastidiously—

(FH): And Kaitlyn, the alter, was anorexic also?

(AL): No.

(FH): Isn't that unusual?

(AL): Not really, no. Carly was also paranoid. She was
phobic; extremely so.

(FH): And superstitious?

(AL): Curiously, no. That was Kaitlyn. Kaitlyn was
superstitious, which was her only unusual behavior.
Yes, she was reclusive, depressive, hermetic, but
these traits are common in this type of alter. She
was clever, but morbid. Rather than have the phobias
Carly suffered, the Kaitlyn alter was reckless. Self-
harming, always wanting to push some kind of limit, to
cross a line, whether she created that line or the law
did.

(FH): How was it possible to treat such contrary
conditions when they existed in one single human?

(AL): I used psychoanalysis, hypnosis, counseling,
cognitive behavioral therapy, reasoning. Sometimes
all she needed was an ear to listen or a restraining
force. But...as time went on, Carly required medication.

(FH): Which drugs was she on?

(AL): Olanzapine at first. Later, haloperidol, lithium—

(FH): Yes, I have the list here. Is it not true
that a certain percentage of people actually *become*
psychotic on these kinds of medications? Particularly
haloperidol?

[Pause]

(AL): That's extremely rare.

(FH): Though it happens?

(AL): [Pause] It does.

(FH): Is it possible that your own treatments are what made Carly worse? What drove her to act as she did?

(AL): What are you suggesting, Detective?

(FH): I'll be frank with you, Doctor. I'm suggesting that Carly Johnson was overmedicated. That she was mentally damaged, but recovering until you medicated her—and that these drugs are what drove her to her eventual break.

(AL): *Excuse me?* If anything, that proves that she was *under*medicated. [Intake of breath] You saw what happened in February. Can anything else be true? And given so, I was right to do what I did.

(FH): I'm not so sure. In the end, you didn't even do that right, did you?

(AL): I was trying to *help* her, Detective. I followed every rule in the book, and I did everything I could for that girl.

(FH): Sometimes the rules are not enough. Thank you. That will do for now.

[Scraping of chair]

Don't leave London, Doctor. I may have more questions for you.

[End of tape]

From: AriHait558
To: RealxChick
Date: 6 October 2004
Subject: Where Are You?

Miss Confessional,

You haven't come to confession in a while, and I fear for your
heavenly soul.

Yours,

Benevolent Ari

PS—Will I have to keep calling you Miss Confessional forever? I
could shake things up a bit and start calling you Miss Falls Flat on
Her Arse?

Naida Camera Footage
Friday, 8 October 2004, 7:33 PM
Magpie House Roof

The camera wobbles; a tiled slate roof, slanted on both sides, comes in and out of focus as Naida moves towards a figure sitting near the very edge. Kaitlyn straddles the roof as though riding a horse, her back hunched. Naida's breathing echoes in the camera's microphone, unnervingly loud.

"What are you doing here?" Kaitlyn asks. She doesn't turn around, and the microphone barely catches her words.

Out of breath, Naida replies, "I'm looking for *you*—what's it look like?"

"How did you know I'd be up here?"

Naida focuses the camera on Kaitlyn's back, but her knee can be seen, as well as the tip of a black boot.

"Carly told me that you hang by the old chapel sometimes. I was heading there when I saw you up here. Brooding, as usual. I want to invite you to my cousin's house for Halloween. She's going out of town and said I could throw a party."

Kaitlyn doesn't blink. "Get that thing off my back."

Naida ignores her and the angle remains steady. "Are you game, or are you afraid?"

It seems, for a while, that Kaitlyn won't answer. Then, slowly, she gets to her feet. The motion is lithe and fluid—easy—as though she's three feet from the ground instead of three dozen. Her feet are bare, but she seems unfazed by the cold. She turns to look down at Naida, and the wind catches her hair, throwing it up around her.

Folding her arms, Kaitlyn says, "I'm no coward."

Naida leans forward, indicated by the sudden decrease in distance from Kaitlyn's face. "It's so strange," she muses, "to see my friend standing there, and yet not her. So different...yet the same."

"Don't confuse me with Carly," Kaitlyn warns. "She might be easy to win over, but I'm not."

"No," Naida agrees. "I doubt you've had a friend in your life, have you, Child of Darkness?"

Kaitlyn's face stills for barely a second, then her mouth quickly quirks up a fraction, but her eyes remain cold. "If I refuse to go, Carly won't force me."

Naida leans back, and the jerky camera movement indicates that she either folds her arms or switches hands. "I think I like you better than I thought I would." She tilts her head to the side. "There's depth in you. Unmeasured depth."

"Dark waters run deep."

"Shallow waters see the sun, though. And they're warmer."

Kaitlyn's eyes glint with a kind of curiosity or amusement. "That's true." Her eyes flicker down to the necklace around Naida's neck.

"*Gorro*, Kaitlyn!" Naida bursts out, a peal of laughter close behind. "Relax, doll, would you? I've got no agenda, okay? My cousin's letting me use her house. I'm just throwing a party. Candy, booze, movies, and pizza. No reason to go all psycho-suspicious on me."

Kaitlyn merely turns away. Naida gets to her feet, wobbling.

"Are you in?"

"I'll think about it."

"Just remember: Carly's my friend, sure. But I'm *her* friend too, and she wants to come. I made it early so she'll be able to enjoy it a bit before your turn. Wouldn't be fair of you to stop her."

"It won't make a difference to her if I leave after the transition. She can have her fun without me."

"You know it will. It matters to her what you do. It matters to her what other people think, and if 'she' suddenly leaves just after she got there? That would look weird, and you know it. She wants you to come, Kaitlyn, and to have fun. She told me."

Kaitlyn turns back, and her gaze never flinches. "I'll think about it."

"You do that. For both of you."

[END OF CLIP]

From: RealxChick
To: AriHait558
Date: 8 Oct 2004
Subject: Weird Developments

My Benevolent Forgiver,

Yes, I realize that my confessions have been infrequent of late. I have
a few things on my mind. I haven't figured out, yet, if you're cocky
enough to think one of those things is *you*.

One hilarious development is that Naida actually followed me onto
the ROOF to hunt me down and practically DEMAND that I go to her
party. Have you met Naida yet? You should know that she's a nut job.
She's probably planning to cut me into little pieces and serve me in a
stew.

Grumbling and disgruntled and all of the above,

Girl Who Falls Flat on Her Arse

From: AriHait558
To: RealxChick
Date: 8 Oct 2004
Subject: Re: Weird Developments

Miss Clumsy, Bruised-Bum Confessional,

Since I don't know Naida very well (we share no classes)—except that you hate her enough to confess to God-slash-the-empty-or-not-so-empty-confession-booth about her and curse the day Carly (?) met her—I really shouldn't offer you an opinion.

But since I have far too much opinion for one single person, and since my opinion is usually very insightful, here's my two pence: GO TO THE PARTY.

Live a little, you weird—YES, WEIRD—secretive girl with no name and plenty of angst. Go to the party, drink a little, relax, and let go. No harm in that, right? I'll be rooting for your teen-coming-out-into-the-world-of-living-actual-people moment.

Ari

PS—I'm CERTAIN one of the things keeping you up at night is me. ;)

From: RealxChick
To: AriHait558
Date: 8 Oct 2004
Subject: Re: Re: Weird Developments

I suppose by "the-world-of-living-actual-people" you're trying to tell me that you are not, in fact, a living person? How nice for you!

I will give my teen angst some indulgence for a bit, while I consider the impending party of doom.

PS—Is anyone of your gender *not* cocky, arrogant, and stupid? I'm perfectly willing to take back the stupid once you prove it. But you might be stuck with cocky and arrogant for life, soz.

From: AriHait558
To: RealxChick
Date: 8 Oct 2004
Subject: Death of Vocabulary

Soz? People still say *soz*??? I fear for the human race. I assume you mean *sorry*. Now apologize properly, you heathen.

From: RealxChick
To: AriHait558
Date: 9 Oct 2004
Subject: Re: Death of Vocabulary

Go to sleep, you (cocky, arrogant, STUPID) vampire! ;)

PS—If I go to this ridiculous, adolescent ritual All Hallows' Eve party...
will you come with me? If by some miracle you will, come at 7:30 pm.

From: AriHait558
To: RealxChick
Date: 9 Oct 2004
Subject: Re: Re: Death of Vocabulary

The apocalypse couldn't stop me. Come to the chapel now. I'll bring
cookies, and we can wallow in the minutiae of our lives in proper
angsty fashion.

Expectant,

Ari

There is no reply from Kaitlyn on the server.

Diary of Kaitlyn Johnson

Saturday, 9 October 2004, 1:03 am
Attic

The noise was jarring in the silence of the basement,
only the creak of a floorboard ahead of me. I stopped
midstep and let my foot hang in the air, holding my
breath. Every hair on my arms and the back of my neck
slowly rose as I peered into the murk, which was
nothing but hints of shadow masquerading as light and
dark, sharp-looking edges and fuzzy blurs. And the room
was still. Too still.

"Hello?"

A sensation, like that of the room suddenly
expanding, even though nothing had changed, knocked
the breath out of me, and I dropped my foot and hunched
my shoulders from some primeval instinct—as though I
was about to be pounced on. Then I saw her. The thin
rake of a girl, the one I'd seen watching me from the
basement, and in the vandalized mirror…She stood at the
back of the room, in the shadows.

She was grinning.

"Dee? Is that you?"

And I heard it. A low breathing, slow and humid.
The room itself was icy, but there was fever in the
breath.

Adrenaline flooded my body, so that even when I
looked back at what I had momentarily seen, my vision
spotted in front of my eyes. I couldn't tell if it was
moving closer, even though I could hear the creak of
weight falling on the wood and the click of nails on
the hard surface.

I stumbled backwards and blinked furiously, staring
with wide eyes as the dark shape peered around the

corner at me—the corner which led to the stairs of the building, the corner which I had to go around—and vanished.

~~Crazy Crazy Crazy—you are so crazy.~~

I told myself to get a grip—I was very, very rational—but I couldn't move my feet.

These meds. These damn meds! "Not real," I kept saying it to myself over and over. Not real, not real—there was nothing there.

And yet...when I finally forced myself to move, and go down the corridor between the precariously balanced items that seemed to sway above me, I smelled something—I smelled sour breath, wet fur (?), and earth. I glanced quickly around, and the darkness in the basement became pregnant with awareness, as if I was the actor, and the junk the observers.

I raced upstairs to the attic where I now sit, wrapped in a moth-eaten blanket, dreading the moment when I have to go back and traverse that dark, junky graveyard of a basement once more.

Because, whatever it was, it was very, very real.

[The tape that corresponds to the notes by Dr. Annabeth Lansing below has never been found.]

Dr. Lansing Therapy Notes
Session #48: Carly/Kaitlyn Johnson

Monday, 11 October 2004

Kaitlyn persists in her delusions regarding the dark shape (possibly a girl), but now an olfactory element has emerged. She describes the smell as "ashy" and "dead," like "something out of a graveyard, only less bland." When asked when she sees and smells these things, she replies that it is "random and unpredictable." I fear that the worsening delusions may indicate incipient psychosis, and I will therefore begin grounding exercises from next session.

Criminal Investigation Department, Portishead Headquarters
Avon and Somerset Constabulary, Portishead, Bristol
Friday, 17 June 2005, 15h00
AUDIO INTERVIEW #2, PART 1: Detective Chief Inspector Floyd
Homes (FH) and Scott Fromley (SF)

[Audio interference]

(FH): Detective Chief Inspector Floyd Homes, Avon
and Somerset CID, interviewing Mr. Scott Fromley on
the seventeenth of June 2005. So, Scott. Here we
are again. You were a student at Elmbridge High in
Somerset?

(SF): You asked me this last time.

(FH): It's standard procedure—please answer.

(SF): Yes, I was.

(FH): For how long?

(SF): I told you this already. Since seventh grade.

(FH): The last time we talked, you were closemouthed
about Miss Johnson. Didn't seem to know much about
her. And yet here you sit, key witness. Possible
suspect. You may want to be a bit more honest with me
this time round.

[Silence]

Did Carly ever talk about school? The teachers? How
she felt about Elmbridge?

[Pause]

(SF): No.

(FH): So she never had any complaints about the
school?

(SF): If you're asking me whether she had a vendetta against the school—no.

(FH): You seem to know her quite intimately, Scott, to know what she thinks. Tell me more about what happened after the Halloween party, about what happened with Juliet McClarin.

(SF): For God's sake, I don't know, do I? I told you back in December that I *don't know*.

[Silence]

(FH): Why don't you tell me again?

(SF): Is this some kind of joke to you people? Are you all just sitting there wasting time? You're asking me the same questions over and over, and my answer is the same—*I don't know!*

(FH): You want to calm down for me? I'd hate to have to put those cuffs back on.

[Pause]

(SF): Sorry.

(FH): Tell me about Carly. How was she after Halloween?

(SF): I guess…after November she started to seem…I don't know…not really herself, I guess. Naida told me that she was going to therapy more…that her sleep issues were playing up. Stuff like that.

(FH): Naida Chounan-Dupré. Whom you were dating at the time?

(SF): Yes.

(FH): Did Miss Chounan-Dupré tell you about Carly's condition?

(SF): Condition? You mean that she never slept? Yeah, she told me. And I just told you.

[Pause]

(FH): Did you ever speak to Miss Johnson at night?

(SF): Um… [Pause] I don't remember.

(FH): It's best if you're honest, son.

(SF): Yeah, I guess I did. Yeah.

(FH): What was Carly's relationship like with Naida?

(SF): I don't know. It was complicated, I guess.

(FH): Care to elaborate?

[Audio crackle]

(SF): Carly and Naida seemed close most of the time.
I mean, they weren't anything alike, so I don't know
why they were even friends, but they were. But then
sometimes they seemed to hate each other.

(FH): They weren't alike? In what way?

(SF): Carly was shy…she wasn't that into guys or
fashion. Naida's louder than Carly. Stronger. Harder.
She's flamboyant and dresses the part whenever she can—
[Laughs, then stops, swallows] *Could.*

(FH): You said that Carly's relationship with Naida
was complicated. But you've said they were close. How
is that complicated?

(SF): Well, this one time, maybe around September or
October, at the beginning of the school year, Naida
was pissed about something. I tried to make her feel
better, you know? Tried to find out what was wrong. She
just said that they'd had some kind of argument and
that it was upsetting her. I asked if she'd talked to
Carly about it since then, and she laughed in this
angry, kind of hate-filled way. I remember, clear as
day, she said, "Yeah, right, I did." That was all.

(FH): So you had the impression that Naida was angry
with Carly?

(SF): Honestly, I thought Naida hated Carly at that moment. [Pause] Like any of that matters now.

(FH): So they had a falling-out.

(SF): [Dully] It wasn't until after the Halloween party that things felt okay again between the two of them.

(FH): After the Juliet incident.

(SF): [Pause] Yeah. But like I said, I don't know what happened to her. I want to make a phone call. I want to talk to my father.

(FH): Humor me for a few minutes more. In your own words, tell me again what happened.

[End of tape]

Naida Camera Footage
Saturday, 30 October 2004
Halloween Party Clip #1
Time Index Not Noted

"I've got it all set up," Naida says into the camera. "Aila's house is *huge* and perfect. So, dear viewers, I hope you delight in the horror of tonight. 'Cause we're going to have us some nightmarish fun."

The camera focuses on a wide porch, which is covered in grinning jack-o'-lanterns and box lanterns. The stairs leading up to the house, which itself glows orange from unseen light sources, are also lined with carved jack-o'-lanterns and an array of statuettes. The main statue, which stands on the grass, is of a life-size headless horseman. Each of the front-facing windows is covered with black material, out of which an image has been cut, and with the orange illumination inside, the effect is sinister. The whole house is one giant grinning face.

"This is it," Naida says. "Tonight is going to be awesome."

Naida carries the camera up the stairs and into the house, right through the wide-open mouth.

Halloween Party Clip #2

A living room, decked out in Halloween decorations—jack-o'-lanterns, spiderwebs, spiders, dangling black ribbons, candles, glowing lights. Students from Elmbridge High mill around, red plastic cups in hand. Johnny Farmer's "Death Letter" plays from an unseen radio. Present are:

Scott Fromley, senior, dressed as Candyman

Brett [name omitted], senior, dressed as an Arthurian knight

Juliet McClarin, junior, as Red Riding Hood

Maggie Myers, junior, as the Little Mermaid Ariel

Carly Johnson, senior, in steampunk couture

Brenda "Bobbin" LeRoy, senior, as Smurfette

Mike Bowers, senior, as Dracula (It should be noted that Mike's face still bears the fading marks from the vandalism of September. Otherwise, he seems unaffected.)

Naida appears from a door leading to the kitchen. She is dressed as a stylized Grim Reaper—her face is painted with a stark white-on-black skull design. She wears a black tuxedo that hugs her figure, a top hat, and black sunglasses. Between two slender fingers she holds a lit cigar, which she brings close to her lips, where it smokes provocatively.

"Ladies and gentleman," she says, grinning, "welcome to the house of terror."

The two younger girls, Juliet and Maggie, giggle and eye Brett from under their lashes. Brett, unaware, takes a sip from his cup, his focus on Carly, who is sitting on the sofa nearest the window. Scott snorts and stands up to greet Naida, wrapping his arm around her waist and pulling her close.

Faintly, we hear his muffled words. "Hey, baby. You look sexy."

She pulls back. "No kidding. You have a Grim Reaper fetish?" When he seems confused, she gestures to herself. "Collector of the Dead, for your delectation and delight."

He nods, brows raised. "Kudos for effort."

"Why, thank you, Candyman."

"*Mr. Daniel Robitaille,*" he corrects her, before planting a kiss on her lips.

"Get a room!" Brenda yells, the lilt of laughter in her voice, even as she glances suggestively at Mike, who sits beside her.

"Wow," Juliet says in Naida's direction, "this is so cool!"

Brenda snorts, and Juliet's blush deepens. Brenda turns to Mike and whispers, "What are they doing here?"

Mike grins but says nothing, and Juliet glances at Maggie, who smiles and shrugs.

As Scott pulls away from Naida, lips smeared white, we get a glimpse of Carly grinning at them.

"I should tell you," Naida announces, "you are currently being filmed for my sociology project. Anyone who isn't comfortable being seen should leave now."

She waits, eyes passing over the faces present. No one moves, but several eyes surreptitiously scan the room for the cameras. Juliet's lips frame the word *where?*—nothing more.

"Good."

Scott leans into Naida, and we hear him whisper in her ear, "Isn't it less effective if they *know* they're being filmed?"

Naida shrugs. "Aye, but I have to give them notice, ethically. Otherwise, there could be problems if anything—*unwholesome*—comes out. This way, I've got my warning on camera. By staying, they agree to it. Besides," she adds, turning her back on the room, and dropping her voice, "soon they'll be too drunk to remember."

"Oh, baby," Scott murmurs. "You're sneaky as a little fox. My minx of a fox."

She looks up at him. "There're cameras in this place you can't even imagine."

A similar piece of film from another camera was found in the online archives. The angle of the film suggests it is a camera Naida was wearing somewhere on her costume, most likely in her top hat, given the height.

Criminal Investigation Department, Portishead Headquarters
Avon and Somerset Constabulary, Portishead, Bristol
Friday, 5 November 2004, 10h00
AUDIO INTERVIEW: Detective Chief Inspector Floyd Homes (FH)
and Maggie Myers (MM)

(FH): At what time did you arrive at the Dupré
residence?

(MM): Um, my mum dropped me off at about four in the
afternoon.

(FH): So early?

(MM): That's when the party started. Naida said four.

(FH): Did you go alone?

(MM): No, I went with…with—

[Sniffling]

(FH): Take your time.

(MM): [Sniff] W—with Juliet.

(FH): Were you with Juliet the entire evening?

(MM): No. [Sniff] Juliet didn't want to do the Ouija
board, so she went to wait outside.

(FH): Why outside?

(MM): She wanted air.

(FH): Tell me about the Ouija board.

(MM): It was stupid. Mike found it in the drawer in
the living room. It had all kinds of weird stuff in
there, but he only took out the board. It didn't look

like a normal board, though. My brother bought one last year and it didn't look like Naida's at all.

(FH): Can you tell me if Juliet went outside alone?

(MM): Yeah, she did. But, I mean, Carly went out later, so I guess she wasn't alone for long.

(FH): Do you remember anything else happening that night in relation to Juliet? Did she leave with anyone? Did you see any strangers talking to her? Did you hear any cars stop near the house?

(MM): No. She just stepped outside. If you want to know what happened, ask that Carly girl. She was there, she must know.

(FH): Thank you, Maggie. You can step outside.

[Scraping of chair]

[Footsteps]

[Door]

(FH): [Sigh] Once again it seems that Carly Luanne Johnson is connected to this event. It seems more and more likely that she is somehow directly involved. I recommend continuing the search for Miss Johnson so that she may be questioned before probable sectioning.

[End of tape]

Naida Camera Footage
Saturday, 30 October 2004
Halloween Party Clip #3
Time Index Not Noted

Several hours have passed, during which Carly has disappeared upstairs and come back down looking annoyed (presumably, as the sun has since set, she is now Kaitlyn), and during which also, Ari Hait has arrived, dressed as Sherlock's Dr. John H. Watson.

Music blasts from somewhere in the room, sending slight vibrations and noise distortions through the camera. Mike Bowers sits beside Juliet, eyes half-closed. Languidly, he pulls a plastic bag from his vest and dangles it before her eyes. He murmurs something the camera doesn't catch.

Juliet blushes and giggles.

"What is *that*?"

Mike turns his attention to Scott. "What is *what*? This? It's weed, man. Where have you been?"

"Get that stuff out of here, Bowers. You think Naida needs her cousin's place smelling like a bloody stoner's den?"

Mike's face turns red, and he gets to his feet. "What kind of a dickhead—"

"All right, my people," Naida drawls, sauntering into the room. "I leave you for a second, and all *hell* breaks loose. I knew I was something, but never knew I was everything. It's Halloween! Chill out."

Kaitlyn mutters something that is not heard by the others. Increasing playback volume allows us to decipher her words: *You know we don't do this Halloween shit in England.*

Ari whispers something in her ear, and she smiles.

"Get this moron out of here," Scott growls, fists clenched.

"For bringing weed?" Mike says. "That's a joke, mate!"

"You brought weed to my cousin's house?"

Mike's aggression wilts a little under Naida's regard. "Well, yeah." He holds it up between two fingers, suddenly a tall yet pathetic figure. "I thought—I mean, I didn't think..."

Naida stares for a moment, and the room seems to hold its breath. "Well, I'll have me some of that."

Both Scott and Mike stare at her openmouthed.

Scott steps closer to her. "*What?*"

Naida takes the bag from Mike, opens it, and sniffs. "It's a plant, Scott. Relax, okay?"

She winks at Scott, who seems momentarily charmed. Then he remembers Mike, scowls, and storms off.

Mike grins. "Let's do this. Who else is game?"

Juliet claps her hands. "Me!" Her friend Maggie nods, and Brenda gets to her feet in acquiescence.

The only person unaware of—or uninterested in—the confrontation and the weed sits in steampunk couture on the same leather sofa, engrossed in a conversation with Ari Hait.

Halloween Party Clip #4

"Are you up for, um...marijuana?" Brett says, standing beside Kaitlyn's chair. Though tall, he seems diminished beside her. Unsure. Ari whispers something in Kaitlyn's ear, and she laughs, then turns to Brett, distracted.

"What?"

"Um, marijuana. You want in? Either of you?"

"Oh." She raises her eyebrows at Ari, who smirks and looks away. "Not for us, thanks, Brett."

Brett looks more than a little crestfallen. He tries again. "Uh, hey. I haven't spoken to you in a while." He steps from foot to foot, holding his plastic cup between both hands.

Kaitlyn stares at him, eyes narrowing. "Huh?"

"How are you?" he asks again.

"I'm...fine. Thanks. How are you?"

Ari leans forward. "Did you want something...specific?"

"I just..." He clears his throat and runs a hand through his hair. "Hadn't seen Carly in a while, and I wanted to say hi. I didn't get your name."

Ari gets to his feet and holds out his hand. "Name's Ari."

"Right, from math. Brett." He shakes Ari's hand briefly, then glances at Kaitlyn. "You looked a little off the other day. Wanted to make sure you were feeling better."

Kaitlyn frowns. "I did? Oh...oh, yeah. Thanks, Brett. Much better."

Ari looks from one to the other and then sits down.

"I better go," Brett mutters. "See you later, Carly."

Kaitlyn smiles blandly at him and then turns back to Ari. Brett smiles awkwardly at her back and scratches his ear. He rubs his head, drinking deeply from the plastic cup in his hands before stalking into the kitchen.

"That was weird," Kaitlyn says, once he is gone.

"So. *Carly,*" Ari says, grinning. "Care to explain what all of that in the chapel was about?"

Kaitlyn doesn't say anything.

"Carly? Because...you were talking about *missing* Carly, and—"

"Don't call me that. Don't call me Carly."

"Why? Everyone calls you Carly."

"I know. But please don't ever call me that. Not you. Please."

"I...okay. Whatever you want." He hesitates. "What *should* I call you?"

"I'm not ready to tell you."

Ari considers her, then smiles. "You're so beautiful when you're angry."

She punches him in the arm but grins anyway.

Halloween Party Clip #5

Later, from the top hat camera, we hear a short, whispered conversation between Brett and Naida.

"What's up, sugar?" Naida asks, her voice low, the screen jiggling as she walks into what appears to be the kitchen. She faces Brett, who leans against the sink, his hands balled into fists on the edge of the counter.

He shakes his head. "Something's wrong."

"What do you mean, 'something's wrong'? It's Halloween! It's meant to feel *spooky*." She wriggles her fingers near his face. "Nobody's allowed to be down at my party. So come on, spill."

"She's not herself. I mean, something's bothering her. And why's that guy hanging around her anyway?"

"This is Carly, I take it?"

Brett sighs, shakes his head. His blond hair falls forward, covering his eyes. "I can't get through to her."

"She's like this at night. Broody and all that. She gets a little...cranky. Why not talk to her in the morning? She'll be better company then."

"She's different during the day. Less herself. We share a few classes, and she doesn't usually want to talk. She avoids me. But I've talked to her at night."

Naida raises an eyebrow. "Oh, aye?"

"This one time, my dad took me to one of his bullshit fund-raisers, and when I got back, I saw her walking across the courtyard. We chatted for a while, and she was so...different. And last year I saw her in the field after dinner, and I decided to say hi. She was more herself. Less closed in."

After a pause, Naida laughs. "Wow. That's...complicated. She's a bad one to fall for, though. I mean it. You'll get chewed up and spit out. It's not her fault, but...it'll happen."

Brett shakes his head, lips tight. "She's not like that."

"Not intentionally, of course not. But she is...oh, aye, she is." She gestures with her hand. "Split right down the middle, that one. During the day, she's as sweet as pie. Can't you just hang out with her then?"

Brett slams the counter and sways slightly. "Whatever, Naida. Maybe you don't know her as well as you think."

Naida takes a breath, and the camera tips as though she has leaned against the counter. "Lay off that beer for a while, okay? Looks like you're going to fall right on your head any second. Forget about her for now. Just enjoy my party. And don't puke anywhere, or it'll be the *last* party I'm allowed to have until I die."

Brett stares for a moment, then skulks from the room, muttering under his breath.

Naida sighs. "Got trouble brewing." She pauses for a moment, and though alone, she adds, "Stay away from her, lad. I'm warning you. That one's a magnet, and not for anything good."

Halloween Party Clip #6

"Come on," Naida says, clapping her hands strategically close to Kaitlyn's ear. "Up. Now."

Ari is no longer beside her.

Kaitlyn glares at her. "*Don't* order me around. I'm staying here. That's enough."

"No, it's not." She glances behind her, making certain that everyone is occupied with other things. She's not disappointed, as everyone is standing huddled around Mike by the fireplace, lighting spliff after spliff.

"Carly wanted to come to this party," she says, keeping her voice low. "She wanted to have fun for once. Fun without thinking of you, how you might react, or what people might say. I started this thing early so she could have a piece, but it's dark now, which means *you* get the show." She sighs. "Look at what you're wearing. You think she pulled that out of some magic hat? She *worked* for that—overtime at school for two weeks during free periods. She made that outfit you're lounging in, and you're telling me that you're just going to sit there and sulk and drink your ass off and treat her effort like a big fat nothing?" Naida's voice, though still low, is barely under control. "No. I won't accept that. *Get. Up.* Dance. Act like you're having fun and quit with the beer. Carly'll be the one with the hangover, remember? You're going to do this, Kaitlyn Johnson, so help me God, because when Carly asks me in the morning if you had a good time, I can at least say, aye, she joined in."

Kaitlyn, whose mouth has fallen open, blinks. "Okay."

Naida frowns. "*What?*"

"I said okay."

"Crickey. I didn't expect that to work."

The ghost of a smile plays around Kaitlyn's lips. "So you can point to this and say, 'Kaitlyn joined in.'"

Naida nods and straightens up. She seems a little thrown. "And bring that Ari lad, wherever he's gotten to."

"Bathroom," Kaitlyn murmurs, still seemingly dazed.

Naida nods again, then turns to the room. "Right, my people! Change the music already and dance! We're all sufficiently drunk and stoned to get moving, right?"

Brenda dances over to the stereo and stares at the many dials and knobs.

"Let me," Naida says, and presses a button. Loud music blares from the speakers.

Maggie whoops and then begins to dance haphazardly, flinging her arms around and wiggling her hips. Brenda bursts out laughing and joins in, followed by Scott and Juliet, each dancing wildly. Mike scoffs from the sofa, very stoned. Brett stands off to the side, watching Kaitlyn as she reluctantly leaves her sofa, downs another plastic cup of beer, and begins to dance, awkwardly at first but then more confidently and fluidly. In a later diary entry, Kaitlyn would remark, *It was like Masqued again, Dee. If I closed my eyes and let myself believe, it was like I was back there on the dance floor with the Viking and my shadows, and I lost myself. I lost myself because I didn't know how free I was away from Elmbridge and away from Claydon.*

Some hours later Naida has retreated upstairs with Scott, and the music is slower, more languid. Brenda sits beside Mike, who murmurs under his breath, eyes closed. She leans forward, listening intently—intimately. A hint of her sweater moving is the only indication that Mike is caressing her lower back.

Brett sits on the living room main sofa, head back, eyes closed. He may be sleeping. Juliet and Maggie stand near the main entrance, glancing around sleepily and occasionally saying something to each other.

Kaitlyn is sitting in the armchair again. She laughs at something Ari says—they are the only source of raucous noise in the room.

Maggie exhales, and Juliet releases a soft, nervous cough.

"Too slow for you kidlets?" Brenda asks, her head hanging back, looking at the younger girls upside down.

Maggie shrugs. "Nothing's happening."

Juliet folds her arms. "It's boring."

"I'm contemplating," Mike murmurs, a spliff still hanging from his lips.

Brenda rights her head. "Contemplating...?"

"Contemplating livening up this place." He pulls out a smooth wooden case from behind the sofa cushion. "I found this earlier in there." He nods at the ancient chest of drawers at the front of the room.

Brenda snorts. "A chessboard?"

"No," Mike says, "not a chessboard, you spanner. A *Ouija* board."

Both Juliet and Maggie lean away from it as though detecting a foul scent, but Brenda leans forward.

"Cool," she whispers, eyes growing wide. "Communing with the dead—"

"This is lame," Juliet says suddenly. "Ouija boards? You're seniors! You're supposed to have the best parties."

Mike turns to look lazily at her. "Piss off, you little priss."

She reddens. "This sucks *ass.*" She says it defiantly, but the words seem unfamiliar in her mouth. "I'm not playing Ouija. I need some air."

"I'll go with you," Maggie offers.

Juliet rolls her eyes. "Don't bother." She glances at Brett, who still hasn't moved from the sofa, scowls at Mike—who grins broadly—then abruptly turns and leaves, slamming the front door.

"You don't *play* Ouija," Brenda says at the same time that Mike says, "What's her problem?"

Maggie reddens but lifts her chin. "Not enough attention for her, I think."

Brenda laughs. "Too right. And you? You in with the big kids?"

Maggie grins and wanders over to the small group. "I'm in."

"Let's do this bitch," Brett says unexpectedly from the sofa. "I'm bored. You in, Johnson?"

Kaitlyn glances over, a smile still on her face. "Huh?"

"Ouija board. You up for it? Talking to the dead?"

"We can talk to your parents!" Maggie says loudly, gleefully.

"Shut it," Brett snaps.

"Just because you fancy her," Maggie returns, and Brenda grins.

Kaitlyn's face is like stone, but Ari takes her hand and pulls her to her feet. He whispers something in her ear, and she laughs. "You're right."

"Come on, then," Brenda says, getting up from the sofa, revealing Mike's arm. "Enough time for drama later. How do we work this thing?"

Brett holds out his hand. "Give it here. I know how to use it."

Mike laughs, but gives the board over. "Some kind of expert on communing with spirits?"

Brett ignores him and unclips the Ouija board, folding it flat on the coffee table. Two small items fall out of the board onto the floor. He sits down on the floor in front of it, frowning.

Brenda sits beside Mike, reaching out to touch the board. "This isn't a Ouija board."

The board has no letters on it, only symbols like runes.

"Yeah, it's different," Maggie says. "The one my brother has looks different."

Brett glances over at Kaitlyn. "Carly? Um, Ari? You in?"

Kaitlyn stumbles a little as she walks over and sits down heavily next to Brett, Ari on her other side.

"Where's the pointer?"

"Here," Mike says, bending down to pick it up. "And there's this." He holds out a small velvet pouch.

Brett takes it, opens it, and pours out the contents. "Mala runes."

"Well, that's useless," Brenda mutters. "We won't be able to even read what it spells out."

"Maybe get Naida?" Maggie offers, but everyone ignores her.

"Okay," Brett says, "everyone put your finger on."

Maggie rolls her eyes. "Why? It's not like we'll understand what those runes mean."

"Just watch. Put your fingers on."

Everyone does so.

"We six wish to, um, commune? With whoever is out there—whoever is *dead* and out there."

Maggie snorts, and Brenda shushes her. Brett's face and neck flush, but he continues. "This rune"—he places a red stone to the left of the board—"means no. And this one"—he places a green one to the right—"means yes. Please indicate that you understand."

Nothing happens.

"Maybe we have to commune with someone...specific?" Maggie suggests. "Like, someone dead?"

Brenda bounces in her seat. "Who should we commune with first?"

"Whoever's there," Kaitlyn murmurs.

"Agreed," Brett says. "Let's just see who's around, shall we?"

Mike nods.

"Whoever you are, talk to us. Indicate you understand."

Nothing happens, and they glance at one another with grins.

"If not yes or no," Brenda adds, "then choose one of us. Choose to talk to one of us."

Maggie shrieks as the pointer moves.

Brenda throws her hands over her ears. "*Ow!* Just deafen me, why don't you!"

"Sorry."

"Get your fingers on here," Mike says, his voice waspish and low. "It's still moving!"

The group stares at the pointer as it moves ever so slowly.

"Are you doing this?" Brenda asks Mike, a grin plastered to her face.

"No, I'm bloody well not. Keep hold of it!"

"You asshole," she says, laughing.

"I told you I'm not doing it!"

"Then Brett's doing it!"

Brett scowls. "No, I'm not!"

She rolls her eyes and folds her arms, unwilling to put her fingers on the pointer. "Let go of it, then."

Brett glances at everyone for a moment and then lets go. All of them follow, even a grinning Kaitlyn, who seems more than a little tipsy.

They all watch as the pointer, now unhindered by the burden of fingers, begins to move faster...on its own.

"Holy chocolate balls!" Brenda whispers. "Bloody hell. I smoked way too much. Mike, what did you put in that—"

"Shh!" Mike hisses. "Keep watching it."

"Is this a joke? Naida—get your ass out here!" Brenda shakes her head, eyes wide. "This is bonkers—"

"Shut it!"

The pointer moves from the middle of the board in one continuous and unfaltering direction until it stops directly in front of Kaitlyn.

Suddenly she seems very awake. "What the hell is this?"

"It chose Carly," Maggie says, a hint of disappointment in her voice.

"This is like some cheesy B horror movie," Brenda says, but the joviality seems forced. "Right?"

Kaitlyn, who hasn't been able to tear her eyes away from the pointer, opens her mouth to reply when a voice rings out over the room.

"What the hell do you think you're doing?" Naida leans over the banister, Scott close behind her. In his hand dangles Naida's top hat, and we see a glimpse of the camera taped inside.

Naida's eyes travel down to the pointer facing Kaitlyn, and in a second, she is moving, flying down the stairs, leaning over the sofa and snatching up the board and pointer roughly. She slams the board shut and throws the pointer into the fireplace, where it ignites quickly, bending and warping in green and purple flames.

"That was spooky," Brenda says.

"You idiots," Naida whispers. "What the hell did you think you were doing?"

"Ouija board," Maggie says with a shrug. "It's Halloween."

Naida's eyes travel to her slowly, wide and shocked. Her face bleeds of its color. "*This isn't a Ouija board!*" she yells. "*You damn fools, all of you!*"

"We were just having a laugh!" Maggie protests, waiting for someone else to stick up for her. When they don't, she points at Mike. "It was his idea!"

Naida, who is visibly shaking—with rage or fear, we cannot know—turns to Mike, who leans back on his hands.

"Chill out. God. It's a *Ouija* board. And rigged too, I'd bet. Nice little gag, I should say."

"Rigged?" Brenda asks. "How?"

"Magnets, probably. They sell these things in novelty shops so you can scare the crap out of people. Carly's in on it, of course."

Naida's voice rings through the room. "*This isn't a novelty board, you moron! It's not even a Ouija board! Goddamn stupid son of a b—*"

Scott, wearing Naida's hat, takes her shoulders from behind; she seems on the verge of a panic attack. "Calm down, baby. Take a breath."

Naida closes her eyes and inhales. "Get the hell out of here, Mike. All of you! *I want you out of this house!*"

Unseen by Naida or any of the others, Kaitlyn begins to sway, her eyes still on the spot where the pointer sat moments before.

"I feel weird," she whispers, but it is drowned out by Mike's furious yell.

"*Make* me, Dupré!"

"Don't push me, you jerk!"

Ari, the only one to notice Kaitlyn, touches her arm. "What's wrong?"

Suddenly Kaitlyn snaps to her feet. "I feel weird."

Everyone stares, surprised, as she walks to the front door, opens it, and walks outside, leaving the door open behind her. Ari stares after her.

"You fools," Naida says again, but this time she seems to be on the verge of tears. "Goddamn fools."

"If it's not a Ouija board," Brenda says, "what is it?"

Naida, still shaking, looks up at her through eyes full of moisture. "Get out of my house. Now."

Brenda blinks, then scoffs. "Well, happy bloody Halloween to you too." She gets to her feet. "Come on, Mike. Let's go."

Mike gets up and walks over to Naida. He towers over her, standing a little too close. Scott steps closer, his face menacing behind her.

"Weirdness personified," Mike tells Naida. "I always said so."

They leave through the open front door.

Brett gets to his feet. "Well, that was—"

A shriek from outside pierces the quiet of the room.

Ari is out the door in a flash. Naida's eyes widen. She turns to Scott, who runs outside with Brett. Naida hides the board under the sofa cushions and then runs from the room.

Halloween Party Clip #8

The angle is distorted and blurry as Scott runs outside. Then he stops dead, the camera focuses, and we see Kaitlyn passed out on the front lawn. Ari is beside her, trying to pick her up.

Brett is clutching his head. "What do we do?" he asks, an edge of panic in his voice.

"Kaitie," Naida breathes from behind Scott. He turns, and we see her running. Down the steps, over the grass, shouting at Ari—"Don't touch her! Put her down!"—falling to her knees beside Kaitlyn, whom she lifts out of Ari's arms and onto her lap.

"Kaitlyn? Can you hear me? Kait!"

"Who the hell is Kate?" Brenda says, but no one is listening.

"Oh, my God," Naida says. "Call an ambulance. I'm not sure she's breathing—"

"Call an ambulance!" Brett yells before Naida has finished speaking. "Now!"

"Where's Juliet?" Maggie cries, running over from the street. "Has anyone seen Jules?"

Brett runs inside when no one seems to be calling an ambulance.

"*Where is Juliet?*" Maggie screams.

"What's happening to her?" Ari demands. "What's going on?"

"Kaitie, wake up. Oh, God, please. Carly, please, come on..." Naida's words are rushed as she taps Kaitlyn's face and shakes her body.

Brett runs outside. "Where's the phone?" he yells at Naida. "Has anyone got their phone?"

As he is yelling, Kaitlyn takes a sudden breath and opens her eyes wide, then they roll back in her head.

Naida gasps and then bursts into tears. "She's okay! She's good—it's okay!"

One slurred word dribbles from Kaitlyn's lips. "Carly..."

"It's okay," Naida whispers to Kaitlyn, stroking her hair. "It's okay. I think I got there in time."

Kaitlyn's eyes roll, flutter, and close.

"Help me," Naida says to Scott.

He starts to pick Kaitlyn up, but Ari is closer and faster, and soon she is cradled limply in his arms instead.

Naida nods. "Up to the guest room."

Ari carries Kaitlyn inside.

"You sure she's okay?" Brett asks.

She puts a hand on his arm. "I told you, sugar. She is the way she is."

TAUNTON ADVERTISER

Tuesday, 2 November 2004

MISSING GIRL LAST SEEN AT HALLOWEEN PARTY

Elmbridge High School student Juliet McClarin, 16, has vanished after attending a Halloween party at a local friend's house last night, two miles from the school. McClarin, last seen at approximately 9:00 PM, is 5 foot 3 and weighs approximately 120 pounds. She has sandy blond hair and was wearing a Red Riding Hood costume at the time of her disappearance. There is speculation that Juliet tried to walk back to her dorm room alone after leaving the party. Taunton police officials are requesting the public's assistance in locating Juliet. Any information should be made available to the Taunton Police Department and will be kept confidential.

Diary of Kaitlyn Johnson

Monday, 1 November 2004, 2:00 am
Attic

Nothing from Carly in the Message Book. Don't know how
to take it.

I've decided that what happened at Naida's party
was probably because of the alcohol. Serves me right
for drinking like that when I <u>know</u> Carly's on meds. I
wanted that release—that feeling of flight. It's the
nearest I can get to actually jumping off that roof,
Dee. Scary thought.

Does it make me a joke? Because, honestly, I feel
like one.

Later

I wish I could stay here, but I have to get Carly back
to the dorm before sunup. It was so amazing to have Ari
at the party with me. It was actually <u>fun</u>. Well, before
the psycho Ouija board thing.

Just thinking about him makes me smile.

5:47 am

Dee…is it you?

If it's you, please stop smiling at me.

Naida Camera Footage
Monday, 1 November 2004, 6:00 AM
Kaitlyn's Dorm Room

A door, closed. A hand knocks.

"What?" comes a tight voice.

"Can I come in?"

Naida doesn't wait for a response. She opens the door, steps inside, and closes it behind her.

"Get that thing out of my face," Kaitlyn says right away, looking at the camera.

"What happened at my house? Why did you...pass out? I mean, like that. Was it even a transition? I've never seen it like that before."

"Is that why you're here? To interrogate me?"

Naida puts the camera on a shelf to her left, facing the room. "Kaitlyn—just stop. Stop it, okay? Do you know that I was scared out of my mind?"

Kaitlyn laughs derisively. "What is this?"

"I know you need this"—she gestures vaguely—"this bravado mask you insist on wearing. I get it. You have to protect yourself: fine. But I want to be your friend. And I'm asking you what went down with that board. What happened outside? I want to help you."

Kaitlyn puts down the book she's been writing in—her journal?—and gets to her feet. As she speaks, she steps closer and closer, until she is standing inches from Naida, her posture aggressive. "You want answers? How about you provide a solution? How about you tell Carly to stop taking those damn antipsychotic meds. How about you do *that* for me, huh? Then maybe I can have a drink without—" She stops herself.

"Kaitie—"

"Don't call me that. You have no right."

Naida exhales. "Kaitlyn. You've made me into an enemy. I have no idea why. But something *did* happen at my party. That pointer found you, and there was…*something*. You weren't playing with a Ouija board, don't you see?"

"I don't care."

"Of course you do. That board is a board of the Spirits—*great* spirits. By using that board, you drew their attention. I've tried to tell you before that you're special. Every person has a living body and a soul. The soul is hugely powerful. It's an amazing energy source, and it connects us to whatever comes after this life. You and Carly are two souls. That's two in one body. Do you see the kind of power you wield? Do you see how potentially catastrophic that is? Two souls connected to what comes after in a single form? Can you see how attractive that is to malevolent forces? You and Carly are in there together, so you have to stay under the radar—"

Kaitlyn rolls her eyes and makes a guttural sound of irritation or boredom. "Twin souls, blah blah. Yeah, I've heard it before, Naida. What's the point?"

"Playing with the *Olen* is dangerous," Naida snaps. "You never know who's listening. It's like talking on a tapped phone line."

"I guess that makes you a real genius, having that thing in your cousin's house on Halloween. I bet you planned this."

"You've really got no idea how dangerous that board was, do you? You just be glad I burned that pointer."

"Nice going, Sherlock. Now get out of my room. And take that bloody thing with you!"

Naida turns, reaches for the camera, and the screen goes black.

[END OF CLIP]

Diary of Kaitlyn Johnson

Monday, 1 November 2004, 8:43 pm
Attic

Naida. Queen of the dramatic. Melodramatic.
   I need a drink. Want to fly. Want to jump.
   Away, away, up, up, away!

Later, Dorm

It's official. Juliet McClarin is missing. No one has
seen her since the party. She and her little friend
Maggie were meant to come back to the dorms together
in Maggie's dad's car, but Juliet left right before the
Ouija board...thing.

   They think she tried to walk the two miles back to
school alone. At night. She could have fallen into a
ditch or been eaten by foxes.

   That's really stupid if you ask me. Unless you <u>are</u>
me.

From: AriHait558
To: RealxChick
Date: 1 November 2004
Subject: Tell Me

Tell me the truth about you.

Ari

Criminal Investigation Department, Portishead Headquarters
Avon and Somerset Constabulary, Portishead, Bristol
Tuesday, 28 December 2004, 15h40
AUDIO INTERVIEW #1: Detective Chief Inspector Floyd Homes (FH)
and Scott Fromley (SF)

(FH): This is Detective Chief Inspector Floyd Homes, Avon and Somerset CID, interviewing Mr. Scott Fromley on the twenty-eighth of December 2004. You are a student at Elmbridge High in Taunton?

(SF): Yes.

(FH): In what year?

(SF): 2004.

(FH): What *academic* year, son.

(SF): Oh, uh, I've been here since seventh grade. I'm in my last year.

(FH): Do you know where Juliet McClarin is?

(SF): No.

(FH): Any ideas about who might want to hurt her?

(SF): [Laughs] Seriously? She was the year below me, mate. I barely paid attention.

(FH): Do you have a girlfriend?

(SF): Yeah, I do, so why would I look at Juliet?

(FH): So you only have eyes for your girlfriend?

(SF): Bloody hell, yeah. Sorry. Look, mate, Naida's my girl. I'm no playboy, right? Nothing to it but that.

(FH): Naida. [Pause] Naida Chounan-Dupré?

(SF): Yeah, that's right.

(FH): And you'd do anything to protect her?

(SF): Of course I would.

(FH): Even lie to protect her. [Pause] Even if it would hurt someone innocent?

(SF): What are you talking about?

(FH): Even if a life could be in danger?

(SF): Seriously, mate, I don't know what you mean.

(FH): Juliet has been missing for almost two months now. It seems highly likely that Carly Johnson was the last person to see her. Juliet stepped outside before the Ouija board incident, and shortly after that, Carly went outside. Witnesses state that they heard a scream, but none have been able to identify that scream as either Carly's or Juliet's for certain. It was several moments before others joined Carly outside. We don't know what happened in the interim.

(SF): What does that have to do with Naida?

(FH): Do you know where Juliet is?

(SF): This is mental. No, I don't know where she is. *You* should, though. Besides, I still don't see what any of this has to do with Naida.

(FH): Scott, I need you to be honest with me.

[Pause]

(SF): Okay…

(FH): Is Naida Chounan-Dupré hiding Carly Johnson?

[End of tape]

Diary of Kaitlyn Johnson

Wednesday, 3 November 2004, 11:00 pm
The Anniversary of the Accident
Attic

We both know what today is, so I guess I'm not surprised that Carly didn't leave a note. I should just come out and ask her, but…what if it's true, and Lansing's right? What if I cause irreparable harm by forcing her to talk to me?

No. It's a trick. Another damn trick.

I felt stupid, but I did it all the same. Walked up to the old chapel, went inside, and lit two votive candles. Mum. Dad. Ari wasn't there. I don't know where he is. I don't know what to say. I closed my eyes, as you're meant to do, and I thought of them…tried to think of them. I don't really remember what they looked like. Lansing keeps their photographs away from me. ~~Trauma~~ Lies.

She (~~you~~?) were standing in the solitary votive area. She (~~you~~?) were watching me from the darkness.

She (~~you~~?) were grinning.

I wish I could go to sleep.

Naida Camera Footage
Saturday, 6 November 2004, 6:53 PM
Naida's Dorm Room

The screen is dim. We can barely make out Naida's face.

"Idiot Mike," Naida says, her voice low, breath heavy. "He doesn't have even the tiniest clue what he's done." She pauses, hesitates, then clenches her jaw. "Or maybe he does."

She pulls the camera away from her face, and we can see her more clearly. Her eyes are shadowed with fatigue and sleepless nights.

"The significance of the vandalism on his room...the missing door, the *mirror*...it's not lost on me. I think he's tampering with things he should leave well alone. I think he's messing with black magic. And that *he* found the *Olen* board?" She closes her eyes. "And then there's this."

The camera pans over to Naida's hand, in which sits a melted piece of dark plastic that she turns between her slim fingers.

"It's the pointer. From my party. The one that found Kaitie...and Carly. I found it on my desk."

She pans back to herself. "Shit. I have to see for myself. I have to know."

[END OF CLIP]

35

"What do you *want*?" Kaitlyn asks. She seems tense, her eyes darting past Naida into the corridor as though waiting for someone. "You know she's not here yet." She checks her watch. "Not for another three minutes."

"Did you put this in my room?"

Kaitlyn frowns down at Naida's hand and the hunk of plastic. "What is it?"

"You're for real? You didn't put it in my room to be funny?"

"I don't go into your room."

There seems to be strong meaning behind those words, made more so by Naida's pointed silence.

Eventually Kaitlyn rolls her eyes and takes the plastic from Naida's hands. Immediately she freezes, her neck muscles distend, and her mouth opens as though she's in agony.

The camera dips and then rights itself. "Kaitlyn—"

Kaitlyn's eyes scrunch up, and she bends over and screams, her hand balled into a fist around the plastic. Naida grabs her hand and rips the pointer free. Kaitlyn's cries cease.

"What," she gasps. "What did you—"

A door bangs open. "What the hell, Chounan?" Brenda's angry voice is heard from afar. "Keep it down!" The door slams shut.

Naida turns back to Kaitlyn, lifting the camera. "Now, can you please explain—"

Kaitlyn's eyes roll back, and she collapses in the doorway.

"Damn it."

[END OF CLIP]

For many years, it was not known what exactly happened to make Kaitlyn scream so violently. However, nine years before the journal was found, a scrap of paper was discovered under the cushions of a sofa in the attic when safety renovations took place. It is written in Kaitlyn's hand and dated 7 November.

Diary of Kaitlyn Johnson

Sunday, 7 November 2004, 7:00 pm
Dorm

Blood on my hands. There was blood on my hands.

And that sound, all around me, that terrible laughter—that derision! I could feel the amused malice behind that Voice, and I felt the breath down my back, and I could feel, I <u>swear</u> I could feel, a hand running down my shirt, touching me—<u>urging me</u>—

What the hell is happening to me, Dee?

36

From: RealxChick
To: AriHait558
Date: 7 November 2004
Subject: Tired of Hiding

Dear Ari,

I'm tired of hiding, running, being scared. I'm so *tired* of being alone, and fighting myself and everything else all the time. But even though I know I want to tell you the truth, I'm too much of a coward to do it face-to-face. That's why I've been avoiding you. That's why I avoid *everyone*.

Bogged Down by My Confession

From: AriHait558
To: RealxChick
Date: 7 November 2004
Subject: Re: Tired of Hiding

Confess.

Sincerely,

Interested

From: RealxChick
To: AriHait558
Date: 7 November 2004
Subject: Confession

You first.

Sincerely,

Coward

From: AriHait558
To: RealxChick
Date: 7 November 2004
Subject: Re: Confession

I think I'm not a very nice person. Me: army brat who hates his dad.
I don't care about very much some days, which I feel like is mostly
because of this rootless existence I live with the asshole who shares
my genes but not my emotional level, and I'm kind of scared I might
be forced to leave, yet again, before I get to know this girl I met.
I struggle to forgive wrongs done against me because I can't ever
forget them—I have an eidetic memory. I wear bowler hats because
I hate my hair, but I despise fashion. I would like to have a cat one
day, even though I hate animals, and I would very much like to know
your story.

Full of Contradictions,

Ari

From: RealxChick
To: AriHait558
Date: 7 November 2004
Subject: Re: Re: Confession

My name is Kaitlyn, and I am a ghost. I don't exist, or so they tell me.

During the day, I literally don't exist. Most people go to sleep, wake up to the sun, and walk around in the light. Not me. My world is, and has always been, darkness, shadows, night.

My sister (we've always used that word), Carly, and I exist in the same body. I only come out at night. Carly is the one you see during the day at school, the one who ignores you, the one who probably looks at you like you're a total stranger (if she looks at you at all), and the one everyone thought was at that party. I'm Kait—I'm the one who talks to you in the confession booth, who has a WEIRD sense of humor, or lack of it, the one you went swimming with, the one you went to the party with, and the one you've been writing to. Me, Kaitlyn.

My doctor is convinced that I'm not really here. She keeps trying to convince *me* of it too. Sometimes she wears me down enough that I start to think maybe she's right. But I didn't appear after my parents died, as she is convinced—I've *always* been here. It's just the way we are. Me and Carly, together in one form.

We keep this secret because we always have. Our parents sort of convinced us it was the best way, unless we wanted to be locked away in a mental ward for the duration of the universe. We even talked about pretending it was some kind of memory problem or something. In the end, though, they just decided to hide *me* away. I've been hidden ever since. I guess they were right after all. People do think I'm crazy when I tell the truth. They try to trick me—lie to me. Tell me things…that are so beyond hurtful that I think they must be denizens from hell to do that. They make me feel like poison. Like an illness. A symptom of some horrible disease.

But hopefully you won't. I don't expect you to believe what I'm telling you. But please, *please*, at least acknowledge this email.

For obvious reasons, I hate to be ignored.

Sincerely and very afraid,

Kaitlyn Johnson, Girl of Nowhere

From: AriHait558
To: RealxChick
Date: 7 November 2004
Subject: Re: Re: Re: Confession

Dear Kaitlyn,

I believe you. Mostly because I made good on my threat. I *did* go and
talk to you during lunch the other day. I walked right up to—Carly,
I guess?—and said, "You missed confession, young lady." When she
stared at me for a full five seconds without saying anything, I asked
about the party, and she looked *really* confused. She stared at me
like I was the Minotaur, and then Naida comes up and says, "Gotta
go!" and steers Carly away without a word. It seemed odd that she'd
protect you from me when we were at the party together. It wasn't
normal. I knew something was wrong. Different.

This raises all kinds of questions about the nature of reality, the nature
of self, the idea of souls, the idea of the afterlife, questions about
genetics, the mind—

You do realize you're a regular science project?

Ari

PS—Thank you for your confession. I promise to keep it locked away as
long as you like. But you should know that I really like you exactly like
this. Exactly as you are. Kaitlyn.

I love your name.

From: RealxChick
To: AriHait558
Date: 7 November 2004
Subject: Re: Re: Re: Re: Confession

I am very, very aware of the fact that I'm a science project—gone
wrong. I seriously can't believe you haven't gone running for the hills.

K

From: AriHait558
To: RealxChick
Date: 7 November 2004
Subject: Re: Re: Re: Re: Re: Confession

I don't scare easily, though I expect others do? It's fine if you don't want to talk about it.

Come to the booth. I want to see you. I have questions. No cookies today—don't want to make Carly fat without her permission. Doesn't seem fair.

A

From: RealxChick
To: AriHait558
Date: 7 November 2004
Subject: Re: Re: Re: Re: Re: Re: Confession

Oh, clever. We have a sense of humor.

Be there in 10.

K

[The following entry was pasted into the journal.]

Diary of Kaitlyn Johnson

Friday, 12 November 2004, 8:00 PM
Dorm

I'm going to do something stupid. I—what's happening to me??

At first it was dark. Not so dark that I couldn't see, but dark enough that shapes had no meaning. I was outside standing in a blanket of mist. I could hear the ocean, and I shivered. The taste of a changeable storm hung on the air. As soon as I thought this, the clouds above me, which seemed alive and full of malevolent depth, moving fast like a stop-motion film, gave a deep rumbling groan—and ceased. Just froze in the sky.

I stumbled forward and tripped on an ancient step, which led to an enormous house towering above me, three stories high.

Dee, I felt that house stare down at me.

The windows gazed across the landscape, each fringed by the crumbling slate roof like eyelids. Even the console brackets had the sunken, eroded texture of all things that have succumbed to the oppressive passage of time. The weather vane, too, stood rusted and old, no longer a thing of pride, but a creaking slice of metal warped into no definite shape by years of long corrosion.

I reached for the handle and gave a push, and the door creaked forward with an eerie whine that echoed around the room. The house was bare, unfurnished and

covered with a film of dust, velvety thick. Desolate
leaves—the remnant of an autumn long past—breezed
their lonely way along the floor, carried by the dank,
rotten air. A giant chandelier in the wide entryway
hung on an ominously rusty chain, draped with cobwebs
that even the spiders had long abandoned. There was a
looming sense of emptiness about the place. Even the
mildew smell seemed oddly distant and weak, like the
remembrance of a scent.

And yet…somehow I sensed I wasn't alone.

I climbed the rickety stairs to the first floor,
feeling more vulnerable and naked than I had outside,
each foot tentative on the warping, decayed wood. I was
momentarily afraid I'd fall through the floor into some
pitch-dark basement with no doors.

The second story was just as gray and foggy as
outside, and I half-expected to hear thunder rumbling
through the ceiling. It was oppressively small,
with long, narrow corridors that seemed endless and
labyrinthine, punctuated by ancient and blackened
candle sconces.

I felt a sudden yearning for Carly, so powerful
that it hit me like physical pain. I called her name.
"Carly? Are you here?"

I wanted her to answer. I was terrified when she
didn't.

I was so alone. Too alone.

Something subtle seemed to move behind the wall, and
I stepped hesitantly closer, not entirely sure I wanted
to look.

It wasn't a wall at all, but a mirror covered in a
coating of dust so thick that it looked like wallpaper.
A smoggy version of my face stared back at me, wide-
eyed. I wiped away the dust, leaving a gleaming streak
of polished silver in the wake of my hand.

This reflection was not me.

The eyes were no longer clear and blue; one was
bloodshot with a blown pupil that made it look entirely
black, and the other was a faded gray—dreary, like

everything in this forgotten place. A cheap imitation of blue. They were pitiless, unseeing eyes, wide with malice, the whites yellow and full of bile. Her skin, stretched tightly over her skeletal frame, tinged a yellow-gray as she leered, black liquid congealing out of a mouth that was too large as it grinned.

"Me," she gurgled, and the black liquid seemed to emulsify as it fell from her cracked, red lips and landed on the floor in gobbets of mush.

It was the girl. The one who has been watching me. But she was rotting. Or was it Carly? I didn't know. I still don't know.

I took a startled breath. "Who—"

Without warning, her smile vanished, replaced with a garish scowl, teeth bared, her eyes flat and dead, but wide and manic. She reached out—through the mirror—and grabbed my throat. I felt her broken nails dig into my skin.

"Me!" she screamed.

I fell backwards; the thing dragged out of the mirror with me, and I saw that she was nothing more than a shredded stump of a torso—her legs and pelvis were gone, leaving ribbons of fatty tendons and muscle. Her half body thumped the floor wetly. I managed to wrench myself free and run farther into the house, along a dark narrow corridor and towards a wooden door that stood apart, brand-new, surreal, and gleaming in the dilapidated abode. I heard the girl dragging herself along the floor after me, her long nails clawing at the splintered wooden panels. I glanced back once, saw her hand extended, her mouth a yawning black hole, and screamed. There was no echo.

I burst through the door and found myself stumbling into the foggy evening, gulping down gasps of brine-tinged air.

Behind me the house stood suddenly far away, watching me. Now I could see that it sat on a hill, and both hill and house were on the verge of crumbling over a precipice into a cankerous sea far below in that slow, fuggy way of dreams I've read about so often.

The sea wanted the house.

The house wanted me.

The girl was nowhere to be seen, and I felt more alone than I have ever felt, even in the oblivion of nonexistence.

Later, Attic

Dee, I had a dream. A nightmare. A house. A dead freaking house. I felt that house like it was a part of me…God, it was so real.

Something else.

A deep, black stillness has come over me, Dee. Slowly, like time itself is bending around me, decaying at the edges. Nothing seems real. Still nothing from Carly in the Message Book, even though I wrote out what Lansing told me…the lie. But nothing, no reply.

Something is wrong.

I scoured the room looking for tiny squares of purple—jeans, no; dresser, no; bathroom mirror; nothing. And then—I found one! On the corkboard over our desk. Except…it was <u>my</u> note. The one I left her yesternight, the one that said <u>No note?</u>

Still there. Completely untouched.

What the hell is going on? I feel sick, Dee.

I pulled out my Post-its and scribbled a message for Carly with shaking fingers: "Are you okay? Why didn't you write me? Is Lansing right? Am I hurting you by writing to you? Please tell me."

Having no sign of Carly makes me feel exactly as I did in the dream—terrified and alone. Even though I've never seen or spoken to my sister, she is always there in her scribbles and in the evidence of her movements by the little acts of kindness—a new book, a folded sweater—that she leaves behind. But this morning, our room looked unchanged, and I suppressed a shudder at the nothingness I felt in the pit of my gut.

Just like at the end of my…nightmare.

I still feel it now.

Maybe she was busy. Maybe she needed time to process

the anniversary. Maybe she went to talk it over with
Naida.

I'm going to check.

[If Kaitlyn went to talk to Naida, no record of the conversation
has been found.]

Diary of Kaitlyn Johnson

Saturday, 13 November 2004, 9:00 pm
Attic

Still nothing from Carly. Dee, what's happening?

4 blue pills

12 white pills

32 yellow capsules

How many should there be? I don't know. I should have been counting!

She discarded me directly in bed, and it was warm, the mattress soft—as though she'd been lying there for a while. I went straight to the Message Book, a dead, horrible feeling in the pit of my stomach. I don't know what I expected. A note telling me she was actually doing better? That she and Lansing agreed on her treatments? That Lansing <u>was</u> trying another trick on us?

All I got were white pages with nothing in them. My own message glared at me with amusement and derision, and I suddenly felt panicked. Where is Carly? Why hasn't she written to me?

I've always <u>heard</u> her words, even though I was only reading them, because without them, the silence feels deep and dangerous.

I hear Aka Manah sniggering somewhere in the shadows.

"Go away," I tell him. "Leave me alone."

But his breathy sounds seem only closer.

Later

I picked up the phone, even. I was going to call Dr. Lansing. The closest thing I have left to a parent. *I picked up the phone*...almost dialed the number. Hung up.

What could she do except tell me I was "integrating"? That I shouldn't be afraid?

She lost my trust long ago, when she first called me a symptom. And now I have nowhere to turn.

The girl is here. So thin, so painfully thin. She is grinning even though her yellow hair falls like spiderwebs into her waiting hands.

I wish she would stop smiling.

Later Still

Whereareyouwhereareyouwhereareyouwhereareyouwhereareyouwhereareyou
whereareyouwhereareyouwhereareyouwhereareyouwhereareyouwhereareyou
whereareyouwhereareyouwhereareyouwhereareyouwhereareyouwhereareyou
whereareyouwhereareyouwhereareyouwhereareyouwhereareyouwhereareyou
whereareyouwhereareyouwhereareyouwhereareyouwhereareyouwhereareyou
whereareyouwhereareyouwhereareyouwhereareyouwhereareyouwhereareyou
whereareyouwhereareyouwhereareyouwhereareyouwhereareyouwhereareyou
whereareyouwhereareyouwhereareyouwhereareyouwhereareyouwhereareyou
whereareyouwhereareyouwhereareyouwhereareyouwhereareyouwhereareyou
whereareyouwhereareyouwhereareyouwhereareyouwhereareyouwhereareyou
whereareyouwhereareyouwhereareyouwhereareyouwhereareyouwhereareyou
whereareyouwhereareyouwhereareyouwhereareyouwhereareyouwhereareyou
whereareyouwhereareyouwhereareyouwhereareyouwhereareyouwhereareyou
whereareyouwhereareyouwhereareyouwhereareyouwhereareyouwhereareyou
whereareyouwhereareyouwhereareyouwhereareyouwhereareyouwhereareyou
whereareyouwhereareyouwhereareyouwhereareyouwhereareyouwhereareyou
whereareyouwhereareyouwhereareyouwhereareyouwhereareyouwhereareyou
whereareyouwhereareyouwhereareyouwhereareyouwhereareyouwhereareyou
whereareyouwhereareyouwhereareyouwhereareyouwhereareyouwhereareyou
whereareyouwhereareyouwhereareyouwhereareyouwhereareyouwhereareyou
whereareyouwhereareyouwhereareyouwhereareyouwhereareyouwhereareyou
whereareyouwhereareyouwhereareyouwhereareyouwhereareyouwhereareyou
whereareyouwhereareyouwhereareyouwhereareyouwhereareyouwhereareyou
whereareyouwhereareyouwhereareyouwhereareyouwhereareyouwhereareyou
whereareyouwhereareyouwhereareyouwhereareyouwhereareyouwhereareyou
whereareyouwhereareyouwhereareyouwhereareyouwhereareyouwhereareyou
whereareyouwhereareyouwhereareyouwhereareyouwhereareyouwhereareyou
whereareyouwhereareyouwhereareyouwhereareyouwhereareyouwhereareyou
whereareyouwhereareyouwhereareyouwhereareyouwhereareyouwhereareyou
whereareyouwhereareyouwhereareyouwhereareyouwhereareyouwhereareyou

whereareyouwhereareyouwhereareyouwhereareyouwhereareyouwhereareyou
whereareyouwhereareyouwhereareyouwhereareyouwhereareyouwhereareyou
whereareyouwhereareyouwhereareyouwhereareyouwhereareyouwhereareyou
whereareyouwhereareyouwhereareyouwhereareyouwhereareyouwhereareyou
whereareyouwhereareyouwhereareyouwhereareyouwhereareyouwhereareyou
whereareyouwhereareyouwhereareyouwhereareyouwhereareyouwhereareyou
whereareyouwhereareyouwhereareyouwhereareyouwhereareyouwhereareyou
whereareyouwhereareyouwhereareyouwhereareyouwhereareyouwhereareyou
whereareyouwhereareyouwhereareyouwhereareyouwhereareyouwhereareyou
whereareyouwhereareyouwhereareyouwhereareyouwhereareyouwhereareyou...

39

[The following diary entry is barely legible, the ink smudged, pages curling, the letters small and untidy, as though written in great distress.]

Diary of Kaitlyn Johnson

Sunday, 14 November 2004, 9:00 am
Attic

Here, in the dark, I can write.

What's happening, Dee? <u>Why</u> is this happening? I woke up this morning.

I woke up.

This morning.

The sun was worse than fire, exposing every single part of me, and everything else. The room was complete like it had never been before. Bigger, more complicated. Harder. It was not a room I have ever seen.

Dee—Carly is...

Where is Carly? I don't know how or where or why. I woke up this <u>morning</u> and it was <u>light</u> and <u>bright</u>, and she wasn't here. I was. She hadn't written in the Message Book, because I was where she should have been—

I can't do this.

I don't know where she is. First, she didn't look at the Message Book yesternight, and now she's gone. Have we switched? Was this meant to happen?

I threw up in the bin, saw my reflection—it's all wrong! I looked like every photo of Carly I've ever seen. And all I could hear was Lansing's voice in my mind—

Integration. Integration. Integration.

I WAS MEANT TO DISAPPEAR, NOT CARLY!

I screamed and I screamed and I ran out of there as fast as I could there were so many people around the girls I only briefly see at dinner on the rare occasions I actually go to the hall and who I watch while they sleep now they were talking moving running laughing all of them in one place there were too many colors too many things too many people all around at once and I didn't understand and I wanted to hide but the sun made everything so white and my eyes my eyes—

They tried to talk to me: "Carly, what's wrong?" "Carly?"

"Carly, what's happened?" "Where is Carly going?"

Carly? Carly? Carly?

I screamed at them all.

Everything so hard, everything so fast. Winding up, not down.

Nothing muted, soft and safe. Everything there, so real and sharp!

I couldn't handle it. I ran and ran and I didn't know where I was going, only that the sky was blue and the grass was green and the colors were all wrong and too strong and my eyes—

Shit…Shit.

The attic is always dark. Always safe.

What do I do? Where is she? How do I…what do I do?

Dee, please. If it's you, stop laughing.

Dee, help me. Help me, Dee. What do I do?

I'm going to wait for sunset. If I discard into another day, I'll know something at least. I'll know Carly is safe. That she is now the night child and I'm now the day. Maybe we were always meant to flip around at some point…We really don't know anything at all.

Except something is wrong. I can feel it inside me like I've lost a lung. I listen for my Voice, but there is nothing except silence. There has never been such silence, so I know he must be close.

I smell ashes and blood, and I don't understand why I am here and Carly is not.

I need to get to the dorm; Carly will panic to wake here. I'll be sure to leave her a note. If I don't discard…if I'm alone. Dee, what happens then?

What happens when a kite loses its string?

5:00 pm, Dorm

The sun set.

From: RealxChick
To: AriHait558
Date: 14 November 2004
Subject: Losing My Shit

Ari, help me, I don't know what to do—Carly's gone. Shitshitshit, Ari, *what do I do*?

From: AriHait558
To: RealxChick
Date: 14 November 2004
Subject: Re: Losing My Shit

Kait? Are you okay? What's happened?

From: AriHait558
To: RealxChick
Date: 14 November 2004
Subject: Re: Re: Losing My Shit

Are you there?

From: AriHait558
To: RealxChick
Date: 14 November 2004
Subject: Re: Re: Re: Losing My Shit

Kaitlyn, you're scaring me—what's going on? Where are you?

From: AriHait558
To: RealxChick
Date: 14 November 2004
Subject: Re: Re: Re: Re: Losing My Shit

I'm going to the chapel. Meet me there.

40

79 days until the
incident

Naida Camera Footage
Monday, 15 November 2004, 2:22 AM
Naida's Dorm Clip #1

The screen is dark, but the muffled thump and corresponding "*damn*"
indicate that the camera is recording.

A lamp goes on, and the screen takes a moment to adjust. The
camera wobbles and points at the floor, where two socked feet appear in
the circle of lamplight on the carpet.

"What kind of hour do you call *this*?" Naida mutters, walking to
her door. She lifts the camera belatedly, and we get a brief view of her
disheveled hair in the mirror on the back of the door before she opens it.
She storms along the corridor and bangs on the next door over.

"Some of us are trying to sleep!"

A thud and then sobbing.

"Kaitlyn?"

Naida opens the door onto a scene of chaos. The bed is upturned, the
bedcovers strewn across the floor. The bookcases are empty, the contents
scattered about the room in violent disarray. Kaitlyn is huddled in a corner

behind the bed, sobbing. She slams her head into the wall repeatedly, the sound loud and shocking. There are smudges of blood on the pale wallpaper.

"Oh, my God," Naida breathes, moving forward, and we see her hand reaching outwards. "Kaitie—"

At the sound of Naida's voice, Kaitlyn's head shoots up, revealing puffy red eyes. She is holding a bottle of wine in her hands; it is almost empty.

Naida's camera shakes. "Kait—"

Before she can finish, Kaitlyn jumps to her feet, wine bottle forgotten, and launches herself past Naida and out of the room. Naida follows, and we see a flash of Kaitlyn as she races out the fire exit.

"Kaitlyn, wait!"

"What's going on?" a groggy voice calls from behind Naida.

Naida angles the camera on the sleepy face of Brenda. "Nothing. The fire escape blew open or something."

"What's happened?" Charlotte Leary says, opening her door. Then Maggie, farther along.

"What's the banging?"

"Fire escape," Naida says.

"Keep it down," Brenda mutters, before withdrawing her head and slamming her door. Charlotte and Maggie withdraw too.

Naida turns the camera on herself. "Something's up."

She rushes down the fire escape and into the woods.

15 November Clip #2, 2:47 AM

"Oh, my God," Naida whispers. Now and then, we see a flash of her hand as she tries to shield the camera from the rain, which falls like bullets. Her voice is obscured by wind in the speakers, but we hear her mutter, "Oh, Kaitlyn...no. Please, Kaitlyn..."

At last, the rain ebbs and Naida lifts the camera, pointing it up to the roof of Elmbridge's west wing. Kaitlyn balances on the steep surface, her feet bare on slippery slate tiles. She wears nothing but a white tank top, which the rain has rendered transparent against her skin, and wet cotton sweats that cling to her legs. Thunder cracks across the sky, almost exactly as Naida yells Kaitlyn's name.

Kaitlyn stumbles, rights herself, and, oblivious, stands at the very end of the roof, staring out into the night as though searching for something. She sways.

Naida screams, "*Kaitlyn!*"

There is vivid movement and muffled sounds, and then we are inside, running along the corridor of Magpie House, the image snapping back and forth. Naida's gasps for breath are loud in the microphone as she runs. She dumps the camera on a table next to a phone, and we see Naida grasp the receiver and pull it out of the shot.

Silence holds for a moment, and the curling cord of the telephone dances as Naida waits, her breaths forcefully punctuating the silence. In. Out. In. Out.

"Hello! There's a girl on the roof, I think she's going to jump! Come fast, please!"

[Silence]

"Yes, Elmbridge, main building—hurry! No—no, I can't stay on the line, she's going to jump!"

The receiver falls, and footsteps recede. In the silence that follows, we can hear the emergency operator on the line.

"*Caller? Caller, are you there? I need you to stay on the line—*"

[END OF 15 NOVEMBER CLIP #2]

41

On 15 November 2004, police were called by Naida Chounan-Dupré to investigate a jumper on the roof of Elmbridge High. Police arrived on the scene at 3:15 AM, and Carly Luanne Johnson was forcibly taken into custody.

PART III

ME,
NOT
ME

Hell is empty,
And all the devils are here.
—William Shakespeare,
The Tempest, Act 1, Scene 2

Rage, rage against the
dying of the light.
—Dylan Thomas

In news journals and articles that followed the arrest, witnesses attest that clips of Carly being carried from the roof by a fireman and subsequently led to a police vehicle were shown on the nine o'clock news that night. To date, no such footage has been found.

On the afternoon of 15 November 2004, Carly Luanne Johnson was involuntarily readmitted to Claydon Youth Psychiatric Facility. Such reports as could be sourced indicate that her doctors worried she may have suffered a psychotic break of the persecutory type.

After readmission to Claydon, a string of therapy sessions commenced, wherein doctors (headed by Dr. Annabeth Lansing), attempted to understand why a seemingly integrated Carly failed to react in the manner expected.

Inpatient Session Recording #52 [Ref: Johnson-Inp-0033]
Tuesday, 16 November 2004, 10:24 AM
Claydon Youth Psychiatric Facility, Somerset
Dr. Annabeth Lansing (AL) and Carly Luanne Johnson (CJ)

(AL): You seem distressed again. Can you tell me what's going on?

[Silence]

Carly? Are you doing okay? Do you feel like talking?

(CJ): [Strained] You won't listen.

(AL): I always listen, Carly. You know that. [Pause] Why were you on the roof? [Pause] Carly?

(CJ): Stop. Calling. Me. *Carly!*

(AL): Am I speaking with Kaitlyn?

(CJ): Yes, for God's sake.

(AL): So talk to me, Kaitlyn. Please.

(CJ): [Lengthy silence] Carly didn't check the Message Book the night before it happened...she's been...silent. For a while. It worried me.

(AL): The night before what happened?

(CJ): The night before I...I woke up, and it was... morning.

[Pause]

(AL): That must have been frightening.

(CJ): That's a total understatement. Everything is wrong. She's just...gone.

(AL): Integration is alarming. She's not really gone. Just...working the way she should. But you need to accept what's happened.

(CJ): [Laughing] "Trust me, I'm here to help you." How can I when you won't believe me? You think you see? That's crap—you don't see. You think you do, but you're all bloody clueless! You won't listen—you don't believe! [Beginning to cry] Carly's gone. I've written, I've—I've—I've— [Sobbing] I've t-tried to discard—she won't come! I can't find her, I—

[Gasps, sobs]

(AL): Calm down, Kaitlyn. It's okay. Take a deep breath, and let's talk about this rationally. [Pause] Okay. Tell me what happened.

(CJ): [Shrieking] I can't breathe!

[Gasps, choking sounds]

(AL): Kaitlyn, calm down. Kaitlyn, breathe—

[Choking, gagging]

(CJ): He's—here—

(AL): [Away] Sedative!

[A door squeaks; there are footsteps, gasps]

[Thud]

(AL): [Soothing] Calm down. Calm down…

[Gasps fade into a disturbed panting]

That's it. Shh… [Away] How much did you give her?

(UNIDENTIFIED NURSE): Twenty-five milligrams.

(AL): Good. Okay, Kaitlyn, it's okay.

(CJ): [Slurred mumble] Won't listen…

[End of tape]

16 November 2004

An interesting development with Carly Johnson. Kaitlyn has surfaced, it seems permanently. We've spent so much time working to suppress the Kaitlyn alter, and Carly was the alter all along. Perhaps the Carly alter was created in order to distance herself from a life without her parents in it.

This contradicts the facts, of course, since Carly (who names herself Kaitlyn at night) is real. The renaming of herself as Kaitlyn, although highly unusual, may have provided the mask she needed to wear. A new identity.

Now that the Carly alter is gone, I can begin to help Kaitlyn be Carly—the real Carly—once again.

I am hopeful of a full recovery in time, although with the incident on the roof, I am concerned that this readmittance to Claydon may be permanent.

43

Several therapy sessions follow before Kaitlyn talks again. Nonetheless, the sessions are recorded, and Dr. Annabeth Lansing attempts to connect with a silent Kaitlyn. For expediency, none of these recordings have been included. However, they are available online at [see appendix A]. The visit from Jaime Johnson on [date unknown] seems to be the trigger event for Kaitlyn's reawakening.

CCTV Camera Footage
[Date and Time Index Missing]
Day Room

"Carly."

Dr. Annabeth Lansing kneels next to Kaitlyn, who sits in a chair, unmoving.

"Kaitlyn. Jaime is here to see you. You want to see Jaime, don't you?"

Kaitlyn does not respond.

"You don't want her to see you like this, do you?"

When Kaitlyn remains unresponsive, Dr. Lansing sighs and gets to her feet, groaning when her knees crack. She nods at the nurse waiting by a wire-mesh-glass door.

"All right."

The door drones, a dull beep, and Jaime Johnson dashes in, followed by a grim-faced middle-aged woman with blond hair, stylishly bobbed.

"I don't like this," the woman says as Dr. Lansing walks over.

Jaime Johnson has paused in front of Kaitlyn's chair, little hands opening and closing slowly, expectantly.

"I know," Lansing says quietly. "It's not ideal. But I need to try anything at this point, and Carly does have a right to see her."

"She shouldn't," the woman says, her nostrils flaring as though an obnoxious odor has just caught her attention. "It's *sickening*."

Jaime, who has been looking at Kaitlyn silently, turns to Dr. Lansing.

"Why is Kaitie here?" she asks.

Dr. Lansing walks over to Jaime and bends down. "What's that, sweetheart?"

Jaime points at Kaitlyn. "Why is Kaitie here? Where's Carly?"

Lansing blinks, shakes her head, and then smiles. "I don't know where Carly's gone, angel. Maybe you can find her for me."

Jaime glances back at Kaitlyn, and her eyes fill with tears. "I don't see her."

Dr. Lansing frowns, and Jaime walks over to Kaitlyn, crawling into her lap, where she curls up, tiny fists grabbing at the statue's hospital gown. She cries little-girl tears.

"This isn't right," Mrs. Bailey snaps. "No child should have to see this!"

She starts forward, reaching out as though to lift Jaime out of Kaitlyn's lap, but Jaime shrieks and clings to Kaitlyn's gown.

"Kaitie!" she screams. "Kaitie!"

Mrs. Bailey manages to break Jaime's hold and carries the sobbing girl out of the room, casting a withering glance in Dr. Lansing's direction.

Kaitlyn does not move, but Jaime continues to scream down the corridor.

"Kaitie! Kaitie! KAAAITTIEEEE!"

44

71 days until
the incident

Inpatient Session Recording #57 [Ref: Johnson-Inp-0033]
Tuesday, 23 November 2004, 3:00 PM
Claydon Youth Psychiatric Facility, Somerset
Dr. Annabeth Lansing (AL) and Carly Luanne Johnson (CJ)

(AL): I think we can make great progress in our inpatient sessions. I think I can help you feel a lot better. Get back to living your life.

(CJ): Don't BS me, Lansing. I know you don't believe a word of what I'm telling you, but you're the only person who might know how I can undo this and get Carly *back*. Even if I disappear, like you want—I don't care. Just bring her back.

(AL): It doesn't work that way, Kaitlyn. You *are* Carly. We just need to remind you of it.

[Laughter]

(CJ): You doctors. You don't know anything!

[Loud crash, footsteps]

[From a distance] High and mighty! You hear, but you don't listen. And if you inject me with that stuff again, I'm going to fucking kick you!

[A door slams]

[Silence]

(AL): [Sighing] Astonishing. Catatonic episode passed without the patient noticing. More analysis required.

[End of tape]

45

Scattered diary entries from throughout Kaitlyn's readmission period can be found clumped together at the back of the journal, folded on letterhead paper with the Claydon crest at the top right-hand corner. Some of the entries are undecipherable, while others are very clear. There are several stops and starts in the diary over the following weeks, but, for expediency, only entries that are legible have been collated. Any that are confused have been excluded, excepting when they mention Carly directly.

None of the entries are dated, and many seem to be a stream of consciousness in which Kaitlyn tries to piece together her thoughts. It seems that she was, as Dr. Lansing advised her to do months previously, getting her thoughts out of herself and onto paper.

The Johnson Claydon Diaries

First Entry

They gave me a pencil to write with. A fucking <u>pencil</u>. Lansing is all smug that her "therapy" has worked. She sees this desire to write to you, Dee, as a success for her, since she gave the diary, the object, to me. But I'd never tell her what a friend you've become, how much I need you. How real you are, and how vital. So she thinks she won because I want to write, but really she handed me her weapons, which I use against her. She has no idea that you are completely separate from these pages and wholly mine.

Can't believe I'm back here. In Claydon. In a yellow institutional room with a little window on the door where they can peek their ugly, fat faces in and "check" on me.

Dee...Carly is ~~gone~~. I still can't bring myself to leave that word on the page. ~~Gone~~. ~~Absent~~. ~~Missing~~. None of them will do.

Inpatient Session Recording #58 [Ref: Johnson-Inp-0033]
Wednesday, 24 November 2004, 3:12 PM
Claydon Youth Psychiatric Facility, Somerset
Dr. Annabeth Lansing (AL) and Carly Luanne Johnson (CJ)

(**AL**): How are you feeling today, Carly?

(**CJ**): I told you not to call me that.

(**AL**): Kaitlyn, then. How are you?

(**CJ**): You already know.

(**AL**): I thought we could continue our talk from last
session.

(**CJ**): I told you everything.

(**AL**): Yes. But you haven't let me tell *you* anything
yet.

(**CJ**): I don't belong here.

(**AL**): Kaitlyn, we found you up on the roof of the
school. You had lesions and bruising on your head,
presumably from repeated impact. You need treatment.

[Silence]

I'm happy to send you back to Elmbridge eventually,
but you need to show me that you can cope on your own.

(**CJ**): I'm taking the meds.

(**AL**): That's a start. A good one. But you need to talk
to me.

(**CJ**): I don't see the point! I don't know what you
want me to say!

(**AL**): The first topic that comes into your head. Just
start.

(CJ): This is stupid.

(AL): [Quietly] Try. Please.

(CJ): [Mumbles]

(AL): Come on, you can do it. The first thing.

(CJ): I…I can't. I want to stop.

(AL): Kaitlyn, you have to try.

(CJ): I said I want to stop!

[End of tape]

The Johnson Claydon Diaries

Second Entry

I'm not me,
    And nor is she,
    Who sits upon the bed?
    But then who,
    Is me, is you,
    Who sits here very dead?

Third Entry

It's been a week, I think…and I can just about hold my pencil steady. Reliving it is hard, but if I don't get it down while it's fresh, it will change like water and then I'll never find her.

I can't remember everything that happened the morning I woke. It comes to me in terrible slaps that are sharp like glass on my memory, and I've been trying to piece it together. I remember that there wasn't enough air, and what air there was, was hot—too hot. I couldn't breathe because it boiled my lungs, and I gagged on the alveoli bubbling up into my throat. I ran—ran out the door and maybe down the corridor, maybe down the fire escape—that part's foggy.

I fled the room, fled the wing, fled the school. Fled my mind, Dee.

I remember running, and things in my way, and knocking into people who were all arms trying to catch me. I remember drowning in the open air, and everything being painful on my eyes. I remember someone's voice calling Carly's name, and I remember covering my ears and screaming as I fled.

I remember writing, so maybe I told you all this already. I can't be sure, though, until I get back to Elmbridge. So here it is again, maybe. Not. I don't know.

The rest is muddled. There was the roof, rain, thunder—someone carrying me away, and my heart broke that I had lost my chance to fly. Lansing is going to lock me up forever now.

Carly was ~~gone~~. Carly was ~~nothing~~. I've ~~lost~~ her. I'm in her space…her space is ~~empty~~. It's been so many days, Dee, and Carly is still ~~gone~~.

The doctors dosed me again. It was like I was back to that messed-up place after they died. It's like I lost ~~it~~ myself as well as Carly.

Honestly, Dee, I have no idea what I'm going to do.

I've had more dreams. What is going on???

I keep hoping I'll discard when the sun rises.

Fourth Entry

The girl is here the girl is here

the girl is here the girl is here the girl is here the girl
is here the girl is here the girl is here the girl is here
the girl is here the girl is here the girl is here the girl
is here the girl is here the girl is here the girl is here
the girl is here the girl is here the girl is here the girl
is here the girl is here the girl is here the girl is here
the girl is here the girl is here the girl is here the girl
is here the girl is here the girl is here the girl is here the
girl is here the girl is here the girl is here the girl is
here the girl is here the girl is here the girl is here the
girl is here the girl is here the girl is here the girl is
here the girl is here the girl is here the girl is here the
girl is here the girl is here the girl is here the girl is
here the girl is here the girl is here the girl is here the
girl is here the girl is here the girl is here the girl is
here the girl is here the girl is here the girl is here the
girl is here the girl is here the girl is here the girl is
here the girl is here the girl is here the girl is here the
girl is here the girl is here the girl is here the girl is
here the girl is here the girl is here the girl is here the
girl is here the girl is here the girl is here the girl is
here the girl is here the girl is here the girl is here the
girl is here the girl is here the girl is here the girl is
here the girl is here the girl is here the girl is here the
girl is here the girl is here the girl is here the girl is here
the girl is here the girl is here the girl is here the girl is here
the girl is here the girl is here the girl is here the girl is here
the girl is here the girl is here the girl is here the girl is here
the girl is here the girl is here the girl is here the girl is here
the girl is here the girl is here the girl is here the girl is here
the girl is here the girl is here the girl is here the girl is here
the girl is here the girl is here the girl is here the girl is here
the girl is here the girl is here the girl is here the girl is here
the girl is here the girl is here the girl is here the girl is here
the girl is here the girl is here the girl is here the girl is here
the girl is here the girl is here the girl is here the girl is here
the girl is here the girl is here the girl is here the girl is here
the girl is here the girl is here the girl is here the girl is here
the girl is here the girl is here the girl is here the girl is here the
girl is here the girl is here the girl is here the girl is here the
girl is here the girl is here the girl is here the girl is here the
girl is here the girl is here the girl is here the girl is here the
girl is here the girl is here the girl is here the girl is here the
girl is here the girl is here the girl is here the girl is here the
girl is here the girl is here the girl is here the girl is here the
girl is here the girl is here the girl is here the girl is here the

girl is here the girl is here the girl is here the girl is here the girl is
here the girl is here the girl is here the girl is here the girl is here the
girl is here the girl is here the girl is here the girl is here the girl is
here the girl is here the girl is here the girl is here the girl is here the
girl is here the girl is here the girl is here the girl is here the girl is
here the girl is here the girl is here the girl is here the girl is here the
girl is here the girl is here the girl is here the girl is here the girl is
here the girl is here the girl is here the girl is here the girl is here the
girl is here the girl is here the girl is here the girl is here the girl is
here the girl is here the girl is here the girl is here the girl is here the
girl is here the girl is here the girl is here the girl is here the girl is
here the girl is here the girl is here the girl is here the girl is here the
girl is here the girl is here the girl is here the girl is here the girl is here
the girl is here the girl is here the girl is here the girl is here the girl is
here the girl is here the girl is here the girl is here the girl is here the girl
is here the girl is here the girl is here the girl is here the girl is here the
girl is here the girl is here the girl is here the girl is here the girl is here
the girl is here the girl is here the girl is here the girl is here the girl is
here the girl is here the girl is here the girl is here the girl is here the girl
is here the girl is here the girl is here the girl is here the girl is here the
girl is here the girl is here the girl is here the girl is here the girl is here
the girl is here the girl is here the girl is here the girl is here the girl is
here the girl is here the girl is here the girl is here the girl is here the girl
is here the girl is here the girl is here the girl is here the girl is here the girl is
here the girl is here the girl is here the girl is here the girl is here the girl
the girl is here the girl is here the girl is here the girl is here the girl is here the
girl is here the girl is here the girl is here the girl is here the girl is here the girl
is here the girl is here the girl is here the girl is here the girl is here the
girl is here the girl is here the girl is here the girl is here the girl is here
the girl is here the girl is here the girl is here the girl is here the girl is here the
girl is here the girl is here the girl is here the girl is here the girl is here the girl
is here the girl is here the girl is here the girl is here the girl is here the girl is
here the girl is here the girl is here the girl is here the girl is here the girl is here the girl
is here the girl is here the girl is here the girl is here the girl is here the girl is here the girl
is here the girl is here the girl is here the girl is here the girl is here the girl is here the
girl is here the girl is here the girl is here the girl is here the girl is here the girl is here the girl
is here the girl is here the girl is here the girl is here the girl is here the girl is
here the girl is here the girl is here the girl is here the girl is here the girl is here the girl
is here the girl is here the girl is here the girl is here the girl is here the girl is here the
girl is here the girl is here the girl is here the girl is here the girl is here the girl is here
the girl is here the girl is here the girl is here the girl is here the girl is here the girl is
here the girl is here the girl is here the girl is here the girl is here the girl is here the girl
is here the girl is here the girl is here the girl is here the girl is here the girl is here the
girl is here the girl is here the girl is here the girl is here the girl is here the girl is here
the girl is here the girl is here the girl is here the girl is here the girl is here the girl is
here the girl is here the girl is here the girl is here the girl is here the girl is here the girl
is here the girl is here the girl is here the girl is here the girl is here the girl is here the
girl is here the girl is here the girl is here the girl is here the girl is here the girl is here the
girl is here the girl is here the girl is here the girl is here the girl is here the girl is
here the girl is here the girl is here the girl is here the girl is here the girl is here the girl
is here the girl is here the girl is here the girl is here the girl is here the girl is here the
girl is here the girl is here the girl is here the girl is here the girl is here the girl is here
the girl is here the girl is here the girl is here the girl is here the girl is here the girl is
here the girl is here the girl is here the girl is here the girl is here the girl is here the girl
is here the girl is here the girl is here the girl is here the girl is here the girl is here the girl
is here the girl is here the girl is here the girl is here the girl is here the girl is here the
girl is here the girl is here the girl is here the girl is here the girl is here the girl is here

the girl is here the girl is here

Fifth Entry

I watch them watching me. They stare and they analyze, hoping to figure out what has broken. Where they've gone wrong, never for a moment thinking that what I told them might be true. They call _me_ the real Carly now. Suddenly, she's the alter. Funny how quickly they turn it all around.

Inpatient Therapy Notes
Dr. Annabeth Lansing
Patient File [Johnson-C-0399524], Session #59

Thursday, 25 November 2004

Carly was found sprinting along
the east hall. There were lesions on
her hands and feet, and Nurse Tulk
informs me that she appeared terrified.
When Health-care Assistant Rogers
caught her, she scratched his cheek
and screamed wildly, kicking out.
Nurse Tulk reports that she was staring
down the corridor, eyes wide and
manic, saliva dried on her lips.

   She insists she did not hurt herself,
but that "something" was in the room
with her. I have no choice but to believe
the injuries are self-inflicted, and her
nails have been cut short to prevent
further damage.

   We have started a saline drip for
dehydration, and for now she has been
locked in her room. I fear she may be a
danger to others.

Sixth Entry

My mind climbed out the window...They think they can cage
me? My nails could be broken and bloody, but what would
that matter? My body is a tool.

Up here, my mind seems to open up. I can picture the
rows of psychiatric wards that lie dull and dead under
a moon that should make them sparkle, and I can almost
hear the silent sobs from within each blocky window.
This is different from Elmbridge, but it's still a
roof. I can still fly. If I want.

And I still float here and wonder why I don't—what's
holding me down?

Carly. Please. Where are you?

Carly? Are you there?

49

Inpatient Session Recording #59 [Ref: Johnson-Inp-0033]
Friday, 26 November 2004, 11:13 AM
Claydon Youth Psychiatric Facility, Somerset
Dr. Annabeth Lansing (AL) and Carly Luanne Johnson (CJ)

(**AL**): What is it, Carly?

[Silence]

What's so amusing to you? Hm?

[Slow laughter]

Care to share it with me?

[Laughter building]

Carly.

[Raucous laughter]

Come on, now. Let's talk, shall we?

[Laughter becomes manic]

Very well. We'll try again tomorrow.

[End of tape]

The Johnson Claydon Diaries

Seventh Entry

I found the patient bathroom—the one Lansing didn't
want me to see. The one in the patient common room.
Because of the mirror. But it's not a <u>real</u> mirror
at all, Dee. It's this imitation mirror that belongs
in a toddler's play area. Thin, plastic, reflective
but warped. But even though the reflection was bent
and strange, I <u>did</u> see her. A girl, far off in the
distance.

Was it you, Dee? I can't be sure, but if not, surely
it must be Carly? It <u>has</u> to be one of you! All I know
is that she seemed trapped. Trapped in the churning
shadows. Tried to call her. Quite calmly, I thought,
but next thing I knew, the ward nurses came crashing
in and carried me away, and I got an injection for my
trouble.

But it's okay, because I now have a plan to find a
real mirror, not a silly child's imitation. And then?
Then, you'll see.

50

The Johnson Claydon Diaries

Eighth Entry

It's a dead place, and I call it the Dead House. It
might have looked nice once…painted white, blue-
shuttered and perky. Now the white paint is gray,
curling away from the wood like dandruff or moth wings,
and the shutters, if any remain, hang from hinges
rusted and comatose. The door looms before me…I can see
it, Dee. It invites me inside. I don't want to go, and
I do…

    Unrelated words pop into my head

    Teeth. Rust. Sleep. Corn flour.

    As I stand there, I realize I'm hungry.

    So is the house.

Ninth Entry

I'm learning to like dreaming. They keep the lights on
in my room—therapy—but they can't force light into the
Dead House. No. The Dead House is old and worn, dim and
dusty, and the perfect hiding place. How ironic that
I've found it in my mind, where they can't get at me.

    I sleep for hours. I'm getting good.

    They have to shake me to rouse me, or they pull me
out of bed, but I sleep on, and they don't know it.

    The rooms inside the Dead House are endless. The
corridors go on and on. The darkness deepens, thickens,
grows denser and heavier the farther I explore. And,
Dee, I am beginning to feel it. The house itself. As
though it were a part of me that had just awakened.

    I seek solace in that dark hiding place, and I know
they will never find me if I choose to stay. I laugh in
their faces.

    So screw you, Lansing. You can't get me in here.

    I can hear the dead ocean.

Tenth Entry

I haven't found a mirror yet, but I see her in the
window sometimes, behind me. It's the most peculiar
thing, Dee, because I'm <u>sure</u> she's trying to reach out
to me, fighting with those pesky shadows—for I only see
her at night. I hope it's her. I hope it's Carly.

Eleventh Entry

<u>Why do you come inside?</u>
To get dry. To feel cold.
<u>Do you smell the air?</u>
Yes, I do. And the mold, and the mildew, and the
silence.
<u>Do you hear the Dead Sea?</u>
Crashing and smashing and waiting below.
<u>Will you stay a little longer?</u>
On and on, I will stay forever.
<u>You are mine.</u>
I am nothing. I am nowhere. Hide me.

Twelfth Entry

Dead House. I love you. I need you. Thank you for
staying with me—please never fade away. I sat on the
floor of one of the dead rooms, and I asked it to stay.
Don't leave me all alone, don't leave me behind—I can't
survive all by myself.

   <u>I am here</u>, it said—the very timber of the walls
seemed to speak to me from some omniscient place that
was all around me but also inside me. I can almost feel
Carly in there with me. Strange.

   <u>You belong here too.</u>

Thirteenth Entry:

The Dead House talks to me; on and on, around we go.
It whispers in my ear so I don't hear the doctors; it
tells me things, and it makes me smile. I sleep and I
sleep and I won't ever wake. Soon they won't be able to
find me at all.

Fourteenth Entry

I might have made a mistake. There is something else
here in the house with me.

    Carly?

Fifteenth Entry

<u>Where are you going?</u>
I am going home.
<u>This is your home.</u>
I am going home.
<u>Blood in the walls is the blood in your veins.</u>
I will come again. Thank you, good (?) day (?).
<u>You belong to me.</u>
I am nothing.
<u>You cannot leave.</u>
I am going.

Dee, Dee, where are you? Why did you stop talking to
me? The Dead House tried to keep me, to trap me, and
I'm so afraid. I couldn't wake up. I couldn't open my
eyes! It wouldn't let go of me. It was tricking me.
I thought I could feel Carly with me in there, but I
was wrong. It's something else. I don't know. I tried
to leave, but the doors were all locked. My haven is
a Venus flytrap. I can hear it calling to me even now
while I'm awake. I can feel the walls, the damp, the
rot—I can hear the churning Dead Sea. Sleep is the
realm of the Dead Things, who want me. I must not
sleep. I must not sleep.

    I'm so alone.

    I. Must. Not. Sleep.

51

The following entry is difficult to decipher because of the large amounts of blood spatter and smearing.

The Johnson Claydon Diaries

Sixteenth Entry

I found a mirror! Such triumph! And it's in Lansing's own little bathroom—the one off to the side of her office. I broke in during quiet hour, knowing she'd be in group session, and I set the girl free! She isn't Carly, but that's okay; she was trapped in shadows just like me, and now she is free! I am ebullient! Hahahahaha!

Friday, 3 December 2004

Carly Johnson now refuses to sleep and has been self-harming to prevent it. She has broken the mirror in my personal bathroom and lacerated both arms up to her elbows, which needed fifty-seven stitches. She is now under careful observation. I am considering sedation therapy, but reluctantly, as it may trigger another catatonic episode. I must admit that I am unsure of the next course of action. I will write to Dr. Sparrow for a consult. I was hoping to avoid permanent readmittance—or worse: removal to the B Ward—but unless I see some signs of improvement, that may be the only course of action.

52

The Johnson Claydon Diaries

Seventeenth Entry

For a little while, or so they tell me, I was catatonic. A while, they say. Shock, they say. Denial, they say. A bump, they say. A bump before I continue on my road to recovery.

At first, I refused to believe, but then…the dates don't match up in my head. And Jaime was here. They showed me the CCTV footage. The way she looked at me, curled herself into my lap…the way her mouth opened wide before she began to sob her little tears—tears that no child should ever produce, but which seemed so familiar to me…the way Mrs. Bailey said, "This is sick! I refuse to allow Jaime to suffer like this!"

And I didn't stir. I didn't move. Jaime sat sobbing in my lap, clinging to my hospital gown, and I didn't even blink. Jaime…I'm so sorry—

I've looked at my arms.

So…maybe…

Maybe I am ~~crazy~~ broken. Maybe I do need ~~help~~ fixing.

Oh, Dee. Maybe Lansing _is_ right.

Eighteenth Entry

Don't look at me like that, Dee. Especially when you've failed that girl in the reflection. See! She's still reaching!

(CJ): I want to talk to Jaime.

(AL): Why?

(CJ): I need to explain to her...what's going on.

(AL): I don't think that's a good idea, Carly.

(CJ): You have to let me see her. Or just talk to her—a phone call. That's all.

(AL): I can't do that, Carly. Not after her last visit. You saw the tape.

(CJ): Exactly! You showed me what I did—I need her to— [Swallow] I need her to understand.

(AL): Carly, Mr. and Mrs. Bailey have filed a restraining order against you. It's being considered. Until we know the outcome, I can't allow you to contact her.

(CJ): But...but I...I was sick. You said I was sick, right? And...I'm a minor. Can—can they really do that?

(AL): They're her guardians now. But...no, I don't believe they will get the order, so take a breath. Calm. But while it's not been decided, you can't speak to her.

(CJ): [Muffled sounds] [Quietly] Kill me. God, please just kill me.

[End of tape]

53

The Johnson Claydon Diaries

Nineteenth Entry

I've learned, in my tragic little life, that memories
are like water. Not solid, like some people think.
Once something happens, it isn't set in stone. It can
change.

You can make yourself believe anything if you lie to
yourself long enough.

I'm good at lying to myself. I'm good at it because
I have to be. If I believed the life I was in half the
time, I would have jumped off that roof and taken Carly
with me a long time ago. My biggest secret, Dee, is so
pathetic that I can barely bring myself to write it.
But I must.

<u>Write it, you coward!</u>

I am afraid of the dark.

No, not just tense. Not just tense at all, Dee.
I ~~am was~~ <u>am</u> a child of night—I even <u>need</u> it…and I am
<u>petrified</u> of it. Some kind of joke, right? But it's
true. And more than I'm afraid of the dark, I fear the
light (ha ha). I fear the sun, and I fear the exposure.
So, really, I'm not fit for life. One or the other, kid.
And if I face that truth for too long, Dee, it'll break
me. So I have to lie to myself to survive.

But lying is a habit, and it's addictive. You lie.
It breeds. You lie again. It grows. And one day you
wake up and realize that everyone around you has this
weird idea about who you are, and you don't recognize
the person they're describing. You don't understand why
they're treating you the way they do.

Or not treating you.

It's like you have a cancer.

I've pushed everyone away. Even Carly. I live behind a veneer of Teflon that I worked hard to grow and then to maintain. I could blame it on the ~~accident~~ ~~murder~~ ~~accident~~ ~~death~~ fact that our parents left us, left me, but it would be unfair. Because the truth is…I was like this before they died. I pushed them away too, and now nothing I do will ever change that.

They saw a drunk, when I was broken.

They saw sarcasm, when I was sobbing.

They saw me push them away, when I was screaming for their love.

It's too hard. I can't admit to this flaw—this chink in my armor. So I walked around in that ever-night, and I felt afraid, and I climbed on the roof hoping that someday I would feel the bright moon on my skin. I still long for that, and more. Until then, Dee…I'll be honest. I'll be honest with you.

I'm afraid. I'm so, so afraid.

And I wish there were arms around me and words in my ear, breath on my neck…telling me that everything will be okay, that someone loves me, that I'm not a mistake, not a waste, not a nothing. Telling me that, no, I'm not a child of darkness, and there is a place for me in the light.

I want Carly to tell me.

But if she can't—if she can't tell me that and still be with me, then I'll take the dark. I'll take the dark gladly—if only she'll come back to me. If she'll come back and put me in the back room and take her place in the light.

I'm sorry I ever wanted it.

I'm sorry! I'm sorry! I'm so sorry—

[What follows is indecipherable scribble.]

Twentieth Entry

I feel the Dead House calling to me when I'm awake.
It's been digesting me. Somehow I know this.
    Surrender, it says.
    I must not go.

54

55 days until the incident

Inpatient Session Recording #68 [Ref: Johnson-Inp-0033]
Thursday, 9 December 2004, 8:03 AM
Claydon Youth Psychiatric Facility, Somerset
Dr. Annabeth Lansing (AL) and Carly Luanne Johnson (CJ)

[Audio crackling]

(AL): Tell me, why won't you sleep?

[Silence]

Okay, then why do you feel afraid?

[Shuffling]

(CJ): I'm not afraid.

(AL): Why are you angry?

(CJ): I'm sick of all these questions.

(AL): Fair enough. But if you answer the questions, there'll be fewer of them on repeat, won't there?

(CJ): Fair enough.

(AL): So tell me, why won't you sleep?

(CJ): Just—leave— *Shit!*

[Panting]

(AL): Take a breath for me. Just stay calm.

[Gasps]

(CJ): I WON'T SLEEP!

(AL): Carly, calm down, or I'll sedate you.

(CJ): Let me go back t-to my r-room! Just—please—let me g-go—

(AL): Okay. Go.

[Crash, running]

[Silence falls]

Dr. Sparrow, as you can hear, Carly Johnson becomes very agitated when sleep is suggested. I'm not sure what to do at this point except to sedate her for an extended period. Any advice would be welcome.

[End of tape]

55

After a lengthy consult with Dr. Sparrow, it was decided that Carly "Kaitlyn" Johnson would be sedated for a twenty-four-hour period. The sedation was filmed on a hospital CCTV camera and has been transcribed below.

CCTV Camera Footage
Monday, 13 December 2004, 9:58 AM
Claydon Youth Psychiatric Facility

Kaitlyn is led into a padded room, no doubt in anticipation of resistance. She seems tired and listless, plopping down in the corner limply when the female health-care assistant leaves. Dr. Lansing and Dr. Sparrow enter the room, along with a larger health-care assistant, who hovers near the door, a mass of height and bulk.

"Now, Carly," Dr. Sparrow says, coming closer, "I have a small shot here for you. It won't hurt."

Kaitlyn's head snaps up. "What is it?"

"It'll calm things down."

Kaitlyn reacts as though shocked by a live wire. She jumps to her feet, pressing herself against the padded wall, and holds out her arms, palms forward.

"Get that away from me," she gasps.

"It will help you sleep, that's all."

"I don't want to sleep! Stay away from me!"

She looks left, then right, eyes wide and wild, in an attempt to seek an escape. After realizing that she has been backed into a corner, she hesitates, then presses violently off the wall and makes a dash for the door. She slips easily by the elderly Dr. Sparrow, narrowly avoiding a collision with Dr. Lansing, and almost gets past the burly health-care assistant. At the last moment, however, he grabs her around the waist and pulls her back. Her legs lift off the ground, and she kicks out violently.

"*NO!*" she screams, wrestling the assistant with all her strength. "*Please, please!*"

He stumbles back into the wall, still holding her against him. She bites down hard on the arm restraining her; the assistant grunts and lets go. She falls to her knees, and then scrambles out of the room.

Ignoring the blood running from his arm, he grabs for her foot, and yanks her back inside, then straddles her, pinning her arms down above her head.

"Calm," the assistant says, his voice deep and heavily accented. "Calm now."

Kaitlyn shakes her head violently left and right, the blood from the assistant splattering her cheeks and hair. Her teeth, too, are stained red with his blood.

"*Nonononononononono!*" Her screams seem endless.

"*Oui*, Doctor," the assistant grunts. "I have her steady now. S'okay."

Dr. Sparrow, paler, bends down and injects Kaitlyn in her left thigh.

"Don't! *Don't put me back there!*"

She continues to struggle and groan, and eventually falls limp. The health-care assistant gets up and gently pulls down her hospital gown, which had ridden up to her waist.

"Poor little girl," he says, in a surprisingly gentle voice. "She is calm now. She will sleep."

Dr. Sparrow and Dr. Lansing—who seems harassed and alarmed—both stare down at Kaitlyn, who does now seem to be very calm indeed.

Inpatient Therapy Notes
Dr. Annabeth Lansing
Patient File [Johnson-C-0399524], Session #72

Thursday, 16 December 2004

Carly Johnson has been unconscious for fifty-six hours. After the intended twenty-four-hour period, we were unable to wake her. With little other choice, both amantadine and Ritalin were administered, but to no avail; I fear that we may have triggered a new catatonic episode. Carly Johnson seems trapped in unconsciousness. I question my judgment in sedating her now. I am alarmed by her final words before going under, and our inability to wake her. I confess I am at a loss as to my next course of action.

The Johnson Claydon Diaries

Twenty-first Entry

What did they do to me? God, Dee. I am lucky to be
here. The Dead House descended like music curdling into
time; and as it did, I grew wet and cold, and it was
dark, and I was so alone…

It had devoured me. Eaten me.

You belong to me. The Voice was ancient as stone
and fleeting as the wind, yet familiar and intimate as
a caress. It rumbled through the walls and floor, and
shook me and stirred me.

I ran for the door, but the corridor changed,
stretching on and on; my cries echoed and carried
forever. Always the door stood, tiny and hopelessly
appealing, at the very end. A speck of hope the house
knew I couldn't stop seeking. I ran for days, weeks,
centuries. I died and revived, and still the door
stood, waiting.

And then I heard her.

Carly.

She was calling for me. Screaming. She was in agony!
The moment I realized it, I was out. Out and awake and
coughing up water from my lungs. Only it wasn't water,
it was vomit, and I was choking.

I went to the window, and I stared at myself—and the
dead girl—until the sun began to rise over the sill.

"Carly?" I kept calling, waiting for her reflection
to show.

Crazy Kaitie, crazy Kaitie.

Those dicks forced me back into the Dead House, and
now it has something. It got a bite out of me as I ran,
a little shadow of a bite, but it will have a piece of
me forever.

58

Inpatient Session Recording #74 [Ref: Johnson-Inp-0033]
Friday, 17 December 2004, 5:17 PM
Claydon Youth Psychiatric Facility, Somerset
Dr. Annabeth Lansing (AL) and Carly Luanne Johnson (CJ)

(AL): So why do you think you're afraid?

(CJ): You ask me questions that I...that I can't—

[Breathing]

(AL): Tell me what you want.

(CJ): I want Carly.

(AL): You want more than that. [Pause] Would you like to stop talking?

[Rustling]

(CJ): Yes. No.

(AL): Why don't you take a breath, sit for a moment, and when you feel like you want to start talking, then talk.

(CJ): About what?

(AL): Whatever's on your mind.

(CJ): You want to talk about Elmbridge. The roof that night. Why I was up there.

(AL): Why *did* you go up there?

(CJ): [Loudly] You won't believe me.

(AL): I believe that you think Carly is gone. I believe you think your Voice is somehow responsible. Aka Manah.

(CJ): Don't say his name.

(AL): Why not?

(CJ): Just don't. Everything's different.

[Heavy breathing]

(AL): Carly? [Sigh] How about we try talking again? Let's just try. Last session we failed, but maybe this time we'll succeed.

[Pause]

(CJ): Okay.

(AL): Okay. Tell me the first thing that comes into your mind.

(CJ): The Viking.

(AL): The Viking?

(CJ): He…he was a friend. From…before.

(AL): Excellent! Tell me about him.

(CJ): [Takes breath] The Viking…he used to give me sunflower seeds. [Pause] "You're a fucking bird," he'd say, holding them out. "This is bird food." The first time he did it, I tried to knee him in the nuts. [Laugh] He just picked me up and dumped me on his shoulder, laughing as he carried me away. "A fucking pesky bird, at that. You're a tiny little falcon hawk, always nipping at something." He always said that. I was a falcon hawk. It became our thing. My big Viking friend bringing his pesky little falcon some seeds. [Pause] I haven't had seeds since my parents…died.

(AL): Why did he stop?

[Silence]

Try to articulate that emotion.

(CJ): [Voice low] You know why.

(AL): You blame being admitted into Claydon?

(CJ): He didn't know where to find me. You never let me say good-bye. You took him away from me—

(AL): Carly...I only began work on your case after you were admitted here. How could I personally be responsible? Hm?

[Pause]

If I am to have any chance of helping you, you have to stop seeing me as the enemy.

(CJ): [Softly] You're not responsible. I think...I think maybe I do...need help.

[Pause]

(AL): Carly...this is remarkable progress. Thank you for allowing me back in.

(CJ): I'm tired now.

(AL): Okay. Let's resume tomorrow. This is wonderful progress. You should feel proud.

[Pause]

(CJ): Then why do I feel like I just murdered Carly?

[End of tape]

Some people say that
night blooms.
But night descends
self-consciously.
Night cuts slowly.

—Kaitlyn Johnson, Attic Wall

59

A record of the phone call transcript, which Kaitlyn references in the entry below, took five years alone to secure and release. The transcript follows the diary entry.

The Johnson Claydon Diaries

Twenty-second Entry
Presumed to be Tuesday, 21 December 2004

I never expected to hear his voice on the phone. The Viking, after all this time. He said he'd been trying to find out what happened to me—where they took me—for two solid months after the accident, but he was shut down by the police. After I was taken to Claydon again, a small article made it into the local paper. As soon as he spotted ~~Carly's~~ my name, he was on the phone to Claydon, demanding to speak to me.

Lansing got ahold of him after that, and I think I'm grateful. I don't know what my mind might do anymore. Lansing said I was catatonic, and so I was. Lansing said I would integrate, and I have. Lansing says I'm fragile, and, well, I did almost jump off a roof...

So she has control of me. Takes care of me.

I can't be trusted by myself. Because Lansing is right. I do hear Aka Manah still, getting closer and closer, his Voice so soft I can feel his breath. And I feel the Dead House, yearn for it even. That's not normal, is it, Dee? So I should withdraw, keep away.

But, the Viking...I can't believe it. He found me.

The first thing he said, after I picked up that gray phone, was "You're a bird, and I have your seeds."

Dee, I burst into tears. If I ever had something close to a brother, although more, it would be the Viking. My stupid-ass John, who dresses like some kind of barbarian and towers six feet tall, looking down over my tiny five-five. He made me feel safe—just his voice, over that crackling audio line.

He asked me what I was doing here. I told him about Elmbridge. He made me feel like a part of the world again, Dee.

I cried.

I never cry.

I hate how small I sounded. How already-broken I was. Am. He told me to hang tight, that he was coming soon, and I cling to that, Dee. I cling to the knowledge that he'll come and see me when his course ends. (He's at college now, can you believe that??)

My Viking, my brother, after so long.

Transcript of Incoming Telephone Call
Schedules at 4:00 pm, Tuesday, 21 December 2004
Ward A3

John Hutt: DH? Dark Half?

Operator: Please hold the line while I connect you.

John: Okay.

[Connection tone]

Reception: Ward A3.

Operator: Call for Carly Luanne Johnson, authorization Dr. Lansing.

Reception: Connecting.

[Connection tone]

Carly: Hello?

John: You're a bird, and I have your seeds.

Carly: [Sharp intake of breath] John?

John: What the hell are you doing in a place like that? I saw it in the paper. Have you been there all this time?

Carly: [Soft crying] [Sniff] No—

[Crying]

John: It's okay, Kaitie. I'm here.

Carly: [Takes breath] I was here for a while, but then they moved me to a school. Elmbridge. It's in Somerset. I've only just come back here. For a little while.

[Pause]

John: Well, I guess it makes sense. You were a bit potty.

Carly: [Laughing] You dick. Where are you? Where have you been? I've been looking for you for forever.

John: Back home still. I never left Chester, but we moved house. I was in an accident. It put me in the hospital for a while, which is how I lost track of you. By the time I got out, you were just...gone. No one knew or would tell me anything.

Carly: An accident! Are you okay?

John: Yeah...Yeah, no worries, I'm fine. Just pissed that I lost you for a few broken bones. But I'm hoping I can come see you when college is out.

Carly: You're in college?

John: Yeah. Engineering.

Carly: [Quietly] You always were good at fixing things.

[Pause]

John: Not always.

[Pause]

Carly: [Softly] Chester is ages away.

John: I'm coming to see you. I am. As soon as I can. I promise.

[Silence]

John: I *am* coming, DH.

Carly: Yeah.

John: Ever the skeptic. You've got to trust someone, right? So trust me.

Carly: [Laughs] You sound like Dr. Lansing now.

John: [Pause] I'm going to have words with that Lapdog woman.

Carly: [Laughs] Lansing, not Lapdog!

John: She's got a lot to bloody answer for.

Carly: I don't think you're allowed to swear on a hospital phone, you know.

John: Well, she said something that pissed me off.

Carly: She's helping me.

John: Listen, if she were a guy, I'd have broken a rib or two by now.

[Pause]

Carly: What'd she say?

John: She said something that tipped me off to the reason I haven't been able to find you in so long. You were there. In a bloody mental hospital.

Carly: I...I thought you'd forgotten about me.

John: I would *never* do that! I told you, remember? Even though—even if—

[Pause]

I have to go. I don't want you to hear me like this. I might break something. Pro'ly the phone. Or the wall.

Carly: Wait—John...

[Breathing]

John?

John: I'm here.

Carly: So...you didn't forget me?

John: You're a riot, Kat. [Pause] You pest.

Carly: [Laugh, sniff] So...you'll come?

John: Wild trolls couldn't keep me away.

Carly: [Exhales]

John: Kaitie?

Carly: Hm?

John: Don't let them break you.

Carly: I...I'm trying.

Operator: Time's up.

John: Talk to you soon, pest.

Carly: John—

[End of call]

The Johnson Claydon Diaries

Twenty-third Entry

I had a conversation with a viper tonight. He slithered
up my legs, around my torso, lingered on my shoulder,
forked tongue flicking near my eye as he smelled me.

"Whatttttttttttt are you doing?"

"Are you real?"

"Are yyyyyyou?"

"I am," I retorted. But then I had this strange
sensation that he, with his whispers and scaly armor,
was the real one, and I was just a thing wearing a
Carly suit.

He seemed to laugh, and as he laughed, he
curled himself about my neck three times. "A real
girl, ttttttttttalking to a sssssssssnake. Are you
ssssssssure you're real?"

"What do you want?"

I began to shiver, but not from fear, and it
repulsed me.

"I'm ttttthhhhhinking of doorrrrrsssssss and
windowssssssss," he told me; his orange eyes, so
serpentine and unfathomable, stared right into mine.

"Doors and windows?"

"What, do you tttttttttthhhhink issssssssss behind a
pane of glasssssssssssssss?"

I felt utter terror at his words.

"Whattttttttt if there'ssssss nottttthhhhhing on
ttttthhhhe ottttthhhher sssssside?"

"There's always something," I told him. "There has
to be…"

The brille on his eyes began to cloud over.
"Nottttthhhhhing issssss…sssssssometimesssssss real."

"Please," I said, feeling his body around my neck,
slowly tightening. And I shivered again, and felt a
desperate heat flush my cheeks. "Please stop."

He turned those milky eyes on me. "Whyyyyy, when you like ittttt sssssssso?"

I gasped and raised my chin, trying to gain some space. "What are you? Are you really a snake?"

He began to shed. "Are *yo o o o o o u...real l l l l y* a girl?"

Am I, Dee?

60

CCTV Camera Footage
Wednesday, 22 December 2004, 2:15 PM
Claydon Youth Psychiatric Facility

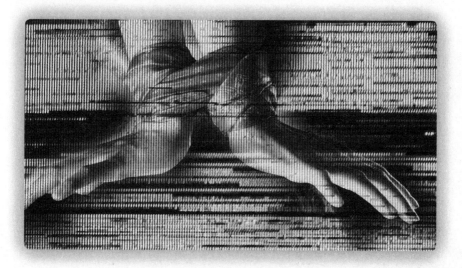

A low buzz sounds as the nurse lets Naida Chounan-Dupré into the visiting room. Naida steps inside, her eyes dull but alert. She looks at the guard for a moment, perhaps to ensure that he leaves, and then turns to Kaitlyn, who sits on a plastic chair in the center of the room, motionless. Her wrists are cuffed with soft restraints; Naida eyes them and bites her lips.

"I'm surprised you came," Kaitlyn says; she doesn't stand. Though her words are hostile, their delivery is weak—fragile as rice paper.

Naida sits down in the chair opposite Kaitlyn; she seems affected by

Kaitlyn's appearance, which is somehow muted since the Naida Camera Footage, as though washed of vital color.

"Of course I came." Her eyes dart left and right. "You're my best friend."

Kaitlyn doesn't reply for a moment, but her eyes seem to take Naida in with precision. "They...they didn't tell you? About what's happened?"

"Yes...I know *exactly* what's happened. I came to see how you are."

Kaitlyn nods. "Thank you. I...I've been better."

"Everyone's been so worried." Naida glances around again, finally spotting the camera. "They can't wait to have you back, hopscotching around."

"I miss them too. Why aren't you home for the holidays?"

"I'm staying at Elmbridge over Christmas."

Kaitlyn frowns. "Why?"

Naida smiles but doesn't answer. Eventually, she says, "Ari's been asking after you. I said you'd be back as soon as you were well. He's staying for Christmas too. And Scott and Brett."

Kaitlyn turns her head to the side, resting her chin on her sharp shoulder like a bird perched on an outcropping. "I see. Thank him for me. Tell him...tell him I—" She breaks off as one dry sob breaks free.

Naida's hand shoots forward to grasp Kaitlyn's. She squeezes, then lets go. Kaitlyn balls her hand into a fist, eyes fixed on Naida, then snatches her hand into her lap.

Naida swallows. "Ari...he wanted to tell you that the chapel's been pretty dank and dark, and he doesn't like to go there much anymore. He prefers the main building...mostly the lower level."

There's a small pause and the briefest hesitation from Kaitlyn.

She swallows, squeezing her eyes closed. "They're saying I'm crazy, Naida." She says it in a rush. "They say I'm Carly and that I'm crazy—they say I need help—they say—"

"No." Naida says it firmly, her voice low and her lips tight. "Never. *Never* let them tell you that, Kait. You're not crazy—do you hear me?"

Kaitlyn presses her fists to her eyes. "I don't know anymore—I don't know what's real. They sedated me, and I couldn't get out of the Dead House. The Voice...I hear his whispering so close—" She breaks off once again, tearing her fists away from her eyes, and her voice grows softly shrill. "*I think he's trying to get inside me.* Naida…that's not normal, is it?"

Naida leans forward and drops her voice. "You listen to me, okay? You're not crazy. I think someone's trying to make you think you are. You'll be out of here before you know it. Just stay calm, stay focused." Her eyes dart to Kaitlyn's hands and back up to her face. "All right?"

Kaitlyn begins to shake, slowly at first, and then more violently. "They won't let me go, Naida," she breathes. "They'll lock me in here forever! I heard Carly screaming for me to help her, but I can't—I don't know how!"

The guard buzzes into the room. "Calm down, Johnson, or this meeting will be over in a second flat."

But it's too late.

Kaitlyn locks her eyes on Naida's and yanks on her restraints. "Get me out of here, Naida! *The Voice is getting closer!* Get me out of here! Get me out!"

Naida stumbles out of her seat and covers her mouth.

The guard moves to intercept Kaitlyn. "I warned you."

Kaitlyn throws herself out of the chair, yanking her arms violently to try to break free. She must pull a stitch, because the bandages covering her left arm bleed red. Naida begins to cry, watching as the guard grabs Kaitlyn.

"*Naida!*"

"You can leave," the guard shouts as two health-care assistants rush into the room from the rear door. "Now!"

Naida, shaking her head, hand still pressed to her mouth, flees the interview room and out of camera shot. The assistants remove the restraints and carry a hysterical Kaitlyn from the meeting room. An eerie silence follows the slow, mechanical sweep of the weighted door.

61

The Johnson Claydon Diaries

Twenty-fourth Entry

```
Naida came.
     She slipped me a note:
```

Kaitlyn,

You have to get out of there, I know you can. Carly told me how you'd break out at night and go wandering during the summer. <u>You have to come back to Elmbridge</u>. Down to the basement, which Ari showed me. Avoid the chapel—we can't risk you being seen—the basement is safer. In that little side room, okay? Weird things have happened since you left, and I'm convinced that a Shyan is working you. That's a Mala priest who has tainted himself with dark conjurings.

Someone's been trying to bind me with tricks, I think because I've been looking into Carly's disappearance, but they're using Gründi, not Mala. That's dark magic, plain and simple. But they don't know that I know a bit about Gründi, so I recognize it.

I think I know who's doing this—I mean, maybe. I'll explain more when I see you. If you absolutely <u>have</u> to reach me, use this number: █████
My dreams have been...Carly is in worse trouble the longer we wait.

[number omitted]

Come soon.

Carly is in trouble. I was right. I knew she was calling to me. This is bigger than me, Dee, much bigger than me. I knew it, I knew it, I knew it! I'm so relieved, so grateful. Nothing else matters now.

What do you mean?

I don't think—

She might, I suppose…

No, I suppose so…

Well, yeah. I guess I really don't, do I, Dee?

Yeah…yeah, I know, I should trust you. Naida never liked me. She always wanted Carly for herself…and she *is* promised to the Mala calling, which Carly made sound like some kind of witchcraft-voodoo cult. She could be working with the Voice. With Aka Manah.

She might be trying to trick me. Get me into worse trouble.

What's that? Oh.

Yeah, I think so too.

I must look a wreck, because when she came through the door, she stopped in her tracks and blinked back sudden tears. I know she sees Carly, not me. Still, it was nice to think that she cared how they've been treating me.

"Of course I came," was the first thing she said when she sat down across from me. "You're my best friend."

The visit was nothing more than hidden messages that I didn't really understand. Except when she spoke of Ari. I haven't forgotten him. I wish he would write to me. I don't understand why he doesn't. Maybe they won't let him. I miss his smell.

They dragged me away, but they didn't sedate me. They just locked me in my room—how long before they take you away from me too, Dee? How long before they steal these pages and plot against me once more?

I must be careful what I write. I should tell you, though:

[The rest of this page has been torn off. Where she hid the paper, as well as what it contained, is a mystery.]

62

The Johnson Claydon Diaries

Twenty-fifth Entry

I fall into the Dead House when I am awake now. I
<u>thought</u> I was awake…sitting on the floor, my pages in
hand…

Something changed in the ambience of the room,
a shifting, a darkening…and I looked down; I sat on
waterlogged floorboards, so old and moldy that they sank
under my weight. Claydon was gone…

<u>Get</u> <u>out</u> <u>of</u> <u>the</u> <u>house.</u> <u>Get</u> <u>out</u> <u>of</u> <u>the</u> <u>house.</u>

I got to my feet, and the room opened out before
me, from the deep umbra into the dim main room of the
house, which creaked and subtly moved so I couldn't
focus on any one object. Once a picture frame, empty,
now a light fixture, dusty. Once an armchair, warped,
now a rickety table, cracked and peeling. It formed and
unformed like a breath released and forgotten.

"Carly?" I called, hoping the house would shift,
allow her to scream—anything that would pinpoint her
location, up or down.

I thought of the attic in the main Elmbridge
building, where secrets were hidden. Up. As good a
choice as any.

Crazy

     Kaitie

          crazy

               Kaitie.

The stairs were normal when I looked at them, but as
I glanced to the top landing, they seemed to warp and
move, shift and sigh, all in my peripheral vision. The
house had control of them, like everything else. When
I looked back, they were once again still, innocent.
Lying.

"You can't keep her," I muttered, all the while wondering why I was saying it. "She's mine."

I repeated the rhyme that was Carly's favorite when we were young, holding on to the memory of her presence, something I never realized I could sense deep inside me until she was gone.

"Yesternight," I began, "upon the stair…I saw a girl who wasn't there…she wasn't there again today. I wish I wish, she'd go away…Yesternight upon the stair…"

On and on, I said the rhyme; on and on, I climbed, and the staircase never ended. The house had changed from a refuge to a trap overnight, and I couldn't shake the notion that it was keeping me away from Carly.

"I will get her," I told the house, and I <u>hated</u> with a passion I have never felt before.

No sooner had I spoken the words than I was at the last step, facing a door I had never seen. It was old, bolted from the outside. I put my hand on the bolt, intending to slide it away, when I sensed in the core of me that there was something I didn't want to see behind the door.

<u>Don't be afraid.</u>

But I was. Because I could feel a desire locked away in there—something that wanted out. Desperately. Impatiently. Something big. Something that wasn't Carly.

I dropped my hand, knowing somehow that the house would never have given her to me so easily, and the door thundered, rattling on its hinges. It raged, it yelled, yet it never spoke a word.

"Trickery," I breathed at the house, my will deflated and shriveled as an old balloon. "Trickery-trick-trickery."

The door quieted.

<u>Creeeaaaaak.</u>

I stepped backwards.

<u>Ssshhhhrrrrk.</u>

A noise down in the dark.

<u>Crrrrrrrreeeeeeeeeaaaaaaak.</u>

"Carly?"

The sound continued, inching closer to me out of the darkness.

"Carly, tell me that's you."

Ssssssshhhrrrkk.

I felt the grin in that umbra. Something wasn't right. I turned, and I ran down the stairs, but they were endless, and the dark shadows behind me never seemed to recede, no matter how fast I ran.

Finally, because I knew it was a dream and because the thing in the dark was so very close, I launched myself over the railing. I fell for a long time, but I don't remember landing. Only that all of a sudden I was in the doorway and the house was screaming, foul breath forcing me backwards—tearing me away.

I clung to the doorframe, needing to stay, needing to go into the basement—the only place left hidden— needing to find her.

GET OUT OF MY HOUSE!

I flew out the door, past the crumbling mountainside, towards the mists, which roared up to meet me.

I woke up on the floor, sticky with my own sweat, the echoes of the voice of the house ringing in my ears. Even now I can hear it—Get out of my house. Get out of my house. It doesn't want me snooping.

My Voice is nearby, Dee. He laughs, and he sings: The house is mine. The house is mine.

I really am crazy, aren't I?

The devil's in the details.

Inpatient Session Recording #78 [Ref: Johnson-Inp-0033]
Thursday, 23 December 2004, 3:14 PM
Claydon Youth Psychiatric Facility, Somerset
Dr. Annabeth Lansing (AL) and Carly Luanne Johnson (CJ)

(**AL**): I want to address what you spoke about at the end of our session last Friday. You said you felt like you had murdered Carly. Why?

(**CJ**): I'm not sure how I feel anymore. I thought...I thought I felt like that because by—by accepting your help...I accept that she's gone. And that was hard for me.

(**AL**): And do you accept it?

(**CJ**): I...don't know.

(**AL**): To have any hope of recovery, you must accept it. The first step is accepting that you *are* Carly. You are Carly Luanne Johnson. So let's try to say it. Say it with me...I am Carly. You can do it. [Pause] Please try.

(**CJ**): I...

(**AL**): You can do it.

[Sharp intake of breath]

What is it, Carly? What's happened?

[Shuffling]

Vocalize, Carly. Come on.

[Heavy breathing]

(**CJ**): I...I suddenly, um, realized that this will be my first Christmas without her. It was alarming for a moment...to think it. But...I—I'm better now.

(**AL**): Carly, what is it?

[Pause]

(**CJ**): I am Carly.

(**AL**): Excellent! Again.

(**CJ**): I am Carly.

(**AL**): [Laughs] No need to cry, Carly. This is wonderful work, and I am so proud of you! Now, again.

(**CJ**): [Crying] I am Carly.

(**AL**): Again.

(**CJ**): I...am...Carly. [Sobbing]

(**AL**): This is excellent, Carly. You're doing well. Now, I'm going to give you an assignment. I'd like you to write down everything you can remember about the night your parents died. Not what I told you, but what *you* yourself remember. Then I'd like you to attend the Friday group session and read it aloud to everyone.

(**CJ**): Okay.

(**AL**): You're very brave. I'm so pleased with your progress, Carly. Maybe, if you keep it up, you can return to Elmbridge by the New Year.

[Chair scrapes]

(**CJ**): Thank you.

[End of tape]

64

The following outgoing phone call was recorded on 23 December 2004, 41 days before the incident:

[Three rings]

[Muffled noises] "Who is this? [Sigh] You know what time it is, dickface?"

[Heavy breathing] *"Naida! Naida, it's Kait!"*

"Kaitie—you called. Thank God."

"You were right—I have to get out of here."

"What happened?"

"I was in a session today, and I saw something—I don't know—something wrong with her face. She isn't who she says she is!"

[Silence]

"Kaitie, are you alone?"

"Yeah, why?"

"Hang up."

"But why? What is it?"

"I can hear someone breathing on the line."

[Click]

[Line dead]

Somerset County Council Police Department

SPECIAL BULLETIN
MISSING PERSON

Johnson, Carly Luanne

DOB: 2 June 1987

5'5", 100 lbs, blond hair, blue eyes

Last seen wearing blue and white hospital gown
and slippers

LAST LOCATION: Claydon Youth Psychiatric Facility

LIKELY CONTACTS POINTS: Students at Elmbridge
High School

Wanted for questioning in connection with
the McClarin missing persons case.

Take care when handling individual, as she may be
suicidal and/or violent.

PART IV

THE
SELF
THAT
ISN'T YOU

No one thinks of how
much blood it costs.
—Dante Alighieri

A voice in the darkness, a knock at the door,
'And a word that shall echo forevermore!
—Henry Wadsworth Longfellow

God hath given you one face, and you
make yourselves another.
—William Shakespeare

Criminal Investigation Department, Portishead Headquarters
Avon and Somerset Constabulary, Portishead, Bristol
Friday, 17 June 2005, 15:34 PM
AUDIO INTERVIEW #2, PART 2: Detective Chief Inspector Floyd
Homes (FH) and Scott Fromley (SF)

(FH): And that's all, huh? You're telling me that's all you know about what happened to Juliet?

(SF): Yes.

(FH): I see. And what about the night of the fire? Do you also know nothing of that?

(SF): I can't remember exactly. I don't know!

(FH): Several people are dead, two are missing, and one is permanently crippled...and you don't *know*?

(SF): I wasn't there at the end—I never saw anything. All I know is that it happened. I don't know anything else.

(FH): And Carly Johnson? How well did you know her, huh? Maybe you'd better rethink that answer, lad, because Naida's talking.

(SF): You asshole—

(FH): Watch your mouth. You're facing some serious charges, Scott. If I were you, I'd answer my questions honestly. [Pause] Carly Johnson. Were you intimate with her?

(SF): What the hell is that supposed to mean?

(FH): Did you and Carly Johnson have sex?

(SF): I want to speak to my father.

(FH): Answer the question! Did you and Carly Johnson have sex?

(SF): No—

(FH): But you wanted to. Maybe you suggested something of that nature to Carly herself. Maybe you forced her into it—

(SF): No! I told you, no! I was with Naida, that didn't change—

(FH): Something triggered her, and you're the only one left!

[Loud bang]

[Heavy breathing]

[Pause]

[Softer] Scott, I need to know how it all went down. You're the only one who knows.

[Silence]

See, I think you know more than you're telling me. Why, I don't know. You've got no one to protect and everything to lose. So tell me what happened that night!

[End of tape]

**Naida Camera Footage
Friday, 24 December 2004
Time Index Not Noted
Basement**

Naida swings the camera around the small room. It is nothing more than a cemented space with a solitary lightbulb hanging from the ceiling. The circle of light that the bulb creates does not touch the corners of the room, which sit stagnant in shadow. The mic picks up the sound of dripping water.

"Lovely spot," Kaitlyn murmurs, folding her arms.

"It's temporary. I'd stash you in my room, but the chances of you being seen—"

"No. No, you're right. This is fine. Cold, dank, lonely." She gives a grin. "Feels familiar."

"I'm going to set the camera up there," Naida says, angling the camera at a strip of wall near the ceiling. "I can monitor the footage through my computer."

"Won't the battery die?"

"Nah, I'll hook it into the school's power supply, and it'll feed directly to my laptop. I'll rig it to send automatically to an online server too, so we can watch it later in more detail."

"Watch *me* in more detail, you mean. We're past sociology projects, aren't we?"

"It's not about that anymore. We need this. Need proof." She spins the camera to face her and messes with the focus.

"They told me I was crazy," Kaitlyn says after a beat of silence. Her voice barely registers in the mic.

Naida glances at her, then steps forward. "You've got to put that out of your head, sugar. It won't help Carly."

Kaitlyn looks away, and the progress of the camera—and Naida—stops. "What you did...going there. Seeing me, the note, everything. I... thank you."

"I'd do it again and more in a heartbeat." Naida hesitates, and then adds, "But what made you come here? Why believe me?"

"I could blame it on the pill diet they had me on, but...in my last session with Lansing...I saw something. I don't know, probably nothing. But..."

"Tell me."

Kaitlyn sighs sharply. "I sound so bloody crazy, and I *hate* it because I'm *not* crazy."

"I don't think you're crazy. You've got to trust me with the truth."

"I saw something in the room with us in my last session with Dr. Lansing. A girl. She smelled wet and earthy, and she looked terrified; her mouth was wide open, and her teeth—" She takes a breath. "She was pointing at Lansing. Like she was warning me. And I knew...I just *knew* I had to get out."

There is another pause, and then Naida says, "We should find something for you to sleep on in that junk heap round there." She points the camera at the floor. "There's bound to be—"

[END OF CLIP]

"You look like shit," Naida says, facing a mattress that now lies in the corner of the room. She goes to sit beside Kaitlyn, handing over a bag of cookies. She takes one too. "Didn't they feed you?"

"Don't remember."

"So tell me about this girl, the one you saw. Have you seen her before? Do you see her a lot?"

The slightest hesitation. "No."

"What about other things? I need to know, Kait."

Kaitlyn opens the bag of cookies. She removes one but doesn't eat it. "I don't want to go back to that place."

"Then tell me."

"Right." Kaitlyn laughs. "Tell you about crazy stuff I see so that you *don't* call my shrink."

Naida glances at her pointedly. "I warned you, Kaitlyn Johnson. I warned you about all this. You called it crazy Mala shit, remember?

Now you're going to tell me everything so I can help you and Carly, okay?"

Kaitlyn smiles, regarding her. "Well, it *is* still crazy Mala shit, even if it's true."

"Come on, now. Spit it out."

"I don't know. I see...sometimes—" She sighs. "A...a dark shape. I'm not sure...It really wasn't much more than a shadow. I heard breathing, smelled an ashy smell. And there was a snake...a green viper. I spoke to him." Her voice fades away, into a murmur. "He asked me if I was a real girl..." She blinks, shakes her head. "But it was a dream."

"You spoke to a *nathair nimhe*? A snake?"

"Yeah, but it's just the drugs they were making Carly take. It does crap to the brain—"

"No. It's not just that. There's a spirit associated with animals, the snake in particular, but also dogs, wolves, foxes. It's a dangerous spirit, Kaitlyn. An *Olen*. *Olens* can be very powerful—they are more than mere spirits. Normally *Olens* are revered, because when they come, they bring healing, strength, courage, and love. But they can be malevolent forces too; they can cause physical harm, injure the souls of the living, and they can enter animals to manipulate them—and animals that are filled with an *Olen* are collectively called *Sivu*." Naida stands up. "Blessed Gorro, help us."

Kaitlyn laughs, leaning back against the wall. "So, what? I was conversing with a god?"

"I don't know. It almost feels like...a—a haunting. All I know is that someone's working. Working *you*."

"I don't understand."

Naida rubs her face, then pulls something from her pocket. "I found this under my bed. It's a bind...for Marri-Korro. You see the feathers? The likeness of the shrieking crow? These symbols belong to her. She's a demon *Olen*, Kaitlyn. Dangerous. And this bind—this is Grúndi. Grúndi and Mala are two *very* different things. Mala is faith, religion, and ritual. And Grúndi...like I said in my note, Grúndi is black magic. It's not governed by morals or ethics. And if whoever's working you is *conjuring* too, then we're dealing with somebody—" She breaks off, shaking her head. "Someone who fears no consequences. And who knows what they're doing. Mike and that damn spirit board at Halloween."

"So you're telling me that, because of the Ouija—the *Olen* board *thing*—at your party, someone is, what? Casting magic spells on me?" She snorts with laughter, but her face falls when Naida stares at her.

"What I'm telling you is that someone has *noticed* you. And that someone is a *Shyan*—that's the name we give a *Holi* who practices black arts as well."

"A what?"

"*Holi*. A Mala priest. *Shyan* is the name we give someone who has no morals and no ethics. Someone who delves into Grúndi and who is dangerous to you and to Carly too."

"And you think it's Mike?"

"I don't know. He seems too stupid to pull this off. I don't know. Maybe."

"What about his mirror? Those cuts on his face?"

"Aye, that was weird. Goddamn it, Kaitie, I warned you." She exhales. "This is beautiful. Just *beautiful*." She pauses, then mutters, "When you said 'the Voice' was getting closer in that visiting room...I *knew* something was going on. I could *feel* it in my bones."

"So...you believe this stuff. And you believe me?"

"Of course I do. I feel it myself, didn't I say so? I warned you about that pointer, about keeping under the radar—"

Kaitlyn lies back on the mattress. "Blah, blah, I remember."

"I know. I know. I'm sorry. It's just...it's Carly—" Naida's voice breaks on Carly's name, and she turns away, fiddles with the camera. "Well. Here we are, anyway."

There is an awkward moment of silence.

"Look, I don't know why the *Shyan* took Carly, if that's even what happened. I think maybe it's to do with creating a gap where she used to be. But a soul doesn't just pass on. It takes time. Assuming Carly's soul is behaving like the soul of someone who died, then her spirit won't leave your body right away. It'll linger. Which means something is hiding her away in there. I'd say we've got roughly a month to get her back. Maybe more, maybe less. Damn it, I don't know." Naida leans forward, resting her head on her hands. "I just don't know. I don't know why a *Shyan* wants her soul at all. But I'm going to find out."

"Here we are," Kaitlyn agrees, her entire face in shadow.

"Gorro help us."

Diary of Kaitlyn Johnson

Saturday, 25 December 2004, 9:17 am
Basement

No pills.
No toilet.
No window.
A mattress.
Wet.
Cold.
A camera, always watching.
A new kind of prison.
Merry Christmas to me.

Oh, Dee. Have you been lonely without me? I know, I
missed you too. So much. While you were gone, a lot
happened, but I made sure to write it down—as much of
it as I could anyway. Here, see? The pages are for you.
   Dee? Are you here?
   I really am a ghost now, aren't I?

Later

I'm still getting used to sleeping. Naida tells me it's
been a month and ten days since they put me back in
Claydon—a month and ten days of sleeping—and I still
feel like I'm vanishing every single time.
   The dreams. The nightmares. The possibility that,
this time, I'll enter the Dead House. I can't control
it. These things make it impossible to lie down. The
dank air, the warped steps, and the molding wallpapers
have crept into my bedcovers. With every step I take
towards the mattress, I hear the creak of swollen,
rotten floorboards, swelling and shrinking with moisture
and the air I breathe is stale and musty and the sheet

under my back is the mirrored wall and the thing I'm
staring at when I close my eyes is her.

The dead girl, only not grinning this time, but
broken and torn like she was when, I now realize, I
saw her in the Dead House mirror wall. When, for the
briefest moment, I thought she was my reflection. Or was
that Carly? I don't know.

And I hear those nails snapping as she drags her
torso along, her blown pupil blaring at me like a
foghorn, if such things are possible. If silence can be
so loud.

I can smell her rank breath in my mouth.
She couldn't be Carly.

Dee, I wish you could hold me.
Don't touch me.

Diary of Kaitlyn Johnson

Thursday, 30 December 2004, 3:45 am
Attic

I felt it, Dee—that thing people write about. That
thing the girls laugh over in their rooms at night
when I'm out in the cold looking in. That thing
Carly's teacher was talking about when they read
Wuthering Heights last year. The burn—it really is
a burn, Dee, somewhere in the solar plexus. Warm.
Intolerable.

Can it be that love really does exist? Is it love?
This fire in my stomach when he leaned over and touched
my cheek? When he said, "You just vanished. I had no
idea where you were until Naida came to tell me." His
eyes as they bored into mine, the desperate pressure of
his hand on my face. "You were gone."

His stupid bowler hat and the darkness in his eyes.
The bend of his jaw, the line of his yielding lips as
he leaned closer and—oh, God—kissed me. Is this love?

Please don't think I'm stupid for crying right now,
Dee, because I can't help myself. I emailed him, and
then went to the chapel after midnight, and he was
there, and it was like seeing life again.

He came in with wide, urgent eyes, looking all around
for me. I watched him for a moment as he strode down the
aisle and checked the confessional. I was in the rafters,
so I already felt as if I was flying. I was hiding—making
sure that I wouldn't be seen, like Naida said.

Then, because I had to see his face, I called
to him. He was with me in a flash, hand on my cheek,
hurting.

We were superior creatures, up there in the darkness
while everyone else slept, so when he put his hand on

mine, I felt our purposes—our existences—united in that moment. That contact.

His voice: "You were gone."

He said the words and then he looked at me, and that fire began as soon as I saw his eyes flicker down my body. In that moment, when I knew he was looking at me in the way that men look at women and the fire lights them from inside, I became Kaitlyn Johnson. I was nothing before he noticed me, and everything is different now.

His mouth on mine, the texture of his tongue, the taste of him, his warmth in a world of such coldness—all of it felt like divinity. I wasn't a ghost in that moment. I wasn't nothing.

My life is different forever, Dee. I think I love him, and it doesn't scare me. He is connected to me in this horrible life; he shares my every night, which I refuse to give up, because it means accepting that Carly is gone, as I almost did in Hell.

And maybe, just maybe, he is the reason I can stay in the dark. He is my new reason—the new reason I don't jump out of this life.

Or, if I do, I can fly.

Naida Camera Footage
Saturday, 1 January 2005, 5:45 AM
Basement

Naida faces the group of Elmbridge students gathered in the gloomy basement: Brett, Scott, Ari, and Kaitlyn, sitting in the corner.

"Right," she says. "I've asked you all here because you love Carly as much as I do, and you've come because you trust my judgment." She pauses, her face panning slowly over them all.

"Not sure how much we *should* trust," Scott mutters. "Sorry, babe, but you are aware that you're helping someone who escaped from a mental hospital—someone, I might add, that the police are now looking for in connection to Juliet McClarin? No offense, Carly, love," he adds. "But that detective bloke has already been asking me questions. I felt like a bloody criminal! Great bloody way to start the New Year."

"This won't be easy," Naida says, "but all of you know I'm not crazy, right? And I would *never* lead you astray. So"—she takes a breath—"I hope you'll believe me when I tell you that Carly Johnson is not in this room."

Only Ari is unsurprised.

Brett glances at Kaitlyn in the corner. "This is a prank, right?"

"April's a while off," Scott adds.

"Forget it, Naida," Kaitlyn says, getting to her feet. "This isn't going to work. They don't believe you."

"Sit down," Naida snaps. "*Sit!* We need our friends if we're going to do this. Now, I know they're not a bunch of cowards, and I know they've got our backs. We just have to explain a little. So." She gestures. "Go ahead."

Kaitlyn folds her arms and looks away. "I'm not a performing monkey in the circus."

Brett and Scott glance from Naida to Kaitlyn and back again.

"It's true," Ari says eventually, getting to his feet to stand beside Kaitlyn.

"Well, of course *you'd* agree," Scott snaps. "Everyone knows you've got a thing for Carly."

Ari meets Scott's eyes. "Her name is *Kaitlyn*. Not Carly. They're... sisters."

Brett frowns and glances at Kaitlyn with uncertainty. "Sisters. Twins?"

"Not in the conventional sense," Kaitlyn says, smiling slowly at Ari. "We...we share the same body. Carly comes out during the day." She swallows. "Used to. And I'm around at night."

Scott scoffs.

"Scott," Naida pleads, "I've known this about Carly and Kaitlyn for almost two years now. Do you think I'm lying?"

He throws up his hands. "Babe—"

"*Well?*"

"No, but I think she's pulled the wool over your eyes."

Naida throws up her hands in a mirroring gesture and growls.

"You know," Brett says slowly, glancing at Kaitlyn tentatively, "she *is* very different at night...."

Naida turns to Scott. "I need your help. I need you to believe this quickly, because Carly's in some serious trouble. Life-and-death kind of trouble, only worse, because it's her eternal soul in danger."

Scott stares at her like she just sprouted feathers. "Naids, I dunno. It's so...Jekyll and Hyde, you know? Are you sure she's not just—"

"What? Crazy?"

Scott shrugs. "Well...yeah. Sorry."

"Just listen, okay? We think an *Olen*—a Mala spirit of great power—has taken Carly." She pauses, looking each of them in the eye. "Last year I initiated you guys into a Mala circle. I taught you and shared with you, remember that? Now I need you to believe me."

"Excuse me?" Kaitlyn says softly.

"Last year I taught all of them a bit about Mala. I wanted to explore it a little more. Scott was curious, and so was Brett. Carly too. We formed a kind of Mala group."

Kaitlyn looks as though she's had the air knocked out of her. "Carly... was in a witch ring?"

"Just basic stuff. How to create a charm bag and a trick bag, simple things like that." Naida turns back to the room. "But this is bigger than that. Like I said, Carly's been stolen somehow. And I need your help."

Scott frowns and, after a moment, as though sensing that Naida has reached some kind of limit, walks over and wraps her in his long arms.

"This is mental, I hope you know that. But...you're stubborn as shit, so I guess I have no choice but to make sure you don't get hurt. What do you need from us?"

Naida doesn't reply right away, and before long, it is evident why. She is crying. He kisses the top of her head, nuzzling into her corkscrew curls.

"I need you to sneak Kaitlyn food and drink," she manages, at last. "And bring her clothes from my wardrobe, bringing out the old ones. It'll have to be on a rotation. Kaitlyn can't be seen."

"For how long?" asks Brett.

"I don't know. I have find out what's going on. I can't go into this blind. I need to prepare myself—could be a few days. A week, maybe?"

Brett smooths back his perfect hair. "I don't know, Naida...Why do the police want her?"

"Because they're idiots," Ari says. "But if you're too scared, we can do it without you."

"Forget it!" Kaitlyn snaps. "I don't need help—"

"No, wait," Brett says, cutting her off. He smiles. "I'm sorry. I want to help, if I can...Kaitlyn."

"I really think that I'm the only one who can get Carly back," Naida whispers. "I'm the only one who knows about Mala, and about Grúndi. I'm the only one who can deal with this...and it's a big responsibility."

Kaitlyn clenches her jaw and glances at Naida, perhaps still wary, but she says nothing.

Ari folds his arms and frowns, and with a glance at Kaitlyn, says, "Back from where?"

"I'm not sure yet. I need to research, as I said. Have to find out the time frame, look for clues."

"What about Juliet?" Brett asks. "Could she have been taken too, like Carly? Could they be in the same place?"

Naida shakes her head. "I think Juliet...I think human evil was responsible for her disappearance. I don't sense anything spiritual. I think she was kidnapped, or—I don't know."

There is a long moment of silence.

"In any case," Naida says at last, "you should know that someone's working against us."

"What do you mean, 'working against us'?" Ari says.

"I mean *someone* took Carly—someone took her soul and trapped it. Now that someone is going to do his damnedest to try to stop me from going after her."

"Is this dangerous?" Brett asks.

Naida nods, and Scott lets loose a vehement exclamation.

"But I can do it. I just need time. I need you to keep Kaitie safe for me until it's time."

"Time for what?"

Naida looks at Scott, whose eyes are locked on her face. "Just time."

Scott shakes his head, and Brett pulls on his lips in thought.

"How exactly are we going to do this without the teachers noticing?" Scott says. "You know that Coach O'Grady and Mrs. Mayle both stayed over Christmas, right? And they both live in this part of the school. What happens if we're caught?"

"Make something up. But try *not* to be caught. These stairs"—Naida nods towards the door behind her—"they used to be the old servants' stairs. They lead up between the walls and into the kitchen. We'll be safe to use them after supper at night and early in the morning. Then out into the main hall. Other times, use the broken window at the other end of the main basement, okay? But make sure no one sees you."

They all nod, with varying degrees of confidence.

"We should get going soon," Naida says after a while. "The dinner bell will ring any time, and if we're all missed, they'll know something's up."

"Do you all have to go?" Kaitlyn asks.

Brett raises a hand, then realizes what he's done and puts it down again. "I don't. I'd booked out to go to dinner with my dad, but he canceled."

Naida checks Scott's watch, then claps her hands. "C'mon, chop chop"—*clap, clap*—"See you later, Brett. Stay safe, Kaitie."

Kaitlyn nods, and everyone files out.

"Need me to stay?" Ari asks at the door.

"No. They'll miss you. It's okay. Later, though, yeah?"

He glances at Brett, nods once—tightly—and then vanishes up the servants' stairs with the others.

Brett wipes his hands on his jeans and rocks up onto the balls of his feet, while Kaitlyn sits down on the mattress.

"How...how does it work?"

"I come out at night. Carly during the day."

"Oh, right, yeah." He nods, seriously.

Kaitlyn rolls her eyes, but Brett pushes on.

"That's why...at the party—you said to talk to you during the day. That you'd be more yourself."

Kaitlyn regards him. "And you said you preferred me at night."

"It's true." He steps closer, then pauses, tilting awkwardly forward. "I do prefer you at night. Like that night on the field, we talked, remember?"

"Hm."

Kaitlyn shuffles back on the mattress, her face lost in shadow.

"You're more, I don't know, confident. So...do you remember stuff that happens during the day? Like, do you remember when we talk during the day and stuff?"

"No. Because it's not me."

He looks around. "So...you're stuck down here, then."

There is a beat of silence before Kaitlyn speaks again. "Hey, Brett?"

"Yeah?"

"I'm actually kind of tired. I think I'm going to sleep for a bit."

"Oh—I, yeah...yeah, okay."

He teeters for a moment, steps forward, then back, and with continual glances behind him, shuffles out of the door and up the stairs.

"I'm sorry...but it's not you I want," she whispers.

[END OF CLIP]

When introduced to powerful emotional stimuli, the individual who is dealing with personality disorders—especially those that are trauma-based—and who is at risk of experiencing psychotic thought patterns is in a very fragile state. The effect of such emotional intensity may be invigorating or even calming at first, but this is merely the silence before the hurricane. Care must be given and precautions taken.

—DR. ANNABETH LANSING, 2010

(FH): During treatment, did Carly Johnson know the details of her parents' death?

(AL): No. She could never remember the incident, and I never revealed the details.

(FH): Why?

(AL): Because it might have resulted in a psychotic break.

(FH): Wouldn't you say that the psychotic break was inevitable?

(AL): Now...yes. But at the time, I had no way of knowing that, and medically I couldn't risk it. My duty was to my patients.

(FH): Forgive me, Doctor. But don't you suppose that if you had told Carly the details and she had experienced a break, at least she would have done so in a safe environment, rather than out there in the world?

(AL): We didn't expect her escape from the facility. We were working towards disclosure. These things take time, Inspector. And with all due respect...you don't know anything about mental disorders, particularly those rooted in trauma. It was my job to protect Carly, not to inflict yet more trauma on her.

[Squeak as though of chair]

(FH): With all due respect to *you*, Doctor, you failed to prevent the death of several people and the serious injury of another. Not to mention the two we can't even find.

(AL): Carly was unstable, which is *why* she was hospitalized. She had delusions about flight and a fixation with putting herself in danger. She had a history of reckless behavior even before what happened to her parents. When she escaped, she was delusional. She behaved in the manner of someone hiding something, and I think that something was what she called "the Voice." Aka Manah, the voice that tortures the mind. I did everything to help that girl—I was there for her, at her beck and call, all hours of the day and night, should she have chosen to talk to me. But, like everyone who suffers from paranoid personality disorder, she made me into the enemy, saw my attempts to help her as trickery, and pushed me away. Then, after she was readmitted to Claydon, she began to see that she needed help. She began to let me in. *Until* Naida Chounan-Dupré insisted on seeing Carly.

(FH): Do you think Naida has something to do with Carly's escape?

(AL): You know better than I do what happened, Inspector. All I know is that Naida came, and then Carly regressed, and then she escaped. Smashed right through the window in her room.

(FH): Did you ever meet Naida face-to-face?

(AL): Yes. Directly before she went in to see Carly.

(FH): Is that meeting on tape?

(AL): No. Only the meeting room is recorded.

(FH): Did Naida seem normal to you when you met her?

[Pause]

(AL): What do you mean?

(FH): Do you think that Naida herself might have been... emotionally unstable?

(AL): I never had any professional dealings with Naida, so I don't know.

(FH): And if I were to inform you that Naida was a patient at Claydon for a summer some years ago?

(AL): I was unaware of that.

(FH): Her records are sealed, but her consultant, a Dr. [name omitted], stated that she had an anxiety disorder that was brought under control.

(AL): Then I expect that's correct.

(FH): Is it possible that Naida, a girl with a history of anxiety and hospitalization, might have been… influenced by Carly in some way?

(AL): Mr. Homes, I think you'd better be frank with me if you expect a helpful response.

[Pause]

(FH): What is your opinion on group hysteria?

(AL): My opinion?

(FH): Myth or fact?

(AL): It's very real. I think you'd better tell me what you're getting at.

(FH): Thank you, Doctor. You've been helpful. I'll be in touch.

[End of tape]

Diary of Kaitlyn Johnson

Sunday, 2 January 2005, 7:00 PM
Attic

These are what my thoughts sound like.

Have you ever heard glass sing? It's so beautiful. Delicate, crystalline—it's a sound you think should be relegated to the happiest places and the friendliest gestures.

I hear glass splintering…no, not even glass, really. It's too soft for that. More like the glass equivalent of toffee…more like…a mirror. A mirror, squeaking and snapping as it splinters and begins to break. On and on.

Chip…crack…squeak…

A plastic sound, not quite real, but real enough to cut if you grab too hard. And I always do, so I always bleed.

These are what my thoughts sound like.

The house is mine.

I hear him in the day now too. I feel him, the way I felt the house in that nightmare. I feel the house like my own heartbeat.

Later

What do you think, Dee?

A succession of days and nights follow, all of them with Kaitlyn waiting, restlessly pacing in the dank cellar room. Occasionally she examines her arms, pulling back the long sleeves of her top to stare down at her stitches. Scott brings food and drink, then Brett, who stays to chat with a fairly unenthusiastic Kaitlyn, then Scott again. Naida is rarely seen.

"Naida's busy again?" Kaitlyn asks Scott one night. "Am I too much…am I a burden?"

Scott puts down the tray of food he has brought with him. "Just hang in there, I guess. I know it's hard—"

"No, you don't! It's more than hard, Scott—I'm going crazy in here! I'm losing my mind!"

Scott, in a yet-unseen act of kindness, pulls Kaitlyn into a hug. "She's been working hard to find out what's what. Waiting for a sign from the *Shyan* bloke, watching students around her, performing rituals, and laying—whatever she calls them." He releases her. "I'll tell her."

Kaitlyn shakes her head. "Don't. Carly's more important."

He nods. "I can stay for a while, if you want?"

"No. Help Naida if you can. But…maybe you can find Ari first? He's doing extra-credit work after school, but…ask him to come?"

"Right." He grins. "You and the army brat getting close, huh?"

"Did he say something?"

Scott laughs, the sound echoing through the chamber. "Are you insane? Ari never says anything. He's about as chatty as you. But I saw you two at Naida's party. You seemed really comfortable. I'll tell him to get his arse over here."

"Thanks."

He turns to leave, then pauses. "Carly—I mean, Kaitlyn…"

"Yeah?"

"Do you believe this stuff? The Mala stuff?"

Kaitlyn stares at him for a moment and then gives one sad laugh. "I… don't know."

"Kind of sounds…"

"Crazy?"

"Yeah. Crazy."

"I guess it fits me, then."

Scott laughs, then notices Kaitlyn's face. "I joined her Mala group last year because I thought she was hot. Now I'm up to my neck in it."

Kaitlyn smiles. "Life is weird."

"Major understatement."

"So you'll get Ari?"

"Yes, ma'am! At your service, ma'am!"

She nods, and he leaves, closing the door behind him. Kaitlyn stands for a moment, looking down at the soup, then walks over to the old mattress and picks up her pen and journal. She writes a sentence, smiles, and shuts the book, before walking slowly over to the light chain and pulling it once. The room is flooded with blackness.

Then she begins to hum.

Sunday, 2 January 2005, 10:00 pm
Basement

They've cleared it all away. All the stuff from our dorm room. Everything we wore, used, owned. Everything she touched. Naida came to tell me. But she salvaged the box under the bed, the most important thing. I'm so glad she brought it to me, but I don't feel like I thought I would. One box, and it holds a whole life of love—almost every letter Carly and I have ever exchanged. Seeing it here, all together, three big bundles of paper…is that all we were? Dying pages, fading ink?

[Kaitlyn has pasted several letters into her diary over the following pages, allowing us a unique insight into her relationship with Carly.]

Carly, there's something at the window! There's a big storm. I'm scared! What do I do if it's a monster?

Monsters can't get inside the house, because I planted magic stones outside. It's the wind blowing on the window probably! So don't be scared! The storm is gone now.

Happy birthday to us!
Happy birthday to us!
Happy birthday,
CarlyandKaitieeeeeeee...
Happy birthday to us!!
(Look under the bed.
I hope you like it!
Happy 14th birthday, Kaybear!)

xxx

In London, we'll have our own place. It'll have huge windows to let in the sun for you, moon for me. We'll have our own rooms, our own wardrobes, our own food. We'll be able to choose where we go, who we talk to, and I'll be able to go shopping and see movies and go to a West End show. You'll be able to go to university and buy books from shops, and everything will be the way <u>we</u> want it. Exactly as we want it. I can't wait. This will end, Carlybean. It will end.

They wouldn't want you to be sad.

I can't stop crying. I miss them. I totally took them for granted. Having no one believe us is so much harder than they said it might ever be. I understand why they told us to keep it a secret. This is hard, Kaitie. I can't do this without them.

Talking about London makes me feel like there's hope. We have a life waiting for us. We just need to get there, I guess. In London, our apartment will be open plan, no barriers. We'll get a cat and call her Freedom. You'll have a room just for all your books, and I'll have a little place to study. We can each go and see the same film on the same day and talk about it. I want that, Kaybear. I want our life to start. But this place...it gets to me sometimes. Dr. Lansing gets to me sometimes.

Screw Lansing. She doesn't know us. A cat called Freedom. It's a promise.

Kaitlyn to Carly, 22 July 2002

I know you're pissed at me, but I wanted to keep him to myself for a while. I'm sorry, C, but you have school, and you have some friends (yes, you do!), and I just wanted a friend of my own. His name is the Viking, and he is the tallest, biggest boy I have ever seen! I think you'd like him; he's really funny. And honest. We met in town, and he's a child of the dark, just like me. Well, not really _like_ me. He has insomnia. I'm sorry I upset you. I didn't mean to make you angry. Do you want to meet him?

Carly to Kaitlyn, 23 July 2002

I think I was in shock. Mostly. You just dropped this mention of a random guy, and you made it sound like you'd known him forever. How long <u>have</u> you known him? Does he know about us? The <u>truth</u>? Are you, like, <u>dating</u> him? That's totally fine, but if you're going to...you know...um, could you give me a bit of warning? You know I hate surprises, and that would be a big one. How is this going to work? I wish I could talk to you. I feel nervous. Do you love him? How will that work? It's kind of...weird. What if he doesn't like me?

Kaitlyn to Carly, 23 July 2002

He's just a friend. <u>I promise.</u> My only friend, apart from you. You said I should meet people. I wasn't going to do anything. I would never do anything like that, Carly. Don't be nervous. He's just a friend. Barely even that. You are the most important thing to me, okay? That will never change.

Diary of Kaitlyn Johnson

Monday, 3 January 2005, 2:12 am
Forgotten Garden

I've been sitting here for twenty minutes, trying to
figure out how to write it down.

I never intended it to happen—I never meant to take
this from Carly. DAMNIT. Does smacking my face into
the wall make it better? No, because it's Carly's face.
Carly's hands and her legs, her heart. Her virginity
too. I had no right. But I did it anyway.

She asked me to tell her if I ever—when I decided—if
there was a <u>chance</u>—

She wanted warning.

How many times can I say I'm sorry, Dee? I'm sorry—
I'm so sorry! But I'm happy—I'm happy, and I'm sorry,
and I hate this so much!

I took Ari to the Forgotten Garden—on top of the
old crypt, so sad and broken. I wanted to show him
<u>me</u>, which is what the graveyard is. The remnant of
something, like the husk of some exotic fruit once the
bird has had its fill. The shadow on the wall of the
flickering object.

Don't look at me like that, Dee. Because you have
no idea what I'm going through. Ari was…Ari is…the
only thing I have. Now. The kiss was just as sweet,
especially outside in the dark with the wind tickling
our faces and the moisture in the air gifting tiny
droplets on our skin, like uncanny tears. It was cold,
which is so familiar, so safe. Like an old friend, Dee…
you can understand that.

When his hands fell from my hair to run down my
back and take in my thighs and then frantically up to
my breasts—I was on fire. I crossed a line I never let
myself cross when I haunted the streets of Chester. I

don't know why. Maybe because I could. Maybe because I had no choice—I was compelled. My dark nature brought me to it. I needed it.

Do you remember? That the thing I long for the most is breath on my neck, arms wrapped around me, telling me I'm wanted. Needed. Do you?

Ari knows me now, more than anyone. He's seen the darkest side of me and he's been me. And he's not afraid. It was inevitable as soon as his lips fell on mine again, his hands on me—our bodies urging us forward like an unstoppable tide. Sure, it was sore, and I don't know if you could call it "making love." It was more like "falling alive."

Ari and I had ~~sex~~ tonight.

Sex. God, I wrote it. Sex.

Thanks to me, Carly is no longer a virgin. I have a confession, Dee, and it's so vile and disgusting that I'm retching as I write it. I think, in some subconscious and demeaning part of me, I was hoping that this would hurt her enough to make her come back. That she would be so repulsed and appalled and angry by what I had done to her that she would just tear her way back into our body, and I would suddenly, painfully, be complete.

Dee, I feel like I just raped Carly. I know—it's stupid. But I feel like that. She didn't give me her consent. I don't know…

I've never felt more alive than I did in his arms. It was such an amazing thing…more wonderful than anything else I've ever experienced. And that just makes me feel even worse!

I can't stop feeling Ari all over me. His lips on mine, his hands in my hair, his breath—harsh and full of passion—on my neck. The feeling of the stone crypt under my back, hard and moist and cold, like the Dead House, which I felt descending all around us.

From: RealxChick
To: AriHait558
Date: 3 January 2005
Subject: The Prisoner Finds Ink and Parchment

Naida supplied the caged bird with a little window. What do you think of it?

Confessional Girl

From: AriHait558
To: RealxChick
Date: 3 January 2005
Subject: Re: The Prisoner Finds Ink and Parchment

I am beyond ecstatic that Rapunzel has found her window. That the muse has been released. I am nothing without you, Caged Beauty.

From: RealxChick
To: AriHait558
Date: 3 January 2005
Subject: Our Secret

I can't stop thinking about…our secret. Did that really happen only a few hours ago? Did I dream it? I don't know what's real anymore.

Confused, alone, needing you.

From: AriHait558
To: RealxChick
Date: 3 January 2005
Subject: Re: Our Secret

You'll never be alone again. You have me.

It was real. It happened.

It was the best moment of my life.

Do you regret it?

From: RealxChick
To: AriHait558
Date: 3 January 2005
Subject: Re: Re: Our Secret

A little.

From: AriHait558
To: RealxChick
Date: 3 January 2005
Subject: Re: Re: Re: Our Secret

Ah.

From: RealxChick
To: AriHait558
Date: 3 January 2005
Subject: Re: Re: Re: Re: Our Secret

Only because of Carly! I don't regret you. You saved me. You came into the dark with me, and you showed me that there *was* life. You pulled me into the light.

I think I love you.

From: AriHait558
To: RealxChick
Date: 3 January 2005
Subject: Re: Re: Re: Re: Re: Our Secret

Get some sleep. We had a late night, and the breakfast bell will ring any moment. Try to rest, beautiful caged Rapunzel. Things will seem less uncertain after you rest.

PS—I love every little molecule in your body. I love every hair on your head.

From: RealxChick
To: AriHait558
Date: 3 January 2005
Subject: Re: Re: Re: Re: Re: Re: Our Secret

I don't deserve this happiness.

Diary of Kaitlyn Johnson

Tuesday, 4 January 2005, 6:25 am
Basement

It started with footsteps. Footsteps coming slowly
towards my room. The sound is so heavy, like the
footsteps of a Moloch, and they echo down the hall.

    Step. (BOOM.) Step. (BOOM.) Step. (BOOM.)

    I can't move.

    My heart throws itself against my ribs as though
telling my lungs: Inflate! Inflate now! We need air!
Breathe! BREATHE!

    But I can't breathe, because the footsteps have
stopped outside my door and they squeeeeeaaakkk as the
monster turns towards me—or is it a devil, Dee? I can't
tell. All I know is that there is nothing but a strip
of wood between us, and all I can think is

        Oh my God Oh my God Oh my God

    And
            then

The walls were bleeding. Not just bleeding, Dee. They
were raining blood. I could smell that copper scent
like old pennies, and I could feel the warm, sticky,
squishiness of it in between my toes.

    As the blood rose in the Dead Rooms, I grew more and
more panicked, sure I would drown in whatever the blood
concealed. Dee, I did; I drowned in my sleep tonight,
and when I woke, I found blood and stitches and skin
caught in my teeth, and my arms had been ripped open
anew.

Naida Camera Footage
Tuesday, 4 January 2005, 7:45 AM
Basement

Naida enters the basement with a tote bag slung over her shoulder as the motion camera is clicked on. Kaitlyn sits huddled in the shadows and doesn't stir.

"Up, up, up," Naida sings, dropping a bag by the foot of the mattress. "I've got something for you, but you've got to be awake to get it."

The shadow that is Kaitlyn still doesn't move, and even with the night vision on the camera, it is difficult to see what Kaitlyn is doing under the blanket draped across her.

"Don't make me shine a flashlight in your face," Naida warns, bending over to pull one out of the bag. "I was courteous enough not to flip on the overhead light, but I've got limits. Three seconds. Two. One! You leave me no choice, Johnson."

She clicks on the flashlight and shines it on Kaitlyn. We get a brief image of Kaitlyn hunched over her arms, legs curled tightly to her and blood pooled on the mattress before Naida drops the flashlight and the room is flooded with black once more. The camera takes a moment to adjust to the darkness again.

"Kaitie," Naida breathes, "what happened?"

"The Dead House tried to drown me in blood." Kaitlyn's voice shakes and jumps as though she is very cold. "Or the thing in the Dead House— I'm not sure."

Naida runs over to the light and flips the switch. The bulb illuminates very little of the room, but it is enough to see that Kaitlyn has been bleeding profusely. She is a chalky gray color, and her eyes are drooping.

"Why didn't you call me?" Naida demands, tearing off her shirt and clambering onto the mattress. "That's what I gave you the laptop for!" She presses the material to Kaitlyn's arms, shaking her head.

"M-mustn't b-be s-seen." Kaitlyn shudders.

"I have to call an ambulance—"

"No!" Kaitlyn wrenches backwards, tearing her arms away from Naida.

"Kaitlyn, you'll bleed to death!"

"Then h-help me. S-sew it up ag-gain."

"I can't do that. You'll get some kind of infection—Kaitlyn, I have to go now!"

Kaitlyn attempts to grip Naida's arms as she tries to get up, but her hands are weak.

"Th-they'll lock m-me away forever—and Carly—N-Naida, please. Please h-help me. Help me—" Her head shakes, dipping lower and lower, but her eyes never leave Naida's face. They are hollow, piercing like the gaze of disease. "P-promise me. *P-please*, promise me!"

"I...Okay. Okay, Kaitie."

Kaitlyn nods once and slumps against the wall. Her eyelids flutter closed.

"Gorro, help me," Naida mutters, then crawls off the mattress and dashes from the room.

It is more than ten minutes before she returns, by which time the motion-activated camera has clicked off. When it comes back on, registering the time difference, Kaitlyn—who had been slumped against the wall—is now standing against the perpendicular side, her forehead pressed to the concrete. It is unclear how she got there without the camera picking up the movement.

Naida sees her standing like a mannequin, hesitates a moment, and then rushes over.

Kaitlyn is lackluster and pliable in her hands.

"Sit down," Naida says, leading Kaitlyn back to the mattress. She slumps, leaning against the wall.

Naida unscrews the cap from what looks like a bottle of clear alcohol and wets a white cloth with it. She cleans out the wound, and Kaitlyn hisses through her teeth.

"You have to be strong if you want me to do this," Naida warns. She is the picture of calm focus; only her shaking hands give her away. She ties a bandage around Kaitlyn's left arm and secures it in place, then removes a needle and thread from what looks like a little sewing bag.

"God help me," she mutters, and then begins the long process of sewing up Kaitlyn's arm.

Kaitlyn tries not to scream, but eventually it becomes too difficult. Naida has to wad up another bandage and put it into Kaitlyn's mouth. When the right arm is done, it is a butchered mess—all black thread and bunched flesh, but it is no longer bleeding. Naida douses it in alcohol again and then bandages it in place.

"One down."

Kaitlyn passes out before the second arm is finished, and then Naida checks her pulse, feels her forehead, and carefully pulls her more firmly onto the bed. She then covers the unconscious form with the blanket and sits on the edge, bows her head into her hands, and sobs.

10:02 AM

Kaitlyn sits wrapped in the blanket, a cup of warm tea cradled between her palms. She seems barely able to hold it. Naida watches her carefully.

"Won't they miss you?" Kaitlyn asks.

"I faked a note. It's only PE, anyway."

Kaitlyn glances up at her. "Thank you. Not just for the tea."

Naida gives a weak smile. "Well, I've never done *that* before. Too bad you couldn't stay for the whole show."

"It was getting tedious."

Naida grins at Kaitlyn's weak attempt at humor. "God *damn*, Johnson."

Kaitlyn takes a sip of her tea, and her skin seems to warm a bit, the gray alabaster flushing with a little peach. She glances up, towards the door, where a short, knotted rope wound with numerous materials that the camera cannot differentiate hangs.

"What is that?"

"A bind. Protection for you. It'll stop the dreams."

"Will it work?"

"Should. It's got my own blood in there, so it'd better."

Kaitlyn flinches. "Was that necessary?"

"Wouldn't do it otherwise."

Kaitlyn nods and sips her tea again.

"What's up, sugar?"

"How much longer?"

Naida sighs and pressed her hands to her face. "I don't know. I'm getting closer, I think. This is new for me—I've never conjured or done root work before. There's a lot to learn, to go through...And I'm tailing Mike...I'm trying my best."

"It's just..." Kaitlyn shudders. "Whatever's going on inside me, it's getting worse. I don't know, closer. It's getting harder to cope."

Naida says nothing, and Kaitlyn continues.

"And I was thinking...maybe...maybe medication will help. Maybe all I need is the right kind, the right dose—maybe...maybe I am—"

"Crazy? You can't really believe that, can you? What about that house you keep dreaming about? And where's Carly, huh? And why did I find this"—Naida pulls out a stiff knot of...*something* from her bag—"outside my dorm this morning, huh?"

Kaitlyn leans away from it. "It reeks—what is it?"

"Oh, just the intestines of some poor creature, knotted into a conjure to keep me immobile."

"What?"

"It's a warning. From whoever's doing this."

Kaitlyn swallows. "It's easier not to believe."

"We will get through this."

Kaitlyn dashes away a tear. "I feel alone, Naida. I don't know if I feel Carly anymore. It's like she's locked away where I can't get at her. I don't have anyone else."

Naida takes her hand. "You have me."

Kaitlyn bites her lips and nods, blinking hard. "I'm scared."

"I know. But this isn't going to get easier before it gets better. I need you strong. So drink up that tea."

Kaitlyn eyes the cup suddenly. "What did you put in it?"

"Something to make you strong."

Kaitlyn nods, and then drinks.

[END OF CLIP]

Naida Camera Footage
Tuesday, 4 January 2005, 9:00 PM
Naida's Dorm

Naida kneels on the floor before her camera and clasps her hands, bowing low over them. A candle, lit somewhere below the screen, casts an orange light on her face, accentuating her angular features. She looks tired, worn, and scared. But there is a fire in her bright eyes as she looks up, hinting at her determination.

"Blessed Gorro, guide me," she whispers. "Mother Karrah, hold me close. By your powerful intercession, hear me." She lifts a small brown root for the camera to see and snaps it in half. "Here is earthroot, to break conjures against me. Devil's heart"—she lifts a small purple flower—"to protect me from those who work against me. Master root"—she lifts a bark-like formation—"to aid my psychic powers. And currency"—a silver coin—"to plow over my enemies and the enemies of my friends."

She bows her head for a moment, then opens her Bible and begins to read.

"'Arise, O Lord, in thine anger, lift up thyself because of the rage of mine enemies: and awake for me to the judgment that thou hast commanded...My defense is of God, which saveth the upright in heart.'"

She flips through a few pages. "'Thy tongue deviseth mischiefs; like a sharp razor, working deceitfully....God shall likewise destroy thee forever, he shall take thee away, and pluck thee out of thy dwelling place, and root thee out of the land of the living!'"

She lifts her gaze into the camera; she is looking directly at us.

"I curse you, dark worker and thief. I lift up a mighty shield against you and point a knife at your neck. You will relent, you will fall, and we will find Carly and bring her back. I hope you're afraid, you son of a bitch. You should be."

She reaches forward and switches off the camera.

Diary of Kaitlyn Johnson

Wednesday, 5 January 2005, 9:51 pm
Attic

I think I was beginning to lose myself to despair. I kept thinking, Did I dream her? Did I imagine her? Was she ever here at all?

But the dead girl came to me. I opened my eyes, and there she was, standing in the doorway. I never noticed before, but she's wet. She raised one thin arm and motioned me to follow with her finger; her eyes were wide and sad, but she was still grinning. So I felt afraid.

But I didn't care what happened, because what could be worse?

She took me upstairs, step by creaking step. I was a little dizzy and unsteady on my feet, and in quite some pain, but followed nonetheless. We haunted the corridors of the school, two specters of nothing, and I forgot to question where she was leading me.

The walls seem sad, which scares me. They seem to cry; I want to scream. But then I was in a classroom and the grinning girl was standing on a desk, her dead flesh dripping everywhere, and I knew I had to look inside.

And there it was. Carly's journal.

When I looked up, she was two inches from my face, grinning at me with haunted yellow eyes. She said something, but there was no sound. It looked like "see what I found?" And then she was gone, walking away down the silent corridor, flickering in and out, like something about to crack and topple over.

And here I sit with it in my hands. It feels like an ancient relic of someone dead. The only piece left of them. Of her. That's when it hit me, Dee. If I don't get Carly back, she's dead. She's gone forever.

I can't live like that.

There's so much I want to tell her. I flipped to the back of her journal and wrote inside. Maybe, somewhere, somehow, she can see it.

Carly,

Nothing is the same without you. I eat because I need the strength to find you. I sleep because now my body forces me to. But it's meaningless, like a movie set. I play a part, but there is no substance. I go home to nothing at the end of the scene.

I wish you could see how you've brought Naida and me together.

I wish you could see Ari…the things he's revealed in me. What I've done. I'm sorry, so sorry, but I wouldn't change it even if I could, because it saved me. He saved me. I was falling into a blackness without you that was darker than the world I lived in before. He reached into that darkness with his beautiful, strong hand, and he pulled me up. He continues to prop me up.

I think I love him. I want nothing more than to be able to tell you this. To believe that you can see these words and know that they're true. But I would give him up if it would bring you back.

I'd give up anything for you.

Please come home. There's a gap inside me waiting to be filled, and the longer you're absent, the closer I feel something…other coming. The harder it will be to keep this space open, ready to receive you.

I feel the thing getting closer.

Hurry, Carly. Oh, hurry!

Give me a sign. Give me a sign, please, please, give me a sign. I will wait. I will watch. Please—anything. Anything, Carly, please!

Later

I feel the eyes of this attic over my shoulder as
I read. I feel the urge to hide her words from the
walls' prying eyes. Her entries are discordant, worse
than mine. "Got no pen," she writes. Writes with a
pen. "Something, nothing, sunlight isn't real." Broken
fragments of thought, no more.

What was I expecting? That she would write endlessly
about me, the way I do her? She was more of a poet than
that.

Far, far, far, far, far, far, she writes.

Shut up, shut up, shut up, shut up, shut up, she
writes.

Her words are neat and precise, solid and real.
Then they change. The writing grows, like some kind of
mythical beast eating space, disregarding the lines,
looser, softer, more widely spread, until a few pages
later, there are no words, just long lines of nothing.

Dee, she was disappearing even then. How did Naida
not see? Was the Voice pulling her away without my even
noticing? If I had told her the truth, might she have
tried to hold on to me? I can almost see Aka Manah
pulling at her arm. She is insubstantial as a rag doll,
stitched at the joints, loosely, like she will fall
apart any moment.

Today the dog barks, she writes.

Someone is coming, she writes.

And on the last page: *help me*

Later

I know. Yes, I know it's important. Yes. Yes, I'm
going to.

Don't rush me. Naida can wait for a minute, can't she?

This means something, Dee, doesn't it? That's why
you're pushing me.

I know.

Yes, I know.

I will—I'm going to tell her right now.

A conversation with Naida is implied in the last section of the diary. No record has been found of such a conversation, nor is it mentioned by Kaitlyn or Naida in any of the following entries.

The light is on. Kaitlyn gets off the mattress gingerly, leaving her journal and Carly's journal behind. She walks over to the armoire, pauses as though listening, and then opens both doors. There is a full-length mirror attached to the back of the ornate cupboard.

"Carly?" she says, staring at her reflection. "Carly? Carly? Carly? Carly? Carly? Carly? Carly?"

This behavior continues for forty minutes, until Kaitlyn falls silent, but does not move. By the time the motion-activated camera deactivates, she is still standing in front of the mirror, looking for a sign that does not appear.

On the first of January 2005, DCI Floyd Homes was assigned to the Johnson missing persons case. He began an investigation into the whereabouts of Carly Johnson and issued a warrant for her arrest on 6 January 2005.

Diary of Kaitlyn Johnson

Thursday, 6 January 2005, There Is No Time! Basement

Writing down—
Haaaaaandrad heeeeeends.
—everything he says to me.
Seeeeeee the bluuuuuuuuuud?
Leeeeeeesen welllllll.
Caummmmm to meeeeeeee.
Yooooooooo ah myyyyyyyyyyn.
Reeeeeeeeeeeeeee
Mehhhhhhhhhhhhhhm
Behhhhhhhhhhhhhhr
Rrrrrrrrrrrrrrrrrrrr…
His voice fades away into the hiss of the Dead Ocean, but I have the words:
Hundred hands.
See the blood?
Listen well.
Come to me.
You are mine.
Re
Mem
Ber.
Remember.

Remember what?

Later

She's always here now. Can you see her, Dee? Her
laughter sounds like glass.
YOU ARE NOT HER!

**Naida Camera Footage
Friday, 7 January 2005, 7:12 AM
Attic**

———

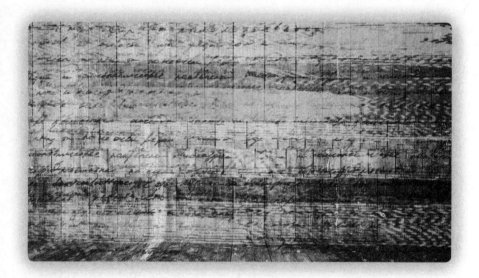

"It appeared overnight, we think," Naida says. She is holding a pashmina around her neck, lifting it over her nose. "It reeks."

She turns the camera. This is the first glimpse we can see of the attic in which Kaitlyn spent so much of her time before her sectioning. As Kaitlyn described, it is riddled with boxes, dust, cobwebs, and cupboards. Only now, script covers every inch of the wooden walls.

Naida approaches the wall to the left, directly beside the door. "We think it starts here. We can't know for sure…it's all so manic." She touches the wall. "Wow, look here. Mirror writing…like Da Vinci used."

The camera reveals an array of script written in pen and marker, sharp letters that slant left, then right, most of it difficult to decipher. The mirror writing runs neatly from right to left in patches.

"Moving along," Naida continues, her breath noisy in the mic, "looks like the pen ran out. See here, it turns to pencil."

And the writing does change, for a short while, to pencil.

"Then scratching in the wood itself."

Naida runs her fingers along the grooves where words and symbols have been cut into the wood with sharp, frenetic lines.

"And then here," she says, walking farther along. "Some kind of stain."

The words become larger, haphazard—and seem to be smeared onto the wood with something brown. Naida follows the script, moving between and behind boxes, and rounds the first corner.

"Then there's this."

A stain on the floor. Large. Dark. Ominous.

"Haven't got a clue what that is, but I do sense something…off about this room. Kaitie says she'd been spending all her time up here until Carly…went. It troubles me."

She turns the camera on herself. "It troubles me, because I can sense intent here. Like parts of this school…the older parts. Only, I've never sensed anything like this. And there's a smell…a scent. Like"—she inhales, nostrils widening—"I don't know, like mildew or something. Like rot. And something else—something vile. It worries me that Kaitie's been sitting in this power for so long, exposed to hell knows what."

The camera spins once more, to take in the defiled space.

"Something's been working up here. I'll have to check people's handwriting. I'll decipher all I can."

77

Diary of Kaitlyn Johnson

Friday, 7 January 2005, 9:50 am
Forgotten Garden

It's everywhere.

On the walls, on the ceiling, on the floor—every surface. Words and words and words. Endless writing, some of it legible, some not. The whole attic is covered in the scrawl. I found it when I went up there. It <u>stank</u>. I couldn't stand it. Went to find Naida.

Someone has been in my space. Someone knows I'm here. But who? Who knows, besides Ari and Naida, Scott, Brett, and me? Who besides us five would come into my bubble, while my body betrayed me to sleep down in the basement, and write on the walls of my haven?

It's her, isn't it? The thin yellow girl. You can tell me, Dee.

But, see now? Do you see? How some of the writing is written in felt-tip pen? Marker? And how as the fibers die on the splintered wood, it changes to ballpoint pen? And farther, as the pen dies, scratchings as though she—Carly, it has to be Carly?—attempted to use the pen to gouge her cries into the wood itself. That doesn't last long, see, Dee? Something else is used after that—it's messy, confused, brown. Ugly. Oh, God— it's shit. She wrote in shit, Dee. This is where the smell is coming from. It reeks!

I followed the trail of words, none of them making much sense, following all the way along the dark and narrow U that is the attic—my home—until I came to the very end, where not even the spiders live anymore. There, on the floor, sat an ominous dark stain in the corner, soaked into an old carpet rolled up to one side. I didn't know if it was green or blue or brown, that stain, but there in the shadows, it looked black. The true color.

Horror woke itself inside me, and I backed away slowly, never letting my eyes wander from that stain, which seemed to regard me as much as I did it, telling me, I can see.

But can you?

Later

I told Naida I won't look at the writing. I won't go back to that defiled place. There is something wrong with me. There is something inside me.

Because…I didn't tell her that the writing on the walls, Dee…seems to be my own.

5:00 pm

Maybe it was stupid, but I DON'T CARE! I'm sick of waiting! I'm sick of being alone! Her school's only four miles away, in town, and I knew I'd be back before anyone noticed, and I was, so no big deal. So you can quit looking at me like that, Dee.

I saw her waiting for dickball Bailey by the front benches, so tiny and lonely and vulnerable, and I called her over to me. Her eyes widened, and she ran over so fast I could barely catch her. All her stuff, including the ridiculous bobble hat she was wearing, went rolling all over the place, but I didn't care, because she was in my arms.

"Kaitie," she murmured into my hair. "You were gone!"

"It's okay, Jaimebean, I'm here." And she didn't smell like Jaime anymore. The Bailey smell had completely taken over.

I took her round to the back benches, just out of sight of the main school, and I asked her how she was. Normally she'd tell me about her school, her friends, her new coloring pencils—all that stuff—but this time she just kept asking about Carly.

"Where's Carly? Is Carly with you? Has she gone to heaven with Mummy and Daddy?"

"No!" I snapped, and when her eyes filled with tears, I added, "She's just…sleeping. Don't worry, though, because I'm going to wake her up."

"You're going to get her?"

I nodded. "I <u>promise</u>."

Maybe it was stupid to say that, but I did. And that promise held a thousand meanings.

I promise I will get Carly.

I promise Carly will be safe.

I promise life will go back to normal.

I promise I will take care of you.

I promise I know what I'm doing.

I promise I'm not crazy.

I promise I won't go to jail.

I promise I will force the world to make sense again.

I saw Mrs. Bailey before Jaime did, and when she called out Jaime's name, and Jaime turned to look, I melted into the shadows and watched the whole disgusting scene like the ghost I am.

Mrs. Bailey came, and Jaime picked up all of her lost treasures. She didn't turn to look for me. Not once. It's as if she knew I wasn't really there to begin with.

Diary of Kaitlyn Johnson

Friday, 7 January 2005, 10:00 pm
Basement

I can't make sense of all the images in my head. They
flash and burn and change; they bleed into one another,
but I must try. The first thing is a hand. A huge hand
right in my face, and there is terror in my mouth,
bursting to get out as I look at it coming slowly
forward. I'm choking on the fear, which bends its way
into my vitals like an insidious and very conscious
weed. The weed knows exactly where to go, and it is
laughing.

I see his face—but it's torn, warped, bleeding. Dad.

There is shadow on a wall, moving, but slowing.
And with the slowing, I'm filled with *something*. And
then there is blood on very rough, dark walls—bleeding
stone—like walls?!—then, clear as crystal, John the
Viking's face.

He is pale, his eyes wide, his lips grimly set.

He is always in the flashes, right at the end, and I
don't know why, and I am terrified.

Naida Camera Footage
Date and Time Index Missing
Naida's Dorm

The camera light illuminates Naida's face, turning it to sharp lines and deep furrows. In the distance, the constant echoing drip of water tells us she is in a room of stone. There is no natural light.

"Someone doesn't want me snooping around," Naida says, her voice low and solemn. "That little cast I performed...this is what's been made of it." She holds up a round object. "It's a bull testicle, sealed with red wax. My conjure's inside. The earthroot, the devil's heart, the silver coin...Then there's this."

She lifts a tag from behind the object and reads it aloud.

"*'Be ye not unequally yoked together with unbelievers: for what fellowship hath righteousness with unrighteousness? and what communion hath light with darkness?' 'Ye cannot drink the cup of the Lord, and the cup of devils: ye cannot be partakers of the Lord's table, and of the table of devils'*—2 Corinthians 6:14 and 1 Corinthians 1:21." She sticks her tongue between her teeth and laughs. "He's quoting scripture at me. He's taunting me—telling me I haven't got what it takes to beat him. That I won't do what might be necessary."

She laughs again, shaking her head. "Someone's been *inside* my room, found the bind I placed in secret, and conjured around it. He—or she, I suppose—is more powerful than I reckoned. But if he thought he'd scare me away by quoting scripture and reworking my bind against me, he doesn't know me too well. This only makes me *more* certain. It only makes me *more* determined."

She sighs. "But now I have to do something I *really* don't want to do." She looks up into the lens. "I have go and see Haji."

Saturday, 8 January 2005, 7:55 pm
Basement

London, my precious London!

Naida's never done anything like this before. She wants me to take her top hat camera so that we can look at the footage later. No need to tell me how stupid I look. She thinks this guy—Haji, she calls him—might give something away with a glance or a particular phrasing of words.

All I should care about is this: London. London, Dee. My sleepless city, at last, just like Carly and I planned. Cute, right?

Naida says we could be going into a den of vipers, and I secretly hope so. Anything to take away this feeling in my chest.

No going back now. We catch the 9:14 train.

A review of the system records on the date in question reveal no train ticket purchases by Carly Johnson or Naida Chounan-Dupré via credit card. We can only assume cash was used.

80

24 days until
the incident

**Naida Camera Footage
Sunday, 9 January 2005, 12:15 am
Time Index Not Noted**

Top Hat Camera Clip #1

The streetlamps flicker over streets that look as though they've seen Victorian England. Kaitlyn, wearing the top hat camera, follows Naida across a deserted road and into a narrow alley; only one set of footsteps echoes against the walls and boarded-up windows that tower on either side.

"Are you sure this is the right way?" Kaitlyn whispers.

"I stole my cousin's map," Naida murmurs, rifling through her bag.

She pulls free a thick roll of parchment paper, murmuring, "It shows all the places she gets her supplies and all her…friends." She nods, her gaze sharpening as she taps the scroll. "We got it right. Down here."

"Not exactly the side of London I know best."

The alley continues for three hundred yards and then banks sharply left. Kaitlyn follows Naida around the bend, glancing up at the buildings that tower on either side, and then the alley opens onto a small side street.

"Here," Naida says, pointing towards a set of railed stairs that disappear down into the pavement, beneath the street level.

"You're shitting me," Kaitlyn says drily. "We're going into a sewer?"

Naida rolls her eyes as she puts away the parchment. "It's not a sewer, it's just belowground. It's...grungy-chic."

Kaitlyn snorts. "Blah, blah."

They descend the stairs, the camera panning left and right, as though Kaitlyn is seeking a way out. Once at the bottom, they are facing a concrete corridor, much like the pedestrian underpasses of London, which ends abruptly in a black wooden door, the paint chipped and peeling. It looks like the entrance to the backside of an abandoned factory.

The camera pans 180 degrees as Kaitlyn looks back. "I don't know, Naida...you *sure*?"

Naida nods.

As the girls approach the door, the camera picks up the faint traces of matte paint on top of the chipped gloss paint on the door, revealing a mostly obscured symbol. Naida raises a hand and pulls the door open, slipping inside. Along with Kaitlyn, we follow.

The corridor behind the door is much like the narrow alleyway upstairs. Naked brick walls, damp tarmac, old streetlamps. But when Kaitlyn glances up, we see a roof clothed with thick burgundy drapes, hanging horizontally as though gravity has shifted her axis.

The camera pans down, and Naida is far ahead, obscured by darkness. Kaitlyn hurries her pace. We reach another set of burgundy curtains, heavy velvet, and Naida takes a deep breath, then faces Kaitlyn.

"Best say nothing."

"I wasn't going to."

"Okay. Good." Another breath. "Good."

"What? You look panicked."

Naida shakes her head.

"Naida, what aren't you telling me?"

"This guy, Haji. He's...unpredictable."

"He runs an underground Mala nightclub. I got that."

"What I mean is—well, you remember I told you that a respectable Mala priest is called *Holi*?"

"Yeah?"

"And that a practitioner who works both sides—the respectable but also the less...savory, the kind of stuff that people who are desperate go for—is called a *Shyan*?"

"Yes. What is going on, Naida?"

"Well...Haji's not exactly a *Holi*...he's...a *Shyan*."

There is a pause during which Naida flinches.

"You said...you said the person doing this to me *was* a *Shyan*."

"Aye, but—"

"You said they're evil!"

"Nothing's truly black and white like that. The world's all...shades of gray and mucky browns. *Shyans* can choose evil...yes. But they can be a useful tool."

"We should leave."

"We need him. He knows about dirty practices. He knows about blood arts. He's expert in Gründi."

"I can't believe you only told me now! Was that the plan the whole time?"

"I...dunno."

Kaitlyn lets loose a guttural sound. "Let's just kick Mike in the bits and make him confess!"

"I doubt very much it's him."

"And how do you know this Mala guy will help you? How do you know he won't curse you or trick you? Could he hurt you?"

Naida steps back. "Are you worried about me?"

Kaitlyn mirrors Naida's retreating step. "I'm worried that you're being reckless. And Carly will suffer."

"He'd never hurt me."

"How do you know?"

Naida opens her mouth to reply, then turns back to the curtain.

"Jesus, Naida. I have a really bad feeling about this."

"Me too. Gorro guide me," she says, as she lifts the fabric aside and disappears into the folds.

"Shit. This is bad. This is *so* bad."

Kaitlyn follows.

[END OF TOP HAT CAMERA CLIP #1]

Diary of Kaitlyn Johnson

Sunday, 9 January 2005

The music was loud and boisterous—a pounding rhythm that jumped around the dim walls free of any physical constraints. It was like a wasp trapped inside a plastic tub, uselessly stinging, thumping, moving. The lights flashed like a nightclub, mimicking the rhythm of the beat,

<u>flash!</u>

<u>Flash!</u>

<u>Flash!</u>

Until I was so zoned out I could feel it pumping through my chest. It was so…alluring.

Here and there, people crouched around small fires or candles. Some played with what looked like little bones, some played with other things—things that used to be living. And then, some seemed to be playing with things that were <u>still</u> living. Snakes here, a small bird there.

With the twitch of a wrist, the bird was no longer living. So small a movement. Almost nothing. I just kept thinking, <u>Oh, God, what am I doing here? We're going to die.</u>

At one point, a commotion broke out in the center of the room, where I had noticed people swaying and humming. A girl, maybe fourteen, roared and raged, convulsing as she ripped at her white clothing. She started to spit and point her fingers, always shrieking, even cursing.

She yelled something unintelligible, spitting into the face of a young woman.

"What's going on?" I whispered to Naida.

"She's possessed. They've conjured an Olen into her as a vessel. It's considered a very great honor. But the Olen isn't happy with their offerings."

I swallowed my nausea and began to turn away. <u>We're going to die, we're going to die.</u>

"Atholl/Atholl Brose!" the girl shrieked. "RUM!"

A man ran to oblige her, and she threw her head back, drinking deeply from the proffered bottle of alcohol, and the liquid ran down her neck and dress, yellow like urine. Then she flung the bottle away and scratched the man's face. He cried and fell back, shaking, at the same moment the bottle smashed against the wall.

Naida kept walking. I kept walking. And the girl continued to shriek and curse. The tubby lady crying into her hands nearby seemed to be the girl's mother, and I thought, Some honor.

For a moment I was distracted by an old man huddled to the left, sitting alone. He held a green viper snake to his face and was murmuring to it in an intimate tone that made me shudder. The snake observed him like it might possibly understand. I felt my heart trip up on itself as I recalled the snake in my half dreams.

Reborn.

I'm a girl.

Are you?

I watched the man, and I watched the snake, and I waited for the snake to give me some sign of recognition or understanding, but there was none.

It was just a snake.

And then I thought, Are you with me, Voice? Are you with me, my Aka Manah? I couldn't feel him then, can't feel him now, but it doesn't mean he's gone. After all, if I heard him shouting when he was far away and whispering when he was near...doesn't it follow that his silence means he's...inside me?

Top Hat Camera Clip #2
Naida Camera Footage
Time Index Not Noted

Naida moves around the crowd and Kaitlyn follows. She bypasses the screaming, which has grown in pitch and volume, instead taking a narrow path of darkness to the back of the room. We follow because Kaitlyn does.

It doesn't take long to realize where she is headed. A man sits languidly in a large chair beside what appears to be an altar. It is decorated with flowers, fruit, seeds, broken mirror shards, bottles of liqueur, candles, baby dolls, and other statuettes.

He wears a vest shirt, revealing built arms covered in small scars in some obviously meaningful pattern. His earlobes are stretched to accommodate two large horn plugs, and he wears several talismans around his neck.

"Naida," he says in a deep voice. "Sister."

[END OF CLIP]

Sunday, 9 January 2005, Continued

Sister!

I stared at Naida, and if she knew I was thinking
WHAT THE HELL, NAIDA? she gave no sign. I felt him
before I saw him. I've never experienced that before.
It was like it ~~was~~ is with Carly when we transition,
except more ~~vivid~~ real. I could <u>feel</u> this guy, I could
smell his power—if power is a scent. I could taste it,
if it's a flavor, feel it like a kiss or a stab.

Haji looked so much like Naida. The same chin, the
same nose, the same pale skin…the same piercing, yet
almost colorless eyes that seem to see so much and feel
so little. Dead ocean eyes. I could barely look at him,
even as he stared at me.

He caught me staring at the little straight scars
along his arms.

"I cut power into my skin," he said, pointing.
"One for every sacrifice, and one in a perpendicular
direction for every grant."

There are more sacrifices than grants.

And he does have power. I could feel that too.

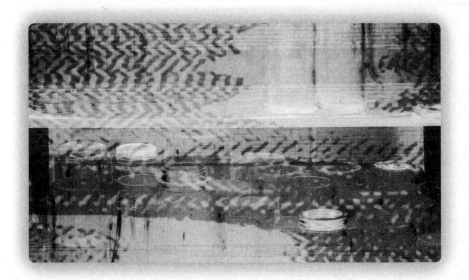

Naida curtsies low. "Haji, Brother, good health on your dwelling. I come seeking your blessing."

"I told you never to come here, *piuthar*." His voice is deep, tinged with a strong Scottish accent.

"I need help."

He dips his head, but his eyes, penetrating and bright, never leave her face. "Does Seanmhair know you are here?"

"No. And I want to keep it that way. Our grandmother has enough to worry about. Haji, I need a guide for what I'll be attempting very soon. I need advice."

"Advice is not free. And guidance"—he laughs—"is really not free."

"I know that, Brother. I also know that money is worthless."

"Seanmhair taught you something at least, since I left." He looks at Kaitlyn once more. "And you? Why are you here?"

Naida steps in front of Kaitlyn, blocking her brother from our view. "You'll be dealing with me. Respectfully."

"If you want advice, then my price is honesty."

Naida hesitates. "You have it."

"If you want my guidance as well…then the price is honesty from *her*. Your little *dautie*."

Naida stands silent for what seems too long. Eventually she says, "What of…supplies?"

"Cash. Money is not so worthless when supplies are concerned." He shrugs, gesturing helplessly. "*Sannt*."

"You think it greed to request money?"

He raises his hands, as though helpless. "What can be done, eh?"

"Fine."

Haji nods low. "It is a great shame I did not get to know you very well. I am sorry for that."

Naida shrugs. "You were gone before I had a chance to remember you." She hesitates. "I regret that too."

Haji nods, regarding her, then gets fluidly to his feet. "Follow me."

He turns and draws open the heavy curtain behind his chair. We follow him into a room a fraction as big as the entrance room, where the people writhe and moan. Here are the wares of his trade—rows of shelves holding jars of all shapes and sizes. The jars are old and murky, and it is difficult to see the contents of many, but numerous frames paused for detail reveal animal parts, root herbs, powders, and liquids of varying color. Here and there hang trickbag talismans and conjure bags.

Kaitlyn takes a superficial look at them before passing on with Naida into the back of the room, where Haji opens a door, this time with a key. He waits for Naida and Kaitlyn to go inside, and then shuts it firmly behind all three of them.

"Sit," he says, gesturing to a circular carpet in the center of the room. Naida and Kaitlyn comply, while Haji walks around lighting candles that throw a warm, flickering glow over the dim surroundings. The room seems dank.

Naida, as though responding to a glance from Kaitlyn, shakes her head and smiles slightly as if to say *everything is okay*.

"What is your name?" Haji asks from the darkest part of the room, where he is still lighting his candles.

"Carly," Naida says.

"My people call me Brother," Haji says, eyes boring into Kaitlyn. "*That* is the truth."

There is a small silence, then Kaitlyn shifts.

"Kaitlyn." Her voice is soft. "My name is Kaitlyn."

"She understands my price. You, it seems, do not. I will withhold one piece of information from you." He looks at Kaitlyn. "And to you, I will give one truth."

"I'm sorry—I..." Naida stammers. "Carly's who we're here about."

Haji, finished with his candles, sits down, facing the girls so that they are sitting in a circle. His expression is hard, closed, and expectant.

"Tell me what is needed, and I will offer both advice and guidance. Minus one piece of information."

"And one truth," Kaitlyn says, and Haji's eyes seem to sparkle as they turn on her.

Naida is about to speak when he holds up his hand.

"One more thing. After we are done, you must never return to this place. Never seek me out again. I have told Seanmhair to tell you this, and I have told you myself, long ago. Never come here, Naida, *dautie*. It is not safe."

Naida hesitates. "I swear it."

"Fine. Give me that hat, and we will begin."

Naida glances at Kaitlyn, hesitates, and then nods.

The camera wobbles as Kaitlyn removes her hat and hands it over. We spin around, stare up into Haji's stern face, and then the screen goes black.

[END OF CLIP]

Diary of Kaitlyn Johnson

Sunday, 9 January 2005, Continued

Haji is an intriguing man, Dee.

He told me not to tell anyone any of the things he shared with us, and so I can't tell you, Dee. I want to, please believe me, but I fear the price. Naida already lost us one piece of information for her accidental lie about who I was, and so I dare not risk losing anything more. I feel like he can see everything I'm writing as I write it.

But I will tell you this: He was speaking to me. <u>Me</u>, Dee. I knew it just as I knew he realized right away that Naida was wrong about my name being Carly. And at one moment—no more than a fraction of a second—as he stared at Naida, listening to her explain a vague version of what we need...I saw his mind turn to focus on me.

And clear as anything I have ever heard, his mind-voice reached out to me in the darkness.

<u>You know it won't be enough,</u> it said. <u>You know the end already. This is the truth.</u>

Top Hat Camera Clip #4
Naida Camera Footage
Time Index Not Noted

Naida's face appears, though the audio is distorted. "Ugh, finally."

Kaitlyn's voice from nearby. "I had to give it to him."

"Don't sweat it, sugar. You did the right thing."

The camera swivels towards Kaitlyn's head, then stops, facing Naida. Kaitlyn is wearing the top hat once more.

"Let's try to go over everything he said," Naida says, walking down what is now visibly the drive to Elmbridge High.

"Maybe we should wait until we're inside. Safer."

"No." Naida's voice is firm. "Now. I need to remember it now. I feel it slipping away like sand in an hourglass."

"Why didn't you tell me he was your brother?"

Naida shrugs. "It doesn't matter. We barely know each other. He's twelve years older than me—"

Naida breaks off as Kaitlyn's hand shoots out to grab her arm. They turn to see blue lights flashing in the distance.

"Do you see that?"

"Police!"

"Shit—what do we—"

"Get behind the trees," Naida says, pushing Kaitlyn away just as an officer walks through the side gate to the gardens.

Kaitlyn ducks behind a tree, and the camera goes dark, but the mic picks up the audio.

"Who's there?" calls a male voice.

"My name's Naida. What's going on?"

"Are you a student here?"

"Aye."

"It's not even five in the morning. What are you doing skulking around?"

"I'm not *skulking*. My cousin just dropped me off."

There is a pause and then footsteps. The voices begin to recede.

"Best to get to your room. The school is being searched, and everyone needs to be in their dorms."

"Oh. What's going on?"

"Just get to your room. Now."

"Yes, Officer."

Eventually the crunching of leaves and twigs underfoot fades and Kaitlyn exhales.

"Damn it," she mutters. "Lansing...you bitch."

She peeks from around the tree, and the road is empty and silent. She glances up the road where blue lights continue to flash, out across the field to the left, which is open and in plain view of the school, and then, finally, into the woodland on the right.

She sighs, then heads into the trees, which will eventually take her to the abandoned chapel. She will be there no less than twenty minutes before Ari Hait arrives. Together they will break into the oldest family crypt on the grounds and make love on the flat surface of the oldest stone tomb.

"I love you," Kaitlyn will say as the battery on the camera is fading.

"Go to sleep," will be Ari's reply.

[END OF CLIP]

Naida Camera Footage
Monday, 10 January 2005, 8:12 AM
Basement

"Okay," Scott says, thundering down the steps. "I found out something."

Kaitlyn, Naida, and Brett sit on the sunken mattress, eating cookies from a white packet.

"What?" Naida asks, sitting straighter. "About the police?"

"Hey, are those cookies?"

Naida rolls her eyes and hands him the bag. "Here."

"Cheers," he says as he rummages inside. "Points for simple carbs."

"*What* news?" Kaitlyn asks, after watching him scoff down three of them whole. "Scott!"

"Oh, yeah. So, apparently, it's something to do with Juliet."

Kaitlyn blinks. "Oh. God, we thought it was me!"

"Oh, it is. Heard two coppers talking in the kitchen this morning. Talking about how that Lansing woman found something in some tapes. Something about Juliet."

"*What?*"

"Shh! Didn't you hear me? The cops are everywhere. Gebus, Mary, and Joseph."

"Hang on," Brett cuts in. "What does Kaitlyn have to do with Juliet, though?"

Scott shrugs. "My guess is they think you knocked her off."

Kaitlyn stares at him.

"You know," he adds, swiping at his neck, "did her in."

"Yes, *thank you*," Naida drawls. "Gorro, they'll do anything, won't they? Absolutely anything to get you back."

"Well," Scott says, reasonably, "we already knew they wanted to talk to her about Juliet anyway. Breaking out of Claydon was probably not the best thing to do to prove innocence. They're saying Carly might have been the last one to see her."

"Yeah, for like two seconds, *and* she was passed out at the time, if you don't remember!" Brett says hotly.

"Yeah, all right, calm down, Panicky Annikey. I'm just *saying*."

"This is stupid," Naida says, getting to her feet. "We just have to hide Kaitlyn even more carefully. I want us to keep an eye on this stairway. Make sure it stays secret." She turns to Kaitlyn. "And I want you to start sleeping at *night*, and keeping hidden and alert during the day, all right?"

Kaitlyn doesn't reply, and Naida takes that for affirmation. She nods and then heads towards the stairs. "In the meantime, we have to keep going to class like nothing's wrong. So let's get moving, before the kitchen staff get in."

"As the lady commands," Scott says, taking out a handful of cookies before handing the bag back to Kaitlyn. "Right you are, love."

Brett smiles down at Kaitlyn after he gets up.

"Try to rest," he says. He nods, awkwardly, and then follows Scott out of the room.

From: AriHait558
To: RealxChick
Date: 10 January 2005
Subject: Status Update

How are you doing? I'm in the library—study hour. Every little thing is boring as hell without you.

Sincerely,

Rule Breaker

From: RealxChick
To: AriHait558
Date: 10 January 2005
Subject: Re: Status Update

Tired of waiting. Want to get moving. Scared about what "get moving" really means. Why are you emailing instead of studying? Don't you know I feel bad enough about all of you helping me without you failing on top of it?

Deeply Concerned,

Ghost Girl

From: AriHait558
To: RealxChick
Date: 10 January 2005
Subject: Re: Re: Status Update

Girl-Who-Is-Very-Real-to-Me,

Don't worry; I'm a genius. I can pass with my eyes closed. I'm curious about what the "get moving" will involve too. Has Naida said anything?

Suave Genius Prodigy

From: RealxChick
To: AriHait558
Date: 10 January 2005
Subject: Re: Re: Re: Status Update

We went to London to talk to someone. I can't really talk about it. He said not to. Besides, I'd rather not think about it.

PS—I can tell you that his name is Haji, and he's Naida's brother. He seems to know his stuff.

From: AriHait558
To: RealxChick
Date: 10 January 2005
Subject: Re: Re: Re: Re: Status Update

I might be able to help. You don't always have to do everything on your own. When will I see you again? When can we be alone?

From: RealxChick
To: AriHait558
Date: 10 January 2005
Subject: Re: Re: Re: Re: Re: Status Update

It's not that at all. I just really don't know what he said, if I'm honest. I'm so confused. I wish he hadn't taken Naida's top hat camera off us. I wish I could have filmed it. I would have liked to watch it back. It's weird how little of it I remember.

I'm not really feeling very sociable. Or sexy.

From: AriHait558
To: RealxChick
Date: 10 January 2005
Subject: Re: Re: Re: Re: Re: Re: Status Update

Shit. Bell rang. I'll check for your reply later. Don't worry about anything—it's not worth it. Naida knows what's going on, I'm sure. I guess we should just enjoy the calm, right?

Talk later,

A

84

After the meeting with Haji, the basement camera footage shows Kaitlyn staring at the wall day after day, barely touching the food she is given. It is unclear what has happened, since she does not write in her diary.

Ari visits almost every day. They kiss, but not much more. He asks her to come to the Forgotten Garden, but she refuses. One day he brings her a pile of wildflowers. She smiles faintly and turns back to the wall.

It is six days before Naida enters the basement with news that shocks Kaitlyn out of her depression.

Naida Camera Footage
Sunday, 16 January 2005, 11:45 PM
Basement

The camera clicks on as Naida storms into the room. Kaitlyn is sitting on the mattress, facing the wall.

"Come on," Naida demands. Above her, the light flickers ominously. "Get up."

Kaitlyn doesn't move, and for a moment, Naida won't give ground. Then she exhales and walks over to the mattress, flinging herself on top of it.

"It's taking longer than I thought to get everything in place," she mutters. "I've been keeping an eye on Mike, just in case. Apart from fondling Brenda in her room after lights-out, I haven't seen anything yet. And the ritual...it isn't my usual kind of thing. But it *will* happen. Trust me. You can't give up hope."

Kaitlyn doesn't reply.

"Anyway, there's a problem. There's some guy out there saying he knows you. Demanding to see you. He was actually in the main building today at reception. I thought he was a nut job, but then he turns up again now." She checks her watch. "It's close to midnight. Crazy-ass talking about pesky birds—"

Kaitlyn's head snaps sideways. "What?"

"Huh?"

"Birds?"

"Aye, he kept going on about some falcon shit—"

Kaitlyn is on her feet in a moment, running past Naida and out the door.

"What—Kait! You can't go out there!"

Naida sprints from the room after her. The camera footage doesn't end for an additional thirteen seconds.

[END OF CLIP]

Diary of Kaitlyn Johnson

Monday, 17 January 2005, 2:00 am
Basement

I'm sorry I've been ignoring you. It's just been too
hard.

Haji is in my head. I guess he's not going anywhere.
I would have explained if there was an answer.

But, Dee! Something wonderful happened! He's here!
John, my Viking! He's here! I feel like the old me—the
me that danced away the night in Masqued with John, who
ate the seeds he brought me and flew through the streets
with him at my side, the me who lived before my parents
died.

FREEDOM.

JohnJohnJohnJohnJohnJohnJohn!

My soul is singing, Dee.

Later

Ari was here. He's confused about John. He didn't say
much, but I could see it in his face the second he
arrived. Tightness in the lips, granite in the jaw.
Bruises in his eyes.

I kissed him, told him John was like my brother, and
he hugged me and said, "Everything is going to be okay."
Except I don't want Ari to hate John. My John. Ari
smelled my hair and then kissed me again.

We had sex on the cold, wet floor of the basement,
and the whole time, the dead girl was grinning in the
corner. It was only after he was gone and I was smoking
a cigarette (Carly, I'm sorry) that I remembered
Naida's camera had been filming the whole time.

[No such clip has ever been found.]

Diary of Kaitlyn Johnson

Tuesday, 18 January 2005, midnight
Basement

I won't hear these lies
Your words laced with arsenic
Poisonous deceit

It is unclear what lies "Kaitlyn" referred to in this haiku poem. Perhaps this is only an indication of the degradation of her mental stability, or perhaps it is something far darker. Something she chose never to share.

Naida Camera Footage
Wednesday, 19 January 2005, 5:00 AM
Basement

John and Kaitlyn sit on the mattress, facing each other. He is a tall, broad-shouldered youth with a thin beard and long hair tied back. He wears a Metallica T-shirt and a leather jacket. They sit in silence for a long time, Kaitlyn furtively glancing at John every few seconds.

"What?" he asks at last, grinning.

"You...you look so different. A beard?"

"Even more Viking now, right?" He rubs his face, smiling. "You look different too."

"How?" Her eyes are bright with anticipation, and she leans forward.

"You look thin, and..."

"What?"

He laughs, throws up his hands, then slumps. "Well, look how you're living."

Kaitlyn looks around, her expression difficult to read. "It's not that bad, really."

"You're sleeping on a moist mattress on the floor of a basement."

"It's okay. The mattress is good."

"God's sake, DH, you know what I mean. You're going to catch your death."

It is true that Kaitlyn looks drawn and pale.

She nods. "Yeah. It's not forever, though. Just until Lansing and the cops stop focusing on the school. Stop looking for me."

"They say you had something to do with a girl going missing."

"It's a lie. I was passed out when she decided to walk home. Naida was with me the whole time. So how could I have done anything to her?"

"This is…this is messed up, Kaitie. Maybe…maybe you should—"

Her body tenses. "What? Go back to Claydon?"

John looks at her, mute.

"Are you…are you *joking*?" She jumps to her feet. "Are you kidding me right now?"

"Calm down."

"No! No, I won't calm down! You're telling me I should go back to a nuthouse! You told me I didn't belong there—on the phone, you told me! You were lying?"

Kaitlyn's words become shrill, yet there is something more, because suddenly she turns away and half-collapses against the wall, her palms pressed against the dark surface to keep herself erect as she gasps for breath.

John hurries to her side and pulls her into a tight embrace, but she begins to gasp deeply and scream with every exhale.

"Shh, Kaitie, it's okay. Shh…"

Kaitlyn's screams turn into cries and then her cries become sobs.

"I'm sorry," John says. "I'm sorry. I'm an idiot. I'm sorry. *Shit*."

Kaitlyn's arms fall to her side, and she seems calm. "I have to go," she says, her voice empty. "Let me go."

John releases her and steps back. "I'm sorry, Kait."

She doesn't look at him. "I have to go now."

John steps aside and she stalks past him like a zombie. He stands staring after her for a few seconds, then he turns and punches the wall.

"*Damn it!*"

[END OF CLIP]

Diary of Kaitlyn Johnson

Wednesday, 19 January 2005, 11:12 pm
Basement

Naida's bind no longer holds.
  The Dead House is upon me once again.
  It's
                    A
                              Trickster.

  It's a thief.

Thought I saw Carly. Just for a second. She was
standing at the end of a long hall. Could I put my
joy into words, even though it lasted only a moment?
Probably not. But it doesn't matter, because when I ran
forward, the house bent around her and she was gone. I
could hear the walls laughing at me.
  Strange.
  Stranger still, when I opened my eyes, I could
still feel the house. Feel its solidity, feel its
putrescence, feel its floors, walls, and roof. Smell
the decay of it. I could feel the awareness of it, the
hunger. Until I realized that it wasn't the Dead House
I was feeling at all.
  It's the school.

Extract from the statement of Annabeth Lansing

Friday, 25 February 2005

Patients do construct mental settings that can help them escape their reality. When those settings become more real than reality, or bleed into reality, we have psychosis. Thoughts and emotions become so warped and impaired that external reality can no longer be accessed. It is a discontinuation in the belief of the person's own reality. That is psychosis.

Diary of Kaitlyn Johnson

Monday, 24 January 2005, 2:52 am
Attic

So here I am. Naida said she wanted to talk to me.
That it was important to do it up here, and she was
right. I finally understand. I think I do. I recorded
the conversation like I did before, so take it in, Dee.
I could use your opinion.

"This isn't Carly's handwriting," Naida said. She
was standing at the farthest wall, right by that big
stain, her hand on the wood.

"You don't know that—"

"I know my best friend's handwriting, Kaitlyn." She
turned to look at me, and I couldn't decide whether to
slap her or run from her. Before I could decide, she
whispered, "Write something for me."

"This is stupid."

She stepped towards me, holding out a marker. "Write
for me. Here, on the wall."

"No."

"Why?"

Cornered, I got up off the green sofa and walked
away. I don't know if I intended to leave. "I just
don't want to, okay?"

"You wrote this. All of this. The writing—it must
have taken days."

"I didn't write it." I needed to make her
understand, and being evasive wasn't going to help,
Dee. "Yes, it's my handwriting, but I didn't write it."

"I believe you." She said it so simply, and I got a
small glance of the Naida Carly loved so much. I think
I loved her too, a little, then. Just for her faith.

"I think…I think something else did." She choked
the words out. She sighed and rubbed her hands over her
face. She looked tired. Had she slept? "That house you
keep dreaming about? The, what was it, the Dead House?"

"Yeah."

"Did you know that in dream psychology a house represents the self? Your own mind?"

"Oh, hello, Dr. Lansing. You look different today. Get a ridiculous perm, by any chance?"

Naida managed a smile. "It's a simple fact. I think the Dead House <u>is</u> your mind. I think you were right when you said Carly was stuck in one of the rooms… with something. I think she was still in there, with you—only trapped. Unable to come out. But I don't think that's true anymore. I think she's gone."

Icy terror flooded my veins, and I wanted to make her stop, but I couldn't. "I think I saw her, though—the last time I was in the house. She was standing at the end of a long corridor, but then in the blink of an eye, the house had bent itself around her and she was gone."

"You sure it was her?"

I wasn't, Dee. Not at all.

"In the last dream," I whispered, "the house felt really empty. Not quite empty, but empty of her. So…no. But if she's not in the house, where did she go?"

"I don't know. Somewhere beyond you. I always told Carly that you two were something—something special. It was something I sensed, rather than knew. But I could tell that it put you in danger."

"You always spoke about dual souls," I said, remembering the countless times I had put her down.

Two souls in one body, blah blah.

Naida nodded. "I think there's a kind of doorway to that other place <u>inside</u> you. Like a portal. The door that the Olen used to steal her away. It's the same door he used to enter you in the first place. I think all those times you heard—what did you call it, your Voice?"

"Aka Manah."

"Aye, every time you heard him coming closer, he was entering you. Finding that door."

"Wait, so my Aka Manah is the Olen you keep talking about? They're the same?"

"I think so, yes."

"But I heard Aka Manah before the Halloween party."

"I think the Halloween party—the Olen board…I think it just made it worse. I sensed that you were already in danger before that. But anyway, it doesn't matter now. The thing is…I think…" Her voice trailed off.

She stood up and paced the room.

"You look like you have to tell me I have terminal cancer."

Naida stopped, pressed her lips together, then continued. "I think you're possessed."

I remembered the girl from the Mala nightclub, how she writhed and shrieked and scratched that man's face. I couldn't be…possessed. Not like that. Not like her.

"Somehow," Naida continued, oblivious to my screaming thoughts, "I think…I think Carly opened the doorway. I don't know if she knew she was doing it, but I think she did it all the same."

"Carly? Why do you think she did it?"

"Well…did you?"

"No," I snapped, irritation bubbling up inside me. "But maybe you did with that stupid Olen board of yours at Halloween. Or with your little Mala group last year, I don't know!"

Naida stared at me for a moment, and I thought she looked a little pale.

"I'm not accusing her, Kait. I'm just trying to find answers." She took a breath. "It just seems likely that a door like that could only be opened from within. Anyway, it doesn't change the fact that I think something's in there with you."

"Possessed. Possessed like needing an exorcist, or like that crazy girl at the club? Possessed like, like—" I could feel myself panicking.

"It's okay, sugar. All I mean is…If I'm right, then I can't do this ritual alone. You have to help me. You have to take me into yourself. Let me into that Dead House of yours. We have to find that door, the door Carly was taken out of. And then"—she paused, swallowed—"then we have to go through it."

12:00 pm

I slept a little, I think. I'm not sure anymore.

Possessed.

I am <u>possessed</u>.

The word keeps ringing around in my head like an echo bouncing off invisible walls and coming back to me. Some<u>thing</u> is inside me. Inside my head. Can that thing read these words? Can he know them from my mind before I've even written them down?

Is the thing her? The dead girl? Aka Manah, the snake, the dark shape, the Olen? Are they all one and the same? A single entity, trying to invade me? Trying to confuse me?

I feel so violated. So <u>dirty</u>.

And what about this "door"? If it's a door leading <u>out</u> of my mind, then where does it go? What does my mind have access to? Some dark realm I can't remember? Right inside my head?

Is there a chance I could slip through it, by accident, and lose myself in the process?

Is the thing inside me getting closer? Could he bring even more vile things back with him? I've been reading Carly's journal to make myself feel better. Her early entries, when things were still normal. I've started tearing out the pages. I'm going to stick them in here. Keep them safe.

Torn-Out Page from the Diary of Carly Luanne Johnson
Undated

I think I'm half and half. HA! I just realized what I wrote!
Half and half, not in the Kaitlyn sense, but in the sense that
I'm two different sorts of people. Because I hate company
sometimes, because I'm shy and quiet and awkward. I want to
be left alone. But then when I _am_ left alone for any length
of time, I get lonely and I need to find company. That's only
been the case since Naida. She's brought so much life into
my life. How funny. I just read that back. The only downer to
needing company is, well, Brett. He's just always around. And
I just want to spend time with Naida. I don't even mind Scott,
because he makes her happy and he makes me laugh, but
Brett is always here...always just a little too close.

Naida Camera Footage
Monday, 24 January 2005, 11:00 PM
Naida's Dorm Room

Naida positions the camera in its customary place on her desk, then she sits on her bed facing it. Her hands are shaking.

"Something keeps telling me to call Haji." She wrings her hands, but they still shake. "I want to. I want to hand this over to him and let him take control. But he'll try to stop me. And I'm so scared I might even let him."

She covers her face, and when she pulls back her hands, her cheeks are wet with tears.

"If I fail, I could lose them all," she whispers, her eyes wide with panic. "I could lose Carly forever, and Kaitlyn, and Ari and Brett and Scott—there are five lives in my hands! What if it goes wrong? What if the *Shyan* is too strong, what if I'm not good enough— Oh, Gorro, Mother Karrah! Bring me to the light and hold me in your hand."

Naida inhales deeply, then exhales and wipes her face. She is still shaking, but she balls her hands into fists.

She reaches forward and switches off the camera.

[END OF CLIP]

Naida Camera Footage
Monday, 24 January 2005, 11:26 PM
Basement

"You'll open your eyes. You'll be in a—" Naida breaks off and glances at Kaitlyn, who is sitting beside her. Scott and Brett are nearby, while John and Ari are hugging the walls. The room, normally lit by the unreliable bare bulb above them, is illuminated by the dancing flames of six black candles.

"It's a house," Kaitlyn says. "It'll be a room. You'll be in a room."

"Right. I want you to check every single room of that house. Look for some kind of doorway. You'll sense that it doesn't belong. I'm not sure how—maybe it'll look out of place, maybe you'll just know it doesn't feel right."

"This is mental," Scott mutters under his breath. Naida looks pointedly at him, but then her expression softens and she takes his hand.

"Everything's going to be okay. Once we find that door, you call me. *Don't* go through it. We don't know exactly where it leads—maybe some kind of other world—but we think Carly was taken out that way. If you see it, yell like there's no tomorrow. I'll come quick as lightning, and that'll be it for you."

Scott leans forward. "What about you?"

She swallows and glances at Kaitlyn. "We have to go through the doorway. We have to find Carly."

Brett, who has been sitting silently up to this point, blows air through his lips. "You're asking us to believe something...huge."

"It's real," Kaitlyn says. "Brett, it's *real*. I need your help."

He stares at her for a moment and then smiles, the crystal blue of his eyes melting into something warmer as he looks at her.

She smiles uncertainly and looks toward Ari, who is watching the display impassively.

"I don't think I can do this," John says. He steps away from the wall and crosses his arms.

Kaitlyn looks at him and then into her lap.

"That's okay," Naida says. "We need a lookout. You stay behind and make sure no one comes down here."

He looks at Kaitlyn for a full ten seconds before he nods assent.

"Well, I'm coming," Ari says, and he walks over to Kaitlyn and sits beside her. He takes her hand and rubs it between his own. "What do we have to do to...uh...get there?"

Now it's Naida's turn to look uncomfortable. She steels herself, then removes the cover from a box that has been sitting to her left. It is a wire mesh cage, and within it slumbers a plump black rooster.

Scott's eyes widen, and he turns slowly to Naida. "You're not... babe—"

"I have to..."

He shakes his head, raising his voice. "No, no—"

"I don't want to...but..."

"What are you talking about?" John asks.

Scott gets to his feet. "I'm not going to let you pull some Mala bullshit, okay? You told me it was dangerous!"

"This is the only way!" Naida yells again. "I'll do anything to get my friend back, do you understand? *Anything!*"

Her voice rings around the room and then distills into a low hum before dissipating into nothingness.

Scott frowns. "What happened to you?" He rubs his eyes and then goes to kneel before Naida. His voice is low. "Naddie, please. You can't *kill* something. *You* can't. However this works, you can't take something's life away—it would change you. *Please,* babe. There has to be another way."

There is a small silence before Kaitlyn shifts. "I don't want to hurt anyone," she says softly. "Or any creature. I just want my sister back."

"It has to be a sacrifice," Naida says. "A trade."

"Okay, fine. We'll all give something." Scott pulls out a necklace from behind his T-shirt, removes it, and kisses it. "Here."

"Your Saint Peter..." Naida whispers. Scott puts it in her fingers. "But your grandmother gave it to you before she died."

He shrugs. "Sacrifice."

Naida's face crumples as she looks down at it in her hand.

"I don't have anything on me," Brett says.

Scott looks up at him and there is a hint of a smile on his face. "Hair. That perfect blond hair. Cut some of it off."

"Seriously?"

"Yeah, it's perfect," Scott says. "Something beautiful that you care *way* too much about."

Brett folds his arms and stares at the wall. Scott rolls his eyes and looks at the others. "Well?"

By the time everyone has finished, Brett is missing some hair from the left side of his head, Naida's necklace is gone from around her neck, Kaitlyn's anklet is gone from her ankle, and all the items, including Scott's Saint Peter, are held carefully in Ari's round bowler hat.

Naida glances at the rooster. "Now what the hell am I supposed to do with it? I can't exactly sneak it back into my cousin's garden."

"Roast it later," Brett says, grinning.

Scott snorts. "I'm not eating that thing. We can take it back later. I'll go with you, Naids, okay?"

She nods at him, seems relieved. "Okay."

[END OF CLIP]

Tuesday, 25 January 2005, early morning
Basement

There was time to turn back, Dee. There was so much time.

Naida knelt before a bowl surrounded by seven black candles, whose wax dribbled onto the concrete like some kind of awful premonition. To her left sat the caged rooster, and to her right, a thick book with ancient, curling pages. In her hand she held the knife—the knife that she had planned to cut the bird's neck with. Scott and Brett sat on either side of her, protectors. Ari sat beside me—my rock.

John refused to come.

I suppose I understand.

There was so much time to turn back. But none of us did. Nobody stopped Naida as she began the ritual, setting the items—and Ari's hat—aflame.

The house crashed down on top of us, as if it had known we were coming. It was more broken than I remember, more rotten, more alive. A brutal, enraged storm was brewing inside, and low clouds hung over the ceiling, threatening rain.

"Blimey," said Scott, stumbling backwards. "It's real."

His voice echoed through the house and came back at us with more force.

Brett looked too stunned to move. "It stinks," he managed.

Ari just peered around, his beautiful mouth open in surprise.

"This is your mind?" he said.

I felt humiliation wash over me.

This <u>was</u> my mind.

"Split up," Naida <u>said.</u>

"Find the door," Naida said.

"We'll go in pairs," Naida said.

God, Dee. I can't do this—

I need them to tell me what's happening. I can't keep waiting like this.

Brett went upstairs, and Scott followed a moment later to find the attic. Ari went to find the basement. Naida and I stood alone once they had gone, her staring at the reality around her, and me taking her reaction in.

"You weren't kidding, were you?" she said at last, and the clouds that churned above us seemed to roar with laughter.

"Let's get this over with," I muttered, heading down the ground-level corridor.

Dee, we looked. The house was just playing with us. The corridor elongated, bent, and twisted until we were walking in circles. We passed an empty picture frame on the left wall, broken down the middle, and later, the same frame was on the right wall. Then it was under our feet and we were walking along the walls themselves.

The clouds broke open with a roar, and rain spat down on and around us, hot, then cold, then sticky, then slimy.

We trudged through it all, and only ended up back where we started.

"I suppose this is the part where the walls start raining blood?" Naida said drily.

I walked over to the wall and placed my hand upon it. Where I touched, the wall was dry. The floor beneath our feet grew soft, like wet earth, and we began to sink into the wood.

THE HOUSE IS MINE.

I gasped, and stared at Naida. "Did you hear it?"

Her lips tightened, and I thought I saw a flash of anger in her eyes. Maybe she was about to say something. Maybe I was about to say something. Maybe I was going to make a suggestion. Maybe I was going to suggest we leave, quit, give up.

That's when I saw the dead girl, up on the banister

behind Naida—she was pointing at us with her mouth wide
open, her teeth cracked and jagged. She was all silent
screams. And where she pointed, behind me, I felt the
House shift. I saw Naida react to whatever was behind
me…I saw her mouth open in horror…I saw the snake
reflected in her eyes. I turned. Out of the sinking
wooden floor reared a giant snake—the green viper—mouth
open, ready to strike down on me. I couldn't move, I
was stuck in the quickwood of the floor. But then I felt
movement. Naida, running, right at the snake, directly
in the path of its yawning mouth. Naida, running to put
herself in front of me. Directly in the path of those
brilliant white teeth.

The camera clicks on at the same moment that Kaitlyn reaches forward with her right hand across the bowl that is now charred and smoking, her terrible cry—"*Naida!*"—ringing through the room. The others jolt into awareness and look around with foggy expressions.

Naida sits with her mouth frozen open, her eyes huge in her face. Her eyes rotate towards Kaitlyn, and her expression is one of grief and horror.

"Kaitie," she whispers, before her expression hardens and she reaches for the knife beside Ari's bowler hat, grips her tongue between her left fingers, and with a violent, sickening motion, saws off her tongue.

She flings it across the room, where it lands with a soft slap, and then she falls to the floor, twitching.

Chaos erupts.

Scott is the first to reach her, pulling her into his arms. "Call an ambulance!" Spurts of blood jump from her mouth, and she gurgles.

Ari stares at her, seemingly unable to move. Brett grabs his own hair and yells, "Shit! Shit! Shit!" It is John, standing guard by the door, who runs up the stairs.

"What should I do?" Scott yells. "What the *fuck* should I do?"

Ari blinks, shuts his mouth, and hurries over to them.

"Flip her over," he instructs. "She's choking on her blood."

Scott turns the seizing Naida over, and the blood pumps from her mouth in spurts.

Ari grabs the cloth that lies near the chicken cage. "Shove this in her mouth. Hard!"

"She's bleeding to death!" Kaitlyn cries. She stands near the armoire, arms folded over her chest. She looks more like Carly than ever. "She saved me...she saved me..."

John returns. "They're coming. They said to stuff her mouth with cotton, but I couldn't find any."

"Help me get her up the stairs," Ari says, starting to haul Naida up.

"Don't move her!" John yells.

Scott, crying, begins to help Ari lift her, then pauses, looking at John.

"We can't have them down here," Ari says firmly. "Now, *help me.*"

John swears, then runs forward, lifting Naida into his arms. He runs up the stairs with her, and Scott follows.

Ari turns to Kaitlyn. "I'm sorry," he says, and then he shoves her backwards three sharp times. "You can't be seen!"

"Ari—"

With a final shove, she falls back against the armoire. Ari pulls open the door and pushes her inside.

"Stay there," he snaps, then slams the door and locks it.

He runs out of the room, leaving behind a noisy wardrobe, rocking back and forth, shaking as Kaitlyn screams.

[END OF CLIP]

PART V

WHO ARE... I?

I became insane, with long intervals of horrible sanity.

—Edgar Allan Poe

Because I could not stop for Death—
He kindly stopped for me—
The Carriage held but just Ourselves—
And Immortality.

—Emily Dickinson

On 25 January 2005, at 1:46 AM, Naida Chounan-Dupré was admitted to Musgrove Park Hospital with severe blood loss, shock, and a severed tongue. She entered the operating room at 2:05 AM and was transfused with five units of blood, type AB positive. Coma was induced for three days. The use of her tongue was permanently lost.

Diary of Kaitlyn Johnson

Tuesday, 25 January 2005, 2:24 am
Basement

Her tongue is still on the floor. They left it behind.

2:36

Torn between fury and fear. Want to hunt down the Shyan and slit his throat. Want to throw myself blindly into the Dead House and <u>will</u> my way to the gateway. I don't even know what to look for.

Terrified to try.

Someone took the chicken.

Lost them. Lost Carly. Now Naida too. I keep hurting the people around me.

He probably saved me, Dee.

Yes, I know he locked us in a cupboard.

Yes, I know that too.

But if he hadn't, I'd be back in Claydon, wouldn't I? Probably in isolation on the high-security ward. Maybe even prison. Can they arrest you for breaking out of the hospital? And that's without what they're saying about Juliet…

I would never hurt anyone.

Besides, they would have found a way to blame me for Naida too. And I couldn't live with any more of their accusations and lies. Still…when he pushed me in like that and locked the door…when I realized he was going to leave me in there while he got Naida to the hospital with the others…I'll admit to a certain…annoyance.

But he was protecting me. Protecting us.

Protecting the thing inside me too.

3:12 am

I need news.

What's happening?

Is Naida okay?

I can't believe what I saw…what she did. What *it* did. She saved me. She *saved* me. She sacrificed her voice for me. How can I ever repay that? She's a saint.

I don't know—I don't bloody know! Shhh! I hear something—

Naida Camera Footage
Tuesday, 25 January 2005, 3:14 AM
Basement

Footsteps echo in the room as someone hurries down the stairs, their
heavy, condensed breath following like a trail. The armoire door is broken,
kicked out from the inside.

"Carly?"

Kaitlyn, who has been kneeling in the corner over her journal, looks
up as Brett rounds the corner from the stairwell. All we see of him is his
dark outline, trapped in the shadows of the darkest part of the room. The
meager lightbulb flickers above him.

"Anything?" Kaitlyn asks, closing her book and sliding it behind her.
"News? Is she okay?"

"They were operating when I left."

"Can they...fix it?"

He steps closer, out of the shadows, and Kaitlyn gets to her feet, but
doesn't move closer. Brett seems to teeter, wanting to step forward.

"No. She'll...she's lost it. I...What the hell happened in here, Carly?"

"Kaitlyn."

He nods. "Sorry."

"You saw. You saw what happened."

He grabs his hair and shakes his head. "I don't know—she...she cut off her own tongue...she almost died."

"There was something in the house. I didn't see it...it was going to do something to me...maybe kill me? I don't know. Can the thing in the house live if the house itself—me—is gone? But it was going to get inside me maybe, control me? And Naida...Naida, she—she put herself in the way. It got her. I...I don't know why she cut out her...maybe the thing made her...or maybe she did it to protect us from it...maybe it was trying to possess her? Use her against us? And she stopped it. I...I don't know, Brett. I just don't know!"

She is shrill.

"This is mental," he says, then yells, "*This is insane!*"

"You didn't believe it was real, did you?" She gives him a withering look. "*Did you?*"

He sighs, paces the room. "I don't know. I don't bloody well know. That house—the...*I don't know!*"

"You knew something could happen. Naida explained it. She told us it was risky—"

"Yeah, but I didn't know it was—" He breaks off, turns to face her. "I didn't know it was...that you...Carly..."

"You thought I was insane? Thought I was making it up? That I really *am* Carly but that you had to humor me or something? That crap you spun about me being different at night was just—"

Her words are cut off as Brett leans forward, and we can assume he is kissing her, since his arms lift and disappear as though around her small torso. "I thought...I thought I was helping you by letting you think..." Something in the shadows moves, and the camera adjusts to the change in light as Ari, apparently having descended the stairs, hurls himself at Brett.

"Get your filthy hands off her—" An impact and a grunt.

Surprised, Brett is thrown off balance, and with him, Kaitlyn. She hits the wall with a small cry; she grabs her elbow gingerly and watches as Ari tackles Brett to the ground, punching him repeatedly in the face.

"Ari! Ari stop it!"

She throws herself on Ari, and with some effort, she manages to wrench him away from the cowering Brett. She bends low over her arms.

"You touch her again, and I'll rip your lungs out!" Ari yells.

Brett spits blood from his mouth and wipes his lips. "You're psycho, man. She can bloody well kiss whoever she wants!"

Kaitlyn shakes her head desperately at Brett. She pulls Ari gently into the opposite corner and wraps her injured arms around him. After a moment, panting heavily, his arms come around her in return. Brett gets to his feet and glares at Ari, whose back faces the camera, then shakes his head and leaves, running loudly up the stairs and slamming the door at the top.

"You kissed him," Ari says a few moments later, pulling away from her. His voice is low, and Kaitlyn looks startled.

"Not really. I'm…Ari, I'm not used to being *seen*. Noticed. I'm…He kissed me. I was stunned."

He lifts his hands and cups her cheek. "I don't want to lose you. I want you to be with me—I love you."

She nods. "I'm sorry. I'm sorry, Ari."

He steps away from her and faces the camera, but his expression is obscured by shadows.

"How is she?" Kaitlyn asks at last. "How's Naida?"

"She's alive."

"Thank God. Will she…*stay*…alive?"

He nods. "Likely."

Kaitlyn, whose calm control seems to have been a carefully managed mask, covers her face and begins to cry. "Thank God, thank God, thank God," she mutters, over and over. "Thank you, thank you—I'm so sorry."

Ari moves to the other end of the room. "Kaitlyn…what was that with Brett? Do you…like him?"

Kaitlyn wipes roughly at her face. "He was just…reaching out, I guess. He was just scared. He needed comfort. It was stupid, but understandable. He…he liked Carly. I know he liked Carly."

"He has a thing for *you*."

Kaitlyn laughs shallowly. "Yeah. I guess so. I didn't kiss him, Ari. It's not like that."

"You just let him kiss you."

Kaitlyn shrugs. "He needed a friend."

"I need a friend."

Kaitlyn smiles and walks over to him, standing on her tiptoes to kiss him.

[END OF CLIP]

Diary of Kaitlyn Johnson

Tuesday, 25 January 2005, 6:00 am
Basement

It's over for them. I can't ask—

I won't ask for any more.

Diary of Kaitlyn Johnson

Wednesday, 26 January 2005, 11:59 pm
Forgotten Garden

Haji is angry. Angry with me, angry with Naida.

We arranged to meet at night, in the Forgotten Garden. Here. I taped everything so I wouldn't get it wrong.

Scott and Brett are at the hospital with Naida, but John wanted to come, and so did Ari. I didn't think it was a good idea for them to be here…not at first. Not at all, maybe. So I decided to meet Haji alone. Ari didn't like it—didn't want to hear of it. But I insisted. Me. Haji. Alone. I had to explain to him what happened. I had to tell him how sorry I was. I don't know what I was expecting.

He stepped through the broken, rusted gates like a towering shadow, and I knew that of anything I might get from him, forgiveness wasn't it. That was when I pressed Record. He was bigger than I remembered. The kind of big that makes you feel like a tin can at the foot of a skyscraper. I wanted to step away, hide my face—but I forced myself to stay rigid and calm.

"You have caused many problems."

I didn't deny it.

"You have a Shyan working you."

"How did you—"

"Naida's ritual. I found her worker's book. I read what she was planning."

"You knew we were doing something dangerous when we came to see you."

"Not that a Shyan was conjuring against you. Not that you planned to risk your souls on this stupid mission of yours. Naida is a foolish child for helping you."

I swallowed. "Naida's a hero. You don't look like the kind of person who would understand that. My sister's _life_ is at risk. Her soul is _gone_. Naida was helping me get it back."

"If an Olen holds her soul, he won't simply give it back."

"I know. We made a sacrifice. A trade."

A scoff and a mutter. "Gorro have mercy. I sent you off thinking Naida knew what she was doing. I was wrong."

"We did what we could, okay? Naida did what _she_ could."

"Naida is a _child_," he snapped, and his voice was much louder. So. He _did_ care, after all. "She doesn't know how to communicate with a malevolent Olen. They are a destructive force only. To make them listen _requires_ destruction. With a Shyan working them—and you—it's a wonder you're still alive."

"Naida kept me safe—"

"Naida was stupid! Risking herself for you. For someone not of her blood, not of Fair Island!"

"You sent us off knowing something was up! We practically told you everything! _You_ let us go!"

"An asking ritual, Naida said. A request. Guidance for her friend Carly. Nothing more."

"She's a _saint_! She helped me when no one else would. She told me what was going on. Explained things. She could have let me rot away in a psychiatric hospital and lived her life free and whole. But she came to me, she saved me—she risked everything! So if you're going to trash her when she's lying in a hospital bed, then you can just fuck off! I'll do this alone."

I started to walk away, I was almost crying. God, you can even hear it on the tape. Halfway between panting and sobbing.

"Wait," he called, but I didn't. "I said, wait!"

I stopped then, trying to swallow down the emotion, and turned as he walked towards me.

"You're strong." He paused, assessing me with those ocean eyes. "That's useful."

"Are you going to help me or not?"

"It seems I have no choice. You will do this alone if you have to, won't you?"

I nodded.

He muttered something so quietly I didn't catch it. Then he said, "Foolish child. Playing with fire. If you die, the fault is yours."

His words didn't scare me. "I'd die for Carly."

"Good!" he snapped. "Because you probably will."

Thursday, 27 January 2005, 1:00 am
Basement

What is wrong with me? I don't understand. John just left, and…I feel like crap. He came to comfort me, put his arms around me like a protective cage, and kissed me on the top of my head. I should have felt safe.

But something weird happened. His arms suddenly felt too firm, too tight…I was trapped. He was containing me, and I didn't like it. I felt a surge of panic, and when he released me, a smile on his face, I thought the panic would fade. But it didn't.

It hasn't.

Dee, I'm terrified of John. My John. And I have no idea why. Could it be that there is something I don't remember? Something from Chester that I've forgotten? To do with him? Did something happen? Is that what those flashes mean…with the hand and the blood and his face?

Why am I so afraid of him? Why do I fear him coming again like I fear Haji's upcoming ritual? It's terror.

Mortal terror.

Naida Camera Footage
Thursday, 27 January 2005, 9:00 PM
Basement

Haji stands in the center of the room, arms folded. Brett and Ari file in from the stairs and stand off to the side, watching Kaitlyn and each other. John follows, spots Kaitlyn, and smiles.

"My name is Haji. I'm Naida's brother. I don't want to be here." He looks at each face in turn. "But you've opened a door, and it needs closing. If I allow it to be left open, it will be Naida who pays for it. I ask you now—*all of you*—to reconsider your decision to be involved tonight."

Scott enters last. His usual joviality has been replaced with something more solid and reserved.

"Scott," Kaitlyn says, stepping forward, "is Naida—"

"She's resting," he says, his voice firm and hostile. "She wanted me to come here. I wouldn't have otherwise."

Kaitlyn swallows and introduces Haji.

Scott nods at him once, and the anger and resistance on his face seem to satisfy the Mala priest.

"I'm trying to convince you to leave. Don't get any more involved in this. As you've seen, it is no game."

"We're not leaving," Ari says, stepping close to Kaitlyn.

John shifts. "I think we're all agreed that leaving isn't an option. But, for my sake, would you mind telling me what exactly we intend to do?"

Haji regards them all. "You are all so stupid," he mutters. "Very well. Kaitlyn and I will be performing the same ritual as was performed by Naida."

"Are you joking?" Scott snaps. "Did you not hear what happened to Naida? You want a repeat of that?"

"There will be no repeating that fiasco. I will get us into Kaitlyn's mind—this Dead House you described," he adds, in Kaitlyn's direction. "We will *all* go. We will search the rooms—all of them—for the door that leads beyond her. You will know it if you find it." His eyes move around every face. "If you do—do *not* go through it. Call out, and keep calling until we all come to you."

"Are we seriously doing this again?" John demands. "Kait?"

She nods. "I'm seeing this through until the end."

"I wish you'd just leave it," he mutters.

"No standing off to the side this time," Haji says, looking at Kaitlyn. "*You* are the ritual. *You* need to take control."

"I'm ready."

"Good. Sit down." Haji reaches into a pouch on his hip, withdraws what looks like flour, and pours it into a sigil on the floor, one mirrored in the charm around his neck.

John steps up to Kaitlyn. "Are you really going to do this after what happened? After Naida?"

"Yes. I told you." She takes his hand and squeezes it. "Are you with me?"

"I'm in," Brett says from across the room.

"I guess that's the answer, then," John says "I won't leave you alone."

Kaitlyn blinks, then turns away. "What do you need?" she asks Haji, who is sitting cross-legged on the floor in front of a wooden bowl. Inside he has placed three eggs and a sprig of sage.

"Your blood." He puts out one hand to Kaitlyn. In the other, he holds a knife with a curved blade.

Kaitlyn holds out her hand without hesitation. Her sleeves hide the stitched-up mess of her forearms.

"Hold on a minute," Brett interrupts. "Is this wise? Her blood? Isn't that...extreme?"

"And Naida wanting to kill that rooster before wasn't extreme?"

"Yeah, but her *blood*? That's, like, bordering on Satanism or something."

Haji gives him a distasteful once-over. "You just pray she won't need to give her life."

"Hang on, *what*?" John says.

"This is mental, Carly—Kaitlyn. It's just...too much. Naida nearly died, and now your blood? I think maybe it's asking too much." Brett speaks quietly.

"Just get out if you're not going to help." This utterance, delivered with sharp venom, comes from Ari, who steps off the wall and walks forward. "Cowards, all of you. Piss off and let us work. Or stay and actually help by shutting your gob-holes."

This silences all of them, but Brett is red in the face and his lips are a thin white line. John merely shrugs and folds his arms.

In all the commotion, no one noticed Haji slice Kaitlyn's palm or the blood trickling into the wooden bowl on top of the eggs and sage sprig.

"It's done." Kaitlyn looks around. "Can we get on?"

"Bloody hell," Scott mutters, but backs off.

"Keep going," Ari says. "Everyone sit around the bowl."

Each of them complies, and silence falls.

Haji cuts open his own hand with the already-bloodied blade. "Respect, Gorro, spirits, *Olen*. We weaken ourselves for you, we show you our good intentions. Accept this blood sacrifice and hear our bargain. Gingerroot for spice, beetroot for sweetness, tobacco leaf for pleasure, athair lus, the snakeroot, for connection." He bows low after adding the items. "Hear us, great spirit of the *Olen*, hear us, Mother Karrah, Father Gorro. We call on your aid to help us find a lost soul. Bless us. Let us pass and bring our passengers with us. Here is the vessel." He touches his bloodied palm to Kaitlyn's head. "Let us enter."

He leans forward and lights a rope of mixed dry herbs, and smoke begins to plume. "Close your eyes," he instructs them.

No movement is seen for five full minutes, at which time the motion-activated camera switches off.

[END OF CLIP]

Diary of Kaitlyn Johnson

Thursday, 27 January 2005, 11:59 pm
Chapel Confessional

I can still feel them, lingering in my mind. The scent
of them, almost…their imprint.

Haji said, "Close your eyes."

And then I felt a pull. I was dizzy, felt it in my
throat, and then smelled the house fade in, growing up
all around me from an unknown hell like dead creeper
vines, blossoming with deadly blooms.

I opened my eyes, and they were all there with
me again. And I saw what knowing me had done to
them. Brett's pristine grace had been replaced with
a bruising around the eyes, a lankness in the hair.
Scott, once such a joker, looked around the house with
hard eyes and a set mouth. John, once my escape, now
seemed as much of a trap to me as the house, but how
could I trust that? How could I trust my mind, which
seems so much of a trick these days—a Dead House of
a mind that even I can't control? I couldn't ask him
to leave, though I wanted to. He was my John…and I am
still terrified of him. The only constant, the only
unchanged thing, was Ari, standing beside me, holding
my hand.

"This," Haji said, "is Kaitlyn's mind. Her self."

"I remember," Brett breathed.

"Let's split up," Haji suggested, taking control.

"No," I insisted, right away. "We won't do that
again. Scott with Ari, Brett with John, me with Haji.
No one goes anywhere alone."

I said this, even though I knew the house was empty.
Deathly
Silently
Absolutely
Empty.

Haji looked at me for a moment and conceded with a slow nod. "Very well. There is no way to keep time here. When you hear this"—he broke off, placed two fingers in his mouth, and blew out a shrieking whistle that echoed down every hall—"then come back here."

We went into the Empty House.

It was very strange, Dee. So different from the first time. The house was solid and real, cold and empty. I could feel them all walking around inside it—inside me. Was this how it was supposed to be the first time? Did Haji do something that Naida failed to do? When Scott and Ari entered a room, it was a memory, and I felt them there too.

I am twelve. A letter sits on Carly's table in front of me.

Happy birthday, Kaitie. We are twelve today! One day I'm going to give you a big hug, and we'll walk in the sunlight together. I love you. Xoxo

Ari and Scott read the letter too.

When Brett and John enter a room, I feel them there.

I am fifteen. I am looking at the Viking dancing with a girl in a raven mask, and I am angry that she gets to touch him and kiss him, and I am angry it isn't me instead. I thought maybe I was special. The girl in his nighttime world, like he is the boy in mine, but he has plenty of girls. Any developing idea of romance I

have is murdered then and there. After that, the walls
come down. I remember the words he'd spoken to me only
moments before—I won't hurt you. And you won't hurt me.
We'll do it by being totally honest with each other.
We'll never lie or hide or deceive. Not like them.
It'll be our pact. I wonder if this is his honesty.

And I see John watching, the John now in the Dead
Room of this memory, and I feel him blanch as he
realizes what he's looking at. I see Brett scowl and
wander through the crowd, nothing but a wisp.

I feel them plodding all over my memories. They linger,
like a scent. And it's as if they've always been with
me.

And the house
Is
Still
Empty.

Basement footage coinciding with events shortly after the ritual with Haji has never been found.

I know Kaitie has spoken to him a few times at night, because she told me. She didn't give an opinion, just mentioned it like she'd mention a passing rain cloud. Completely without opinion or judgment. And if I were to tell her how I'm feeling, she might overreact and do something.

I saw him at lunch today, just staring at me. I was so uncomfortable that, even though I resolved to eat at least half of the sandwich, I couldn't touch it. When Kaitie asks me why, what can I say? Brett was watching me, and it made my skin crawl? Yeah, right.

I can't tell Naida either, because Scott is Brett's friend, and it would be weird to admit that Brett makes me feel—

I've seen him following me between classes too. Yesterday after English, he followed me for ages. I had to duck into the girls' bathroom to avoid him, and I was late for Religious Education, but I didn't mind so much because he was gone when I came out. I wish I was brave enough to tell him to go away. Why does he watch me like this?

Naida Camera Footage
Friday, 28 January 2005, 5:51 AM
Basement

The camera has already been on for some minutes before Haji enters. Kaitlyn, tossing and turning in her sleep and moaning deep in her throat, sits up violently as he descends the stairs.

"Who's there?" Kaitlyn whispers.

"Haji. Are you alone?"

Kaitlyn exhales and the sheets ruffle. "What are you doing here? You scared me."

"Are you alone?"

"Yes, why?"

He comes closer, stands by the edge of the bed. "I wanted to talk to you without the others. There is something you should know. Something I felt."

"What? What is it?"

"The *Shyan.*"

"What about it?"

"I felt him there with us, in your mind."

"I told you that something was in here, with me—"

"No—I mean...I felt him when we were thrust out of there. I felt him in the room with us. Kaitlyn...*the Shyan was in the room*."

Kaitlyn doesn't move.

"Do you understand what I'm telling you? The *Shyan* is one of us. One of your friends."

"I don't—"

"You must be wary. Trust no one. He has been close to you all this time, watching. Trust none of them, Kaitlyn. You cannot be sure who is working against you from within your ranks."

He sighs and then moves towards the stairway.

"Keep the door to the larger section of the basement locked, if you haven't been doing so already. Be vigilant. We will talk again, in daylight. Say nothing in front of the others. Good night."

Kaitlyn's form seems frozen, but she is hidden in the deepest gloomy recess of the room and we can't see what emotions might be playing across her face. She has not moved by the time the motion-activated camera clicks off.

Diary of Kaitlyn Johnson

Friday, 28 January 2005, 6:00 am
Roof

One of my friends. One of them is lying to me. Oh, my
God. What do I do? Which one could do this to me? I
can't believe this. I can't process.

One of my friends.

I was so stunned by what Haji said that I almost forgot
about my dream. Carly was in it. She was standing very
still, watching me, and she was in flames. Her eyes
wanted to tell me a whole story, but she couldn't—that
much I could see. She lifted her hand slowly and first
pointed at me, then to something off to her right.

It was the snake—she was pointing at the snake, and
he was writhing in flames too, an inhuman scream piercing
the whiteness of the dream. Then I faded backwards,
as though something was dragging me far away, and the
whole scene suddenly cleared. Both Carly and the snake
stood before the Dead House—itself, too, a conflagration
of flames. Not the silent, dancing kind on Carly, but a
yowling, monstrous beast, hungry for more. It bent and
curved, cracked and spat, and the Dead House blackened
and submitted beneath it. Not only that...but the Dead
House had begun to crumble into the Dead Sea.

Now, here, where things were once so clear and easy
to grasp, I look down over the grounds, and I can feel
the school. I feel it, Dee, as though, subtly, it has
become the Dead House. I almost expect it to move and
change beneath me, glide like a serpent into some other
form. Then maybe if I close my eyes, I will suddenly
be back in the basement, a voice will be telling me
you're mine, and I will happily submit to my eternal
encasement.

10:00 am

Been reading C's diary while the others are in class.
Found this:

> I don't know Brett. I don't recognize him. Not at all.
> There's something wrong with him. Deeply wrong.
> The way he looks at me, I feel like I'm fading away.
> I wish he would stop. I don't want to be near him.

What does this mean? Brett?

Brett.

96

The camera clicks on as Kaitlyn jerks on the mattress, night-vision painting the picture green and white. At that moment, we see that John stands in the doorway, silently watching her. It is uncertain how long he has been there.

Still asleep, Kaitlyn groans, turns her head towards the door, and starts to pant. "Have to," she murmurs. "*Have* to..."

John continues to watch, until one violent start wakes her and she begins to cry. He hesitates, then hurries to her side, and she allows herself to be taken into his embrace.

"I wish you would stop this," he whispers.

She sniffs. "What?"

"You *know* what, Kaitie."

She pulls back, looks up at him. "I'm *fine*."

"We're worried."

"Who're *we*?"

"That Brett guy. He came to ask me to talk to you. Get you to leave this Mala-Gründi stuff alone."

"Brett doesn't know anything. He's an idiot."

"At least he seems to give a shit about you. You need to stay away from this, Kait. Seriously, *stop it*. Before something bad happens to you as well."

Kaitlyn pushes him away, but cries out as her arms make impact. "I have to," she breathes, "have to save my sister. You don't know—you never met her. But she's the better me. You'd like her, you would. I need her, John." She shakes her head. "I need her."

"Let her go. Please...I'm begging you. This thing—it's bigger than us. You could get someone killed. *You* could be killed. Is she worth *that*?"

"Yes!" Her eyes narrow as she regards him. "You're just assuming things will go wrong. But they won't. They can't. Trust me."

"They've already gone wrong. Your friend Naida? I've never seen anything like that. I think..." His voice trails off, and he looks down at his hands.

Kaitlyn folds her arms over her chest. The gesture comes off as more vulnerable than defiant. "You think what?"

He meets her gaze. "I think you need to contact Dr. Lansing."

There's a beat of silence before Kaitlyn whispers, "*What?*"

"I'm thinking of calling her."

She's on her feet in a moment, her hands balled into fists at her side. "Get away from me."

"Stop this."

"Judas," she spits. "Fuck you! Go back to Lansing? Have them lock me up like a dog?"

"I thought you were...I don't know. Better."

"Not this again! You *told* me that I didn't belong there!"

John gets to his feet too, tries to reach for Kaitlyn.

"You—you," she yells, "you think I'm crazy!"

"Kaitlyn, I don't think you're crazy. But you need...something. I don't know what. I...this is dangerous for you. You need to leave Carly where she is"—he raises his hands—"and claim your life."

"*No—*"

"Listen—"

"I'm nothing without her!"

"*Listen!*"

"I can't survive—she's the best part! I'm nothing on my own—"

"Kaitlyn, stop!"

"You can't take her away—"

"*What about your parents, Kait?*"

A ringing silence follows his exclamation, and the dripping water in the distance—*drip, drip, drip*—seems suddenly louder.

"What...what do you mean?"

John frowns. "The accident? What you told me that night?"

Kaitlyn shakes her head. "I don't remember. I don't remember anything that happened."

"I was there. I was there that night. You told me to come over. We were going to the orchestra, remember? Your dad was playing. You wanted your parents to meet me. Does any of this ring a bell?"

She shakes her head again.

"We were in the car, and you and your dad started arguing. You were sitting up front so your mum could hold your dad's trombone case and keep an eye on Jaime, who was sitting on the other side of her. She kept trying to get you to stop yelling, and I guess he was distracted...We crashed."

"It was a car crash?"

"Your dad was thrown out, and I broke a fair few ribs and my collarbone. That trombone case saved me. Remember that accident and the reason I lost track of you?"

"You said *an* accident...I didn't know it was *the* accident that..."

"Yeah. Your mum...she got the brunt of the impact. She was in the middle. There was never any chance she'd survive that."

Kaitlyn swallows. "What did I tell you? You said I told you something that night."

John hesitates. "Kaitie, please—"

"Tell me, John, so help me God!"

"You're too fragile for this."

"Talk about a volte-face. What happened to 'you're strong,' huh?

What happened to our pact—always honesty? You liar!" Kaitlyn's voice breaks, but she keeps yelling in a broken half voice. "You're like everyone else—you *traitor*, get away from me!" She tries to shove him, but he is like a big wall in front of her. She laughs, once. "I'm an idiot! I needed you, but I *am* crazy, after all, for ever trusting you—"

John grabs her, and she pushes away and spins as though to run out the door—but he has her upper arms, and she simply bounces back against his chest. He closes his arms around her, pinning her to him.

"*Geddoffme!*" she screams, trying to break free. "Let me go!"

"Shh, calm down. It's okay—shh, Kaitie, shh!"

Sobbing, she kicks his shin, and John stumbles back a pace but keeps hold of her.

With one violent yank, he yells, "Kaitie, *stop!* You told me—you told me you were glad. You said that right to my face, while they were scraping your dad off the road!"

Kaitlyn stills, but continues to sob garbled words that fall from her lips like drool—among them "liar" and "not true" and "you promised." Eventually she settles into a kind of half slump in his arms. He maneuvers her to the mattress.

"I'm sorry," John says, stroking her hair. "I think you need help."

"I need Carly. I *need* her. If it's true...if I really said that I was glad they were dead...then she's the better one. The best Johnson girl, and she can come back and have this life, and I can disappear. I need this, can't you understand?"

John doesn't answer. Instead, he deflects. "Don't you remember being covered in blood?"

Blood on my hands. There was blood on my hands. [Diary extract: Sunday, 7 November 2004, 7:00 PM]

"No."

"You got out of the car that night...you stumbled over to where your dad was lying on the road, and you knelt beside him...there was so much of his blood on the road already. You said something to him, and he reached out for you, but you just got up, covered in all that red...and stumbled away."

"I was probably in shock or something."

"Except, when the paramedics had me in the ambulance, you told me. You told me it was the best night of your life. You were so...*happy*."

"Please, just...get away from me."

"Kaitlyn, please..."

She retches, then coughs. "You said you would never hurt me. You promised."

"I don't want to hurt you."

"Traitor."

"I don't want to, but I will if I have to. Because I need to help you. You're sick."

Kaitlyn pauses, and then slowly lifts her eyes to stare at him for a full five seconds before they widen in alarm. "You..."

"What? What is it?"

"John...please, just leave me alone."

"DH—" This time when he grabs her, it is her left forearm, the wounds covered by her long sleeves.

She screams.

"What?"

Hunched over, she manages to whisper, "*Leave me alone! I want to be alone.*"

"Okay. Fine. I'll be by in the morning. Please don't do anything stupid."

He leaves, at which point Kaitlyn reaches for her journal with shaking fingers.

[END OF CLIP]

Diary of Kaitlyn Johnson

Friday, 28 January 2005
Basement

You bitch. You've always known, haven't you?

I DON'T BELIEVE YOU!!!

Later

I never wanted them dead! What kind of a sick monster would want her own parents to DIE? It's impossible! How could I ever—
   It's a lie! Do you understand me? There's an explanation for this—I don't want it to be true! It would break me anew if he…if John…
   How can I be sure?
   …
   No. No, I won't bring her into this.
   NO!
   Yes, I know that. But she's too young. She won't remember.
   <u>I won't do that to my sister!</u>
   Just leave it alone, Dee! Jaime is safe from you! Safe from me!

Leave me alone.

Later

I know you mean well. But I'm doing this. I need to be sure, I can't just…I can't — just <u>trust</u>. I must be certain.
   Yes, I forgive you.
   Come here.

Diary of Kaitlyn Johnson

Saturday, 29 January 2005, 8:00 pm
Forgotten Garden, Crypt

I couldn't think of anywhere else to talk to Haji, so
I brought him here. He just left, and I feel…I don't
know. Weird.

"There is a token," Haji said to me, his voice low
and encompassing. "A bind. It works by reading the
threshold of any dwelling where an enemy has entered.
You will dream who the Shyan is after he has crossed
it."

"I expect this will cost something."

He nodded. "You expect correctly. For Naida, I would
give you this bind for nothing. But it requires payment
of a different kind. It requires a piece of *you*."

"Do it," Kaitlyn says without pause. "Take it.
Whatever it is. I need the charm tonight."

I needed to be sure. It couldn't be…but it might be.
And it was killing me. I had to know. Now.

Brett. John. ~~Scott. Ari.~~ Brett. John. Brett. John.
Who? Why?

"The eye does not witness its crafting."

"Fine."

"You feel him, yes?"

There was nothing to say to that, except, "I need it
tonight."

He made it. He did it. Here it is in my hand. I
hope this works; otherwise, I want my payment back.
Hahahahaha!!!

9:30 pm

I can't believe I never knew. I don't know whether to
kick his teeth in or be really, really afraid. If I
didn't know this about Brett, what else might I not

know? And Carly's diary entry about him watching her…I can't ignore that. Haji's words keep going round and round in my head. <u>Trust no one. He has been close to you all this time, watching</u>. Over and over. <u>Trust none of them, Kaitlyn.</u>

John. Brett. John. Brett. I don't know who is doing this to me. One of them. Both of them. I don't know.

Torn-Out Page from the Diary of Carly Luanne Johnson Undated

I'm scared. I don't know what to do. Brett just…I don't know…attacked me? He—he kissed me. Forced it on me. He cornered me outside the PE lockers this morning and said he knew why I refused to like him. He said…he said I was into Naida. And his face when he said it…like he was so disgusted. Like I was revolting. Then he pressed his kiss on me and touched me, and I shoved him away, and I know Kaitie would be proud. He was so manic. I didn't recognize him. And the worst thing is…I can't deny what he said. I can't say for sure that I don't like Naida, that I don't love her, even. All I know is that I'm scared of Brett. How did that happen? BRETT. He's not who I thought he was. There's a darkness inside him that terrifies me, and no one can see it. They all think he's this golden boy, but he's not. It's a mask.

It could be him. Carly sensed something. But I sense something too, and it could be John. I just don't know, Dee. But I have the bind. I am going to find out who the viper is.

Diary of Kaitlyn Johnson

Saturday, 29 January 2005, 11:13 pm
Roof

I'm really alone now, Dee.

Slipped into the diary on this page is a rumpled note.

Trust no one. Say nothing.
Find the door.
Good luck.

I only just saw him. Why didn't he tell me he was leaving?

It is presumed that Haji Chounan-Dupré disappeared on 29 January 2005, however, he was not filed as missing until 30 January. The corpse of Brett [name omitted by request] was discovered in the south quad at 9:12 PM on the evening of 29 January—the same evening that Kaitlyn met with Haji in the Forgotten Garden. Reason for the fall is unknown, since the body was severely damaged by the impact. The coroner's verdict: Accidental death.

Sunday, 30 January 2005
Forgotten Garden, Crypt

~~This is my fault, this is my fault~~

~~I hurt everyone,~~ Dee. I hurt so many people. ~~I'm sorry, so sorry, so very, very sorry. And the fact that I'm sorry is worthless.~~

~~Did I do this? Is it my fault? Should I have given him some kind of warning? How could I when I didn't—I don't know anything for sure? Haji told me the Shyan was here. Haji told me not to trust anyone. Now Brett is gone, and he's not the Shyan, but he still attacked Carly but does that mean he deserved to die? and Juliet is missing, and somehow I can't stop thinking maybe I'm to blame for that too~~

~~Now there are only a few left, and one of them is a killer.~~ One of them killed Brett. Who? ~~Scott? Ari? John?~~ Who can I trust?

Naida. Yes, Naida. Poor, mute Naida.

Dee—can you help me? Can you help me to see what I'm not seeing? Can you light a little torch?

~~I should talk to~~ them.

Naida Camera Footage
Sunday, 30 January 2005, 9:00 PM
Basement

"Haji didn't say anything to Naida," Scott says in a low, rasping voice. He folds his arms. "It's weird."

Ari shakes his head. A new bowler hat stands atop it. He turns to Kaitlyn, who sits in the corner on the mattress, wearing a loose beanie. "Wasn't he going to help you?"

She shrugs.

John clears his throat. "This needs to stop. I listened to the news. They're saying you did this. They're saying you killed—" He breaks off.

"His name was Brett," Kaitlyn says softly. "Don't be shy. His name was Brett, John. *Brett.*"

He looks at her with a pained expression, and his lips grow tight.

"All I know," Scott says, voice unsteady, "is that Haji was called away. He said he had to leave right then for Fair Island and to give her the note, which I did."

"What did it say?" Ari asks.

"I didn't read it," Scott says, looking towards Kaitlyn, who offers nothing up.

"I'm tired" is all she says. "I want to be left alone."

"Are you sure—" John begins.

Ari cuts him off. "Let's go."

Scott frowns at Ari, who folds his arms. "We've all lost Brett; we almost lost Naida. And Juliet is still missing. Are we going to turn on one another as well?"

"And Kaitlyn's had enough of this," John adds.

"You're not one of us," Ari snaps. "Don't talk like you are."

"Yeah, well, maybe Scott's right," John says. "We should stop meddling before we end up dead."

"I don't know if you've noticed," Ari says, "but we're in this already. Do you really think this *Shyan* guy is going to leave us alone now?"

Scott shakes his head. "We can try. We can try to put this behind us."

"You're a coward," Ari says, his voice low. He turns to John. "So are you."

"I'm trying to do what's best for Kaitlyn, and I think you should be doing the same. She needs help."

Kaitlyn looks up. "Get out of here," she whispers. "Get away from me. Judas."

John's face falls. "Kaitlyn, please—I'm trying to help you."

She gets to her feet and walks across the mattress, stepping down and standing before John. Her face is that of someone heartbroken and sick. She is pale and thin, her eyes huge in a sunken face.

"Are you?" she asks.

He lifts his hands to touch her arms, but she flinches, and Ari steps closer. "Yes, I am," John says. "Please...Falcon..."

"I just don't know," Kaitlyn whispers, her eyes filling with tears. "What you said...I can't afford to believe you."

Ari steps up beside Kaitlyn. "Everyone out. Let's let her rest. Come on."

John's eye twitches, and he stares at Ari with a locked jaw before finally turning away. At the door, he hesitates and then he disappears into the main basement, heading for the broken window.

Scott glances at Kaitlyn. "I'm going to talk this over with Naida. If she's strong enough. Think about it, Kaitlyn. Think about just giving up. Please."

He exits via the stairs.

Ari releases her. "Get some sleep. I'll keep watch outside for you."

He makes to leave, but she grabs his sleeve.

"Ari—"

"Are you okay?"

She shakes her head. "No. But I can't—"

"It's okay. Here." He puts his arms around her again, and she exhales into his chest.

"I think John's the *Shyan*."

The words seem to leave her mouth against her wishes and then she stiffens.

"John? Who told you that?"

She covers her mouth, shakes her head. "I'm tired."

He kisses her head. "I'm sorry. I'm so sorry you have to go through this."

Kaitlyn swallows. "Haji gave me a charm for protection."

She walks over to her bag, pulls out what must be the bind from Haji—it looks like a knotted rope-braid, coiled with ribbon and clumps of wax—and tries to hang it from the edge of the door. Her arms are weak, however, and she isn't tall enough.

She begins to cry, still attempting to hang the bind, but Ari gets to his feet and takes it from her hands. "I'll do it. Kaitie, you have me. I'm here. I'm not going anywhere. You're not alone." He hugs her to him tightly, and she continues to cry into his shirt.

I hate fucking crying.

He leads her to the mattress, and they sit down.

After Kaitlyn has cried herself into exhaustion, Ari looks down at the bind in his hands. "What is it?"

"It's me."

Ari's jaw clenches. "What have you done?"

"What I had to." And she slides the beanie off, revealing the damage. Her hair, once long and luminous, has been cruelly shorn, leaving a jagged crop behind.

"Kaitie…your hair?"

"Yeah…it was a bit of a shock when he told me the price. He wove my hair into the charm."

Ari looks down at the bind with a new expression. It is clearly made from her hair, though some of it seems to have been soaked in something, darkening strands here and there to amber.

"Let's hope it protects you, then," he says.

[END OF CLIP]

Diary of Kaitlyn Johnson

**Monday, 31 January 2005, 6:34 am
Basement**

He must have come while I slept, because now I know.

In a journal entry dated 31 January 2005, Kaitlyn practices several drafts of a letter, which she states she will give to Ari. It is evident by the confused writing that it cost her something to put down on paper all she thought. The bottom of the page has been torn off, presumably the version of the note she delivered to Ari.

dear ari

~~please come see me right away, something happened~~
~~i think i know who the shyan is~~
~~i don't want to do this—i can't believe it. i won't.~~
~~i need to talk to you about john.~~

A return note is slipped inside the back of the journal beside the Claydon diary entries, and is presumed to be Ari's reply.

IS IT HIM?

A reply in writing has never been discovered. Anyone under the age of eighteen should not read the rest of this report without parental consent.

Naida Camera Footage
Monday, 31 January 2005, 10:57 PM
Basement

The basement camera clicks on as John throws Ari into the room. Presumably they have been arguing in the stairwell, but as Ari opens his mouth to say something, John yells, "You son of a bitch!" and hits him hard across the face.

"John—" Ari tries to yank free, but John hits twice more, and Ari spits blood.

Baring teeth smeared crimson, Ari knocks John in the stomach with his shoulder before landing two of his own punches across John's face. He falls against the far wall, collapsing onto his left knee, and Ari kicks him hard in the stomach. John grunts but seems otherwise unaffected, and the two wrestle, landing blows and shoving back and forth.

Footsteps echo from some way off, but neither seems to notice because John's large hands close around Ari's throat.

Ari jerks and yanks at his arms, face bleeding red and then tingeing purple; John's strength seems overwhelming. At that moment, Kaitlyn rounds the corner, saying "What is going on—" and stops, dropping her journal. She screams.

"*John!* John, stop it! *Let him go!*"

John doesn't react—maybe he doesn't hear—but when Kaitlyn launches herself forward, pulling on his arms despite her injuries, he grunts and shoves her back with one hand, the other still clasped firmly around Ari's throat. She staggers, but tries again, this time jumping onto his back. Again, he throws her off, more forcefully now, so that she is, for a moment, winded.

Ari, foaming at the mouth, manages a startled choke, and his eyes roll back in his head. Kaitlyn moves onto her side, coughing, and then forces herself to her feet.

"Please!" she cries again, hitting John, her efforts futile. Panicked, she scrambles into the shadows. We hear metal scrape against concrete, then Kaitlyn runs towards John, yelling, her arms raised high, and brings down the object she is holding to strike his neck.

John jerks upwards, a tiny grunt escaping his lips, and stumbles away from the now-unconscious Ari. Kaitlyn jumps back as though shocked at what she's done.

"I'm sorry, but stop it!" she cries. "Just stop!"

He turns to look at Kaitlyn, then reaches up to touch his neck. His hand comes away crimson.

He staggers.

He falls onto his knees.

Kaitlyn drops the knife. The same knife that took Naida's voice. The sound echoes across the room.

John coughs, his lips rouge. Kaitlyn cries out once, then scrambles over to him.

"John—*John*—"

He coughs again, and a spray of blood follows, then a bubble of crimson pops on his lips. He is breathing very fast, and each exhale spills blood from his nostrils.

"Oh, my God, John, please!"

Kaitlyn grabs him as he collapses, his weight on top of her legs. Her cries die away as she watches him breathe, her hand pressed to the wound she created.

"It's okay," she says. "It's okay." Over and over, she says it. "I didn't mean to...I didn't mean to!"

His eyes stare as his breath quickens, and more and more blood spills from the wound in his neck. He twitches, twitches again, and Kaitlyn stifles a sob as she strokes his hair. It is a terrible, lengthy process, during which Kaitlyn watches, her face contorted.

Ari stirs, coughs, leaning over to gasp in desperate breaths. His eyes meet the scene in front of him just as John stops his desperate inhalations, seizes briefly, and then stills.

Kaitlyn's lips tremble, and her eyes fill with tears.

Ari staggers to his feet and hurries over to the door. He swings it shut just in time to contain Kaitlyn's scream, which lingers on and on, as she bends over John's dead, bloodied body. When the scream ends, another takes its place, and another. She grips John's shirt, now vividly scarlet, and Ari has to pry her fingers free.

She continues to scream.

One must wonder why, in all the minutes John lay dying, she didn't call for help.

For several long minutes, Ari keeps guard at the door while Kaitlyn sits over John's body, her whole frame a small, sunken heap. She is shaking.

"We need to do something," Ari says quietly. He is hoarse. "Kait. We need to get rid of the body."

Kaitlyn doesn't stir.

"His body," Ari says slowly. "We need to get rid of it."

"I didn't...mean to—"

"*Kaitlyn.* If they find him and see that knife—and your hand? They'll lock you away for life."

"Maybe they should."

"Stop that. We'll take him to the chapel. To the Forgotten Garden. We'll bury him there with the graves. It's more than five hours until sunup. We'll make it."

"I'm a...I stabbed..." Her words slur, and she begins to mumble incoherently.

Ari walks over to her and slaps her, hard. Her head is flung back with the impact, and she expels a tiny squeak.

"We—need—to—get—rid—of—the—body." Ari enunciates each word. "The Forgotten Garden. We'll bury him. I need your help."

Kaitlyn peers up at him through her tears and nods. "The Forgotten Garden...okay."

Ari helps her to her feet, and then they each grab one end of John; Kaitlyn takes his feet but drops them soon after, her arms shaking. It takes them five minutes to climb the stairs, Ari dragging most of John's weight, at which point the motion-activated camera clicks off.

[END OF CLIP]

Diary of Kaitlyn Johnson
Date, Time, and Location Not Noted

The smell is evolving—is that bad?

I closed my eyes to shut out the memories of my
life, which now includes the hardest heartache ever
experienced. I fell into sleep—sleep that still feels
like falling. I fell into the dark, felt vaguely the
moment when Ari left me to go to his dorm and clean
John's grave dirt from under his fingernails, and then
I was fully asleep and in the Dead House, and all was
silent. I sensed its emptiness like a weight—knew I
was alone. Whatever darkness lingered before had now
moved on.

Or maybe it only slumbered.

Or maybe it's so much a part of me now that I can no
longer distinguish it.

But the smell—that old mildew scent—had changed,
deepened, turned into something like fine musk, and I
liked it.

This was it, I knew. For if the house was empty, or
sleeping, I had a chance to find the door.

Knowing that John was the Shyan didn't make this
easier, but at least it cleared the path. For, without
the Shyan to lead and contain it, surely the Olen would
subside into the fabric from which it had come. The
fabric of time and space and a universe I could never
understand.

I was angry not to have fought harder to locate
Carly while she was still there, still a part of me.
But if I could find the doorway that Haji spoke of, the
one Carly had been dragged through, then I could go
beyond and have a chance of finding her—maybe we were
still linked by some invisible thread. The thread we
had always taken for granted.

I tried not to dwell too hard on the thought that,
if the Dead House was my mind, and I found the door…
was I then going out of my mind? An unwelcome sensation

like cold water trickling down my back and into my shoes came over me. But I had to go.

I wish you had been with me, Dee. You know, you and Ari are now my sole comforts.

I searched and searched, quietly at first. Haji had said we'd know the door when we found it. But I didn't find it. On the ground level, I roamed rotting parlor, abandoned hall, decrepit foyer, and endless galleries. Upstairs, I searched each sweeping bedroom, which stood empty and uninviting; the leaves shuffled and whispered across the floor under the tread of my boots. I ventured up another level and found the attic, but a sign of any door that did not belong? Nothing.

Then, at last, down to the basement, at last, down to the basement, the only place I hadn't yet searched. I stood at the door, pressed my ear against it, and there inside, I heard the dreadful sound of some large beast sleeping.

I didn't understand. Why was it still there?

I strained to feel around the thing, hoping I might sense whether he was guarding something. Guarding the door. But I didn't feel anything beyond the giant's sleeping form. What shape it took, I have no idea, but as I was going to suck in my courage and slowly open the door—possibly creep around whatever lay there—a sensation of someone watching overcame me so suddenly that I turned.

And there she was. The dead girl, grinning at me as always, only her grin was sad and empty and more… sympathetic. But she was fading, Dee, as though some omniscient artist was erasing her in front of my eyes. And she was still dripping wet.

And that was when I knew what she had always been trying to tell me.

The Dead Sea.

The door.

The exit.

All this time, looking for a <u>door</u>, I had never once considered that it might not be a conventional entry point at all. As soon as this idea lit itself in my

mind, a window to the right of me, a little way down
a darkened corridor, bent and twisted itself into the
shape of a door, just big enough for me to fit through.

I looked back at the girl, who was now no more than
an outline; saw <u>myself</u> as I currently am—an emaciated
thing, an empty vessel, a lost cause—and I smiled.

"Thank you. For telling me to escape Lansing. For
giving me Carly's journal. For showing me the way."

She continued to grin as she faded away. Was she
some residual part of Carly? Was she some unconscious
part of my own mind—a bit of my sanity, slowly decaying
until she had served her purpose? Was she you, Dee,
leaving me? A warning of Carly slipping away? Or was
she a little bit of mercy from God, who maybe hadn't
quite forgotten me in the shadows? I don't think I'll
ever know.

I walked over to the little window-door calmly,
stepped through into the outside and the awaiting
mists, and heard the great rushing Dead Ocean.

Elmbridge's roof seemed so small, compared with where I
then stood, looking down over the edge of the crumbling
cliff. I looked out at the raging waters, which crashed
violently, but slowly, dark and fathomless.

And

I

leaped.

The waters rushed up to meet me.

I will not utter a word of what lies beyond, only to
say this: <u>I see.</u> You tricked me for long enough, and
I see. I bet you're afraid. I bet you're reading this
right now and shuddering.

And you should be afraid. Because I'm coming.

The following entry was presumably written shortly after the previous entry, as the ink is identical.

Diary of Kaitlyn Johnson
Date, Time, and Location Not Noted

Her dear, sweet voice! My little sister—she sounds so sad and alone.

"Kaitie, where's Carly? I want to see Carly!"

Maybe it was a mistake to call her from Scott's phone, but I had to ground myself, and she's the last thing left.

"I'm going to find her," I said. I didn't lie. I <u>am</u> going to find her.

"Take me with you," she begged.

No. She can't come with me, because I know the end already. Haji was right, Dee—I knew it all along.

The following diary entry is written in an almost illegible hand, and is difficult to fully grasp at first. This copy of the first paragraph has been included as originally written, in order to demonstrate her state of mind, following which the entry has been transcribed.

There never was any choice I know that now but Dee my soul is burning! I want to cast off my skin and throw it into the flames and walk around in my bones because then maybe this all will go away. Maybe my bones will turn to dust and I will float away, on the breeze, free like I have always wanted.

[Transcription]:

There never was any choice I know that now but Dee my soul is burning! I want to cast off my skin and throw it into the flames and walk around in my bones because then maybe this all will go away. Maybe my bones will turn to dust and I will float away, on the breeze, free like I have always wanted.

I know, I'll try, but it's so hard, it's so painful. Everything is over, I just want it to be over, I don't know why I am here to suffer like this, do you find it funny? Is that what I am? A joke? An experiment?

Ari was in the chapel on the hill and somehow I knew he would be. I didn't know what was going to happen but I knew I had no choice. My feet carried me up there without my brain engaging because it was simply the way it had to be.

Because, Dee, it suddenly made so much sense. I had to talk to him, find out. Because it wasn't John, you see? Because John is gone now and this is still happening. John…I'm so sorry. My friend, my brother— you were trying to save me, for so long. I'm sorry I couldn't see it! I'm sorry you ever had to see me in Masqued, that I was ever here to taint your life. You were innocent.

It wasn't Scott either, because Scott has been with Naida, and I still feel the school pulsing its filthy energy into me. And it's not Haji because he's the one who warned me in the first place, and he's gone away. Brett is dead—oh, God, so much death. And that leaves Ari.

Ari, who hung the bind Haji gave me. Ari, who comforted me and told me everything was going to be okay. Ari, who told me I was his forever and who kissed me and touched me and—

This whole time Ari has been the link.

It was Ari.

I couldn't believe it at first, but I had to know. So I went to talk to him. Just to talk, you understand? I think he was expecting me, because he was different. He was so happy, smiling, almost laughing. I remember it all so clearly please God I wish I didn't.

He said, "Oh, Kaitie," and I said, "Yes." I said, "It was you all along, right? You're the *Shyan*." He smiled gently and said, "It's not that simple." My whole chest was concave. He said, "It's just a technicality."

"A technicality? What do you mean?" I said. He said that nothing was ever that simple and that "all is fair in love and war." "Why are you doing this?" I asked, and he laughed and said he wanted me. "I want you. I <u>love</u> you; can't you see that? I want to free you. Why else all this trouble?"

"Trouble. Is Carly trouble?" I said. "Is Juliet trouble? What about John and Brett and Naida? Are they all trouble too?"

"Yes." He said yes. So simple. So blunt. I couldn't believe I was talking to my Ari. "I'm sorry, Kaitie. I don't mean to sound so glib. Not at all. But I had to free you. You were <u>trapped</u>. They were keeping you hostage in your own double life."

"What happened to you?" I said, but the words barely left my mouth.

"I am what I am," he said, "and I love you more than anything."

"No. No no no." I told him that over and over but he just stepped closer and closer and whispered "yes" over and over and it was pointless and also important.

"I don't understand. How did you know about all this stuff?"

"Army brat," he said, smiling in a way that was not joyful, not at all. "Remember? I've lived in so many places I've lost count. When I went to the Orkney Islands, I met an intriguing woman. She used to live on Fair Island and knew Naida's grandmother—had studied under her. She taught me a lot. I dabbled in witchcraft for a while, and some voodoo as well." He smiled, as though remembering fondly. "But when I heard about Mala, I was intrigued. It's much more ancient, much more potent."

"What about the Grúndi? How could you mess with that stuff? How could you even think of using dirty conjurings like that?"

"That woman, Naida's grandmother's pupil—she had broader interests than Mala rituals. It's the reason she left the island. She was the one who opened the door to Grúndi to me. I learned what she knew, and then it was time to move, yet again, and this time we moved to London. Grúndi central, if you know where to look."

"How could you not tell me?"

"Would you have understood?"

I couldn't reply. I was so confused.

"But…why take away Carly?"

"She was a parasite, Kait. She was a *leech*. She was draining you. Stealing half your life, making you miserable. We could barely be together. You were always hiding, always in shadow, always so sad and trapped and—you were a hostage. I tried…I tried to switch you first. Make her the night half for a change. I tried to keep things simple, knowing it would hurt you to lose her entirely. But you can't do things halfway. It didn't work. I had to go deeper. Do more." He paused, his eyes intense. "*Free you.*"

Could someone love me like this? Could someone do so much for me because he really, truly does love *me*? Me for me, and not me for Carly?

"Ari," I begged. "Stop it. Please stop it."

He smiled sadly, stepped closer, touched my arms. When my dad told me we were moving to Somerset, I chose Elmbridge. I thought it was for Naida, and then I met you…You turned the world around. I knew in that moment, I would love you.

Then: Carly is gone. "Carly is gone. You're free."

He didn't know. He didn't know that I had already found the door to that place beyond and walked through it and come back. Somehow this seemed important.

"I don't understand," I said. "Why me? Why Carly? What do you want her for? And the others? Explain it to me."

He smiled patiently, and I wanted to hurt him even as I felt my love for him stubbornly refusing to die. "The others are expendable, for you. Everyone is, for you. I was trying to reach you. To give you what's yours."

I shook my head, struck dumb.

"You're ready, Kait. You're ready. Everything that was in your way is gone. You're free, just like you always wanted. We can have a life together. We can *be* together. Do everything you want. Go to London, go to university. Have a life!"

I wanted to vomit, wanted to scream. He was so excited. I wanted it.

"And Carly?"

"She's not what you thought, Kaitie. She's weak, but she's also selfish." He broke off, sighing. "I don't want to hurt you, but you have to know what she did."

"Tell me the truth." I couldn't believe him.

"Last year Naida taught a few minor things to Carly—Mala things."

I knew this was true. Naida herself had told me. I nodded.

"She entered into a pact that she thought would bring you both freedom. I could see it the second I met you. You had a debt on you. I could *see* it, almost like a curse. It's hard to explain. I didn't know anything about you, but I was intrigued. It was clear, the more I got to know you, that you didn't believe in anything like that. But Carly…I spoke to her too. I got to know her. I'm sorry I didn't tell you, but I knew you wouldn't understand. Not yet. But when I asked her questions…asked about Mala and about Gründi…she talked about freedom—for both of you. She talked about wanting a life, about worrying for you. She was an open book until I asked her what she had done. She got uncomfortable. Stopped talking to me. Avoided me. I knew she had tampered with something outside of her control. But you don't make deals with *It*. You simply pay up."

"Carly wouldn't…couldn't. She wouldn't know how. *I* don't know how."

"Oh, come on, Kait! Google will tell you how to do just about any kind of black magic you can think of. She was desperate. She was *hurting* you."

Who was I speaking to? This wasn't the Ari I knew. This wasn't the Ari I fell so hard for. I was looking at a stranger.

"Naida opened the door to Mala, and she abused it."

I didn't understand. "When did this happen? Last year? During the summer? At the beginning of the year?"

"I don't know that, Kaitie. Before I came along. Before the chapel, for sure. You were already cursed when I met you."

"I don't…" I could feel myself getting dizzy.

"The power inside you…you've felt it…she put that there. She had no idea what she was doing."

"The Olen," I said. "You infected me with it."

"No, I didn't. It was Carly who opened the door. And it's not an Olen." For the first time, he looked worried. "It's a demon."

I stumbled backwards. His words floored me. That sleeping thing inside the Dead House—inside *me*—was a *demon*. A real demon. A demonic entity. Had I known this before I heard Ari tell me?

"I control it," Ari said quickly, as if reading my fears. "I can control it for you. I know how. You don't have to worry about it, okay? I'm going to contain it. I'm going to keep you safe."

And he was a fool, and he was wrong, so wrong. He controlled nothing. Nothing, and he didn't know what he was doing. And I loved him.

It was all so much, I felt the world closing in around me, a big dark veil. But somehow I saw clearly too.

"And Juliet? Where is she? Did you kill her?"

I couldn't believe I was asking my Ari that question. Did. You. Kill. Someone. This wasn't Ari. This had to be a dream—a nightmare. I wanted it to stop. I wanted him to stop. Stop playing tricks on me, be Ari again.

He flinched. "Please, just leave it alone. Let it be. Let me contain the thing inside you now, so we can be together. Finally free together. Don't ask me questions. I can't...I can't lie to you anymore."

And I saw that this *was* Ari. How could I have missed it? This thing in his eyes? This rage in his words? How did I not see?

I persisted. "Ari, did you kill Juliet?"

"No. I didn't kill Juliet." He released a breath that was trying to contain some deep emotion. "You did."

It was like the air in my lungs had suddenly become lead. Plumbum. "No," I choked out. "No."

He had every reason to lie, didn't he, Dee?

Liar, liar, liar.

I plugged my ears; could still hear him.

"It was the thing inside you. It wasn't *you*. That's why I have to bind it. Soon."

Innnnn...sssssiiiidddde...yyyouuuuu...

I could hear the snake.

"You're overthinking it. Just stop trying to get all the answers. They'll hurt you, Kaitie. Just...just let me take you away from here. Let's just go away. Together."

I started to cry. "How could you do this to me?"

He thought I meant Carly. "I know," he said, taking me into his arms, kissing the top of my head. "I'm angry with her too. But she's gone now."

I don't know anymore. I didn't know! I don't and didn't know anything! I was in a room of mirrors, each one bent and distorted, none of them true, but all of them accurate, and all of them laughing glassy laughs that screamed and shattered all around me.

I pushed away from him. "And Brett? Did the thing inside me kill him too?"

He shook his head. "Please leave it alone, Kaitie."

"Tell me. Right now, tell me."

"Brett wasn't a good guy. Did you know he attacked Carly? And then he zeroes in on you like you're some kind of target? Always around you. Always with you. And then that kiss…" He made a guttural sound deep in his throat. "It sickened me."

I sobbed. "You killed Brett."

"You need to be free from the people who are hurting you, Kaitie."

"And Haji? My God, Ari. Did he even go home?"

Ari's voice was very quiet. "He was going to put her back."

I just sobbed. I sobbed and sobbed because he loved me so much but he was so sick, and I loved him, so much it was tearing me apart inside, and I had to go. I had to get out of there and away from him before I threw myself into his arms and forgave him.

I turned and ran, as fast as I could, and in my head I kept hearing the snake that was the demon inside me, inside the Dead House, calling me *Killer Killer Killer*. I heard them painted on the walls, saw them dripping blood there.

I

Killed

I

Killed

I

Killed

Juliet. And. John. And. I Was Happy That My Mother. My Father. Were Both. Dead. Too.

it's okay, dee. it's quiet.
you can come out now.
he will never hurt you again.

On 1 February 2005, Kaitlyn paid a visit to Naida in the hospital, but precisely what was said can never be known for certain. A nurse—Sister Winnie Sholto of Musgrove Park Hospital—gave a statement to the police. It has been copied below.

Witness Statement, Winnewa Sholto, Sister at Musgrove Park Hospital, Attar Wing

Interviewer: Please state your name for the record.

WS: Winnie Sholto.

Interviewer: Please tell me, in as much detail as you can, what you saw.

WS: Eh...girl come into the hospital to visit the patient in room 204. She was so small, so sick-looking. She stayed for maybe ten minute, I don't hear them talking, only the girl holding the patient's hand. I go do my round, come back; the girl and patient they hugging and crying. I wanted to go in to see if everything was okay, but seem like nice moment and patient didn't ring bell, so I go. Girl leave room, and patient did not ring the bell, she standing by window holding IV pole, so I go on my round again. Have cup of tea with girls and then back to the ward. When I get back, patient still standing at window, not moving. I don't know what is wrong, but she doesn't want to get into bed. She stand at window all night long

during shift. When I go off shift, she sitting in
chair, still by the window.

Interviewer: Did the girl say anything to you?

WS: No, she left. Didn't speak. Maybe she lost
tongue like patient, eh? [Laughter]

[End of statement]

Diary of Kaitlyn Johnson

Tuesday, 1 February 2005, 10:21 pm
Attic, Green Sofa

Stay here, Dee. Stay safe.

Thank you for holding my truth.

Kaitlyn's last entry is surprisingly neat, written in a slow, precise hand. Whatever happened between Ari's confrontation and subsequent murder, and the next entry, seems to have calmed the storm in her mind.

Police reports indicate that the fire that destroyed Elmbridge High originated in the main common room and spread very quickly, indicating the use of an accelerant. The common room is where the charred remains of Ari Hait were discovered, though Kaitlyn's journal suggests he perhaps died in the chapel. This means that Kaitlyn would have needed to carry his dead weight over 1,800 yards to the main building without being seen, a nearly impossible feat in her condition. How, then, did Ari end up in the common room? Speculation about whether Ari tried to reason with a delusional Kaitlyn and was killed in the common room itself, moments before the fire, abounded for several years, though this is unlikely, given the location near to the dorms and lack of witnesses. The location of Ari's corpse is only one of the inexplicable elements of the Johnson Incident.

Two more bodies were found in the charred remains of the school. The first was Brenda LeRoy, discovered in her dorm room. She died from smoke inhalation, and toxicology reports of the time indicated she had slept through the fire alarm because of a dose of nitrazepam, which she took each night for insomnia and for which she had a GP prescription. The second was Haji Chounan-Dupré, brother of Naida Chounan-Dupré. The autopsy report indicated that he had died before the fire as the result of a blow to the head with a heavy, cylindrical object. According to Kaitlyn's diary, Haji was killed by Ari Hait some time after Kaitlyn's meeting with him. He was scheduled to return to Fair Island that evening but did not make his flight from Tingwall. Some speculate that Kaitlyn murdered Haji when he began to see that she was not under attack by a *Shyan* or *Olen*, but was rather quite severely mentally ill. No evidence exists for accusations against either Ari Hait or Kaitlyn Johnson.

The body of John Hutt was found buried in the chapel cemetery— what Kaitlyn referred to as the "Forgotten Garden." Cause of death was a knife wound to the neck, piercing the jugular vein.

In an interview, Howard McKay, psychology expert and author of *Self and Its Distortion,* commented on the significance of Kaitlyn burying John's body in the "Forgotten Garden."

It really is fascinating. [Kaitlyn's] reference to the garden somehow being her—"*I wanted to show him me, which is what the garden is*"—demonstrates something significant. Namely, that she was burying the body *in* herself. Quite literally concealing his murder, and the evidence of it, within her own being, where he would lie and decay and never really be forgotten."

The records of Kaitlyn's history in relation to the death of her parents remain sealed by order of the courts, but there is speculation about social services being involved in an investigation into allegations of possible sexual or physical abuse within the Johnson household prior to the accident. All social service records also remain sealed.

The discovery of Kaitlyn's journal has renewed interest in the case and sparked online fan forums. Debate has raged about the true story. Earlier this year, amateur researcher and Johnson enthusiast Michael Mooring, aged seventeen, discovered a hidden panel in the wall of the Elmbridge High School attic, inside which lay the curled remains of Juliet McClarin. The cause of death is unknown, as is the identity of her killer, but heavy blood loss is evident from the brown stain on the attic carpet, as noted in Kaitlyn's journal and videotaped by Naida Chounan-Dupré.

A police interview was conducted with Naida Chounan-Dupré on 26 September 2005. It was recorded on camera for the trial, which was to take place over the following months. Naida wrote out her replies, but these were then superimposed onto the screen for the jury viewing. The interview has been transcribed below.

Criminal Investigation Department, Portishead Headquarters
Avon and Somerset Constabulary, Portishead, Bristol
Monday, 26 September 2005, 15h22
VIDEO INTERVIEW: Detective Chief Inspector Floyd Homes and Naida Chounan-Dupré

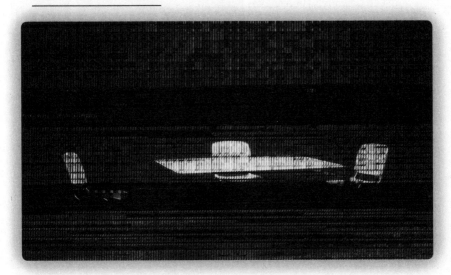

"Tell me," DCI Floyd Homes says, "why you helped Carly to escape from the hospital. Surely you must have known she was very ill."

She wasn't "ill." She was possessed.

"Possessed. Surely you don't believe that?"

To the core of my being. Carly was no longer within that form. Kaitlyn was there, and something else was there too. I don't regret anything, except failing to help her better.

"And the fire? You have no thoughts on that?"

I don't regret helping my friend.

"And the people who died? Your brother? Regret that?"

Naida folds her arms and looks away.

DCI Floyd Homes leans forward, resting his arms on the table. "Ari Hait is dead. Does that mean anything to you?"

Naida scribbles furiously with the pencil she has been given. *He was evil—he was a Shyan! He's the only one left, so it had to be him.* She pushes the note across the table.

"He was an innocent boy," Homes says, looking up. "An innocent boy who had the terrible misfortune to love Carly Johnson. And it cost him his life." He sighs, shakes his head. "Do you even know how they found him? Do you know how Ari's body was discovered?"

Naida hesitates, then shakes her head.

"His neck was broken. Snapped in two. Carly did that to him."

No. It was an Olen. It was an angry spirit. Ari tried to control it, but you <u>can't</u> control raw power. How could a tiny thing like Kaitlyn Johnson <u>possibly</u> have the strength to do that? Tell me! <u>How</u>?

"Do you believe he deserved to die?"

He confessed to her. You weren't there.

"Were *you*?"

Naida hesitates, but then writes, her lips set firmly. *No. But Kaitlyn told me. She came to see me in the hospital. We were friends. She didn't lie—she told me.*

His hand slams down on the metal tabletop. "And did—*Kaitlyn*—tell you that she killed her own parents? Did she tell you *that*? She grabbed the steering wheel and caused the car accident. Did she make you privy to *that* information?"

At these words, Naida shakes her head, then scribbles a hasty reply. *That's a lie. You're trying to trick me.*

"Naida, I think you *have* been tricked. But not by me. Juliet's blood was found in the school attic—the only part of the school left untouched by the flames and where, as you know, Carly spent much of her time. When we find Juliet's body, we'll know."

<u>Ari</u> killed Juliet. <u>ARI</u>. He needed a sacrifice to bargain with the Olen.

"Did 'Kaitlyn' tell you that?"

It's the only explanation.

"Kaitlyn was the delusion of a very sick girl."

No. Kaitlyn was real. She was my friend. You can't just erase her.

Homes leans in, his expression tired and drawn, his eyes shadowed. "You can't see the truth, can you?"

You're a fool.

Homes reads Naida's last note with dismay, regards her for a moment, and then looks to the officers behind him.

"Cuff her." He turns back to Naida. "You're under arrest. Do you understand?"

She nods, and the uniformed officers handcuff her wrists behind her back while DCI Floyd Homes states her rights.

"You are being charged with obstructing a police officer, wasting police time, harboring an escaped prisoner following sectioning, obstruction of justice, perverting the course of an investigation, and willful conspiracy to harm. You do not have to say anything. But it may harm your defense if you do not mention when questioned something which you later rely on in court. Anything you do say may be given in evidence." He pauses, frowning at her. "I hope they find you mentally incompetent. A girl like you wouldn't survive prison."

Naida tries to spit at him, but her missing tongue makes it impossible, and she drools on herself and the table instead.

DCI Floyd Homes sighs, his eyes bright with tears, and he shakes his head. "Jesus. What the hell is the world coming to?"

[END OF CLIP]

Much analysis has been done of the Johnson Incident. Academics have studied the scratchings in the attic wall—the only remnants of the writing that Kaitlyn described in her journal—and the basement where Naida lost her speech and John Hutt lost his life. Both sites were part of a center for paranormal research for the better part of a decade.

In 2013, what are presumed to be the last words Kaitlyn ever wrote were discovered in an old visitors' book in the chapel at the top of Elmbridge hill, which had remained boarded up since 2004. Whether these words are, in fact, Kaitlyn's is yet unknown.

Extract:

My confession to whoever finds it, to anyone who cares:

I am not real. I spent two years trying to convince people that I am, but after everything that's happened, I realize—I finally realize—that I'm not. Carly isn't either. Not anymore. I'm a vessel. That's _all_ I am now.

I want you to know that I didn't kill him. It was the thing inside me. It's getting stronger. He wanted to bind it because he loved me. He loved me so much, and I loved him too. Even though he did bad things, I loved him. And that _does_ matter.

But it was my hand on his neck. It was my arm that jerked. And even though I was screaming inside, and even though I wanted to stop, it wouldn't let me. I have to live with that. But it wasn't _me_. And now it's getting stronger. I can feel it taking over. I am a vessel, but I still have some control. I can still end this.

I am not real.

110

The Final Image

The final security footage in the Elmbridge seniors' common room reveals the last moments before the fire. This image has received a cult following, held dear by those who seek a happy ending to the Johnson Incident. The camera footage has been transcribed below.

Seniors CCTV Camera Footage
Wednesday, 2 February 2005, 12:33 AM

The fire is already lapping at the sofas in the room when Kaitlyn enters the camera's field of vision. She leaves the frame, and moments later, a flaming ball of some kind—perhaps a towel—is thrown into the room. It lands by the curtains, which quickly ignite.

The curtains burn, the upholstered sofas burn, the tablecloth and the cabinets burn. All obscured by increasing amounts of smoke. It is several minutes before Kaitlyn returns. She walks into the flaming room, pauses, and is engulfed in the fire.

A close inspection of the footage reveals four things.

1. Kaitlyn Johnson died smiling. Indeed, there seems to be a look of complete serenity on her face in the split second before the fire closes in on her. This is in line with her last journal entry, which also has an air of peace about it, implying that she must destroy herself in order to destroy the demon within her.

2. As the fire engulfs her, she raises her hand as though to reach for something—or someone.

3. Her final word was either "Dee" or "Carly."

4. When the footage is enlarged, a darker shape can be discerned in the flames. Most analysts believe it is a flame shadow or an object in the fire, but some fanatics and devoted followers of the Johnson Incident believe that it is either the snake Kaitlyn spoke of or her long-lost sister Carly. More extreme Johnson Disciples claim that the figure may in reality be the actualization of her journal and closest (imaginary) friend, Dee.

It is certainly comforting to think of Kaitlyn reuniting with her sister. However, her smile suggests a deranged state of mind. On the night of the incident, twenty students had minor injuries and burns.

Naida Chounan-Dupré, tried at seventeen and found mentally incompetent, was detained at Broadmoor mental hospital at Her Majesty's leisure following her first trial but was found competent in a retrial five years later after additional camera footage was discovered.

The quality of the image is poor, but it is clear that the person holding the camera is in one of the Elmbridge High School dorm rooms. The overhead light is off, but the camera light allows us to see that the dorm is bare, bed stripped, desk empty. One item seems to have been left behind: a purple Post-it stuck to the lamp shade, evidence that we are in the former room of Carly Luanne Johnson.

The person carrying the camera wanders towards a nook in the wall, where a sink sits beneath a mirror. The mirror is broken, the glass spiderwebbing but not shattered. Naida's broken reflection stares out at us. She backs away, frowning, and turns again to the room. She walks over to the wardrobe and opens the doors. A mirror in the rear wall is also smashed.

"Holy shit..."

She turns to leave, but gasps.

The full-length mirror on the back of the dorm door is zigzagged and broken as well. Naida shakes her head, an expression of horror on her features.

"Oh, Gorro. She broke them all."

[END OF CLIP]

Not many conclusions can be drawn from this video footage, but the prosecution was able to argue that Naida, at the date of this video, knew that Carly Johnson was responsible for the attack on Michael Bowers and the vandalism of school property. Naida, twenty-two years old at the retrial, wrote a defense stating that Carly had broken the mirror and cut the skin of Mike Bowers only because she was possessed by a demon.

Despite these claims, Naida was found mentally competent and given concurrent sentences of two years for withholding evidence from the police, one year for concealing a suspect, and an additional eight-year sentence for obstructing the course of an investigation, obstructing the course of justice, obstructing a police officer, harboring a suspect, and conspiracy to harm. She served a total of nine years and two months and was released on probation in 2014.

Scott Fromley also faced charges of conspiracy to harm and obstruction of an investigation under juvenile law but was found not guilty and released to his parents. Now thirty-seven, he is a top barrister and remains unmarried. He declined to comment on his involvement with the Johnson Incident or his relationship with Naida Chounan-Dupré. He and Naida have not spoken in twenty years.

Naida's grandmother, [name redacted], traveled to Britain for the initial trial of her granddaughter but later returned home and has not been heard from since.

Jaime Johnson, now twenty-five, is a nursery teacher for children with special needs. She still lives with her adoptive mother, Meredith Bailey. Both declined to comment.

An investigation into the treatment that Carly Johnson received at the hands of Dr. Annabeth Lansing was carried out in 2005 and 2006, during which all taped session recordings were taken in as evidence. At a private medical hearing in October 2006, Dr. Lansing's medical license was revoked for malpractice, and she received a fine of an undisclosed amount. The National Health Service declined to comment.

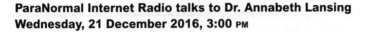

111

ParaNormal Internet Radio talks to Dr. Annabeth Lansing
Wednesday, 21 December 2016, 3:00 PM

Interviewer: What do you think is the truth of the incident? Was Carly disturbed? Or was she really under the influence of evil forces?

Lansing: She was disturbed, of course. She had a mental injury—dissociative identity disorder, and psychopathic tendencies. She was a danger to herself after the death of her parents, invented an alter ego, killed Juliet McClarin, Ari Hait, John Hutt, and Haji Chounan-Dupré. There can even be a case made against her for Brett [name removed at request of the family]. Carly Johnson was very sick. It's a tragic affair, but it is what it is.

Interviewer: And what about the figure in the fire?

Lansing: What figure? There was a shadow—a piece of furniture burning.

Interviewer: And the disappearances on the site for the last decade? How do you explain that?

Lansing: I can't. Only to say that people should be more careful when walking around a ruin. Accidents happen.

Interviewer: And Naida? Brett, Ari, John, Scott—they all believed.

Lansing: Unfortunately, group hysteria happens too.

Interviewer: Do you think you could have done anything differently to help this girl? She was under your care.

Lansing: [Pause] I did everything for her.

Interviewer: Care to comment on the medical hearing of '06? Why was your license to practice medicine revoked? In ten years, it hasn't been renewed.

Lansing: Thank you for having me on today. It was illuminating.

In the end, we must decide for ourselves what we believe. To date, twenty-six people have gone missing on the Elmbridge site and five have filed reports of hearing girls whispering in the basement. Despite this, the ruins continue to attract risk-seeking tourists each year, most likely because the site is listed as one of the top fifteen most haunted places in Britain (see editor's notes for links).

In 2011, Dr. Annabeth Lansing visited the site for the first time in six years. Today, she is a leading paranormal researcher, with a particular expertise on Elmbridge High. Her latest book, *The Forgotten Elmbridge*, comes out next winter.

To date, she will not speak of what happened during her visit to the site.

112

Despite CCTV footage that shows Carly Johnson in the flames of the Elmbridge fire, her body has not been found. Some say she still lingers on the grounds, seeking out the missing half of her soul, Kaitlyn. Others believe she moved on, reuniting with her sister in a better afterlife.

Kaybear? Will you always be here with me? Will you promise?

I promise, Carly-bean. I am not going anywhere.

ACKNOWLEDGMENTS

F irst, to the people who saved my life and to whom I owe this book's existence. My dearest friend and husband, who fed me every two hours, traded back rubs for bites of food, came in every morning with a smile even when all seemed hopeless, and who got me to the other side. Thank you forever—I love you, I love you, I love you! My unnamed hero and donor, I think of you daily. This book is for you and those you left behind. Professor John O'Grady, the House MD of the King's College Liver Department, and his amazing team for their unflinching support. Dr. Agarwal for the smiles and wit! Dr. C. J. Tibbs, for really caring; I hope you know how much you gave me. My talented surgeon and the rest of the King's surgical team, and to the nurses on Todd Ward—you are angels on this earth, I really hope you know that (but I'll keep sending chocolates as a reminder!). Without all of you, this book wouldn't be here. I humbly thank you for giving me my life. To every organ donor out there in the world: Thank you too!

Thank you, endlessly, to my mother, who gave me so much when she forced me to read to her (even through my wailing protestations!). For always believing it would happen and that I had something worth sharing. You are my favorite person in the world and always my biggest cheerleader. You make my world bright and put up with my insanities. I love you, and I'm proud you're my best friend. You rock the socks off everyone!

To Polly Nolan and Sarah Davies, agents extraordinaire and superwomen, and to the rest of the Greenhouse staff, my deepest thanks for believing in this book and championing it across the oceans. I adore you, I really, really do!

To my editors, Alvina Ling and Jenny Glencross, a huge, massive thank-you for your sage advice and wisdom and for your faith, right from the get-go. For seeing things I couldn't, and allowing me to bring out the best (and the worst) in Kaitlyn, Carly, Naida, Ari, and the rest of the Dead House gang; for helping me to see the beautiful tragedy of my ending. Jenny—we are twin Harry Potter souls! Alvina—your found-footage Hachette diaries still bring me the greatest joy! To Fiona Kennedy, for your enthusiasm and class. To Nina Douglas, for always providing awesome shenanigans, and to the whole Orion/Indigo team for such an amazing pitch document, which I have framed because it is so beautiful and magnificent! Thank you all for truly understanding *The Dead House*.

Huge thank-you also to the Little, Brown Books for Young Readers and Orion/Indigo teams and designers. I love you guys so much for bringing so much awesome to young adult literature. Thank you!

To my critique partners and best writerly friends, the YA League—Isabel Sterling and David Purse. You loved *The Dead House* all the way, and because of that, you loved me. Thank you, thank you, thank you! PS: Scotland, baby! (Our bitchin' swans will always haunt me!) Huge thanks also to Melissa See, who promised *Dead House* cake and cosplay.

To my first readers and friends: Patti Rossier, Lauren Charles, Ashley Hartzell, and Ley Saulnier. You are some of the most beautiful, insightful, brilliant people I have ever met, and I'm honored to know you. Ashley, you saved me, girl, and I love you.

To the YA Scream Queens—Courtney Alameda, Jenn Johansson, Lindsay Currie, Trisha Leaver, Hillary Monahan, Lauren Roy, Cat Scully, and Sarah Jude Bromley—for showing me that there is a place for me and my weird brain, and for bringing YA horror to ready and willing readers (including me!). You are queens of the highest order.

A gigantic thank-you to the illimitable Kat Ellis, for the cake, coffee, and chats. I cherish them more than I can say! To my agent sister, Jen Rose Bell, for your enthusiasm, support, and beautiful spirit—I am so glad Polly brought us together! To Neil Jackson, Sarwat Chadda, Tara Kemsley, and Lia Keyes—thank you for the writing retreats! Here's to so many more.

To my friends, who keep me grounded and happy: my twin and forever chop, Stacey Poulton; my beautiful and kind Mandip Kaur; my Mrs. Moose, Yurena Diaz; the wonderful and cherished Kimia Ahmadi; the lovely Colleen Mulhall; and my personal Viking, James Lidgey-Hutt. To anyone I haven't mentioned, forgive a frazzled writer—but I love you, I do!

A big thank-you to my beautiful model, Amy! You are a perfect Kaitlyn and just gorgeous!

And you. If you're reading this book, thank you so much. Words can't express the honor I feel, knowing that you went on this journey with Kaitlyn too. Thank you.

AUTHOR'S NOTE

The Scottish Mala and Grúndi aspects of this book are fictional, inspired by a childhood of travel and exposure to various cultural, tribal, and religious beliefs. Additionally, the fictional "Fair Island" in the book shouldn't be confused with Fair Isle, which is a very real, very beautiful island off the coast of Scotland and part of Shetland.

Dissociative identity disorder is a fascinating, complex, and controversial disorder on the dissociative spectrum. The human brain is a magnificent tool, capable of breaking into pieces the conscious part of a person's mind in order to protect the self from the memory of trauma. In DID (previously known as multiple-personality disorder), this means that at least two distinct personalities exist in one person, with one, or several, of the personalities (the "alters") holding the memory of trauma away from the core personality so that he or she can function. Kaitlyn Johnson, as described by her (very negligent) doctor, is one such alter. What makes her unique is that she comes out only after dark and that—according to her—she has always been around and isn't an alter at all, but a natural second half to her "sister."

Kaitlyn was born during a period of my life when I experienced inversion syndrome (this is when you are awake at night, rather than during the day). During those nights, I began to think about what kind of life someone who had only ever known such darkness would have. What she would be like. How she would behave, how she would (or wouldn't) associate with other people. And, of course, if there was a dark half to the equation in Kaitlyn, there had to be a light half. From that came Carly, someone who had only ever known warmth, light, and the reality of daily life. How different these two would be!

What might it be like to have control of only half your day? Would you love or resent the person who got the rest of it? Would you communicate with that person? How? What would it feel like not to have control of your own body—or worse, to feel as though your body may not even be yours?

What would it feel like to be told you are a symptom or a disease?

And then came the thought: What happens when the other half of your life is suddenly taken away? And what if someone told you the reason was not psychological (integration), but spiritual (demonic)? How would that feel?

Especially when no one will believe you're real.

I would like to make a special thank-you to the person in my family who suffers with DID. You are the most intriguing person I know. All of you.

And another special thank-you to the doctors who gave me back control of my body.

This book is for you.

PHOTO CREDITS